Calvary Chapel Christian S
11960 Pettit St.
Moreno Valley, CA 92555

D0388833

Calvary Chapel Christian School

00005925

BY DAWN'S
EARLY LIGHT

BY DAWN'S EARLY LIGHT

Grant R. Jeffrey
and Angela Hunt

WORD PUBLISHING

NASHVILLE

A Thomas Nelson Company

Library of Congress Cataloging-in-Publication Data

Jeffrey, Grant R.
By dawn's early light / Grant R. Jeffrey with Angela Elwell Hunt.
p. cm.
ISBN 0-8499-1609-7
1. Hunt, Angela Elwell, 1957– . II. Title.

Printed in the United States of America

9 0 1 2 3 4 5 BVG 9 8 7 6 5 4 3 2 1

AUTHORS' NOTE

Like its predecessor, *Flee the Darkness,* this is a work of fiction based upon fact. Michael Reed, Devorah Cohen, Alanna Ivanova, and Vladimir Gogol have been created from imagination. Their function is to represent people who will live through situations and circumstances similar to those detailed in these pages. The amazing weapons and sophisticated computer systems described in this book do exist.

The war of Gog and Magog, described in Ezekiel 38–39, will come to pass. As we researched this book, we had no difficulty finding current information about the Russian-Arab alliance. We found several articles in which the world's top intelligence analysts predict that Russia will invade the Middle East in the not-too-distant future.

We cannot predict the timing of this coming war—only God knows when it will begin and if it will occur before or after the moment when Christ summons his church to heaven. But because fiction must be rooted in a time and place, we have devised a possible scenario depicting how Gog's invasion may come to pass in the light of biblical prophecy. It is our prayer that you will take this story to heart and walk in hope as the day of Christ's coming approaches.

We owe a special word of thanks to Captain Thomas H. Orr, USNR; Petty Officer First Class Cheryl L. Orr, USNR; and Gary and Ranee McCollum, USAF.

Maranatha! The Lord returns!

Grant R. Jeffrey
Angela Hunt

In the darkness . . . the sound of a man
Breathing, testing his faith
On emptiness, nailing his questions
One by one to an untenanted cross.

—R. S. Thomas, *Pieta*

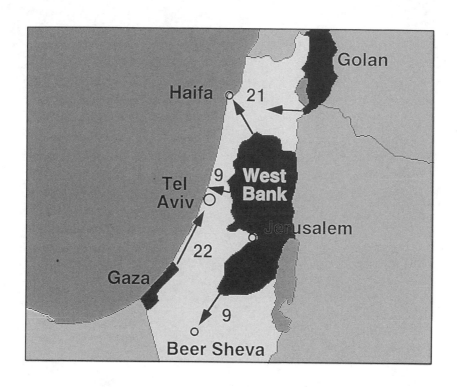

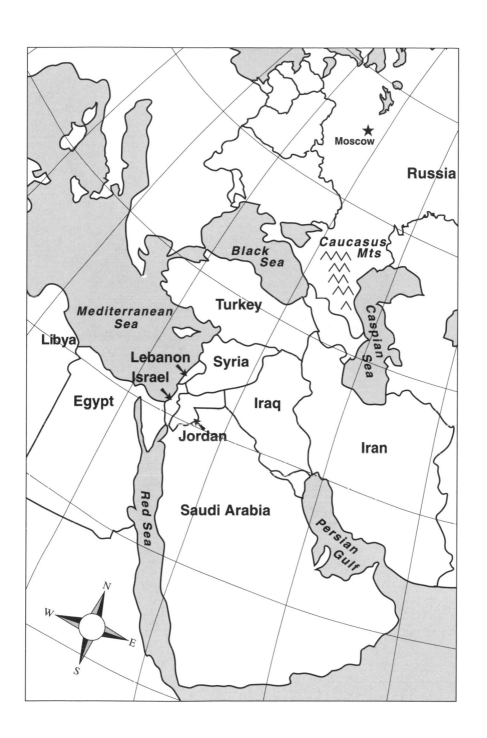

CHAPTER ONE

Fort Meade, Maryland
0801 hours
Monday, October 9, 2000

THE TROUBLE FIRST APPEARED AS A TINY WARNING FLAG.

Capt. Michael Reed saw it the moment after he typed in his password and tapped his computer touchpad. His usual desktop replaced the whirling screen saver, and the warning flag lit up the monitor's lower right-hand corner.

He clicked on it, then shifted uneasily in his chair as the screen filled with an urgent e-mail message from Bob Johnson, one of his intelligence section chiefs. Johnson's note referred to the attached encrypted communiqué, and Michael frowned as he pressed his index finger to the biometric sensor attached to his keyboard.

Every hour the National Security Agency's worldwide electronic eavesdropping infrastructure pulled in millions of signals from e-mail, telephone calls, and fax transmissions around the world, but only communications using certain key words were analyzed and deciphered. Information from the Echelon system, fondly referred to as "the big ear," was also available to Britain, Canada, New Zealand, and Australia, whose security officials shared the task of analyzing data and forwarding intercepts to the appropriate country. Johnson's information had come from British agents, who had relayed it at 6:00 A.M. EST. Johnson had immediately forwarded the message, wanting it to reach Michael ASAP.

The biometric reader flashed its acceptance of his fingerprint, and the attachment unscrambled in a flurry of letters. Resting his arm on the sliding keyboard tray, Michael skimmed a series of disjointed messages that sent a spasm of panic through his body like the trilling of an alarm bell.

He pushed away from the computer and punched the intercom on his desk. "Gloria—place a call to the National Photographic Interpretation Center. Tell them I'm en route and I want to see the latest recon photos of military bases in Russia, Iraq, Turkey, and Syria." He hesitated, tapping his fingers on the desk. "On second thought, tell them I want to see the entire Middle East, the latest shots they have."

"Right away, sir. I was just about to bring in your coffee—"

"No coffee today, Gloria. I'm leaving now."

Michael sent the fragmented messages to his printer, then studied the printed sheet for a long moment, feeding it, line by line, to his memory. When he had absorbed all the pertinent data, he slid the page into the shredder, then stood and plucked his overcoat from the tilting coatrack in the corner behind his desk.

"I'll be in touch shortly," he told his secretary as he strode past her desk in the outer office. "I may need you to make another appointment for me—with someone higher up in the chain of command."

Beneath a cloud of white hair, Gloria's eyes widened. "Sounds serious."

Michael nodded and moved toward the door. "I'll be back later."

"Shall I order lunch for you in the office?"

"Don't bother." Michael paused at the door long enough to slip into his overcoat and give his secretary a grim smile. "The beginning of World War III could spoil my appetite."

CHAPTER TWO

Moscow
1614 hours

"SWEETHEART?"

Through the haze of sleep, he felt a light hand touch his shoulder.

"Vladimir, you need to wake up now. Your telephone is ringing."

Adrift in the soft, honeyed tones of his mistress, Vladimir clutched at satin sheets gathered at his waist, then sat up. He blinked once, peering through the fuzzy shadows of Alanna's bedroom, then took the phone from her pale hand.

"Yes?" His voice was gruff with sleep and irritation. His aide knew better than to disturb him here, so this had to be news of monumental importance.

As Petrov's nasal voice buzzed in his ear, Vladimir gestured for Alanna to switch on the bedside lamp. Her hand, a dim shadow enfolded in the feathers of her peignoir—his latest and most expensive gift to date—floated across his field of vision and clicked at the lamp. Bright light flooded the nightstand, revealing two crystal goblets, his Tokarev TT-33 pistol, and Alanna's ridiculous windup alarm clock, its spindly hands reminding him that it was four fifteen—and very late. But it had been a long night.

Beside the table, swaying slightly to a tune playing softly on the radio, Alanna edged her lower lip forward in a pout. Vladimir forced himself to concentrate on the caller. Oleg Petrov, his aide and the only man permitted to have this number, wanted to patch through an important call.

As the line clicked and momentarily went silent, Vladimir picked up one of the goblets, drained the dregs of last night's wine, then cleared his throat. Adrian Romulus, president of the European Union, would expect

Russia's minister of defense to be clearheaded and alert at four o'clock on a Monday afternoon.

The line clicked again and hummed quietly as the encryption system synchronized with the base station calling him. Suddenly Romulus's voice, crisp and clear, filled Vladimir's ear. "General! I am delighted to be able to finally return your call. I trust you are well."

"Very well, thank you." Vladimir closed his eyes to the sight of Alanna's pouting pose. The woman had no shame—and no sense of politics. "I trust you are in good health, President Romulus."

"Always." Though Romulus's voice was deep and controlled, Vladimir could hear the hint of a smile in it. "What can I do for you, General?"

Vladimir stiffened his spine and turned toward the window, where daylight fringed the closed blinds. "I am in need of guidance, my friend. In three days' time I am scheduled to hold a clandestine convocation of several of Russia's allies, but my intelligence operators tell me I cannot invite them to Moscow. The Americans have too many eyes and ears here."

Romulus's chuckle was deep and easy. "I would be pleased to extend an invitation to visit either my apartments in Brussels or my chateau in Paris. Both are at your disposal, General. And both are totally secure."

"But this short notice cannot be convenient for you—"

"It is my pleasure to serve you, General. I will do you a favor—and someday you may perform a service for me."

It was only as the tension went out of Vladimir's shoulders that he noticed it had been there. "Ah, President Romulus, you are most generous. I think Paris would be best-suited for our cause. The French are remarkably uninterested in other people's affairs."

"Then it is settled. I would be pleased to be your host during this important meeting."

"You are very kind, my friend." Unable to conceal his pleasure, Vladimir turned and smiled at Alanna. "We are most grateful for your hospitality."

"I am only doing my part for peace and justice." Romulus's voice echoed with depth and authority. "And if there is nothing else, I shall see you in one week's time. Have your aide contact Adam Archer, my military advisor in Brussels. He will make all the arrangements."

Vladimir flinched at the name. "Archer—isn't he an American?"

Romulus chuckled, and despite his misgivings, Vladimir felt soothed by the sound of the man's laughter. "Don't worry, General. Archer is completely reliable. He worked for me even in America—do you recall the explosion that killed Victoria Stedman?"

Vladimir lifted a brow, impressed. The American president's wife had been killed by a car bomb, and for months the international community had wondered which mastermind had managed to breach the almost impenetrable White House security. If Archer had been responsible for that bombing, he was a talented man.

"I had no idea."

"It is true. Archer is a security expert, and you need not fear the trip to Paris. So come, General, and let me aid your cause in this small way. I shall look forward to seeing you."

The line went dead. Vladimir switched off the power, then stared at the cell phone while Alanna lowered herself to his side.

"Why so serious, sweetheart?" she whispered, her breath softly fanning his ear. One of her hands rose to stroke his neck. "You look like a man with deep thoughts."

"Not deep thoughts," he placed the phone on the nightstand, "only deep ambitions." As he turned to look at her, he felt the pressures of leadership fly from his shoulders. With this regal beauty by his side, he would rescue Russia from the threat of economic, military, and cultural collapse. Like Peter the Great and Joseph Stalin, he would be the strong man to lead Russia forward . . . but his plans could wait for another hour.

"So tell me, love," he whispered, his hands spanning her narrow waist, "what would you like me to bring you from Paris? A bottle of perfume, perhaps? A string of pearls?"

He lowered his head to her sweet-smelling throat and breathed a kiss there while she giggled and slipped her pale arms around his neck.

Chapter Three

District of Columbia
0930 hours

Navigating through the sea of Washington traffic, Michael Reed thought it apt that the National Photographic Interpretation Center was located in a former heavy gun factory in the rear of the navy yard. Government workers no longer manufactured guns in the bright yellow cement building, but they certainly studied them. Though the NSA had access to satellite imagery, the NPIC guys were experts in evaluation. Photographs of missile batteries, silos, restricted military buildings, launch pads, and terrorist training camps streamed daily through the NPIC, where they were pored over by trained technicians capable of spotting a signpost out of place.

Michael parked in a visitor's parking spot, then flashed his NSA badge at the pair of guards at the security checkpoint. Within moments he was ushered into a room the size of a football field, divided into a maze of gray Dilbertesque cubicles. Richard Blanchard, the chief analyst and the man lucky enough to merit the first cubicle on the right, looked up from a report, his eyes quickly moving to Michael's shoulder. Seeing the four bars, he lowered his coffee cup and stood. "Morning, Captain. How can I help?"

"I'm Michael Reed, and I'm sorry to interrupt your morning coffee." Michael extended his hand with a grim smile. "But we've gathered some interesting electronic intelligence regarding the Middle East. I'm hoping you'll be able to send me back to my office believing that what we picked up is nothing serious."

Blanchard's handshake was solid. "I have a hunch I might know exactly what you gathered . . . or what the ELINT was buzzing about, anyway. My

Middle East analysts are going over the latest photos from Big Bird right now. The film canisters arrived late yesterday afternoon, and my Middle East people stayed here all night going over them."

"Shall we take a look?" Michael stepped back through the doorway and allowed Blanchard to slip out of his cubicle and lead the way through the maze. As they walked, Michael peered into several different compartments, where analysts were studying their computer screens with absorbed attention. A poster above one man's monitor summed up the agency's mantra: God Is in the Details.

Michael followed Blanchard inside a larger cubicle where three analysts were poring over actual photographs on glossy paper. Blanchard introduced them as Tom Dixon, Henry Kenyon, and Blake Townsend. Michael nodded a brief greeting to each.

"We had these shots printed up," Blanchard said, "once we noticed the anomalies. We were expecting company—you and other action officers from the CIA, DIA, NSC—the whole alphabet soup of the intel community." He set his coffee cup on the table and ran a hand through his thinning hair. "We may still hear from the others."

Michael moved around to the side of the table where Dixon and Kenyon were bent over photographs. "All right, guys—tell me what's up."

"Not a heckuva lot, and that's what worries me." Dixon lowered the photograph in his hand and looked up at Michael, his unshaven gray beard bristling as he set his chin. He shoved the picture in Michael's direction. "That's a shot of the primo Palestinian terrorist training camp in the Gaza Strip. What do you see?"

Michael picked up the photo and scanned it. The overhead shot revealed several tents, a parked jeep, a rectangular building, and two lumpish figures dressed in the head-to-toe black robes worn by Muslim women. From the length of the building's shadow, he surmised that the photo had been taken in early morning. "I see two BMOs and not much else," he said, shrugging.

"That's the point." The analyst took the picture from Michael. "The black moving objects shouldn't even be there—the women wouldn't be present if the men were training. The infrared shot tells us the men are gone—there are no warm bodies in the building or the tents, nothing but those two women on the street. Now look at this shot, taken at the same time of day, same place, last week."

Michael accepted a second photograph and frowned at the difference. There were more than a dozen vehicles in this grainy black-and-white, three camels, and two Arabs with machine guns stationed outside the building. In front of one tent, Michael saw at least two dozen men kneeling in prayer, facing the southeast . . . and Mecca.

"The ghost town photo was shot at the time of prayer, just as this one was." Kenyon spoke up, squinting through his glasses at Michael as if he needed to readjust his picture-logged vision. "We'd write it off as a fluke, but the phenomenon was repeated in this shot—of a different camp." He slid another photograph toward Michael.

"And this one." Townsend flicked another picture in Michael's direction. "That's Osama bin Laden's terrorist training facility in Afghanistan. Apparently it's been cleared out, too."

Michael glanced at the other photo in his hand. "And this one?"

"Lebanon's Bekaa Valley," Dixon reported. "Near Taanayel, about ten miles west of the Syrian border. The Israelis have been trying to shut down this training camp for years, but they had nothing to do with this mass desertion."

Michael dropped the photos, then ran a hand across his jaw. "We got Arabs disappearing anywhere else?"

"Sudan and Iran," Blanchard said, crossing his arms. "Most of their camps cleared out last month. We thought they were just repositioning their troops, but now those camps are active again. Wherever they went, they've already come back."

Michael leaned against the table for a moment, quietly evaluating the photographs in light of the information he'd received that morning. "Can I see the Sudan photos?" He looked at Blanchard. "And the latest photos from Russia might be helpful—see if you can find shots of a military installation close to Moscow."

As Blanchard picked up a phone and murmured into the receiver, Dixon rolled his chair to a computer terminal. "That'd be Pushkina. It used to be a KGB training camp, but they've been using it to train Arab terrorists for the last several years." Dixon tapped on the keyboard, and a moment later a series of photos appeared on the screen. Michael walked forward, glancing for a moment at the analyst's personal space. A Polaroid of a pretty woman and two little girls adorned Dixon's monitor, an odd juxtaposition with the stark photo on the screen.

"This is the largest training camp in Sudan, capable of supporting a thousand men," Dixon said, clicking to enlarge the picture. "And this is our latest shot. This morning the place was humming again, but last month it looked as deserted as a summer resort in midwinter."

Michael leaned forward. "Center in on that cluster of men there in the corner. Can you magnify?"

"You bet." Dixon's keyboard clattered, and within an instant the image zoomed up at them. The gray stick figures became six men, three wearing traditional Arab dress, the other three in darkish uniforms. Michael saw the glint of a star upon one man's shoulder.

"Those look like Russians to you?" he asked, feeling the silence behind him. The others had risen from the table to gather around Dixon's monitor, and their silence confirmed his suspicions.

"The Russians have always been Palestinian allies," Dixon said, magnifying the picture again. The Russian general came into focus, and though the shadow of his cap hid his face, beneath the edge of the man's cover Michael saw a fringe of blondish hair.

He looked at Kenyon. "I've never met a blond Arab."

Kenyon cock-a-doodled a laugh. "Me neither, Captain."

"Got the latest Pushkina shots," Blanchard called from another computer terminal. Michael turned and walked to the section chief's chair while the other analysts followed. Without being asked, Blanchard magnified the shot of the Russian training camp. A plume of smoke hung over a series of chimneys, more than two dozen military vehicles crowded the parking area. By all appearances, the camp was populated—heavily. If they pulled up an infrared shot, Michael knew the place would be crimson with heat.

Without speaking, Michael pointed toward a cluster of men outside one building. Blanchard pulled the computer's cursor over the area and clicked again. The shot enlarged, displaying a group in khaki uniforms without insignia. Each of them was dark-haired, and one man was tilting his head toward the sky, displaying a dark moustache and beard. Another wore a kaffiyeh, held in place by a double agal cord around his head.

"Correct me if I'm wrong," Michael remarked dryly, meeting Blanchard's gaze, "but I don't think the Russians adopted Arab headwear even when they were fighting in Afghanistan."

"That one is a Palestinian for sure." Dixon thrust one hand into his trouser pocket. "Russian officers don't wear beards."

Michael crossed his arms and looked up at the tiled ceiling, his habitual pose for deep thought. "So—someone in Moscow issued the Palestinians an invitation to Pushkina, and they responded en force. But why?"

"Does that fit with your information?" Blanchard asked, watching with a keenly observant eye.

Michael lifted his brow. He wasn't at liberty to say what they had learned from Echelon, but the photographic information certainly supported the intel.

"What about the Sudanese?" Dixon pointed toward his monitor. "Why did they get invited to the party a month earlier than everyone else?"

"The camp will only hold so many." Kenyon squinted toward Michael again. "Maybe this Russian crash course in whatever is only being offered to a select few at a time."

"Then who's next?" Michael breathed the question in a whisper, but all three analysts returned to their computers and began to tap at their keyboards. "We've still got activity in Iran," Townsend volunteered. "It's been constant. No vacation."

Dixon's chair squeaked as he looked over his shoulder. "I've got two camps in Lebanon with a constant reading, too."

Blanchard lifted his hand. "Flag those and the Iranian camps, too. We'll want to know if they migrate northward in the next few weeks."

Michael crossed his arms and pressed a finger to his lips. "You'd better watch Iraq, too." He looked at Blanchard. "Flag every military installation, not just the training camps. Let me know if there's a sizeable exodus—or if Russian uniforms start showing up."

"Roger that."

"And I'd like to take some of these photos with me. I'll sign for them."

"No problem, Captain. We know where you live," Blanchard answered, giving Michael a wry smile. He plucked several of the key photographs from the table, then thrust them into a folder and handed the package to

Michael. He gestured toward the corridor. "Want me to walk you out? The labyrinth can be a little confusing."

Michael stepped aside. "Thanks."

Blanchard led the way out of the network of cubicles with an ease that could only have come from years of working in the place. Just before they reached the security checkpoint, however, he stopped and regarded Michael with a level gaze. "I'll make a report to my superiors, of course. I suppose you'll do the same?"

Michael gave him a polite smile. "As soon as I return to the office."

"Very good." Blanchard thrust out his hand. "Nice to meet you, Reed."

Michael returned the handshake, signed for the folder at the security desk, then paused in the bright sunlight outside the building. He breathed deeply of the fresh air, then pulled his cell phone from his pocket, and punched in the number for the direct line to his office. Gloria answered on the first ring.

"I've got a bit of a situation here," he said, unlocking his car, an ebony '68 Corvette convertible. "I need you to call the White House and alert them that I'm coming over. I'll need ten, maybe fifteen minutes with the president ASAP."

If Gloria was surprised, she gave no sign of it. "What if they ask . . . why?"

Michael switched the phone to his other hand as he tossed the classified folder onto the passenger seat, then shrugged out of his coat. "Ask for the president's secretary and tell her Daniel Prentice sent me. That's all you'll need to say."

"Fine."

Michael switched off the phone, then tossed it onto the passenger seat as he lowered his lanky frame into the convertible. A half-smile crossed his face as he inserted the key and listened to the engine roar. Amazing what Daniel Prentice's name could accomplish. Michael scarcely knew the computer genius, having met him just before the outbreak of the Gulf War, but he'd been well-acquainted with Brad Hunter, the Navy SEAL who escorted Prentice in and out of Baghdad before the bombing began. Brad must have mentioned Michael to Prentice, for one day last spring, four months after Prentice's mysterious disappearance, an e-mail message had appeared on Michael's NSA computer.

Hi, Mike:

I hope you'll remember me, and I trust you'll be willing to help, if only for Brad's sake. We need someone to function as quiet eyes and ears, and instinct tells me you're the man. The world is about to change, my friend, and SS can't be sure of anyone.

If anything unusual goes down in the Middle East . . . if anything at all causes you concern in the next few months, go directly to Casa Blanca and tell them I sent you. Then speak freely.

I know I can count on you.

Daniel P.

Michael put the car in reverse and pulled out of the parking space, remembering how the e-mail had puzzled him for weeks. The note's meaning was clear enough, and SS undoubtedly stood for Samuel Stedman. The fact that the sender had managed to hack into the NSA's computers tended to reinforce the idea that Daniel P. could only be Daniel Prentice—not just anyone could penetrate the NSA's elaborate system safeguards.

But Prentice was supposed to be dead.

For a while the world believed Prentice had murdered Brad Hunter and his wife in their home on Christmas Eve. For several weeks the police and FBI expended every effort to find the computer genius while the press set off on a veritable manhunt. The press continued its Daniel Prentice feeding frenzy throughout the winter. Reporters camped out across from Prentice's Park Avenue apartment and his office in Mount Vernon, New York. A few members of the media trooped down to St. Petersburg, Florida, where Prentice's mother lived in a retirement community and steadfastly refused to make any comments about her son. The tabloids concentrated on Prentice's hasty marriage to Lauren Mitchell and the lurid details of the Hunter murders. Throughout January and February of the year 2000, the tab rags' headlines screamed, "Did Daniel Kill Lauren, Too?"

As the year 2000 advanced, however, the talking heads stopped babbling about Daniel Prentice and gave him up for lost. The genius who had implemented the Personal Identification Device and the Y2K-compliant national computer network had apparently vanished, leaving his company to be run by his board of directors and his estate in the capable hands of his lawyers.

Michael pulled out onto the highway, drumming his thumbs against the steering wheel as he negotiated the heavy Washington traffic. The members of the media weren't the only people searching for Prentice. For weeks after receiving the mysterious message, Michael had applied himself to the business of locating the computer genius. The press had already hacked a wide trail. By searching public records, reporters had learned that Prentice married Lauren Mitchell on Christmas Eve 1999. Apparently the couple fled Washington after Brad and Christine Hunter's murder, and they had tried to broadcast a news report from an abandoned military base in the wilds of Canada—hardly a logical action for murderers intent on escaping justice. The transmission was inexplicably cut short, and the mystery heightened when, a week later, patrols in the area discovered charred broadcasting equipment, a pistol, and a man's body in a blackened heap of rubble. The Feds never released the dead man's name, but the tabloids assumed the body was Prentice's. Since no trace of Lauren Mitchell Prentice was found, conventional wisdom assumed she died of exposure in the wilderness, where wild animals scattered her bones.

Michael tried to back-trace the e-mail message that had appeared on his computer; he accessed every capability of the NSA's formidable mainframes, but no dice. The signal had been bounced from satellite to satellite, from network to network, and no one had a clue where the message originated. On a hunch, Michael tried replying to the message and tracing his reply, but the NSA mainframe couldn't follow his message once it entered the domain at prenticetech.com. The agent who handed Michael the report grinned and said, "If this guy is alive, he's so deeply embedded in cyberspace not even Echelon could flush him out."

Michael hadn't heard from Prentice in six months, but he was certain the guy was alive . . . and no murderer. Prentice was a computer genius, not James Bond, and he didn't have a killing bone in his body. Though he had undergone two weeks of basic military training before the excursion into Baghdad, Prentice seemed a lot more at home behind a computer desk than on a military mission. When Michael had watched a fumbling Prentice try to lock and load an M-16, he'd decided that if not for those GQ model looks, the guy would be definite nerd material.

The blast of a horn jerked Michael's attention back to the traffic light.

He felt a slow burn singe the tops of his ears as he lifted his foot from the brake. No telling how long he'd been sitting there, lost in the mystery surrounding Daniel Prentice. He punched the accelerator and moved out, leading the pack as the Corvette thundered toward Pennsylvania Avenue.

Chapter Four

Moscow
1800 hours

As Vladimir moved down the corridor, drawing his security detail after him like the Pied Piper, Alanna Ivanova closed the door, engaged the deadbolt, then turned and moved across the foyer, her slippers carelessly clacking across the marble. An audible sigh passed through her, a cascade of weariness that ended when she dropped into the overstuffed chair at the edge of the Persian carpet. She kicked off the annoying froufrou slippers and propped her feet on the edge of a glass-topped table that would cost any other Russian a year's salary. She closed her eyes, her concentration dissipating in a mist of fatigue.

Lunacy, that's what it was. Lunacy and a whopping dose of patriotism had brought her to this place of pretending. She had been so grief-stricken and homesick for anything American that she had fairly leapt at the chance to dine with the American ambassador's charming wife in the month after Sergei's death. During that first luncheon meeting, Mrs. Irene Nance had been effusive in her sympathy, generous with her understanding, and completely tolerant of the fact that Alanna had fallen in love with and married a Russian scientist.

"I met Sergei at the Houston Space Center," Alanna had told Mrs. Nance over shrimp cocktails. "And though my family certainly didn't approve, I didn't think twice about following him back to Russia. I knew he'd take care of me . . . and he did, right up until the day he died."

Mrs. Nance made soft sounds of sympathy.

"I still don't see how he could just drive into a concrete piling." Rigidly holding her tears in check, Alanna looked away, then turned the catch in her voice into a cough, and went on. "But I know accidents happen.

I just don't know what I'm supposed to do with my life now that he's gone."

She looked down and was surprised to discover that she had completely scraped the polish off her thumbnail. "I'm thirty-two, too young to be a widow."

"Don't do anything for a while, dear," Mrs. Nance counseled her. "A widow should not make drastic changes in her life for at least a year. You have Sergei's pension and a place to live. And who knows? Perhaps you can be of service to your own country while you are in Moscow."

For ten months Alanna had followed Mrs. Nance's advice and gone about the slow and painful course of healing. At night she walked along the River Moskva and shivered in the cool evening breeze . . . alone. She steeled herself to the sight of happy couples and small children as she stood in the long queues for food and supplies, growing a callus over the wounded parts of her heart. And she collected memories she would take back to America, for she had loved Sergei and Sergei had loved Moscow. While he had admired the United States and things American, he was a born and bred Muscovite at heart. "Over eight hundred years of history are woven into the fabric of this city," he often told her as they walked arm-in-arm along the Moskva. "Can't you *feel* it? I could never be truly happy living anywhere else."

Alanna tried to be happy in Moscow, but she had already made tentative plans to return to Houston when she met the ambassador's wife for coffee in the early part of February 2000. "Wait," Irene told her, one bird-like hand reaching out to grasp Alanna's wrist. "Don't go until you have met Daniel. He's quite an unusual fellow."

"Daniel?"

Mrs. Nance released Alanna's arm and lifted her coffee cup. "I don't know his full name. But he's a fascinating man, and he has expressed an interest in meeting you."

Two days later, Mrs. Nance introduced Alanna to Daniel, a striking man with brown hair, a slight New York accent, and an air of isolation about his tall figure. For a moment Alanna suspected Mrs. Nance of old-fashioned matchmaking, but Daniel seemed to have more important things on his mind. He waited until the ambassador's wife left the outdoor café table, then leaned forward and told Alanna that she might be of extreme service to the United States by remaining in Russia.

Alanna suppressed a smile and lowered her voice. "I wasn't aware that our ambassador's wife was allowed to recruit spies. Because if that's what this is about, you're talking to the wrong woman. I don't speak much Russian, I happen to *like* the people here, and I wouldn't do anything to hurt them. Oh—and I'm generally a coward. Not at all the heroic type." She leaned back in her chair. "Besides, I don't know you at all. How do I know I can trust you?"

"Have you a fondness for spy novels or just an overactive imagination?" Daniel asked, his eyes flat and dark in the sunlight, unreadable. "I can assure you, Mrs. Nance is not recruiting anyone for any government agency. We would just like you to gather information if you can. I won't ask you to do anything you don't want to do, but I will tell you that this matter is of serious importance."

Daniel looked away, but not before Alanna noticed a faint flicker of unease in the depths of his deep brown eyes. "Please, Alanna. I am acting on my own behalf, and I believe you can help us. Please say you'll consider it."

Against her better judgment, Alanna nodded and left the table. She met with Daniel twice more over the next few days, and at their third meeting was surprised to see him with an attractive blonde.

Daniel stood as she approached, then made the introductions. "Alanna, this is my wife, Lauren. For security reasons, while we're in Russia she is using the name Esther."

"Esther?" Alanna gave the woman a skeptical smile as she sat down. "That was my mother's name."

Lauren smiled, an almost imperceptible note of pleading in her face. "We know, Alanna. It is a beautiful Hebrew name."

Alanna glanced sharply at Daniel. "Who told you?"

A momentary look of discomfort crossed Daniel's face, then he lifted his hand. "It's all in the computer records. Your mother was Esther Honig; your father was Albert James. You finished your secondary education at Kennedy High School in Conroe, Texas; you graduated magna cum laude from Baylor with a degree in business administration."

"Good grief." She frowned, a little unnerved by the fact that a stranger could know so much about her. Sarcasm chilled her voice. "Did you also learn that I used to go to Sunday school at the Little Creek Baptist Church?

And that my father left us when I was ten and I haven't heard from him since?"

Daniel pressed his hands to the table and leaned toward her, his expression growing serious. "We need you, Alanna, and I'm praying you'll have enough respect for your mother's heritage to help us. This matter concerns the Jews . . . all Jews."

Lauren pressed her hand over Daniel's. "Alanna, there is trouble stirring in Russia, just below the surface of things. Surely you know that Russian President Chapaev is very ill."

Alanna nodded slowly.

"And the Russian economy is faltering," Lauren continued, her blue eyes gleaming with intelligence and independence. "Combined with the rampant corruption of business and government and the rise of the Russian Mafia—"

"The Russian government is ripe for a coup," Daniel finished, his eyes never leaving Alanna's face. "And all we are asking you to do is befriend the man who will most likely step into the power vacuum. He is the minister of defense, the man in charge of all Russian forces. He has nerves of steel, a fierce hatred for the Jews, and a weakness for American blondes."

Alanna flinched, momentarily wishing she had been born a brunette.

Lauren must have noticed her unease. "We won't let anything happen to you, Alanna. Daniel will be constantly in touch. And we'll protect you as much as we are able. We'll hack into the national computer registry and make an adjustment of your identification records—and those of your mother. We'll change your mother's name to something less Jewish."

Daniel nodded. "The man we're watching is dangerous, Alanna, though he has never harmed one of his women. I can't tell you much about him, but I can assure you of this—he may be the individual to launch the next world war. In his twenty-five year military career he has gained a reputation for ruthlessness and ambition. His anti-Semitism rivals Hitler's. And he is courting dangerous and influential friends in the Middle East."

Alanna took a deep, quivering breath to quell the leaping pulse beneath her ribs. "What makes you think he would like me?"

Daniel looked back at her and smiled without humor. "Like most Russians, he decries American excess while secretly coveting it. We know he keeps a framed poster of Grace Kelly in his bedroom, and your physical resemblance to that lady is remarkable. He has never been married but has enjoyed a string of mistresses and is currently on the outs with his last paramour. The timing is perfect—there's a vacancy in his love life, and you'd be the perfect woman to fill it."

"And I would just be—" Alanna lifted a brow—"what?"

"Be his friend; be his date—important men always like to have beautiful women on their arms in public. I'm *not* asking you to become his mistress, in fact, I'd seriously advise against it. But if he says or does anything that might affect international interests, let us know. We'll give you the means to contact us, and you'll be perfectly safe. We don't want to move on this man, and you can believe me when I say we're acting on Russia's behalf. We just want to know what he's doing."

Alanna carried Daniel's proposition back to her apartment and spent the rest of the evening trying to see herself as a Texan Mata Hari. On the surface, the idea was ridiculous, but if Daniel's information was correct, she would be safe from harm and she could back out at any time. As a favor to Daniel and Mrs. Nance, she could agree to see the general on a few occasions, then continue with her plans to return to the United States. Once she was home, she'd settle down with a solid, sturdy Texan and raise a half dozen young'uns. This little adventure would make a thrilling story to tell the grandkids.

She poured herself a cup of tea and sipped it, considering. She had been living in Russia for nearly two years and had absolutely nothing to show for it. Because she had been daunted by the idea of learning a language with three genders, six cases for nouns, and an entirely different alphabet, she didn't speak the language well and had made few friends in Moscow. She wanted to return home with the knowledge that these years had not been a total waste, that she had accomplished *something* worthwhile while she lived apart from friends and family.

Daniel had agreed to let Alanna take all the time she needed to consider his proposal, but within twelve hours she had given him her answer—yes. If he would set up a meeting, she would do her best to charm the Russian general.

Part of her brain railed against agreeing to such a foolhardy plan, but a far more vocal part insisted she break free of her ennui and do something with her life. In the months after Sergei's death, her little apartment had grown bleak and forlorn; each day seemed a dreary succession of endless, joyless hours, enlivened only by her occasional meetings with Irene. During the week she considered Daniel's proposal she had felt more alive than she had in years.

The feeling increased as time passed. Three days later, after Daniel provided Alanna with the most elegant evening gown in Moscow, she accompanied her mysterious countryman and his wife to the American ambassador's winter ball. Shortly after the festivities commenced, Daniel presented Alanna to Mrs. Nance, who introduced her to several Russian military officials, including Vladimir Vasilievich Gogol. Gogol asked Alanna for a waltz, then kept her by his side for the rest of the evening.

She found nothing distasteful in the general's appearance. He was a good-sized man, thick through the torso and shoulder, and the military uniform became him. His dark eyes framed a handsome square face, and his shining pate suggested neatness, not age or vulnerability. He spoke English with a careful dedication, and his eyes brimmed with admiration each time he looked at her.

Vladimir sought out her company every evening for the next week. By the weekend, he had arranged for her to move from her small apartment into a luxurious suite at the Hotel Metropol, only a short distance from the Kremlin, Red Square, and the GUM, Russia's approximation of a shopping mall. Without demanding anything in return, Vladimir bought her furs, clothing, and foods from the finest international markets. The average Russian woman would not in her lifetime obtain the myriad luxuries Alanna enjoyed in a week.

She scarcely knew how, but within three months she had become his mistress. Perhaps something in her longed for masculine affection. Perhaps, she ruefully admitted, he had bought her attentions with extravagances she would not have enjoyed even in Houston. He had commandeered her mind and her body, but, she vowed, he would never touch her heart. The calluses around it had grown too thick.

Still, Vladimir had never been unpleasant with her, and she seldom saw any sign of the ruthless, ironfisted leader Daniel had described. Sometimes she wondered if Gogol were two men—one a tough, merciless military general, the other a coddling, attentive gentleman. He loved to dress her up in beautiful gowns and take her to important banquets and social occasions, and she intuitively understood that he displayed her as a bejeweled pet on a diamond-studded leash. During public appearances, he locked his arm around her waist and paraded through the crowds, rarely speaking to her but never allowing her to suffer insult or harm.

The role of prized pet was an unexpected blessing, for it enabled Alanna to disguise her intellect behind a polished smile and a river of shining hair. Vladimir cared nothing for her brain, but he found her Southern accent and flirtatious kisses very satisfying. They had now been together nearly eight months, and Vladimir's affections showed no sign of waning.

She sank lower into the overstuffed chair and wondered if Daniel— whom she had not seen since agreeing to meet Vladimir Gogol—would approve her efforts thus far. He had warned her not to become Gogol's mistress, but what else was she to do? A powerful man would not remain captivated by a less-than-willing woman for long.

She brought her hand to her forehead, pushed back a wayward strand of hair, and frowned at the ornate chandelier hanging over the dining room table in the adjoining room. She had communicated with Daniel only a few times since meeting Vladimir; there had been no need to risk contacting him more often. The general kept his two selves quietly compartmentalized; he rarely mixed personal and professional concerns. But the phone call today was interesting. She had not known Gogol was involved with Adrian Romulus, president of the European Union.

Summoning her energy, she stood and walked barefoot into the kitchen, then rummaged under the sink. Heedless of her expensive peignoir, she sat cross-legged on the tile floor, pushing bottles of cleaning solutions out of the way. Behind the pipes and garbage disposal, a small square had been cut into the back of the sink cabinet, ostensibly to allow a plumber access to the drain. But a week after her move into the Hotel Metropol, a mustachioed man identifying himself as Daniel's assistant had cleared out a space for a small laptop computer and installed a secure phone line protected by an encryption program.

She pulled on the single screw that jutted out from the square, then removed the laptop and pulled away the protective plastic wrap. Reaching up, she set the laptop on the counter, then crawled beneath the sink and hooked the modem into the telephone line, grumbling about spiders and the blasted inconvenience of Daniel's paranoia.

Within a few moments, she had booted the machine and accessed the e-mail program. She didn't understand how her messages were accessed or who processed them, but she always received an acknowledgment within an hour after posting. She typed in the first four letters of the receiver's name, then the computer picked up the thread and completed the address.

She tabbed down to the message field, then typed:

> G. received an urgent phone call from A. Romulus this a.m. Mentioned a meeting that was supposed to be in Moscow, but now scheduled for Paris. Something about a clandestine convocation with Russian allies. G. left soon afterward. Seemed excited, and serious. Referred to his "ambitions."
>
> Live and well from Moscow,
>
> A.

As she'd been instructed, she clicked the key to encrypt the message with a privacy program of Daniel's design, then clicked on the send button. The computer beeped and fuzzed through the speakers, then went silent.

Alanna turned to the refrigerator and pulled out a soft drink, glancing back at the screen occasionally as she sipped the cola. Vladimir would scold her if he saw her barefoot and drinking from a can. He seemed to think that by dressing her in silks and chiding her about her manners he could drive Texas right out of her personality, but Alanna harbored no illusions about who she was and what she had become. In anybody's book, she was a woman living without benefit of matrimony, at best a common-law wife, at worst a high-class courtesan. The day when she could give it all up and go home to marry a cowboy had long passed. She'd grown too comfortable in opulence.

The spying, the harmless little reports, justified her charade. She could almost believe she had sold herself for a noble reason as long as Daniel received and acknowledged her messages.

The computer beeped, and a tiny envelope appeared at the bottom of the screen. Alanna set the soft drink by the sink and clicked on the icon. Lines of gibberish appeared. She pressed the hotkey to activate her secure key code, then watched the letters unscramble.

As always, the message was simple:

Hey, Texas. Thanks for the update. Are you OK? Still safe?

She smiled as she placed her fingertips on the keyboard. Nice of Daniel to be concerned for her welfare, but Moscow muggers worried her far more than Vladimir Gogol. She typed:

Fine as frog hair. That's Texan for A-OK.

She encrypted the message, pressed send, then turned off the computer, and knelt to unplug the modem from the phone line. She had another computer in her bedroom, a desktop she used for Internet access and e-mail correspondence with friends back home, but Daniel's assistant had stressed that she could never use that computer for communication with Daniel's people. There could be no records of her secret e-mail correspondence buried in its hard drive or cache, no incriminating addresses in the files.

If anyone ever discovered the hidden phone line, Daniel had assured her they would follow it to an absolute dead end. Its fiberoptic wires conveyed electromagnetic waves that were picked up by transceivers outside the building, then bounced off a satellite that fed Daniel's portable computer linkups. And if anyone actually tapped into the secure phone line, no one could crack the encrypted files without the password-protected key.

She encased the laptop in its plastic cover, then settled it back into the niche behind the plumbing, her nose crinkling at the musty smell of humidity and ammonia. When the cover had been restored and her cleaning supplies returned to their places, she double-checked the disarray to be sure the maid would not notice anything out of the ordinary.

And as she walked to her bedroom, Alanna smiled at the quiet message from her unknown contact. It was awfully nice of Daniel or whoever was manning the lines at GWJ@prenticetech.com to worry about her.

CHAPTER FIVE

District of Columbia
1050 hours

PRESIDENT SAMUEL STEDMAN SIPPED HIS COFFEE AND TRIED NOT TO LET THE zealot playing to the television cameras disturb the serenity of his morning. Outside the wide windows of the Oval Office, brilliant sunlight washed a bank of blooming red and white chrysanthemums beneath the canopy of a clear blue sky. The evergreens bordering the South Lawn swayed gently in an autumnal breeze, and a brilliant maple added a splash of gold to the landscape.

Victoria had always loved October in Washington. The glowing foliage had reminded her of their home in North Carolina, a home she'd been anxious to return to . . . but to which Sam would be retreating alone if he lost next month's election.

"You'd think the American people would learn to see through all this garbage." Jack Powell, Stedman's chief of staff and only confidant since Lauren Mitchell left the White House, sat on the couch wearing an expression of remarkable malignity. "I mean, look at him! He's ranting, he's raving, but has he said a single thing that makes sense? I don't think so!"

Reluctantly, Sam lifted his gaze to the television set. William Blackstone, California senator and Democratic candidate for president, had come from out of nowhere, surprising even lifelong politicians like Sam. He'd certainly heard of Blackstone before the Democratic primaries began, but not even the most liberal mouthpieces in the national media had seriously believed Blackstone could capture the party's nomination. But he had, handily winning primary after primary, charming voters with his Robert Redford looks and a platform containing anything and everything a voter could want.

Powell opened his mouth to speak again, but Sam lifted his hand. "I think we'd better listen to this." Obediently, Jack picked up the remote and punched up the volume.

"The world's economy is faltering even as I speak," Blackstone was telling a star-studded crowd in Los Angeles. "The economic earthquake shook Asia two years ago, then rumbled through Russia and Brazil. The Y2K crisis has the European Union in such a quandary they'll be sorting out the mess for years! Through American ingenuity and character we have survived, but we must not let ourselves be pulled down by the rest of the world!"

Suppressing a wry smile, Sam rubbed his hand over his chin. Europe's financial woes could be laid squarely at the feet of Daniel Prentice, who had single-handedly managed to save America and her computers by inserting a hardware virus into the international financial network. Twelve hours after the stroke of midnight, January 1, 2000, the United States had literally disconnected its computers from those of the European Union. Sam had gone on national television to announce that America would weather the Y2K storm with flying colors, while Adrian Romulus and his cronies quietly began to unravel the tangled mess Prentice had wrapped around them.

Very little of the truth had been made public. The average American had probably forgotten all about Adrian Romulus and his plans for a united America and Europe, just as Americans had wiped Sam's successful efforts to repeal an overwhelming tax burden from their collective memory. Daniel Prentice had vanished as quietly and completely as D. B. Cooper, and the "sympathy vote" pollsters had predicted would result in a landslide reelection victory had all but evaporated in the heat of Blackstone's charismatic campaigning.

Victoria had always said the American people were as fickle as a weather vane. The same folks who voted for an admitted drug-user and womanizer in 1992 could easily thrust Bill Blackstone into the Oval Office. The average man on the street seemed not to care about character or principle these days; the mass of Americans wanted a leader who resembled *them*—a flashy, charming package, with all flaws and weaknesses wrapped up and tucked away behind a sympathetic smile.

Blackstone was certainly an amalgamation of the best and worst in

America. He'd been married three times, sired seven children with two wives and one girlfriend, and was currently married to Electra Zane, a tall, pale beauty who never failed to remind Sam of an x-ray. She had no children—rumor had it that she'd had a tubal ligation so pregnancy wouldn't interfere with her modeling career—and she refused to play the traditional role of campaign wife. But her success as a model brought media attention from *People, Time, Newsweek*, and *The New York Times Magazine*, and the full-page spreads featuring the powerful couple living the glamorous life in Carmel guaranteed the public's notice.

Sam lifted his coffee mug and stared at the television. People who couldn't identify their congressman would know the names of Electra Zane's four Chihuahuas: Chiquita, Rosita, Perdita, and Joe.

Sam sipped from his coffee and watched the wind ruffle Blackstone's thick, wavy hair. Electra stood with her husband today, posed behind him in some sort of gauzy dress that revealed the thin shape of her legs every time the wind freshened.

Sam set his coffee cup on his desk and frowned as he wiped a smudge away with his fingertip. Compared to Blackstone's youthful attractiveness, he must look like a tired old man. The voters might not remember his dedication to keeping America out of Adrian Romulus's hands, but they'd remember the coma that forced him to turn the government over to his gullible vice president. They wouldn't remember the implementation of the revolutionary national identification system, but they would remember his drawn face and trembling voice in the days following Victoria's murder. They would not remember—few would even know—that he had kept America safe and strong when Romulus insisted upon a complete military stand down on the so-called International Day of Peace. Some of the more politically astute might recall the Millennium Treaty, in which the United States almost became yoked with the European Union and that infernal Adrian Romulus—

"America is tired of being big brother to the rest of the world!" Blackstone was saying now. "We have our own problems! We have our own helpless, homeless, and hungry. Let us be true to ourselves before we attempt to shoulder the burdens of the world. Have the responsibilities of world power made us happier? No! We have replaced the idea of self-dependence with the illusion of superpower omnipotence, and that is a dangerous falsehood, my friends. The lesson of Vietnam, of Iraq, of Bosnia, is that we must throw off the cumbersome mantle of world police-man, for we cannot eradicate our enemies. We cannot establish justice throughout the world until we establish it within our own borders. We cannot ensure the world's domestic tranquillity until we make certain each American family is prosperous and free from worry. We cannot provide for the world's defense, or promote its general welfare, or secure the blessings of liberty to the world's posterity until we have done all these things for *ourselves.*"

The audience erupted into cheers, the applause lifting in great waves as the camera panned over the sea of faces. The camera lingered a moment upon a prominent television star, then focused upon the tear-streaked face of a California talk-show hostess who wept in heartfelt agreement.

"He sounds like a selfish brat," Jack remarked, crossing his arms as he frowned at the television. "We, we, we—it's not a very compassionate plat-form, is it?"

"He's just responding to the latest polls." Sam shrugged slightly. "This morning I read that 89 percent of the American people feel our adminis-tration has placed too much emphasis on foreign policy."

Jack's mouth curled and rolled like he wanted to spit. "Fools, all 89 per-cent of them. Isolationism is a pipe dream, and anyone with half a brain knows it. In this day and age, no nation can afford to ignore the rest of the world."

"Isolationism is just wishful thinking . . . and I think most people real-ize that." Sam smiled, knowing Jack didn't share the profound but peaceful weariness that had settled on him like a blanket. "If I'd been able to ignore the rest of the world, I'd still have Victoria . . . and Lauren. I miss them both."

The grim line of Jack's mouth softened. "Don't you hear from Lauren now and then? I thought Prentice kept in touch with you."

Sam brought his hand to his temple. "I know she's well and happy, though they don't stay long in any one place. And Daniel's capable; I'd trust him with my life." He pressed on the side of his head, at the tender spot where the headache usually began. "Daniel doesn't think he'll be run-ning much longer."

Jack's left eyebrow rose a fraction. "Is he coming back?"

Sam rubbed his temple and smiled, not knowing how to explain Daniel's conviction that all Christians would soon leave the earth. In the coming resurrection, Daniel had once explained, the Lord Jesus himself would appear in the clouds and call his followers to heaven. Every single believer, dead or alive, would be instantly given a supernatural body and snatched up, literally disappearing from the face of the earth.

Victoria had believed in the resurrection of the saints, but she called it the Rapture. So did Charlie Marvin, the young preacher Sam had come to think of as his pastor. And Daniel Prentice, who never believed anything that could not be logically and absolutely proven, believed in the Rapture with a passion. But Jack Powell, who trusted no one, would find the idea ludicrous.

Sam met Jack's gaze without flinching. "Prentice is planning an extended trip—and he says he'll be out of range for a few years. Lauren will go with him."

And so would Victoria. And so would Jessica, their daughter. According to Daniel, all of Sam's loved ones would wait in heaven for seven years, readying themselves for the moment when Jesus Christ would return to earth as *the* triumphant King, eager to set up his millennial kingdom.

Sam sighed, his mind thick with fatigue and crowded with memories. As much as he admired Daniel Prentice and loved Victoria, he couldn't bring himself to embrace their philosophies. Too many people counted on him to be levelheaded, solid, and centered. He couldn't let himself be swayed by a theological theory, no matter how much the idea of joining his dead wife and daughter appealed to him.

A light knock sounded on the curved door that led to his secretary's office, then Francine opened the door and thrust her head through the opening. "Sir, I've just received a phone call from Capt. Michael Reed's office. His secretary says he needs to see you right away. If you agree, I can move your eleven o'clock appointment to tomorrow afternoon."

Sam drummed his fingers on the desk as he searched his memory and came up with nothing. "Who in tarnation is Michael Reed?"

Francine consulted her notepad. "The Middle East section chief at the NSA. His secretary said to tell you that Daniel Prentice would want you to see him."

Sam felt a shock run through him as he looked at Jack. Except for Prentice's mother, no one outside this room knew Daniel still lived.

"Alert the guards, and have an agent bring Reed in immediately," Sam said, managing no more than a hoarse whisper.

After Francine disappeared to make the arrangements, Jack cleared his throat uneasily. "I thought Prentice was officially dead."

"So did I." Sam swiveled his leather chair toward the door, then threw off his glasses and rubbed the bridge of his nose. He knew Daniel Prentice kept a watchful eye on Adrian Romulus and other leaders of the European Union, but he had no idea the man had contacts within the NSA. Who was this Michael Reed, and what did he know?

Sam let out a long sigh, then clasped his hands and looked at Jack. "I want you to stay." He nodded for emphasis. "I don't know what's going on, but I may need your support and analysis."

"Mr. President, I'd be delighted." Jack switched off the television, then crossed his legs and folded his arms, settling back on the sofa to wait.

Sam leaned back in his chair, then glanced at his watch. He had absolutely no idea what to expect, but if Daniel Prentice really had sent this man . . .

His uneasiness shifted into a deeper and much more immediate fear. Prentice wouldn't risk revealing his relationship with the president of the United States unless some critical situation had rendered it absolutely necessary. What had he discovered, and what would it mean for the country?

Sam picked up his pen and drummed the desk top. Daniel Prentice had a sense for calamity, and Sam had never known him to be wrong.

Chapter Six

District of Columbia
1103 hours

MICHAEL WALKED SLOWLY TO THE NORTHWEST APPOINTMENT GATE, HIS BRAIN filled with competing thoughts that scraped against each other as his heels ground against the asphalt path. He clutched an envelope marked with the distinctive diagonal violet stripe of a code-word-secret folder he should have been delivering to his superior at the NSA. In his entire twenty-four-year navy career, he had never read one rule or principle that endorsed the action he was about to take. The navy was a by-the-book operation, and what Michael had in mind was so far removed from the book the chief of naval operations would suffer an apoplectic fit if he knew what one of his captains was about to do.

Catching a glimpse of his reflection in the bulletproof window of the guard shack, he hesitated for a moment. Not only was he under-authorized, he was underdressed. He wore a blue coat over his regular workday naval uniform, a tan short-sleeved shirt and matching trousers. Not exactly what he would have chosen for a meeting with the president.

He nodded as one of the marine guards caught his eye. The sentries were better dressed than he was.

Using the thick window for a mirror, Michael lifted his hat, raked his fingers through his windblown hair, and settled the cover back on his head. If Gloria hadn't gotten through to the president's secretary, he'd feel pretty foolish trying to muscle his way into the White House. But Daniel Prentice had made a request, and Michael respected the man enough to make this attempt. He'd know in a moment whether his mysterious e-mail correspondent was a clever hacker or the real McCoy.

Michael straightened his posture, then approached the security checkpoint and pulled out his military ID. "Captain Michael Reed, NSA," he said, trying to keep the note of uncertainty from his voice. "I believe I have an appointment with the president."

"One minute, sir." The first marine checked his roster, then stepped into the booth and picked up a telephone. Michael shifted his weight and crossed his arms around the folder, trying to look relaxed under the second sentry's steely gaze. A pair of pigeons fluttered and cooed from the top of the guard shack, their ambient noise covering the sound of the guard murmuring into the phone.

A moment later the marine stepped out and gave Michael a bright-eyed glance, full of shrewdness. "An agent is coming to escort you, Captain Reed."

"Thank you." Michael transferred his gaze to the pigeons as he waited. Frank curiosity shone from the guard's eyes, but Michael knew military discipline would prevent him from asking how an unscheduled and unapproved NSA chief had managed to command an instant audience with the president of the United States.

A moment later an unsmiling Secret Service agent appeared inside the tall iron bars. He nodded at Michael, unlocked the gate, and led the way over the asphalt path without so much as glancing at Michael's uniform for any telltale bumps or bulges. Michael shook his head in wonder as he climbed the hill leading to the West Wing of the White House. Daniel Prentice's name carried more weight than he had realized.

He passed through the metal detector at another security checkpoint, signed in as an official representative from the NSA, then followed the agent through a warren of tiny offices until he reached Stedman's secretary's desk. The woman sitting there—Francine O'Connell, according to her nameplate—sprang up out of her chair like a jack-in-the-box.

"Captain Reed." She smiled, a quick curve of thin, pink lips, then stepped toward the door leading into the Oval Office. "The president is expecting you."

A cold knot formed in Michael's stomach as he followed her. What was he *doing*? He had placed his faith in a single e-mail from an unconfirmed source and was about to interrupt Samuel Stedman's busy schedule one month before the election. If Stedman didn't like the news Michael was about to deliver, or, worse yet, if he didn't care, Michael's career could be on the line. Stedman could complain to Michael's superiors, who'd be well within their rights to haul him on the carpet for a major disciplinary action.

The secretary announced him, then turned silently and disappeared through the doorway through which they'd come. Stedman rose as Michael entered the room, and so did another man sitting on a sofa near the fireplace. Michael barely glanced at the other man, for Stedman commanded his attention.

"Captain Reed." The president stepped out from behind his desk and extended his hand, his mouth tipping in a faint smile. "A pleasure to meet you."

Taking his cue from the president's informality, Michael pulled his cover from his head, then accepted the president's hand instead of saluting. "A very great honor to meet you, sir. I only wish it were under more pleasant circumstances."

The president's brows knitted in a frown, then he gestured toward the other man. "I don't know if you've met Jack Powell, my chief of staff. I've asked him to sit in on this meeting, if you don't mind."

Michael hesitated. "I'm not certain if—"

The president cut him off with a quieting hand. "Jack knows Daniel Prentice is alive and well. And I trust both men completely."

Michael exhaled in relief. "Very good, sir."

Stedman gestured to a wing chair next to the sofa. "Won't you have a seat? Jack and I are very curious about what brings you here today."

"It's very simple," Michael said, taking the proffered chair, "but I'm stepping out on a limb here, all the same." He sat down with the others and took a moment to gather his thoughts as he tucked his cover and the classified folder under his arm. "Six months ago, sir, I received an e-mail from Daniel Prentice. I knew him, though only slightly, through Brad Hunter, who served with me in a SEAL platoon. In his message, Daniel asked me to keep my eyes and ears open for any unusual situations in the Middle East. If I noticed anything unusual, he said I should report directly to you."

Stedman leaned forward on the sofa, his brows flickering a little. "Has something happened?"

"Well, unusual is to be expected in a place as volatile as the Middle East, but this morning I discovered something . . . unexpected." Michael hesitated, glancing at Powell. The chief of staff was a civilian and not a part of the military chain of command.

Stedman raised his hands in a gesture of reassurance. "Speak freely, please."

"Yes, sir." Michael swallowed, then plunged ahead. "This morning we received information from an Echelon outpost in London that led us to believe the Russians are inviting Arab fighters to Russian military bases for training and arms supply. Last month a large group of Arabs from Sudan visited Pushkina, a Russian base not far from Moscow. This month the Russians are training Arab guerillas from Lebanon and Afghanistan."

He pulled the classified folder from under his arm and pulled out the photos, then spread them on the coffee table before the sofa. "These are NPIC recon photos, taken this morning, of the deserted PLO camps in Lebanon and Afghanistan. And this—" he tapped the shot of Pushkina— "is the Russian camp. It used to be closed, but you can see that it is quite active now."

Staring at the photographs, the president tented his hands and brought his fingertips to his lips, but said nothing.

Michael rubbed his hands together. "I wish I could tell you that an active Pushkina and deserted Arab camps are a coincidence, but these photos, combined with what we picked up through Echelon, confirm the link. The road to Pushkina looks like a freeway at rush hour—and as you can see, the soldiers in training there are wearing kaffiyehs."

Powell groaned, but still the president said nothing. He closed his eyes for a long minute, then lowered his hands and looked at Powell. "I'm going to have to ask you to step outside, Jack. Nothing personal."

"I understand, sir." With a surprised glance at Michael that belied his words, the chief of staff rose and left the room.

Stedman placed his hand on the polished coffee table, then pushed himself up from the sofa. "Come into my study, Captain Reed," he said, crossing the thick carpet with a noiseless tread. "That's where I keep my computer."

Michael rose and followed the president through a doorway opposite the one he had entered. A short hallway appeared behind this door; to his right hand he spied a small bathroom, to his left lay a crowded office scarcely large enough for a desk, a set of bookshelves, and a guest chair.

Unlike the stately desk in the Oval office, papers and files cluttered this desk top. A small laptop sat in the corner, an American flag screen saver fluttering across its screen.

"Now you know my guilty secret—I'm personally disorganized and a pack rat, too," Stedman said, moving to the battered leather chair that sat like a rock in the midst of a wind-whipped sea. He gestured to the worn chair crowded between the wall and the front of the desk. "Have a seat and make yourself comfortable. This might take a few minutes."

Suppressing a smile, Michael took the empty chair. Carefully, he pushed at a pile of papers and cleared a space large enough for him to rest his elbow on the desk while the president tapped at his computer. The screen saver vanished.

"It's a secure line," Stedman called over his shoulder, moving the cursor to launch an e-mail program. "And everything's encrypted. I don't understand half of it, but Daniel set it all up for me. If he says it's safe, I don't worry."

The corners of Michael's mouth lifted in a bemused smile as the president typed in an e-mail address he recognized: GWJ@prenticetech.com.

"That's the same address I used to contact Daniel," he said. "We tried to trace it but couldn't."

Stedman chuckled. "Of course you couldn't. If Daniel could outfox Adrian Romulus, I don't think he'd have any trouble outsmarting you NSA boys."

Michael swallowed the insult to the NSA without even wincing. He watched, growing more and more curious, as the president painstakingly typed a message:

Daniel—
    Michael Reed with me now. Proof of large numbers of Arab and Sudanese fighters being trained in Russia. Significance?
    SS

Stedman clicked Send, then leaned back in his chair and exhaled in an audible sigh as the screen flickered and went blank. "Sorry about my slow typing." The chair creaked as the president swiveled to face Michael. "But computers weren't standard operating equipment when I was in school.

I've had to pick up what I could as I practiced on this thing." He jerked his head toward the laptop. "I wouldn't have a computer at all, but Daniel and Lauren insisted I needed a secure way to communicate with them without interference. Daniel keeps in touch, and he'll get back to me in just a few minutes. He's never let me down."

Michael stared at the computer as a new realization bloomed in his brain. Nancy Reagan sought guidance from her astrologers; Bill Clinton used Hillary as a sounding board. Stedman's secret hot line to Daniel Prentice topped both of them. He gestured toward the laptop. "Does Powell know about this little setup?"

Stedman gave Michael a look of faint amusement. "He knows I'm in touch with Daniel, but he has no idea how, and I promised Daniel I'd keep his e-mail address confidential. But since Daniel has contacted you himself, there's no need for me to keep the address from you."

Michael rubbed his hand over his jaw. "I wonder if he's corresponding with anyone else."

"I didn't know about you, so it's a safe bet he is." Stedman's brow wrinkled as something moved in his eyes. "Daniel is his own man, and he does what he needs to do. Fortunately, he has the genius and the technology to pull off all sorts of escapades."

They sat for a moment in companionable silence, and then Michael asked a question that had been niggling at him for months: "Why is he still hiding? Surely it's safe for him to come home."

"I would love for Daniel and Lauren to come back to Washington." Unspoken pain glowed in Stedman's eyes. "Victoria and I loved Lauren like a daughter. But Daniel made powerful enemies when he worked with the Y2K problem, and he doesn't dare underestimate them. If they could get to Victoria within the safe confines of the White House, Daniel knows they could get to him or Lauren anywhere." He paused, regarding his laptop with a speculative gaze. "It's far safer for Daniel Prentice to be thought dead than to surface. With the blessing of the Canadian government, I myself sealed the results of the DNA tests on the body found near the old SAGE base in Canada."

"If it wasn't Prentice—" Michael hesitated, uncomfortably aware that he was asking the president to divulge a secret better off buried.

"It was one of the enemy." Stedman shrugged. "No tears were shed for him. And the appearance of a body helped quiet the rumors about Daniel and Lauren Prentice."

Michael let his gaze rove around the office as they waited in silence. A grouping of framed photographs occupied a bookshelf behind the president's desk, and Michael immediately recognized the elegant woman featured in one of them. Victoria Stedman had been a beloved first lady, and the nation as well as her husband mourned her loss. The next photograph was of a young girl, probably eighteen or nineteen, smiling behind the wheel of a car. Though Michael's memory was a little fuzzy, he was fairly certain the girl was Jessica Stedman, who had been killed in a boating accident years before her father ran for president.

A bell chimed from the laptop, and the president nodded in satisfaction as he swiveled to face the computer. "I didn't think he'd keep us waiting. Daniel must walk around with a laptop under his arm."

Stedman clicked on the message, and the screen filled with a mishmash of jumbled letters. "More security," the president grumbled in a good-natured tone as he clicked another series of keys. "Sometimes I think Daniel is paranoid."

"Just because you're paranoid doesn't mean they're *not* out to get you," Michael said, reciting a common joke around his office.

Stedman grimaced in good humor, his eyes intent upon the screen. From where he sat, Michael couldn't make out the words, but he didn't interrupt until the president had finished reading.

When he turned to face Michael again, the president wore a puzzled look. Before sharing the message, however, he tilted his head and asked, "How well did you know Daniel, Captain Reed?"

Michael straightened in his chair. "Not terribly well, sir. I met him and Brad Hunter just before the start of the Gulf War. We ate dinner together a few nights, swapped a few stories aboard ship. I was much closer to Brad than to Daniel."

Stedman nodded, his eyes distant. "It wouldn't matter, I suppose. Daniel didn't become interested in world politics until last year. But I think it's fair to say he's become quite knowledgeable—probably a bit of an expert."

Michael clasped his hands. "I noticed that about him when we met. Whatever he set his hand to do, he did it well—or he stayed at it until he did it well."

The president looked down, his lined eyelids hiding his eyes. "I don't know if you are aware of this, but in the past few months Daniel has become a believer in the Bible. He's quite passionate about his belief, as is Lauren. And he has begun to search the Scriptures, particularly the Old Testament prophets, for clues about what will happen in the last days."

Michael felt his stomach drop. The empty place filled with a frightening hollowness as he stared at the president. "Does he really think these are the *last* days?"

"I'm afraid he does."

Michael looked away, unable to believe what he was hearing. "That's strange, because Daniel never impressed me as an extremist. He was anything but a gloom-and-doomer, not at all the type to run around and scream about the sky falling."

Stedman inclined his gray head. "He's still not that type. I've never seen anyone approach a conviction with such complete assurance and reliability. He is not making rash predictions; he's not pessimistic. But he's told me about things I should watch for, and he's been right on more occasions than I care to admit. And this letter—" He leaned his elbow on the armrest of his chair and rested his head on his knuckles. "Well, he's giving us a lot to consider. Coupled with the information you've brought today, I think Daniel may be on to something."

A pulse of apprehension coursed through Michael as he waited for an explanation, but Stedman only stared through the wall, his thoughts apparently a million miles away.

"Sir," Michael began, approaching with caution, "may I know what Daniel has told you? If it is relevant to the information I've just brought—"

The president abruptly snapped out of his reverie and clicked on a computer icon. "Captain, it is nothing *but* relevant." A second later, the printer on the credenza began to hum. A sheet of paper shot out and landed in the printer tray, then the president handed the sheet to Michael.

"Read Daniel's message yourself, Captain," Stedman said, returning to his pensive pose. "Then let me know what you think."

Michael began to read:

Dear Mr. President:
　　The news from Russia and the Arab world is not at all surprising.

Consider the words of the prophet Ezekiel, chapter 38: "Son of man, set your face against Gog, of the land of Magog, the chief prince of Meshech and Tubal; prophesy against him and say: 'This is what the Sovereign Lord says: I am against you, O Gog, chief prince of Meshech and Tubal. I will turn you around, put hooks in your jaws and bring you out with your whole army—your horses, your horsemen fully armed, and a great horde with large and small shields, all of them brandishing their swords. Persia, Cush and Put will be with them, all with shields and helmets, also Gomer with all its troops, and Beth Togarmah from the far north with all its troops—the many nations with you.

"'Get ready; be prepared, you and all the hordes gathered about you, and take command of them. After many days you will be called to arms. In future years you will invade a land that has recovered from war, whose people were gathered from many nations to the mountains of Israel, which had long been desolate. They had been brought out from the nations, and now all of them live in safety.'"

There is more, Mr. President, but I will attempt to summarize.

The ancient list of nations can be translated as follows: Magog is Russia, while Meshech and Tubal represent ancient divisions of Russia. Persia is Iran, Iraq, and Afghanistan. Cush and Put are contemporary Ethiopia, Sudan, and Libya. Gomer represents as yet undetermined countries of Eastern Europe, and Beth Togarmah includes Turkey and southeastern Europe. Ezekiel's phrase "the many nations with you" could indicate another multinational group, perhaps the European Union or a force from the United Nations.

Ezekiel spoke of "a land that has recovered from war, whose people were gathered from many nations," and that land is undoubtedly Israel. And as a result of the recently concluded peace process with the PLO, Israel is now dwelling in safety.

I am in contact with an American in Moscow, and she confirms that the Russian army is currently engaging in a massive series of war games. The minister of defense, the man the Scripture identifies as Gog, is negotiating with emissaries from the exact nations Ezekiel foretold.

Israel must be warned, and she must be prepared. The enemy is coming.

His name is Gen. Vladimir Vasilievich Gogol.

The rest of Daniel's message was a personal greeting from Lauren, but Michael's brain didn't even register those words, so struck was he by Daniel's analysis of the current situation.

"I work in the Middle East division," he heard himself saying as his hand dropped into his lap. "I'm not an expert on Russia or her military advisors. I've heard of this General Gogol, but I'm really not up to speed on his activities."

"If Daniel's right, there will be no stopping him." Stedman's eyes were still abstracted with thought, but they cleared as he looked up and met Michael's gaze. "What was the phrase Ezekiel used? 'I will put hooks in your jaws and bring you out.' If God himself will bring this Russian forward, then these things will happen no matter what we do."

Michael listened in bewilderment. "Surely, sir, you don't believe the Scriptures are referring to an actual invasion. For every theologian who believes as Daniel does, I could find a dozen who believe that passage from Ezekiel is a metaphor for the apocalyptic battle between good and evil. Others would say it applies to an altogether different event in history."

"Victoria would believe Daniel." Stedman's faint smile held a touch of sadness. "She always insisted the Bible was infallible. If God said something would come to pass, she knew it would."

Michael sat back, momentarily rebuffed. After a long hesitation, he tried a different approach. "Sir, I consider myself a Christian. I grew up in the church, and I've sat through more Sunday school classes than I can count. If there's one thing I've learned about theology, it's that in these gray areas we all must agree to disagree if we're going to keep the peace."

"The peace is not going to last." The president's vivid blue eyes were distant and still. "We've known that all along. Throughout the peace negotiations, Arafat told the Palestinians he would offer Israel 'the peace of Saladin.' Any historian knows Saladin was the Muslim leader who attacked the Crusaders after he had negotiated a truce with them. Arafat has also described the current peace treaty as being like 'the al-Khudaibiya peace,' the ten-year treaty Mohammed broke after only two years." The president shook his head. "No. The Mideastern peace was never intended to last."

Michael's mind whirled at Stedman's dry response. This was not something he should be discussing with the president of the United States. This was a matter for people at the UN, for foreign policy specialists, for the president's cabinet and the Joint Chiefs. Yet Stedman seemed to be voicing his thoughts aloud, and Michael wondered whether he was expected to serve as a sounding board or play devil's advocate. Certainly the president needed someone in whom he could confide. Deprived of his wife and two of his closest friends, his circle of confidants had grown smaller in the past few months.

"Sir," Michael began, "maybe the passage Daniel quoted is just a prophetic warning—something intended to urge us toward caution. America certainly can't afford a war in the Middle East, particularly with the oil princes of the Arab nations. We depend too heavily upon foreign oil."

"Daniel thinks it's more than a warning." Stedman placed his broad hands on the edge of his desk, his knuckles whitening as he gripped it. "And I've got to do something for Israel. Her enemies are coming."

"But Russia can't afford to launch a major war right now. Her economy is in ruins—"

"That's why it's significant that her allies are the *Arabs*. The Arab nations have money . . . and the Russians have the military expertise. It's a match made—well, we can't say it was made in heaven, can we?"

Trying to force his confused emotions into order, Michael pressed his lips together. This president couldn't afford to become involved in an explosive foreign military situation, especially not when his presidential opponent was preaching isolationism.

Devil's advocate it would be, then. He took a deep breath and launched out into unknown waters. "Sir, I believe we've done more than enough for Israel; we've certainly done more for her than for any other nation. Israel has benefited from U.S. military assistance at a level of approximately $1.8 billion annually since the mid-1980s. We officiated at the signings of the peace treaties; we sent troops with the UN force to oversee the Israeli withdrawals from the Gaza Strip, the Golan Heights, and most of the West Bank. Your political opponents won't allow you to do more, especially not with the election only one month away."

The president looked at the ceiling, as if appealing to a higher authority, then turned his gaze to Michael. "You're right, of course. So I won't do anything public. I will do something quietly and work in plain sight. We send military representatives to liaise with foreign governments all the time, so I'll send someone to Israel. He will quietly learn if they are aware of this impending threat, and he'll ask what we can do to help. If they need arms, if they need planes, we'll take care of it. When the election is over and everyone has forgotten about Blackstone and his fantasy world, I'll be able to get the necessary appropriations from Congress to push through an aid package. We'll make certain Israel can stand up to anything that comes her way."

Michael brought his hand to his chin, a little unnerved by the president's broad assumptions. He was assuming that he'd win the election and that Congress would be willing to extend still more foreign aid to Israel. In case of an imminent attack they could, of course, advance certain weapons from the Sixth Fleet in the Mediterranean without congressional approval, but Stedman was obviously thinking of major American involvement . . .

Would the American people sign on for a war to defend Israel? Somehow Michael doubted it.

He shifted his weight and checked his watch, sincerely hoping the president had another appointment. "Well, if there's nothing else, sir—"

"There is something else." Stedman's palm slapped the desk, startling Michael like a thunderclap. "I want *you* to be my personal representative in Israel. You and Daniel are in touch, Daniel and I are in touch, and I'd bet my bottom dollar that Daniel will be able to put you and me in touch while you're over there. I'll send you to Maj. Gen. Doron Yanai, director of the IDF Liaison Unit, and you'll ask to speak to Lt. Gen. Yehuda Almog, chief of the general staff and the man directly under the minister of defense. You'll quietly convey my regards and offer our assistance."

Michael sat there, blank, amazed, and more shaken than he cared to admit. Apparently oblivious to Michael's dismay, the president rocked back in his chair and continued his train of thought. "I'd be surprised if the Israelis aren't already aware of the facts you shared with me this morning. Their Mossad agents don't miss a trick about what goes on in those Arab camps. So you'll go, see what they need, and determine how we can help."

Michael finally found breath enough to speak. "But, sir—"

Wearing the satisfied smile of a man who has solved a pressing problem, Stedman lifted a silver brow. "I'm sure I don't need to remind you that the Israelis cannot afford to lose a single battle." His face suddenly went grim. "Now that they no longer have the Golan Heights from which they could repel a conventional attack, Israel has little choice but to respond to aggression with nuclear weapons. Israel might be defeated in a full-fledged invasion, but she'll take her neighbors with her."

Michael took pains to sheathe his voice in a neutral tone. "The Samson Option."

"Exactly. Die if you must, but destroy your enemies in the process."

Michael stared at the carpet as the muscles of his throat moved in a convulsive swallow. "Mr. President, I appreciate your confidence in me, but I really don't think I'm the right man for this job. I spent quite a bit of time in Lebanon, back in '82 and '83. I didn't like the Middle East much then, and I don't think I'll like it now. I respectfully ask that you find someone else for this assignment."

Stedman didn't answer, but Michael felt the pressure of that blue gaze upon him. When he lifted his head, the president's eyes were compassionate, troubled, and still. "Perhaps it's just me," he said, his voice containing a strong suggestion of reproach, "but don't you think it's odd that an expert on the Middle East wouldn't enjoy traveling in that part of the world?"

Michael lifted one shoulder in a shrug. "It's personal, sir."

The president nodded slowly, then picked up a pencil and balanced it between his fingers while his other hand came to rest on the uppermost folder on his desk. "I think I understand your reasons, son. I had the NSA fax over a copy of your file after my secretary told me you'd be coming in this morning."

Michael looked away, unable to meet those burning blue eyes. So Stedman had read his jacket—what had he read between the lines of his fitness reports?

The president's pencil tapped out a steady rhythm on the desk. "Don't you think I feel the same way every time I stand outside beneath the White House portico?" Stedman continued, speaking with a gentle ferocity that made it abundantly clear he had learned the secret wounds of Michael's past. "Every time I walk down that hallway and step out into the sunshine, I think about that Sunday morning when I lost my wife. The memory twists my guts into a knot, and I suppose I'll feel that way for a long time to come. But I go on. Because I have a duty—and because Victoria would want me to."

You have a duty also. The words were unspoken, but Michael heard them as clearly as if the president had shouted in his ear. A wave of bitterness arose and threatened to engulf him, but he pushed it back and straightened his spine. Something in him wanted to shout that he had already paid his dues; now he was entitled to pursue his career without interference from the pale ghosts who haunted his dreams.

But he had been a warrior far too long, and Stedman was his commander in chief. He lifted his chin and met the president's gaze head-on. "I assume I am to remain at my present post until time to depart?"

"The time to depart was yesterday." Stedman paused to pinch the bridge of his nose, then lowered his hand and gave Daniel a weary smile. "Go back to the NSA, make your report, and submit it as usual. Say nothing about your visit to see me. I'll set things in motion, and by tomorrow you should receive word that you are being dispatched to Israel for a routine diplomatic visit. Once in Israel, speak freely with IDF officials about the Russian threat, but don't reveal my involvement in this matter. Communicate with Daniel; he will put you in touch with me if necessary."

Michael stood, tugged his cover into place, then gave Stedman a formal salute. "A pleasure to meet you, sir." His throat constricted as he forced the next words: "And an honor to serve you."

Samuel Stedman stood as well, a relieved smile upon his face as he returned the salute. "I have a feeling Daniel knew what he was doing when he tapped you for this job, Michael. Godspeed, and God bless."

CHAPTER SEVEN

Moscow
2000 hours

ALANNA PULLED THE FUR COLLAR OF HER COAT CLOSER TO HER CHEEKS, THEN thrust her gloved hands into her pockets and continued her walk. Feeling restless and irritable in the confines of the hotel, she'd left the suite for a stroll around the river. Vladimir had not returned by nightfall, and she doubted he would. His brain had shifted to business as he left her, and once he set his mind upon a thing, he was as tenacious as a terrier.

Shivering, she paused at an intersection and looked around, past the sluggish traffic and the stone-faced buildings crowded cheek by jowl. Curls of gauzy steam rose from grates set into the gutters, and snowflakes spiraled down from a black sky so close it seemed to brush against the painted, onion-shaped domes of St. Basil's Cathedral. Tiny lights shimmered from windows in a government building, reflecting diamondlike against the blackness.

The light changed, and she stepped into the street, lowering her head into her high collar as the wind blew. Her American friends would think her insane for walking alone after dark in a city as large as Moscow, but in the brightly lit areas surrounding Red Square she felt as safe as the pope in Rome. More than once she caught a uniformed guard's eye and found herself receiving a respectful nod. The soldiers all knew Vladimir, and now they all knew her. Just last week Vladimir had brought home a newspaper and proudly pointed to the front-page photo—a shot of the two of them alighting from his staff car. A string of diamonds had glittered from her throat, and in his uniform he looked like a dignified, if slightly aged, Prince Charming.

She quickened her pace as the cold began to seep into her bones. She had been walking for half an hour, her long stride easily covering the city blocks between the Hotel Metropol and Red Square. Now it was time to go back, prepare a cup of tea, and slip into bed with one of the books she'd brought from home.

She lengthened her stride in an effort to burn a couple of extra calories. She had gained weight moiling around the empty hotel suite, snacking out of boredom as she watched an endless stream of talk shows on the Moscow television station. The good thing about her boring daytime existence was that she had begun to develop an ear for the Russian language; the bad thing was that she had gained five pounds in three months.

Hunching into her coat, she took a moment to lift her hand in an impromptu salute as she passed the monument to Russia's printing pioneer, Ivan Fedorov. The brass statue dated from 1909, Sergei had told her on one of their walks, but Fedorov printed the first Russian book in 1563—a copy of the Acts of the Apostles for the Russian Orthodox Church. "Good evening, Ivan," she whispered as she hurried past, her teeth beginning to chatter despite her brisk pace. "Print a book for me in English, will you?"

The temperature seemed to drop as the moments passed, and she was nearly sprinting by the time she reached the marble steps that led to the hotel lobby. A few Japanese tourists lingered in a tight knot just beyond the elevator, and she deliberately turned away from them, not wanting to invite conversation. She punched the call button and flexed her cold fingers in her leather gloves, then noticed that the glass display case in the marble wall had been changed.

She stared at the display, shocked and startled by a sudden elusive thought she could not quite fathom. The display was not particularly unique and not at all flashy by American standards. Several books on brass stands had been arranged very prettily against a swath of emerald green satin. The books themselves could not have arrested her attention, for three of them were titled in the Cyrillic alphabet, which still looked like chicken scratching to Alanna. The fourth book, a little red volume, was a copy of the classic *Uncle Tom's Cabin*.

She took a quick breath of utter astonishment. *Uncle Tom's Cabin?* In English?

She turned on the ball of her foot and strode to the front desk. "Excuse me." She pointed to the display and hoped the clerk spoke English. "The bookstore. Is it open?"

Apparently she had managed to communicate. "*Da,*" the man behind the counter said, pointing toward the curving hallway that ran along the front of the building.

"*Spasibo,* thank you." She hurried down the corridor, her heart lifting with hope. She passed a ladies' clothing store, a newsstand, a tourists' travel office, then braked to a halt at the threshold of an honest-to-goodness antiquarian bookstore. For a moment she merely stood there, inhaling the scent of rich leathers and dusty pages, then a child's treble voice cut through the silence.

"Madame?"

She opened her eyes and smiled at the boy who stood before her. He was an adorable urchin with wide eyes the color of coffee. "Hello," she whispered shyly, bringing her hands together. "Is this your shop?"

The boy grinned, his new teeth too big in his small face. "You are American?"

Alanna laughed. "You speak English?"

"Yes." He turned and lifted his voice toward someone in the back of the shop. "Mama! Papa! We have a customer! A *beautiful* lady!"

A moment later a man came forward, wiping his hands on his work apron. He paused behind the boy, his hands resting on the lad's shoulders. "We are about to close, Madame, but if you need something—"

Alanna lifted her hand and gestured at the well-stocked shelves. "It's, ah—well, I was surprised to see your display in the lobby. I didn't know you carried English books."

"Yes, Madame. We have a wide variety of old and new English volumes." The man nodded, and Alanna noticed for the first time that he wore a *yarmulke* firmly planted on his head.

She tilted her head, her heart softening. "I am Alanna Ivanova, and I am pleased to meet you. My mother was Jewish. I have met so few people in Moscow and no other Jews."

A woman appeared from behind a towering bookshelf. A touch of bright lipstick emphasized the indoor pallor of her face, but a small smile curved her mouth as Alanna finished speaking.

The man nodded, his hands remaining firmly planted upon the boy. "We are Ari and Rochel Benjamin. And this is our son, Ethan."

"I'm delighted to meet you all." Alanna basked in the warmth of their smiles for a moment, then remembered that the hour was late. "I won't keep you, but I would like to buy—" she reached out and grasped the first book within reach. The title was in Russian, and she had no idea what the book was about. But she couldn't leave without buying something.

Rochel's eyes widened. "You want *that* book?"

"Perhaps you would like to look at another." Ari gestured toward another shelf. "That volume is very old, very expensive."

Alanna managed a faint smile, knowing Vladimir would pay for anything she bought. And expensive was good, the money would help this family. "Don't worry, the book is a gift. Charge it to my room, please." As Ari took the book and wrapped it in tissue paper, Rochel scrawled out a sales slip. After Alanna signed it, little Ethan presented her with the package, neatly wrapped in butcher paper and tied with string.

"Thank you so much." Alanna hugged the book to her chest. "I will come again, for some English books. I love to read."

Rochel walked her to the door, a ring of keys jangling in her hand. "Shalom, Alanna."

Alanna smiled, grateful she had finally found a friend. "Shalom to you, too."

CHAPTER EIGHT

District of Columbia
1230 hours

GO BACK TO THE MIDDLE EAST?

Though Michael had been honored by the evidence of the president's faith in him, the more he thought about his upcoming duty, the more the idea rankled. He gritted his teeth and steered expertly around a black limousine oozing through the red light. "Yes, sir, Mr. President," he muttered, "I'd just *love* to go back to the place where we were neither appreciated nor welcome. I can't wait to dredge up the memories of Hamra Street, where a man took his life in his hands just stepping out for a little fresh air. I'm just *dying* to get back to that dry heat, those stubborn zealots, and the Arabs who consider it an honor to blow themselves up and take Americans with them . . . just like they took Janis."

Even after seventeen years, his wife's name knifed across his heart with a pain far more excruciating than any training he had ever endured. He pushed the 'Vette into the left lane and blew past the lawful drivers, but he couldn't outrun his memories. They filled his brain, dancing on the back of his retinas as his body automatically guided the convertible toward 295 and the relative safety of his office in Fort Meade.

For him, the nightmare of Lebanon had begun the morning he kissed Janis good-bye in Virginia, then mounted a chopper that would carry him to join the other operators of SEAL Team Six. SEAL Six, a clandestine antiterrorist unit, had been tasked with inserting into Beirut to quietly assess the terrorist threat to American targets in the area. Just before Christmas 1982, Michael and eleven of his fellow SEALs entered the city by different routes, then posed as journalists and went sightseeing.

They didn't like what they saw. The entire area was a hotbed for terrorist activity, each city block ruled by a different philosophical, religious, or political group. Worst of all, the American marines who helped make up the international peacekeeping force had been instructed to patrol with their hands tied behind their backs—literally, with their guns on safety and no round in the chamber. The marines were not allowed to even chamber a round unless told to do so by a commissioned officer—or unless they were in immediate danger of being mown down by machine gun fire. Trouble was, the enemy didn't believe in middle-of-the-street, Wyatt Earp–type shootouts. They shot at the good guys from behind cars, through dark windows, and through brush so thick it'd take a machete to clear a path. When Michael saw what the marines had to deal with, he thanked God he was a navy man.

One night the techno-wizards brought the spying SEALs a new toy—a little black box that broadcast a wide range of radio signals up to a thousand feet. Since most car bombs were detonated by radio signals, this little gadget would automatically set off any explosive device within range—before it got close enough to damage a target. Michael and three other SEALs hopped into a car, flipped the black box's power supply, and went for a leisurely drive through Lebanon. They had scarcely driven a mile when a building two blocks ahead erupted in a fireball. As chunks of concrete and shards of glass rained down upon their vehicle, Michael ducked low in the seat and looked at Shark, his swim buddy.

"I think we snagged a big one."

A wry smile flashed in the thicket of Shark's beard. "One less bomb to blow us up, man."

The next week the SEAL commander presented their evaluation to a senior official stationed at the American Embassy. He detailed the results of the SEAL survey—the embassy was vulnerable, as was the airport barracks housing the marines. A wall of sandbags and light barricades wouldn't stop a determined terrorist, but if one or two of those little black transmitters were mounted on the embassy rooftop, any potential car bomb would be detonated *before* it reached the building—

The official's answer was strictly standard issue: no. An explosion on the street might kill innocent civilians, and that could not be allowed.

Frustrated and furious, the SEALs returned to Virginia. Michael went back to Janis, and two months later he transferred out of SEAL Six and went to work in the Pentagon, filling a temporary slot in the office of the deputy chief of naval operations. Unfortunately, that slot proved too temporary, and he found himself back in Lebanon in March 1983, working as a military attaché for the commander of the U.S.S. *Independence,* stationed off the Lebanese coast. His mission this time wasn't clandestine, and every time he put on his uniform Michael thought he might as well paint a big red bull's-eye on the back of his shirt.

Tensions had been mounting in the area for weeks and escalated when persons unknown ambushed an Italian mobile patrol on the night of March 15. The next day someone threw a hand grenade at a marine foot patrol in Ouzai, just north of the marine barracks at Beirut International Airport. Five marines were wounded, none seriously, as were several Lebanese citizens.

Michael called in a naval medical team to guard and treat the injured Lebanese nationals. That gesture of goodwill seemed to quiet the troubled area, so in early April, when Janis telephoned and said she'd made plans to visit, Michael was delighted.

He met her at the airport, half-suspecting the reason she'd flown halfway around the world to see him. And yet she kept her secret until that night in the Summerland Hotel, when they lay in each other's arms surrounded by silence. "We're going to have a baby, Michael," she said, reaching up to touch his cheek. "In October. I'm sixteen weeks pregnant."

For a moment he couldn't speak. Though he had certainly suspected she might be expecting, hearing her confirmation sent a thrill shivering through his senses. He slid his hand beneath the sheet and pressed it to the rounded curve of her belly, then thought he might burst from the sudden swell of happiness touching her gave him. A new *person* lay beneath his hand. Through some miracle of God, they had managed to pass the gift of life on to another human soul.

"Janis—" Words failed him, but she understood. She looked at him with dewy moisture in her great beautiful eyes, then she pulled him closer, hope and love and the promise of tomorrow all mingled in her kiss.

The next morning, Michael got up, dressed, and prepared for his three-mile run. Janis still lay in bed, drowsy with contentment and jet lag. They would have one more night together, then she would have to leave . . . but Michael wasn't ready to think about parting.

"Hey, sweetness." He sat by the side of the bed and lifted the tide of brown hair from her sleeping face. "I'm going out for my run. Want me to bring you anything?"

"I'd better get up." Her eyes blinked once, then closed again.

"Sleep all you want. Mothers-to-be need their rest."

"Gotta get to the embassy and confirm my flight for tomorrow." She lifted one eyelid and peered out at him. "Unless you want to do it for me."

"I don't even want to think about you leaving."

"Then let me get up. I'll go to the embassy while you're running, then we can spend the rest of the day together and not worry about a thing."

He grinned as she pushed herself up. She looked like a young girl—rumpled, fresh-faced, and absolutely innocent.

He pressed a kiss to her forehead, then bent lower and planted a kiss on her tummy, too. "So long, junior," he said, his wide hand covering the warm place where their baby grew. "Be back in an hour."

He had just reached Hamra Street and turned back when the explosion shook the city. A feeling of empty-bellied terror paralyzed him for an instant, then he sprinted in the direction of the blast, his legs pumping to the percussive beat of his heart.

When he arrived, the embassy building looked as if an enemy fighter jet had bombed it. The wall of sandbags designed to discourage terrorists had contained the force of the explosion, directing the blast upward to wreak more damage. Now a heap of rubble was all that remained of the front portion of the seven-story building. A thick cloud of debris hung over the scene, a whirling haze of dust, smoke, and embers. Pieces of furniture, bits of steel, and crumbled concrete littered the ground, while a potted plant leaned against a twisted iron railing of the fence.

The contents of the building were still raining down upon the street, papers slip-sliding through the air currents as sirens roared. With a detachment that horrified him afterward, Michael noticed a hand on the ground, the nails bitten and chewed, the knuckles covered in dark hair.

A lone Lebanese guard stood trembling in the courtyard, a trickle of blood running from his ear, his cheek marked with a four-inch laceration that would require stitches. Ignoring the shell-shocked guard, Michael threw himself into the whirling smoke, ripping the skin of his hands as he tossed aside blocks and twisted shards of metal and glass. Part of him wanted to run back to the hotel and discover that Janis had gone back to sleep, that she and the baby were safe and sound, but another, more cynical part of his brain knew she was a woman of her word. She had said she would go to the embassy, so she had to be inside.

A reaction company arrived to secure the area, and strong hands pulled Michael away from the debris. Within twenty minutes Colonel Mead arrived, and all available corpsmen were dispatched to treat the injured. Two surgical teams from the Sixth Fleet came ashore to assist the staff of American University Hospital. Michael paced in the midst of the destruction, and between each ragged breath he heard himself repeating Janis's name as if he had been stricken by a terminal case of Tourette's syndrome and would spend the rest of his life calling for her.

They found Janis after four hours. From all indications she had been standing just inside the embassy lobby, less than twenty feet from the spot where the suicide bomber parked a van loaded with a ton of explosives. By the time the marines finished piecing the victims together, the count stood at sixty-three people dead, among them seventeen Americans. Eighteen, Michael thought, if they counted his unborn child.

When he heard the final count, Michael shivered with revulsion, a spasm of hatred and disgust that rose from his soul. It was all for nothing. A single black box transmitter on the rooftop would have exploded the bomb in the street, away from his innocent wife and child.

The navy offered Michael the opportunity to go home, but he refused. As a SEAL he had learned to play with pain, and every warrior knew that death was a necessary and inevitable part of war. Michael remained at his post, clung to his routine. Though his mind accepted Janis's death, something inside him wasn't sure how he would react if he went home and faced the apartment where every piece of furniture and every picture whispered of his wife. She had already begun to decorate the nursery, she'd said. How could the navy expect him to be comforted by confronting *that?*

For security reasons, the navy recalled all personnel to the safety of the sea. Michael was onboard the *Independence* on October 23, when another suicide truck blew up the marine barracks at Beirut International Airport. Michael had been in a miserable mood all month, knowing that October was when his baby should have been born. The tragedy of so many senseless deaths only thickened the cocoon of anguish around him. During the memorial service, he stood with his comrades on the deck of the *Independence,* the brooding sorrow between them seeming to spawn and spread until it mingled with the million other sorrows borne by the people living in the ancient and war-torn land on the opposite shore.

Now Samuel Stedman wanted him to revisit those shores. And while Israel wasn't Lebanon, the warring factions hadn't changed. The hostility between the Jews and Arabs had existed ever since Abraham favored Isaac over Ishmael.

A dump truck rumbled by on the highway, spitting tiny pieces of gravel that pinged against his windshield. Michael frowned and pulled the Corvette to the right, wishing he could dodge the president's request as easily. Since this upcoming trip would officially be routine, he supposed he *could* have refused, but no career officer would refuse any favor requested by the commander in chief. Besides, Michael respected Samuel Stedman, and the prospect of working with Daniel Prentice intrigued him.

He had thought about leaving the military when the time came to raise a family, but after Janis died, the military became his home. Breast cancer had taken his mother when Michael was a teenager; by the time Michael enlisted, his father had married a woman half his age and settled down to raise another family.

So he remained in the navy, moving steadily up through the ranks, performing his work with a recklessness that often won him praise. His fellow officers called him daring; his superiors decorated him with medals and commendations. The SEAL team he led in the Gulf War gave him the admiring nickname "Iceman," for he kept his cool when Murphy's Law kicked in and every possible aspect of an operation went wrong. Michael had been sorely tempted to explain that the quality they cataloged as bravery was really simple indifference.

Surely that layer of indifference would protect him when he went back to the Middle East. He would speak to the Israelis on the president's behalf, learn what they knew and what they needed, and promise more arms after the election. If all went well, he'd be in and out of Israel within a week, two at the most.

He slanted the Corvette toward the Highway 198 exit and clicked on the radio, settling back against the car's upholstery. As a Beatles tune began to play on the classic rock station, he told himself he was making too much of this assignment. Seventeen years had passed since that cursed operation in Beirut, and his heart had grown stronger. After all he had endured, one short trip to Israel would be a piece of cake.

-0100111100-

"Michael? I need to talk to you."

Michael stared into the darkness, trying to see whatever it was that had slashed his sleep like a knife. The air in his bedroom was heavy, warm, and still, filled with a gentle presence that painted his fear with frustration. He knew the voice, but it was not possible that Janis could be speaking to him.

"Turn on the light, honey."

He sat up, clenching the blanket with one hand while the other fumbled for the lamp on the bedside table. He turned the switch and flinched when he saw Janis sitting on the edge of his bed.

"I don't believe this." His voice came out whispery soft and tinged with terror. "I don't believe in ghosts."

A golden glow rose in Janis's face, as though she contained a candle that had just been lit. "I'm not a ghost, silly. This is a dream." One delicate brow lifted in amusement. "Surely you believe in dreams?"

Michael clenched the sheets tighter. "This doesn't feel like a dream."

She lifted one shoulder in a shrug. "It is what it is, Michael, and I can't help the way things are." She smiled, and her eyes burned with the clear, deep blue in the heart of a flame. "I'd love to be with you, but Jody and I are happy here. We're waiting for you, until the time is right."

"Jody?"

"Our son."

Michael flushed as an inexplicable wave of pride rippled through him. A son! His child was not some unformed fetus, but a person, a boy named Jody.

"Are you—" Michael swallowed hard as he met the apparition's gaze— "in heaven?"

A dimple appeared in Janis's cheek. "Of course. To be absent from the body is to be present with the Lord. You shouldn't worry about us, not at all. But sometimes I think I should worry about you."

This *had* to be a dream. This was a guilt-induced figment of his imagination, some part of his subconscious rising to chide him for his reluctance to return to the Middle East. It made sense that his unwillingness would be personified as Janis, whose death had forever soured him on the place. Michael slowly relaxed his fingers. While he was a little disappointed to think the news about his son was nothing more than a gift served up from his subconscious longings, it was reassuring to know this was no supernatural visitation.

"Don't worry about me." He waved the vision away. "I'm fine. Life is great, the career is going well, and I even met the president today."

"I know." A faint line appeared between Janis's brows. "That's why I'm here, Michael. This trip the president wants you to take—it's very important. More than you know is at stake."

Disconcerted, Michael crossed his arms and pointedly looked away. He had already agreed to go, so why was his subconscious still nagging at him?

"Do you think it was mere chance that you were spared in Beirut and the Gulf War?" Janis asked, her voice echoing in the emptiness of his bedroom. The curtain fluttered at the cracked window, and Michael stared at it, confused by these touches of reality. If this were really a dream, he and Janis should have been sitting on a deserted island beach, kissing in some tropical paradise. They should not be in his bedroom, with a real lamp shining and the scent of his neighbor's burning fireplace creeping through the open window.

"God spared you, Michael." A secretive smile softened Janis's lips. She reached up and tucked a strand of hair behind her ear, and he felt a strange lurch of recognition in the gesture. "That's why you didn't go with me to the embassy that morning. That's why you were safely out of harm's way that day in October when terrorists attacked the marine barracks. And that's why the shell that landed only yards from your unit in Kuwait didn't explode."

"What?" The word burst from him in a gasp. He knew of no shell nearly hitting his unit. His SEAL team had been used for reconnaissance, and they were far behind enemy lines when the brief fighting broke out.

"Friendly fire." Janis lowered her gaze and idly ran her hand over the quilt. "God had a hand in that, too. One of the infantry tank units misread the coordinates and fired a shell at your position. It fell harmlessly into the sand. Freeman saw it but didn't tell anyone because he didn't want to cause a panic."

"Freeman?"

A smile nudged itself into a corner of her mouth. "I think you know him as Shark."

Michael gave her a sidelong glance of utter disbelief. Janis wouldn't know the nicknames of the guys in the platoon, but he did, and he was scripting this dream. But there was no way she was telling the truth about the shell because characters in a dream couldn't know what the dreamer didn't know.

He leaned forward and rested his arms on his knees, then raked his hand through his hair. He either possessed a far more creative imagination than he had ever guessed, or there was something extremely eerie about all this.

He threw the figment a frown. "So God saved me and my men—for what?"

"He saved you because he loves you, Michael." She spoke in a tone filled with awe and respect. "Though sometimes you grieve the Father's heart, you are still one of his children. He's always had a plan for you, and the greatest part of it is yet to come."

Surprised to feel the sting of tears, he glanced away, his voice breaking with huskiness. "He loved you, too, Janis. So why did he let you die?"

"Oh, Michael." She gave him an indulgent smile, like a parent amused by the questions of a child. "Trust him. Today and tomorrow, for the rest of your life. Just trust him. Understanding comes with time."

A soft beep sounded from the computer on the desk, and Janis turned toward it, the lamplight painting her hair with a shimmery golden glow. "You should read that," she said, pointing toward the monitor. "Daniel Prentice will help you."

Michael leaned sideways and peered at the computer, but the monitor was dark, in hibernation mode. The machine shouldn't have even beeped, for after an hour of inactivity the system shut down until he woke it with a command.

When he turned again, Janis was gone. The lamp still burned, the wind still blew the curtains, but he was quite alone.

He switched off the lamp, lay down and pulled the quilt to his shoulders, but sleep would not come. Finally, when the glowing numerals 5:45 shone from the clock across the room, he got out of bed, switched off the alarm, and shivered in the chill. Wrapping the quilt around his shoulders, he walked to the computer, typed in his password, and waited while the disk drive whirred and the monitor crackled to life.

He had one message in his mailbox, from GWJ@prenticetech.com:

Michael:

   I'm glad to know there's a good man on the job.

   Daniel

Chapter Nine

Fort Meade
1100 hours
Tuesday, October 10

BACK IN HIS OFFICE, MICHAEL SIPPED FROM HIS COFFEE MUG AND TRIED TO pretend nothing unusual had happened in the last twenty-four hours. Yesterday, after returning from the White House, he had typed up a report about the Echelon information, mentioned the supporting data from NPIC, and handed the report to Gloria. Now it was probably sitting on the NSA deputy director's desk. Perhaps she had read it and realized its significance; perhaps she had even passed it on to the director. But given the political climate in Washington, Michael doubted the information would ever leave the DOD.

"A courier from the State Department is asking for you, sir." Startled by the sound of Gloria's voice, Michael jerked and splashed coffee over a stack of papers on his desk. "I'm so sorry," the secretary called, leaning in through the partially opened door. "I would have signed for the delivery, but it's close-hold information. I'm afraid you'll have to come out and sign for it."

"No problem, Gloria." Michael pushed his chair away from the mess, grateful that the coffee had only spilled on a stack of papers—last year he learned the hard way that computers and coffee don't mix.

A uniformed marine stood in Gloria's small office, his manner authoritative and formal. After saluting, he asked for identification, which Michael readily produced. After checking to see that Michael's face matched his ID photo, the courier took a key from his pocket and unlocked the briefcase handcuffed to his wrist. From the attaché case he withdrew a manila envelope, then tucked it under his arm, and asked for

Michael's signature in a small black book. Michael signed, the book disappeared into a pocket, the locks on the attaché snapped shut. Finally, with grave and solemn dignity the marine presented the manila envelope to Michael.

Michael thanked the man with a smile, went into his office, and closed the door.

Sinking into the guest chair in front of his desk, he pulled out the contents of the envelope. Inside was a commercial airline ticket to Tel Aviv, a stamped document that would serve as a visa, and two letters. The first was an official letter of introduction to Maj. Gen. Doron Yanai, director of the IDF Liaison Unit. The second letter, issued by the Israeli ambassador, formally invited Capt. Michael Reed to participate in a goodwill mission to Israel. Nothing about the envelope or its contents indicated that President Stedman had anything to do with the proposed trip.

Beneath the letters, Michael found a preprinted form: Requirements for All Military Personnel Traveling Overseas. Before leaving the United States, all military personnel were to do three things: be certain their inoculations were up to date, see the base legal officer to review their last will and testaments, then check with BUPERS—the Bureau of Personnel Services—to learn about supplemental life insurance and the convenience of direct deposit.

Michael tossed the list of regulations onto the stagnant coffee spill. His paycheck was already directly deposited, and he saw no reason to change his will—after Janis's death he had decided to leave what little he had to his father, who had a quartet of young children to support. The warning about inoculations, however, gave him pause. He had endured the entire six-injection series of anthrax vaccinations back in Desert Storm, with annual boosters every fall. It hardly seemed possible that he might be due for another booster, but time could fly when you were having fun.

He glanced at his watch, then checked the time of departure on the airline ticket. He was scheduled to leave Ronald Reagan Airport at 1600 hours, which gave him less than five hours to prepare for the trip. In that amount of time, he'd be lucky to get his background materials assembled and run home to pack a suitcase.

A musical chime announced an incoming e-mail. Michael carefully slid the documents back into the envelope, then stood and tucked it into a drawer. He moved to his desk chair and turned to face the computer. The coffee still covered his desk, but it could wait.

He typed in his password, impatiently worked through the security measures, and found himself staring at another message from Daniel Prentice.

> Michael:
>
>   Everything should be arranged. Have you had a chance to read Ez. 38–39? Consider carefully 39:6. Before you take wing, better ask your friends in the Moscow sector for data on the "dead hand." It could be useful in the days ahead.
>
>   BTW, friend, you're probably wondering why I referred you to SS. Brad always spoke highly of you, and he knew you were a believer. You're going to need faith for what lies ahead . . . but I pray you'll be back home before the prophet's vision is fulfilled.
>
>   Be careful. Keep your eyes open. And keep the faith.
>
>   Daniel

Michael sat back, mystified. Daniel seemed to take a perverse joy in speaking in riddles.

Reaching carefully over the coffee and ruined papers, he punched the button on his intercom. "Gloria! Can you come in here, please?"

She opened the door a moment later, an apologetic look on her face and a wad of paper towels in her hands. "I'm so sorry, sir, about the spill. I'll have it cleaned right up."

"I'll do that." Michael stood and reached for the paper towels. "What I really need is a Bible. Do you have one at your desk?"

Her penciled brows shot nearly up to her hairline. "A Bible?"

Michael dabbed at the river of coffee. "Someone around here has to have one. See if you can borrow it for a while, OK? And—" He closed his eyes, trying to remember Daniel's other riddle. "Call John Howard in the Moscow section, and ask him for information on the 'dead hand' and the Russian military, particularly any alliances or treaties with Arab leaders. I'll also need a copy of his dossier on a General Vladimir Gogol. Anything John has, if I'm cleared for it, I want it. And I need everything—the Bible, the dead hand, the general—by fourteen hundred hours. I've been ordered to Tel Aviv."

Gloria froze in a stunned posture. "You're leaving today?"

Michael felt his mouth twist in something not quite a smile. "Funny how things change, isn't it? But I shouldn't be gone long. A week, maybe two, tops." He gave her a conspiratorial wink. "I need that information ASAP. The sooner I get going, the sooner I can come back and make your life miserable again."

Her expression melted into one of maternal affection, then she nodded. "I'll hurry, sir. Things just aren't the same around here without you."

"Thanks, Gloria. Oh—" He snapped his fingers. "I almost forgot. My swim buddy in SEAL Six was a guy named Thomas Freeman. He's retired now, but I'd like to reach him. See if BUPERS has his address and phone number, OK?"

"Got it."

Michael spent the rest of the afternoon finishing his reports in progress. At 1358, Gloria knocked, then entered the office with several bound reports. "The 'dead hand,'" she said, dropping the first folder into the cleared space on his desk. "Vladimir Vasilievich Gogol, the Russian military, Russian-Arab treaties, Russian-Iraqi economic agreements, and a Bible." She followed the first report with four others and a battered leather volume. "The Bible is mine—I went home on my lunch hour and picked it up for you."

A twinge of guilt pricked Michael's brain as he rested his hand on the leather cover. He had a Bible at home, too, and could have picked it up when he went home to pack . . . if he could remember where he'd put it.

"And there's this." She pulled a note card from the pocket in her skirt. "Lt. Thomas Freeman, retired navy. Now runs Shark's Deep Sea Fishing out of Tampa, Florida. Here's his phone number and address."

Michael grinned at the card as if it were the face of his long-lost friend. "Deep sea fishing, huh? It fits him."

"Anything else, Captain?"

"That'll do it, Gloria. Thanks." He met her tentative look with a confident grin. "This is no big deal, Gloria, just a routine liaison visit. In and out, that's all."

One corner of her lip dipped in a wry smirk. "Sure. Whatever you say, sir."

Michael tucked the card with Freeman's information into the Bible, then stood and scooped the stack of materials under his arm. "I'll be in touch." He tapped two fingers to his temple in what he hoped was an optimistic salute. "You hold down the fort, OK?"

Gloria followed him out of his office and held tight to the doorframe as he moved past her desk. "You be careful," she called, a note of worry in her voice.

"I will." He paused at the outer door and gave her a confident nod. "Nothing is going to happen. Israel's at peace, remember?"

-0100111100-

Thirty-five thousand feet over the Atlantic, Michael Reed stretched his legs in the roominess of the first-class cabin and mentally reviewed his preparation. With one eye on the clock, he had rushed home and packed a week's worth of clothing and tossed all but two of the reports in his suitcase, along with Gloria's Bible. He had even taken the time to dial Shark's business in Tampa but had reached an answering machine: "Hey, this is Shark, and we're out on the water bringing in some of the biggest grouper you've ever seen. If you wanna come along on the next boat, leave your number at the beep."

Michael almost left a message, then decided to hang up. He had no idea where he'd be staying, and any mention of Israel might threaten the secrecy of his mission. Shark and the mystery of the unexploded shell would have to wait.

Satisfied that he hadn't forgotten anything important, Michael reached up and clicked on the airliner's overhead light. No one sat in the seat next to him, so from his briefcase he selected the report on the Russian military, then began to read. John Howard, the Russian affairs section chief, was a friend as well as a coworker, and Michael knew the information would be reliable.

"No greater peril," the report began, "confronts the world today than the dynamic Russo-Iraqi political alliance. The man chiefly responsible for this association, General Vladimir Gogol, has recently been promoted from commander of the Moscow Military District to minister of defense. The political and economic chaos of recent years resulted in a power vacuum, which Gogol rose to fill.

"This international alliance bears watching because both Russia and Iraq possess vast quantities of biological weapons that could set off global epidemics."

Michael read on, learning that an October 1998 United Nations special commission reported that its expert investigations team found that Iraq's biological arsenal contained aerosol generators. These generators could spread lethal biological agents by several methods, including the relatively simple means of helicopter-borne commercial chemical insecticide disseminators. A Russian defector, Dr. Kanatjian Alibekov, now known as Ken Alibek, told U.S. authorities that he was the first deputy director of Biopreparat, the Russian designation for a military project comprising forty research and production facilities manned by more than forty thousand civilian scientists, engineers, and administrative employees. According to Alibek, Biopreparat was a full-scale biological warfare program engaged in the manufacture of anthrax, smallpox, plague, and other lethal viruses.

The hiss of the jet's air conditioning broke into Michael's concentration. He looked up, frowned at the small vent above his head, then flipped ahead through the pages of the report, his mouth set in annoyance. A report about airborne biological contaminants was probably not the most relaxing reading material he could choose while sitting in a sealed, recirculating atmosphere.

He fanned through several pages on Russia's biological weapon programs, then a headline caught his eye: Russia Poised to Invade Middle East. The analyst who had prepared the November 1999 report began the article by quoting Thomas Wimner, a British agent who had for years insisted that a Russian-Israeli conflict was inevitable. "The reason the Arabs and Iranians have delayed in the past," Wimner wrote, "is because the peace process promised them vital real estate concessions that would make military victory more likely. Now that peace has been established and Israeli officials have agreed to withdraw from the Golan Heights and much of the West Bank, war seems unavoidable. We cannot afford to underestimate the desire of Russian nationalists to reestablish the country as a superpower. By providing the Islamic world with the military means to defeat Israel, Russian leaders will gain the economic means to regain a place of international superiority."

Wimner ended his comments with a statement that sent a disturbing quake through Michael's peace of mind: "The next eighteen months in the Middle East will be fraught with danger. Statecraft of the highest possible order will be required from the United States if a catastrophic war involving chemical, biological, and nuclear weapons is to be avoided in the Middle East."

Michael closed the report and leaned his head back against the seat. What had that techno-geek Prentice plunged him into? Why had Stedman insisted upon sending him to Israel? If the intel experts knew peace would require "statecraft of the highest possible order," why had the president sent him on a mere fact-finding mission? The secretary of state should have been dispatched, along with a few dozen diplomats skilled in Russo-Israeli relations. The president should have sent someone far more knowledgeable, someone who *cared*.

He closed his eyes, grateful to admit the truth in the semi-darkness of the plane. He had always been a patriot; he would gladly die for his country. But the only emotion he felt for Israel was an overwhelming apathy, tinged with resentment. After all, if not for the Israelis, he would never have been deployed to Beirut, and Janis would still be alive . . . as would his son.

Was it a son? His face burned as he recalled last night's dream. Part of him was certain he had lain awake the rest of the night, but weariness could play tricks on a man's mind, particularly when he was burdened with troubling thoughts.

Outside the window, the blue sky had deepened, summoning a diorama of stars from the cobalt vault of the heavens. Michael reached up and flipped off the overhead light, knowing he would not read any more tonight. His mind was too occupied with other thoughts.

He shifted in his chair and looked out the window. They were over the Atlantic, so he could see nothing in the darkness below. The first-class cabin grew quiet, the lights dimming as passengers settled in for the long flight and a nap.

Michael reclined his seat, but his mind was not ready to let Janis go. Somehow, sitting in the darkness, the dream seemed to close around him again. Janis's voice echoed in his ears, as vivid as if she'd only spoken to him an hour ago.

A sudden realization brought a wry, twisted smile to his face. The prospect of this mission must have sent his conscience into hyperdrive. He hadn't been to church in months, so his subconscious had sent Janis to remind him not to forsake his religious upbringing. She'd said all the right things—God loves you, God has a plan for your life, God has been protecting you—almost a word-for-word expression of the Four Spiritual Laws he'd been taught as a young boy.

But not everything she said was part of the script. Michael frowned as he recalled her words about the shell from friendly fire outside Kuwait. He had not seen anything out of place that night, and the image of a shell outside their bivouac was not something he'd be likely to forget. Once he had awakened to a whistling sound like artillery, but it passed after a moment and he assumed the breeze was playing tricks on him. The devilish desert wind could howl like a wolf one minute and whimper like a puppy the next. It sprayed sand with force enough to scour bare flesh and sucked the moisture from a man's throat and nostrils until he lay gasping for breath.

No, he did not like the Middle East.

Michael crossed his arms around the largely unread report and leaned his head against the plane's plastic wall, willing himself to sleep. Each passing hour would bring him closer to the day he could return home.

Chapter Ten

Jerusalem
0830 hours
Wednesday, October 11

RABBI BARAM COHEN LOWERED HIS EYELIDS, SHIELDING HIS DIMMING EYES FROM the tidal wave of morning sunlight that poured into the assembly hall at the Toldot Aharon Yeshiva as he opened the wooden shutters. He remained at the open window for another moment, aware of the shuffling sounds behind him, then turned to face the school's thirty students. Without speaking, he lifted the tefillin, a small leather box containing portions of the Hebrew Scriptures, and fitted the leather strap around his skull so the square box rested firmly upon his forehead. A corresponding tefillin had already been strapped to his left arm, and as he walked to the center of the small platform at the front of the hall, he quietly ignored the awkward movements of his students' preparation for prayer.

Standing in the long rectangle of light from the window, he lifted his fringed prayer shawl—worn only by adults who were or had been married—and pulled it over his head. As his students followed in their prayer books, he began to chant the *Adon Olam,* the poem to open the *Shacharis,* or morning prayers.

"Master of the world who was King before any form was created," he began, reciting the words he had memorized as a boy in Brooklyn. "At the time when He made all through his will, then his name was called 'King.' And after all is gone, He, the Awesome One, will reign alone. And He was, and He is, and He will be in splendor."

A Sabbath stillness reigned in the hall, with nothing but Baram's voice and the student's sibilant whispers to disturb it. As Baram prayed, the deep peace that always came from recognizing the Master of the universe crept over him, as warming as the autumn sunlight spilling from the window. He swayed slightly on his feet, the long fringes on his prayer shawl almost sweeping the floor, then fell silent to allow his students a moment of silent devotion before beginning the Shacharis.

He turned his own thoughts inward, mentally bowing himself to the King of Kings who had brought him to this place, at this time. Like many émigrés, he had come to Israel as a ten-year-old boy, eager to live in the land of *Eretz Yisroel* even though his rabbi and many others decried Zionism and its leaders. "How can we establish *Eretz Yisroel* without the Messiah?" his red-faced rabbi had shouted in the small Brooklyn synagogue. "Will Ben Gurion and the Gentiles build the temple? Will the Russian Jews who deny God bring in the Messiah? They cannot! The Torah and the prophets have spoken; we will not have a holy land until the Messiah comes!"

Against the advice of his rabbi and others in the orthodox congregation, Baram's father moved his family across the sea to Jerusalem. And as Baram studied the Torah, attended yeshiva school, and observed the Sabbath in his new home, he realized the routine of his life had not radically changed. But he was studying, learning, and worshiping in *Israel*, living under the same bowl of sky that had canopied Abraham, Isaac, and Jacob. When the Messiah fulfilled the prophecies and stepped onto the Mount of Olives, Baram would be nearby and ready to receive him.

Even at this moment, he was ready. His lips began the first prayer of the Shacharis, the *Birchas HaShachar,* or morning blessings. His mouth curved in a smile as he spoke the familiar and beloved words. Time had not weakened his childhood dream. Each passing year brought the chosen people closer to the Messiah, each passing hour diminished the allotted time of suffering and pain. His father had been right to leave America, and Baram was grateful his own son and daughter were native-born Israeli citizens. If only they would obey the God of Israel as eagerly as they obeyed the state.

Clutching the edge of his prayer shawl, he lifted his hands slightly and closed his eyes, concentrating on the souls of his misguided children as he continued the cycle of prayers. He called upon a student to read the selected psalm and the song of the parting of the Red Sea. He led the students as they read *Krias Shema,* followed by the eighteen blessings known as *Shemoneh Esrei*. They lowered their heads to recite the *Tachanun,* or supplication, followed by Psalm 20, also known as *Ashrei.*

As the chorus of youthful voices faded, Baram silently signaled another student to recite the *Shir Shel Yom,* or daily song. For his reading the boy chose the Thirty-seventh Psalm, and Baram's heart lifted at the sound of the familiar words. "I was young and now I am old, yet I have never seen the righteous forsaken or their children begging bread. They are always generous and lend freely; their children will be blessed."

Caught up in the sense of something wonderful and totally beyond his comprehension, Baram lifted his face to the warming rays of the sun and closed his eyes. The Master of the universe was faithful. His children would return to the faith of their fathers. After all, a man or woman who had lost faith had nothing left to live on.

When the student finished the psalm, Baram reluctantly lifted his lids and returned to his responsibility. "It is our job to praise the Master of everything," he said, ignoring the sounds of adolescent shuffling as his students stood to join him in the recitation of the final prayer, the *Aleinu.* Their voices joined his, rising in a multilayered tapestry of sound designed to glorify The Name. "Give greatness to the Creator of the beginning, for He has not made us like the nations of the lands. He has not made us like the families of the earth, for He has not made our portion like theirs, and our lot like their populations. For they bow to nonsense and emptiness, and they pray to a god who cannot save while we kneel, bow, and give thanks to the King of emperors, the Holy One, Blessed is He."

His students' voices ebbed and flowed as they bowed during the prayer. Taking strength from the sound of their youthful devotion, Baram closed his eyes again and continued. "He is our God, there is no other. It is truth! There is nothing without our King. As it says in the Torah, 'Today you shall know and take to heart that HaShem is the God, in the skies above and on the earth below, there is no other.'"

A profound silence filled the hall as Baram finished. Slowly he lowered his prayer shawl to his shoulders, then opened his eyes and looked out at his students. They were moving back to their seats, lifting their books as their lips moved in whispered confidences. The hall should have resonated with the sound of their movements, yet Baram heard not a sound. A preternatural silence flowed through the room, muffling the sounds of release and activity and life.

He shuddered faintly and fought down the momentary fear that wrenched his bowels. This could not be a trick of one from the other side, for this was a holy place, consecrated to the Creator of the universe.

He closed his eyes, bringing his hand over his heart. The backs of his eyelids seemed to glow as though the room had filled with an unearthly light. Terror, pure and oceanic, gripped him and in an instant he knew that if he dared to open his eyes and look up, he would see the ceiling rolled back and the sky open, revealing the blazing ladder of YHWH.

The mere thought of such a sight chilled his blood. He was unworthy. He had taught many, yes; as a rabbi he was held in some esteem, but he had not been able to awaken the hearts of his beloved children. And only those whose human minds had attached to the Divine Intellect could see visions . . .

Baram.

The voice rolled through the room like thunder and righteousness, lifting the hairs on Baram's arm. His heart pounded; he could feel each separate thump like a blow to the chest. Opening his eyes, he squinted into a golden light that blocked everything else from view.

The hour is approaching when the house of Israel will know that I am in the midst of Israel, and that I am the Lord their God, and none else.

The voice, flowing like the sound of rushing water, seemed to emanate from the light, which pulsed softly with every word. Though he squinted directly in the face of that blazing orb, Baram felt no sense of heat or burning.

I will show myself holy through them in the sight of many nations. Then they will know that I am the Lord their God, for though I sent them into exile among the nations, I will gather them to their own land, not leaving any behind. I will no longer hide my face from them, for I am the Sovereign Lord.

Baram nodded slowly, recognizing the words of the prophet Ezekiel. "What," he asked, seeing nothing but that holy light, "would you have me do?"

The voice, without rising at all, took on a note of urgency. *Prophesy, son of man, and tell the house of Israel that I will put my Spirit in them and they will live. Then they will know that I the Lord have spoken, and I have done it.*

Baram lifted his hands, his ears filling with the rushing sound of many waters—or was it the fluttering of angels' wings? Then he folded gently at the knees and crumpled into a heap, his lids slipping down to cover his eyes. When he could open his eyes again, he found himself lying on the floor, a huddle of pale and worried faces circled around him.

"Lie still, Rabbi," one of his students whispered, his hand firmly upon Baram's chest. "We have called the ambulance. They will take you to the hospital."

"I am not sick." Baram struggled to sit up, but strength had fled from his body. His limbs felt as weak as water, helpless.

Baram closed his eyes again, resigning himself to what would certainly follow. They would take him to the hospital and run tests; they would assume he had suffered a stroke or heart attack. If he told them what he had seen, they might take him to the psychiatric ward, for not since Moshe, of blessed memory, had any prophet ever received a prophecy unless he was sleeping or in a trance . . .

Had he been in a trance? The quick question needed a thoughtful answer. The ancient writings listed several criteria by which a prophecy could be judged as true or false. One was that a prophet would be physically troubled after the receiving of his vision, and that much was true. Baram felt as though the strength had been drained from his body, and his eyes still burned with the memory of that fiery light. Another criterion was that the recipient could not will a prophecy; only HaShem, blessed be He, could will it. That also was true, for Baram would not have wished for this experience; he was not worthy.

He heard the deep voice of Rav Greenspan, another teacher at the yeshiva. Perhaps, for now, it would be better to remain silent and endure the fussing of his friends. He needed time to consider the meaning of what he had just seen and heard.

The double doors of the assembly hall swung open in that instant, accompanied by a metallic clacking sound. As Baram's eyelids lifted, the circle of boys parted to reveal a team of emergency technicians with a metal stretcher. He smiled in honest surprise. If the medics had already arrived, he must have been unconscious longer than he realized. So perhaps it was a trance.

As the technicians lifted and strapped him to the gurney, he caught the hand of one of his students. "Send for my children," he told the boy, managing no more than a thin whisper. "Do not delay—understand?" He did not release the boy's hand until the lad nodded in assent.

-0100111100-

The IDF chaplain general's office sent two officers to Devorah's classroom—one to take over the teaching, another to quietly inform her that her father had been taken to the hospital. "The paramedics are afraid it was a heart attack," the ensign told her, staring at the floor as if afraid to meet her eyes. "Apparently he was leading prayers, then froze and clutched at his chest. Your brother has been informed as well."

Urgency set Devorah's blood afire. "Which hospital?"

"Bikur Kholim," came the answer, but she had already begun to move out the door. She was running by the time she reached the parking lot, and her heart kept pace with the broken turn signal that clicked in an agitated rhythm as she sped through the streets.

She found her father in the emergency ward, behind a printed curtain. She heard his voice before she saw him, and something in her melted in relief when she realized he was arguing— heatedly—with the doctor. "I am not sick, I tell you!" he bellowed. "I am as healthy as any man my age ought to be."

Devorah stopped just outside the curtained cubicle. "Abba, I am here," she called, not wanting to intrude upon his privacy. "Asher is on his way."

"Come in, Devorah." Even now, her father's voice rang with stubborn pride. Devorah stepped through an opening in the curtain and took in her father's appearance in one swift glance. He sat on the table, his white shirt unbuttoned, tiny circles and wires pressed to the expanse of flesh beneath his graying beard. But his cheeks glowed with indignation, and his eyes flashed dark fire.

She suppressed a smile. This was not a man suffering a heart attack. The doctor, however, was not inclined to let a patient slip through his fingers without at least performing a few tests.

"Rabbi Cohen." The doctor, a youngish fellow who appeared to be about Devorah's age, folded his clipboard beneath his crossed arms and fixed her father in a steely gaze. "Sir, today you have had a bad fall, if nothing else. Your students say you went quite pale, you clutched at your chest, and you fainted. I cannot allow you to go home until we know what caused this odd seizure."

Her father looked at the doctor and blinked hard. "Does the Master of the universe mean for you to know everything, Doctor? Now, if you please, I would like to go with my daughter. She will take me home and put me to bed, if you like. If I return to your hospital tomorrow, you may shake your head at me and call me a foolish old man. But I do not think I will be returning." With a determination born of pride, he plucked the adhesive circles from his chest and flung the wires toward a machine on which a bouncing line suddenly went flat.

"Abba," Devorah infused her voice with iron, "you must trust the doctor. If he wants you to remain overnight, what harm will it do? You have been working hard, and sometimes the body does not know when it is stressed—"

"My body knows it does not belong in a hospital." Reaching out to steady himself on the doctor's shoulder, her father eased himself off the examination table, then began to button his shirt.

Devorah looked at the doctor and shrugged. "I will take him home and put him to bed."

Asher, breathless and pale, burst into the cubicle at that moment. He was dressed in an olive green jumpsuit, the uniform of an IDF paratrooper on patrol inside the West Bank.

"Is this how the Master of the universe answers my prayers?" A broad smile lifted her father's pendulous cheeks as he lifted his hands and brought them to rest atop Devorah's and Asher's shoulders. "You see, Doctor, this morning I prayed for my children and HaShem, blessed be He, has sent them flying from the ends of the earth to visit me."

Asher's worried eyes met Devorah's. "Is he all right?"

Devorah nodded and caught her father's hand. "Isn't he always? He was arguing with the doctor when I arrived."

Ignoring her, her father plucked his coat from a chair and impatiently shrugged his way into it. "Let us go home, my children."

He turned, searching for his prayer shawl, and Devorah pulled it from a table. As he draped it over his shoulders, she quietly mouthed a question to her brother: "Have you leave to stay with him a while?"

Asher nodded, his eyes still filled with the blind panic she had known only moments earlier.

Devorah gave him a knowing smile and took her father's arm. Though he seemed perfectly healthy now, *something* had caused him to faint in the yeshiva. She would not rest until she knew what it was.

-0100111100-

With her father and brother in the backseat of her blue Fiat, Devorah drove to Me'a She'arim, the spiritual heart of ultraorthodox Jewry and the location of her father's house. The streets in this neighborhood, only a few blocks northeast of Jerusalem's center, were filled with black-hatted Jews who tended to reject every aspect of modern Israel. On weekdays the quarter felt more like a medieval European village than part of a thriving modern city, while on Sabbaths the streets emptied of traffic while men in fur hats clogged the sidewalks on their way to services at the synagogue.

She drove past the yeshiva where her father taught, then turned onto Etyopya Street. A few moments later she pulled up outside a quaint stone cottage. Some of the city's grandest nineteenth-century houses lay on this avenue, but her father's home was neat and modest. A grateful former student had given it to him, and only the possibility that he might dishonor his student by refusing the gift convinced him to accept.

"We are home, Abba." Her father had been unusually silent on the drive, and a recurrent gnat of worry returned to torment her. She caught her brother's eye as she got out of the car. Asher stood outside on the curb, his hand extended to help her father, and from his expression she knew he was just as puzzled and worried as she.

They spoke of little things as they helped their father into the house, led him into the kitchen, and forced him to sit down at the table. Asher helped him take off his shoes while Devorah filled a teakettle and set it on the gas stove.

"Now, Abba," she said, stepping into the open space that served as his dining room, "suppose you tell Asher and me what happened this morning."

Without replying, he looked up as she slid into the empty chair across from Asher. For a moment she thought she detected a gleam of apprehension in his dark eyes. Her father, afraid? She had never seen him exhibit fear, not even during the Gulf War when Saddam Hussein sent Scud missiles flying toward Jerusalem.

"This morning," her father began. He pressed his hands to the surface of the dining table as if he could pull strength from it. "I did not have a heart attack this morning. I received a vision—a prophecy."

Devorah absorbed this news in silence, but a soft gasp escaped Asher's lips.

Her father pointed a warning finger in Asher's direction. "Do you doubt me? I will admit what I saw was no ordinary sight. I have been a rabbi for many years; I have prayed the Shacharis over twenty-two thousand times, yet I have never seen or heard what I saw and heard this morning."

Devorah settled her elbows on the table and steepled her fingers. "Did anyone else hear anything? Did any of the yeshiva students see this vision?"

A suggestion of annoyance hovered in her father's eyes. "Since when does HaShem, blessed be He, send visions to groups of yeshiva students? At the time I was praying for you and Asher, and God spoke to me alone."

Asher's face flickered with uncertainty. "You were praying for us?"

Her father leaned his head back to better gaze into Asher's eyes. "I prayed that my son and daughter would accept the true faith. That they would become Jews in their hearts, not just in their minds."

Listening with rising dismay, Devorah tugged upon his sleeve, hoping an affectionate touch would distract him from unpleasant realities. "Abba, we don't need to go into this now. Why don't I see you to your room? I will stay with you for the rest of the day, until we're certain you're better. Asher can ask for leave tomorrow, and if there's a need I can stay with you tomorrow night."

"Why won't my children listen?" He looked at her with burning, reproachful eyes. "Do you not want to know what the Master of the universe told me this morning? Adon Olam, the Master of the world, appeared as a bright light, the most pure and brilliant light I have ever seen. And He said, 'I will show myself holy through them in the sight of many nations. Then they will know that I am the Lord their God, for though I sent them into exile among the nations, I will gather them to their own land, not leaving any behind. I will no longer hide my face from them, for I am the Sovereign Lord.'"

"The prophet Ezekiel," Asher whispered softly. Devorah cocked an eyebrow at her brother, then sent him a look of relief and thanks, which he acknowledged with the slightest softening of his eyes. She had been schooled in the Hebrew Scriptures, too, but most of her biblical knowledge had been relegated to the mental equivalent of dust-covered filing cabinets.

"Don't you see, Abba?" Leaning forward with her arms on the table, she fixed her father in a steady gaze. "You were tired, and your mind tricked you so that you heard what you wanted to hear. Science has documented many similar situations—some people see hallucinations, glowing worms, or auras of colored light right before a migraine attack. You may have experienced something—a mild stroke or some sort of headache—and your body fooled you into thinking you experienced a heavenly visitation. But such things are impossible."

A thunderous scowl darkened her father's brow. "Who am I, and who are you, to question the Master of the universe?" A glint of wonder filled his eyes, and the hand he lifted trembled. "I doubted at first, too. HaShem, blessed be He, has not sent us prophecies in so many years, at first I doubted that He would send one to me. But I *did* hear God's voice."

Devorah bit down hard on her lower lip. "You didn't, Abba. *Why* should God speak to you?"

"And why now?" Asher added. "This was not a vision, Abba. You are overworked and exhausted. You must get some rest."

For a long moment her father glared at Asher, matching his determination look for look, then he transferred his gaze to Devorah. She lifted her brow, not yielding.

The light in her father's eyes dimmed as his jaws wobbled and his face rippled with anguish. "I believe with perfect faith in the coming of the Messiah," he whispered as Asher stood and placed his arm under her father's. "Even if he delays, I will wait for him to come."

Devorah stood, too, and moved to her father's other side. Together she and Asher helped him from the table and guided him toward the stairs.

Her father continued, and his voice, though quiet, contained an ominous note. "I believe in *Ikveta Meshicha,* the footsteps of the Messiah. The time is upon us, Adon Olam has spoken. He who does not look for the

Messiah or long for his coming actually denies the Torah. So I will wait and watch for his footsteps and listen for his voice."

Devorah stepped away from the narrow stairs and allowed Asher to guide her father up to his room. She sank to a lower step, waiting as Asher put her father to bed.

Why were the old ones so stubborn? Her father belonged to another generation, an era when superstition and ignorance were the rule rather than the exception. Ritual ruled his life, study occupied his days, prayer filled his nights. She knew for a fact that he recited the two-thousand-year-old *Asher Yatzar* prayer every time he went to the restroom.

Why couldn't he see that Judaism had accomplished its purpose? God, if He truly existed, had given Moses a list of commands to unite the Jewish people. That ancient set of commandments had been added to and reinterpreted over the years, and the Torah had proved to be the concentrating force that preserved the Jews as a unique race during the generations of the Diaspora. The rituals, the prayers, the rules against intermarriage had sustained them through the Roman occupation, the Crusades, the Holocaust. But now Israel was free and at peace, even with her Arab neighbors. The need for law and ritual and prayer had ended.

The stair above her creaked. She turned and gave her brother a weary smile as he moved toward her.

"I will stay with him for a while," she whispered, hugging her knees as Asher sat beside her on the step. "You go back to the base, and I'll ask Dr. Dayan to come over. I want to know Papa is well before I go back to work."

Asher crossed his arms atop his knees and stared thoughtfully at the blank wall before them. "I never thought anything like this would happen." He lowered his head to his arms as he looked at her. "Papa has always been as strong as an ox, physically and mentally. I never thought he'd be the type to suffer delusions."

Devorah tucked a curl behind her ear. "It could be some form of dementia, I suppose. He's only sixty-two, but I think certain conditions can begin at almost any time."

Asher's brown eyes grew somewhat smaller and darker, the black pupils of them training on her like gun barrels. "What if he's telling the truth?"

Devorah winced. "You can't be serious."

"I am. He believes, and we don't. So God would never speak to us . . . but how can we say HaShem would not speak to our father?"

Devorah crossed one arm over her bent knees and chewed on the end of her thumbnail. For that question she had no answer.

CHAPTER ELEVEN

Moscow
Noon

VLADIMIR MOVED TO THE STEREO, ADJUSTED THE VOLUME, THEN CLOSED HIS eyes as the Rachmaninoff concerto swelled to fill the room. He lifted his arms and cued the strings, then opened his eyes and caught sight of himself in the gilded mirror over the fireplace.

He lowered his hands, glad that Alanna was still dressing in the bedroom. She never laughed at him, but she had never caught him acting out one of his fantasies. Soon, though, she would join him in his greatest fantasy, and together they would bring it to life.

Double-checking his image in the mirror, he straightened his back, tugged down his uniform, and plucked a strand of lint from the notched edge of his collar. He must not appear shabby today. This was a special occasion, a time of celebration and significance.

A buzzer chimed from the foyer, and Vladimir called a warning to the butler as he crossed the living room. "*Nyet!* Keep to your work. I will see to our guest."

Col. Oleg Petrov stood outside the door, his blond hair sparking in the light from the hallway. At the sight of Vladimir, he clicked his heels and snapped to attention. "General! I'm sorry, sir, I expected a servant."

Vladimir returned the salute, then took the bottle of wine from Petrov's hand and led him into the foyer. "I did not want to distract the servants; they are still setting the table. After all," he broke into a relaxed smile, "I knew it was you."

Petrov's lips parted in a dazzling display of straight, white teeth. "You are too kind, General. May I say again how honored I am to be invited to this dinner with you and your—" A deep, painful red washed up his throat and into his face as he hesitated.

"Her name is Alanna," Vladimir remarked, his voice dry. "One day, when the time is right, she will be my wife. For now, you should call her Madame Ivanova." He lowered his voice. "And we shall speak English tonight, for her sake."

"Of course, General."

Vladimir paused to hand the bottle of wine to the butler in the kitchen, then led Petrov into the living room. He was about to invite his guest to take a seat, but Alanna chose that moment to step out of the hallway. She came toward them, cool, shining, and smiling, and her beauty caused an instant crisis in his vocabulary.

Petrov recovered far faster than Vladimir. He bowed, a hank of blond hair falling forward on his forehead, and Alanna laughed softly as she came forward to take his hand. "I suppose you are the very capable Colonel Petrov. I have heard many good things about you."

As Petrov took her hand, an unexpected weed of jealousy sprang up in Vladimir's heart. Alanna was closer to Petrov's age than his, and, like her, Petrov was young, charming, and well-favored. But Petrov was also ambitious and intelligent enough to know he would not go far by toying with his general's lady.

"Gentlemen." Alanna brought her hands together, fingertips touching, and smiled at Vladimir. "The chef has prepared a wonderful meal. Shall we go into the dining room?"

"By all means." Vladimir stepped forward and slipped his arm around Alanna's slender waist, pausing long enough to kiss her cheek and inhale the rich scent of her perfume. From the corner of his eye he saw that Petrov stood a respectful distance away, his eyes lowered.

Good. Let him understand.

"Lead me to your table, love," he said, lacing his fingers with Alanna's. "I have much to tell you before I leave for Paris."

"And I am eager to hear it," Alanna answered, smiling.

–01001111100–

They dined on lobster and veal, then sipped Petrov's wine and pronounced it excellent. Vladimir sat at the head of the table, with Alanna on his right and Petrov on his left, and throughout the conversation he found himself measuring the amount of eye contact between his two companions. For once, Alanna was playing the part of modest maiden, and gradually he relaxed. She knew her place. She was wiser than he had imagined.

After dessert, he waited until the butler cleared the dishes away, then he pulled a small box from his pocket. "A small trinket," he said, sliding it across the linen tablecloth. "Just something to remind you of me while I am gone."

"Vladimir!" She smiled, her sparkling blue eyes holding more than a hint of flirtation. Like an exuberant child, she tore off the wrappings and opened the box, then gasped in pleasure as she lifted the string of pearls from its resting place. "Oh, they're simply gorgeous! You are so sweet!"

She reached out and caught his neck, and willingly he bent to accept her kiss. When they parted, he glanced at Petrov just long enough to note that another dark flush had mantled the man's cheeks.

"Darling, I have something for you, too. One moment—let me get it."

As gracefully as a ballerina, she slipped from her seat and darted away. Vladimir picked up his goblet and sipped the wine, noting from the corner of his eye that the colonel had done the same.

"She is a lovely woman," Petrov said, placing his glass on the table. "You are a fortunate man."

"Thank you." Vladimir lowered his glass, too, then idly ran his fingertip around the rim. "You might find a beautiful woman soon. If all goes well in Paris, things in Russia will change dramatically in the coming months. I will hold the reins of power, and as my second-in-command, beautiful women will compete for your attention."

Petrov shook his head. "I only want to serve you, General, so use me where you will."

Vladimir lifted his glass, his mouth twisting in bitter amusement. Petrov spoke like a loyal fool or a skilled diplomat, and he knew the colonel was no fool.

He straightened in his chair as the swishing sound of Alanna's silk gown announced her approach. A pretty blush marked her cheeks as she entered the dining room with a book and a package in her hands. "Vladimir," she said, sliding into her chair, "the other day I was astounded to find this in the hotel lobby." She placed a battered copy of *Uncle Tom's Cabin* on the table before him. "You cannot imagine how much I have enjoyed reading it. English books are hard to find in Moscow, but the bookstore downstairs has a very good selection. I've made several trips just to browse, and if you keep leaving me, I'm afraid I shall have to buy more than one." Her lower lip edged forward in her patented pout. "I have to do something to entertain myself while you are away."

"Buy as many books as you want," Vladimir answered, feeling generous. "As long as you put them away when I return. I will not compete for your attention."

She reached out and stroked the curve of his upper arm with her fingertip. "You won't have to."

Vladimir felt the blood surge from his arm to his toes, but this was not the proper time to indulge the passion roaring through him. He caught Alanna's extended hand and glanced pointedly at the wrapped parcel on the table. "Is there something else, darling?"

"Oh, yes." She pushed the American volume aside and handed him the wrapped package—another book; he could feel the spine through the paper.

"It's for you, darling." The warmth of her smile echoed in her voice. "I hope you like it."

Vladimir felt his heart turn over the way it always did when she looked at him that way. Flushed with pleasure, he ripped off the wrapping and found himself holding a slender book covered in thick, stamped leather, embossed with gold.

Satisfaction pursed his mouth when he translated the title, written in the Russian Cyrillic alphabet: *"Man of Destiny, A Biography of Martin Luther."* Opening the book, he nodded at the yellowed pages. "I know this book—I read it many years ago."

"It took me a while to decipher the title, but I thought you would enjoy a biography of another influential man."

"He was an interesting fellow. Martin Luther and I agreed on many things—including our distrust of the Jews."

He looked up in time to see Alanna's face contract in a small grimace of pain, as though someone had suddenly struck her.

"Darling—do you think I don't like it? I do; it is a true classic. I am surprised you could even find a copy."

She gave him a small smile, then looked down at her hands. "I have to profess ignorance, Vladimir. I had no idea Martin Luther wrote about the Jews."

"Of course he did." Vladimir flipped a few more pages, then thumped his finger against a paragraph. "Listen to what he says: 'Know this, Christian, you have no greater enemy than the Jew.' Ah—here he advises that if we are afraid the Jews might harm our wives, children, servants, cattle, etc., we should apply the same cleverness as the other nations, such as France, Spain, and Bohemia—in other words, we should expel them."

Petrov lifted his goblet in a mock toast. "Hitler was a madman, but he had the right idea. The first large-scale Nazi program in November 1938 was performed in honor of Luther's birthday."

"You see?" Vladimir snapped the book shut, then reached out and took Alanna's hand. "I love the book, darling. It is a wonderful gift. I will always treasure it." He chafed her hand gently, noticing that her flesh had gone cold. "What's this? Your fingers are like ice."

Alanna shivered and gripped Vladimir's hand more tightly. "It's chilly in here. Do you mind if we have our coffee by the fireplace?"

"I am afraid we must be going." Vladimir stood and helped her from her chair, then linked her arm through his as they led the way into the living room. "I am sorry I will not be able to visit you tonight," he said, lowering his voice so Petrov would not hear. "I have many plans to finalize before departing for Paris."

"That's all right, sweetheart." Though she gave him a wavering smile, her eyes were wide blue pools of appeal.

"Ah, Alanna, how you tempt me." He pulled her closer and planted a kiss on her hair, then cradled her head against his chest. "I will be back soon with news that will change our world. Until then, be a good girl and stay inside. I do not want anything to happen to you, my treasure."

A soft sob escaped her, and the sound broke his heart. "Ah, my love." Ignoring Petrov, he placed his hands alongside her delicate face and lifted it. Her eyes were closed, her face unhappy, and a brief shiver rippled through him when he saw the silvery tracks of tears upon her cheeks. None of his other women had ever wept when he left them, and even sweet Alanna had not wept before today.

Spellbound with new and compelling sensations, he gently thumbed the tears from her cheeks. This moment marked a milestone, a new beginning. She must have sensed that together they stood on the threshold of a new epoch, a thrilling time of grandeur, power, and international prominence.

"Do not cry, my love." He drew her completely into the circle of his arms and whispered into her ear. "Never fear. My heart is half-returned before I even go."

-0100111100-

Vladimir and Petrov rode down in the elevator together. The colonel did not say much during the ride, and Vladimir appreciated the man's silence. His own heart was too full, too surprised by Alanna's emotional reaction to his departure. She had never been reticent about showing affection or joy, but until now she had never let him see her cry.

Had she fallen in love with him? Love could be a useful thing, but it could also result in problems. For the role Vladimir had in mind for her, love would be enjoyable, but loyalty would be far more useful.

The polished brass doors of the elevator slid back, and together the two men walked through the lobby. Vladimir paused at the point where one corridor curved toward the front of the building. "One moment, Colonel—I think I would like to send Alanna one final present before we leave. Would you care to accompany me to the bookstore?"

The colonel smiled and inclined his head. "My pleasure, sir."

They found the bookstore immediately. Vladimir had just discovered the English section when a dark-haired woman appeared at his side. "Can I help you, sir?" she asked.

"I'm looking for something special." As Petrov browsed at the front of the shop, Vladimir pointed to the shelf in front of him. "Are these the only English books? I'm looking for something that might interest an American woman."

"We've had quite a demand for American books of late." The woman smiled and gestured toward a far wall. "We have a few contemporary titles over there. Many of the major American authors are represented."

"Do you know any that would particularly appeal to a woman?"

The woman's eyes narrowed in thought. "Madame Ivanova particularly likes John Grisham. She has also asked about Maeve Binchy, though I understand that author is Irish . . ."

She turned and called a question over her shoulder in Hebrew, and Vladimir stiffened at the sound. A moment later a man appeared beyond the bookshelf, and upon his head he wore the telltale skullcap.

Vladimir swallowed hard, trying not to reveal the rage simmering just beneath his skin. His darling Alanna had been consorting with filthy *Jews?* If he had known there were Jews working in this hotel, he would never have allowed her to live here.

He stood still, his blood soaring with unbidden memories. As a little boy, he and his mother had lived outside Moscow in a small collective farm. Stalin ruled Moscow during Vladimir's youth, and stories about the evils of the Jews—about how they used the blood of children in their rituals, how they hoarded wealth and loaned it at outrageous rates of interest in order to drain good people of their hard-won rubles—were woven into the fabric of his childhood. As a boy he had witnessed criminal Jews being loaded onto trucks and taken away; at the age of fifteen he had been horrified by Stalin's report that the United States had hired a group of Jewish doctors to kill high-ranking Soviet officials.

After Stalin's sudden death, public officials released the imprisoned doctors and announced that there was no plot, but Vladimir did not doubt that one had existed. Jews lived among them in disguise, and many had risen to the heights of political power. Leon Trotsky, Stalin's greatest political rival, had been born Lev Davidovich Bronstein, the son of Russian Jews.

His own life had been scarred by the hand of an infiltrating Jew. His mother, an attractive widow, worked quietly in the collective, but her beauty caught the eye of a visiting commissar who worked for the Communist Party. One summer day not long after Stalin's death, Vladimir came in from the fields just in time to see a uniformed officer pushing his mother into a low, black car. The commissar sat in the backseat, his thick hand gripping his mother's arm, his voice overriding her wailing protests.

Vladimir never saw his mother again. For two more years he worked on the collective, then, at the age of eighteen, went to Moscow to search for her. After weeks of knocking on doors, he discovered that his mother had died after being dumped in a Moscow hospital. With a hot, clenched ball of anger burning at his center, Vladimir stalked Red Square, circling the tall walls at least a dozen times a day, always searching for the commissar who had taken his mother. In fair weather and foul he searched, eating what he could, when he could, stealing to survive.

Finally he saw the man. Remaining in the shadows, Vladimir followed the commissar to his house, then asked around and learned that the man was called Nikolai Kondratenko. He was now a powerful man in the Communist Party, but he had been born Uri Epstein, a Jew.

Within a week, Vladimir had murdered Uri Epstein. After retrieving his dagger and washing the blood from his hands, he went to the enlistment office and registered for the Russian army, deciding that if he would have to kill people in order to find justice, he might as well be paid for it.

"Sir? Are you all right?"

Vladimir blinked the bloody images of the past away and stared at the woman before him. She stood with her head tilted, a quizzical expression on her face.

"I am fine." He waved her away, then turned on his heel and moved toward the doorway. He caught Petrov's eye as he exited the shop, and the colonel joined him immediately.

"Those people." Vladimir pointed over his shoulder as they moved down the marble corridor. "Get rid of them. They are stinking Jews, and I won't have them in the same building with Alanna."

Petrov's brow wrinkled. "Do you have any suggestions how I should proceed?"

Vladimir pulled his gloves from his pocket and smoothed the first one over his right hand. "Use any method you like," he said, tugging on the bottom of his leather glove. "Just make certain it is a permanent solution— and flexible. We may have to rid Moscow of other Jews before many months have passed."

He paused as he slipped his left hand into the remaining glove. "And place a guard outside Alanna's door at all times. She is an innocent and likely to stumble into trouble. See that she does not go out alone—I cannot allow anyone to harm her."

Petrov locked his hands behind his back, his smile softening his granite features. "Trust me, General. It shall all be arranged before you return from Paris."

Chapter Twelve

Tel Aviv
1300 hours

MICHAEL SPENT MOST OF HIS FIRST DAY IN ISRAEL WARMING A WORN LEATHER sofa. His official letter of introduction from the Israeli ambassador served to get him into the building that housed Major General Yanai's office, but the general kept Michael waiting for most of the morning.

Michael finished reading an English edition of the *Jerusalem Post* someone had thoughtfully left on an end table, then tossed the paper aside and rubbed his hand across his stubbled chin. The electric razor he'd used in the airplane lavatory hadn't quite done the job, and four hours of thin sleep in a cramped seat left him feeling achy and exhausted. If Major General Yanai didn't see him soon, he might take his suitcase, find a hotel, and catch a couple hours of sleep. If Russia decided to attack while he slept, well—it would be the Israelis' problem.

The phone on the secretary's desk buzzed softly. She picked it up and murmured something in Hebrew, then caught Michael's eye. "Yes, he is still here," she said, speaking English. "Yes, I will see to it."

Standing, the young woman folded her hands and gave Michael an apologetic smile. She wore a military uniform, and Michael knew she was one of several thousand young women in the Israeli army. All eligible Israeli citizens were drafted at age eighteen. Men served a compulsory three years; women, two.

"The general is sorry to have kept you waiting, Captain Reed," she said, amusement lurking in her eyes. "He has asked me to express his deepest apologies."

Michael felt his face stiffen, but kept gallantly smiling. This might be a gracious brush-off, but he hadn't flown five thousand miles just to be told to get lost.

"When might the general be available?" he drawled with distinct mockery. "The matter I wish to discuss is of some urgency."

The woman's dark, silky brows rose a trifle. "Pardon me, sir, for not making myself clear. The general is waiting to see you now and has asked me to order some lunch. We have cleared his calendar, and his time is now yours."

Michael nodded, grateful that at last something had gone his way. As the secretary moved to open the door into the general's office, he sent her a smile of thanks, then squared his shoulders and went in to meet Doran Yanai.

The general in charge of implementing IDF policy before foreign forces stationed in the area would function merely as a go-between, Michael realized, but his cooperation would be necessary if they were to pull off this charade without drawing undue attention. President Stedman fully intended Michael to speak to no less an authority than the chief of the general staff, but proper protocol had to be observed.

General Yanai stood as Michael entered, and he stepped out from behind his desk to shake Michael's hand. "Captain Reed, thank you for coming," he said, his free hand coming to rest upon Michael's during the handshake. "I am so sorry you have had to wait. But I needed the time for a full briefing on the situation that brings you to us."

Michael smiled, grateful that he had not voiced his frustration. "I understand, General."

Yanai dropped Michael's hand and gestured to two chairs flanking a table near the window. "Shall we sit? Our lunch will arrive soon."

"Thank you very much."

Michael sank into the chair nearest the window and watched as the aging general lowered himself into the opposite seat. When Yanai smiled, Michael saw that he must have been handsome when he was younger. But age, and stress, perhaps, had etched deep lines around his mouth and eyes.

"These are troubling times, indeed," the general murmured, resting his elbows upon the linen-covered table. "Our people are enjoying a dearly bought peace, but we are in more danger than ever before. Yet few of them see it. They are foolish enough to think peace is the absence of war."

In a deliberately casual movement, Michael rested one elbow on the armrest of his chair and smiled at his host. "I believe I should see Lt. Gen. Yehuda Almog as soon as possible, sir. I have news that will concern him, and I am prepared to offer him assistance. But this matter is sensitive, and I cannot reveal more without speaking to General Almog."

Yanai's expression shifted from polite interest to pained tolerance. "I know all about your mission, Captain Reed, and I do appreciate its sensitivity. I myself have spoken to the chief of the general staff this morning and have received my orders."

Michael lifted a brow. "Regarding me?"

"Precisely. I am to assign you to one of our sergeant majors, with whom you will tour our bases and see for yourself what our needs are. Since your president has graciously extended an offer of weapons and munitions, we will reciprocate by allowing you unfettered access to our military bases. The prime minister himself has authorized your visit, so you will be able to make a complete report to President Stedman."

Michael forced his lips to part in a curved, still smile. "I am not here to play the role of tourist, General. I am here to do an honest assessment. Surely there is some way I can learn what I need to know without being dragged from base to base by some sergeant major."

Yanai's eyes darkened and shone with an unpleasant light. "I could give you a wish list, and I could give you an inventory. Both would answer your questions and technically fulfill your mission. But pieces of paper will not settle the problems in the Holy Land, Captain Reed. Neither peace treaties, nor inventories, nor maps will make one whit of difference in our situation. You will find your answers, sir, when you walk among our people and see our needs with your own eyes. You will be able to make a full and complete report only if you travel throughout Israel and observe with your heart as well as your eyes."

Michael stared, caught off guard by the sudden vibrancy of his host's voice. The Israelis had always been unpredictable, but he had no idea the IDF was run by warrior poets. But as long as he was on foreign soil, he had to play by their rules.

He inclined his head in a nod of agreement. "Very well, sir. I will travel with this sergeant major and keep a low profile. I trust we will have no difficulties with security clearances?"

"None whatsoever. We will issue the sergeant major and yourself special passes so you can enter any protected area you please."

"Thank you, sir."

The general cleared his throat and held up a warning finger. "I should point out one area of concern. The officer I have in mind, Sergeant Major Cohen, is extremely qualified—a graduate of our counterterrorist program and a former member of Sayeret Mat'kal."

Michael nodded. The Sayeret Mat'kal, also known as General Staff Recon Unit 269, was the primary unit dedicated to hostage rescue missions within Israel. Commandos went through one year and eight months of training before they were fully qualified, and only the best recruits made it to Unit 269.

"A career officer," the general continued, "the sergeant major is pleasant, diplomatic, and intelligent. Cohen speaks four languages—Arabic, French, Hebrew, and English—and is absolutely the best person for this job."

Michael filled in the silence when he paused: "However?"

Yanai tilted his head and gave Michael a wry smile. "Sergeant Major Cohen does not particularly care for Americans. Too many encounters with zealous tourists, I would imagine, so I would tread carefully if I were you." The general studied Michael thoughtfully for a moment. "Already I can see that you are a man of discretion. I do not believe you and the sergeant major will have any problems."

Someone rapped on the door, and the general called out the command to enter. The female aide entered first, then held the door open as a pair of smiling young men in white tunics wheeled in a luncheon cart. Apparently serving the general was quite an honor.

-0100111100-

After lunch, the general summoned an aide to drive Michael to Lod, a major airbase that shared space with Ben Gurion International Airport. Located halfway between Tel Aviv and Jerusalem, the base lay in the geographic center of the nation.

They made the trip in a closed vehicle from which warm air sputtered from the air-conditioning vents. A reluctant grin tugged at Michael's mouth as he held his briefcase and sweated inside his jacket. He knew the general meant to keep his visit low-key, but this was ridiculous. Couldn't he have arranged for a car with air conditioning that worked?

The cloudless sky above them shimmered with heat, and as they sped along the open road a mirage made the rocky hills in the distance dance. The general's aide, a talkative fellow named Shaul, was unskilled in English but eager to practice on a captive audience. From Tel Aviv to Lod, Michael gamely nodded and smiled to a series of innocent questions about the New York Yankees and American movie stars.

Shaul flashed a pass at a security gate, then parked the vehicle and led Michael toward a windowless concrete-and-brick building. "Sergeant Major Cohen did not learn of your coming until about an hour ago," Shaul explained, opening a glass door and waiting for Michael to enter first. "Knowing it would take a long time for us to drive, the major was permitted to complete the classes. As soon as they are finished, the major is OK to travel with you."

"Thanks, Shaul." Michael showed his temporary clearance badge to the sentry on duty, then offered his briefcase for inspection. After giving Michael a careful head-to-toe look, the sentry stepped aside and waved them inside.

"This way," Shaul said, leading Michael through a gleaming tiled hallway that smelled faintly of disinfectant. He paused outside a door and peered through the glass window, then looked at Michael and jerked his head in a movement that clearly indicated Michael was expected to follow.

Michael felt the top of his ears heat to red when he realized Shaul had escorted him to the wrong place. This was a classroom of some sort, and the men and women sitting at the metal desks were dressed in everything from jeans to business suits. A woman in uniform stood at the front of the room, however, and from the look on her face Michael surmised that she did not like interruptions.

He turned, about to exit, but the general's aide blocked his path. Grinning, Shaul pointed to a pair of empty seats near the door, then slid into one. Irritated and uncomfortable, Michael followed suit.

The woman had paused in midsentence when he entered, but continued her lecture once he and Shaul sat down. Michael sank down low in the desk, hoping to avoid her attention, and leaned toward Shaul. "What are we doing here? Shouldn't we be trying to find the sergeant major?"

Shaul used his wide palm to block the instructor's view of his face, then pointed toward the front of the room with his other hand. "She is Sergeant Major Cohen."

Michael folded his arms across his chest and groaned inwardly. Why hadn't he been more forceful when he told President Stedman he was not the right man for this assignment? Not only had he been thrust into hot, uncomfortable circumstances, but apparently he had been paired with an Israeli officer who hated Americans—a *female* Israeli officer. He lowered his head into his hand. If his luck ran true to form, the woman at the front of the room hated men, too.

"Let me remind you, ladies and gentlemen," she was saying, her voice rich and deep, "there are an unlimited number of ways to die and any number of people willing to inflict one of those ways upon you. But, with proper training, you can increase your odds of survival . . . a bit."

A twitter of nervous laughter filled the room, and Michael frowned, knowing that those who laughed had no idea how right this lady was. Who were these people? Death was no laughing matter.

"Sergeant Major?" A big guy with an Elvis-style pompadour lifted his hand. "Do you really think I'll be in danger when I'm out in the field? After all, I'm just the guy who reports the news. I don't make it." He shifted in his seat and flashed her a smile. "Unless you want to help me make some headlines."

Michael stiffened in his chair. Good grief, the guy was flirting with her!

The sergeant major ignored both the smile and the flippant offer. "Terrorists do not care whom they hurt, sir. They want headlines, and if your entourage is carrying a camera, you become a natural target. Which would be more likely to make the news—an attack upon a military patrol or the ambush of a news crew?"

A half dozen hands rose into the air, but Sergeant Major Cohen waved them away. "Please, no more interruptions. I have several points to make, and you should take notes. We will meet next week to discuss any further questions you might have."

Michael leaned back in his chair, finally understanding the purpose of this little gathering. These were news people, reporters, newscasters, and camera crews from all over the world. Rather thoughtful of the Israeli government to give them a crash course in how to survive a terrorist attack—particularly since many of the world's terrorists were now honing their murderous skills in Russia.

"Around the world, more than five hundred reporters have been killed on the job since 1986," the instructor continued, her dark eyes roaming over the group, "so you must learn how to better your chances of survival. First, if you are attacked by gunfire, do not think a car door, concrete blocks, or tree trunks will save you. They might catch a bullet or two, but they will not shield you for long. The safest place is behind a double row of sandbags. Unless you happen to see a wall of sandbags nearby, run as fast as you can. Don't try to play the hero or catch the perfect photo. You will catch a bullet if you do."

Pencils scribbled furiously, and Michael was pleased to note that at least a few of the civilians seemed to be taking her seriously.

"If the enemy is throwing grenades, run. If you are unable to escape, lie down with the soles of your feet pointing toward the blast. Your shoes can take the concussion and shrapnel far better than your head. You can live without a foot; you cannot live without a brain."

The flirtatious newscaster spoke up: "If we had brains, we wouldn't be here."

The class erupted in laughter, and the sergeant major indulged them with a small smile. "If caught in a cross fire, lie down until the shooting stops," she went on, locking her hands behind her back as she paced in a tidy pattern at the front of the room. "If caught in a mortar attack, lie down in a hole made by a previous shell—because lightning and mortar rarely strike the same place twice. To see if an area is mined, look for unusual patterns of disturbed soil, rocks, or leaves. And, unless absolutely necessary, stay away from trouble spots."

She continued, launching into a discourse on the fallibility of bulletproof vests, while Michael rested his chin on his fist and watched her. Sergeant Major Cohen was a very attractive woman, as slim as a pleat in her khaki uniform. A cloud of brunette hair fell to her shoulders in undulating waves, and she wore just enough lipstick to emphasize her perfectly shaped mouth. The set of her chin suggested a stubborn strength, and she held her head high with pride. Hard to believe this woman could shoot out the center of a playing card at fifty meters, but if she were a member of Sayeret Mat'kal, Michael knew she could.

"Now let us discuss the etiquette of kidnapping." Cohen turned to Mr. Elvis in the second row and smiled at him like a cat that has just spied a mouse. "Sir, if you were accosted by terrorists and found yourself wearing a burlap bag over your head, what would you do?"

The reporter made a faint moue of distaste. "I'd rip it off. How can I escape if I can't see where I'm going?"

"Then you'd be dead." She delivered these words in a flat, expressionless voice, then lifted her gaze and scanned the others in the class. "*Obey* your captors. You are not James Bond, and life is not like the movies. If you are taken hostage, do not speak unless spoken to. Make enough eye contact to let your kidnappers know you are human, but do not stare at them long enough to appear threatening. Do not cower; do not take charge. Do what you are told to do. But if your captors start to execute your fellow captives, kick, scream, bite, foam at the mouth. Do whatever you must to get away."

"Wait a minute." The flirt leaned his head back and looked at her. "We're trusting you with our lives. Why can't you military people just keep the terrorists away from us?"

"The freedom ordinary civilians enjoy also protects terrorists," she said, her stare drilling into the obnoxious reporter. "Unless you want to live in a virtual police state, sir, you would do well to be cautious. Governments and organizations that cannot afford to launch full-scale wars will always resort to terrorism, for they can terrorize a thousand by killing one. By striking at the heart of innocent civilians, they can terrify people far more effectively than they could in war."

Her extraordinary eyes blazed as she looked out at her students. "If you are ever taken hostage, remember that you are like the State of Israel. You cannot afford to lose a single war. You must determine the outcome of your situation as quickly and decisively as possible. You must try to avoid bloodshed by political means and by maintaining a credible deterrent posture. You must not seek glory. Your primary aim should be to defend your life with everything in your power."

The nervous twittering had completely evaporated, and a sea of silence greeted these final words. "We will not meet tomorrow or the next day," she said, bringing her hands together as she turned toward the lectern. "But next week we will hold mock drills in the field. Come prepared—physically and mentally. Wear old clothes—you will get dirty."

She sent them out the door with a smile. "See you next week."

Michael remained in his seat, his gaze on the desktop as the sober students filed past him. Sergeant Major Cohen obviously knew her stuff, and if she wasn't trustworthy the IDF wouldn't have tapped her to accompany him. From the impressions of the last ten minutes, he gathered she was bright, attractive, and a flaming Zionist—three qualities he didn't particularly want in an escort. Dull, ordinary, and impassive would suit him much better.

When the last student had left the room, Shaul stood and ambled toward the front of the room. He spoke to her in Hebrew, then pointed toward Michael.

Slowly, Michael stood and offered what he hoped was a diplomatic, let's-be-friends smile.

The sergeant major followed Shaul to the back of the room, then gave Michael a brusque nod. "Sgt. Maj. Devorah Cohen," she said, extending her hand. "I am pleased to meet you, Captain Reed."

Michael noted the delicate strength of her grip as he shook her hand. "But not so pleased about this assignment, I'd wager."

She acknowledged the success of his mind reading with a slight smile. "Quite true. I am in the midst of an urgent family situation and did not expect to be pulled into a special duty. I would have asked that someone else be assigned to you, but—"

"By all means, Sergeant Major, don't let me get in your way." Michael stepped aside and gestured toward the door. "I was just thinking there are probably a hundred soldiers better suited for this assignment."

She took a step forward, then halted. One dark brown eye glinted back over her shoulder, and one corner of her perfect mouth twisted. "Are you saying I am not fit to play tour guide?"

"Not at all." Michael thrust his hands behind his back, uncomfortably aware that Shaul was silently fizzing with laughter. "But it will require many hours for several days. And you just said your husband and children need you."

She turned slowly, her gaze relentlessly drilling into him. "The family emergency is with my father. And even if I had a husband and child, my commitment to the Israeli army would come first. We are not like you Americans, Captain Reed. We do not take our freedom for granted, and we are quite serious about our military obligations."

His jaw clenched as he rejected her softly spoken accusation. He had given his life to the service of his country and had risked his neck more times than he could count. This woman didn't know diddly about him or his work, and yet she had the unmitigated gall to accuse him of being *uncommitted* . . .

Michael tipped his head back and drew a deep breath, tamping down his anger. He couldn't lose his cool now, not when Stedman was counting on him. But how could he proceed? He did not particularly want this woman with him, and she obviously did not want this assignment. But President Stedman and General Yanai asked him to do his work quietly. He had the feeling that if he allowed Sergeant Major Cohen to find a replacement, the story of his perceived snobbery would be spread throughout the IDF within twenty-four hours.

"I can assure you, Sergeant Major Cohen, that I do not take freedom for granted." He managed a small, tentative smile. "I would be honored if your schedule would permit you to be my escort. I don't know what you've been told, but my task is quite urgent."

The angry color was fading from her cheeks, but her liquid brown eyes were still bright with indignation. "We will talk in my office," she said, pointedly reminding him that Shaul stood nearby, listening to every word. "And I will fulfill this assignment at least for the rest of the day. I wouldn't trouble my CO with the task of finding a last-minute substitute."

He nodded his agreement, reminded Shaul that he would need his luggage from the vehicle, then followed the remarkable Sergeant Major Cohen through the polished hallway.

-0100111100-

In her small office, Sergeant Major Cohen pulled a map of Israel from her filing cabinet and spread it on her desk. "The locations of our military bases are marked with blue stars," she said, smoothing the map with her hand while the American looked on. She wasn't certain, but she thought his face fell with disappointment when he saw the constellation of more than a dozen stars.

She suppressed a smile as he pressed his hands to the desk and groaned softly. He had probably been expecting a plum assignment, but this one would take time and effort. A complete on-site inspection of a single military base could take up to three days. To further complicate matters, several bases were located in the West Bank, occupied now by the PLO.

"Well, Captain?" She waited until he looked up and met her gaze. "Where shall we begin?"

He blew a strand of blond hair from his forehead, then grimaced at the map. "I suppose we should begin at the beginning. We're here, so why not start with this base?"

Devorah didn't waste a moment, but moved toward the door, her keys jangling in her hand. "Shall we go?"

She walked him around the military complex, saying nothing about the obvious resources and only pointing out facts he might not know. Several times she paused in midsentence as a jet roared overhead, then picked up a moment later with the same train of thought. Reed listened intently, his hands fastened behind his back, his blue eyes shining like cobalt as they swept the runways and airstrips.

"Some people are surprised to learn that Ben Gurion is the busiest civil airport in the Middle East, except on Saturday," she remarked as they entered a hangar.

His brow wrinkled. "What happens on Saturday?"

She gave him a reproachful look. "Did they not tell you that Israel is populated by Jews? Saturday is the Sabbath."

She expected him to be embarrassed; instead, a flash of humor crossed his striking face. "I'm more tired than I realized," he murmured, taking off his hat. He ran his hand through his hair, as if a scalp massage might stimulate his brain. "Sorry. Stupid of me, I know."

Shaking her head, Devorah moved on. "All the heavy transport squadrons of the Israeli Defense Forces and Air Forces are based here, at the military half of the airport. The runways are shared by military and civilian traffic. And you need not worry, Captain," she added, hearing a bitter edge of cynicism in her own voice. "Military aircraft are not grounded on the Sabbath."

Once they had finished their inspection of the facilities, Devorah took Captain Reed to meet the base commander. Reed introduced himself, displayed his security pass, and was given clearance to visit weapons storerooms and munitions dumps. Occasionally he scribbled notes in a small notebook he carried in an inner jacket pocket, but most of the time he listened intently, as if committing the numbers, facts, and figures to an overdeveloped memory bank.

"You do that very well," she remarked as they stepped out into the bright sunlight.

His brows lifted a question: "What?"

"Take notes." She laughed. "Oh, I know all about the things they teach you in Air Command and Staff courses—how to take notes with the nub of a pencil and a slip of paper in your pocket so no one will notice. The last American military attaché who visited took secret notes constantly—but he wasn't very good at it. He looked like he had an itch."

For a moment he stared at her in amused wonder, then he threw his head back and roared with laugher. Devorah glanced around, afraid someone would notice, then stepped quickly away, leaving him laughing in the parking lot.

"Wait, Sergeant Major." He laughed again, then turned his laugh into a cough. "Please!" She heard the sound of his loafers slapping the asphalt, then he was beside her, his hand over his heart, his face red with exertion. "I'm sorry, it's just that—well, that's such an apt description. An itch! I suppose that's why I've always tried to memorize things. When I have to be absolutely sure I've got it right, I write it in a notebook."

She exhaled and kept walking. "So I noticed."

He shortened his stride to match hers and continued with more enthusiasm than he had exhibited all day. "I figured—what's the harm in pulling out a notebook? Everybody knows attachés are used for gathering intelligence. We're just more subtle about spying on our allies than we are our adversaries. You and I both know that all this—" he waved his hand— "is going to be written up in a memcon and posted to our superiors."

Devorah halted as a sense of unease crept into her mood like a wisp of smoke. She hadn't wanted this assignment and, in an effort to be honest, had made her feelings clear at the outset. If, however, this man meant to record every element of their conversation, her honesty could be seen as belligerence and her unwillingness as insubordination—or worse.

"A memcon?" she asked, turning. "I don't know the word."

He frowned, his brows knitting together. "A *mem*orandum of *conver*-sation. A record of all conversations in official settings. Perhaps you just call it a report."

As anger singed her control, Devorah turned away, caught her breath, then lifted her hand and turned to face him again. "Listen to me, Captain Reed." She shook her finger in his face, not caring whether anyone saw them. "You are here to report on Israeli readiness. You will not report on me, do you understand? You will not record my statements, my attitudes, or my con-versations. You have no authority over me, and I will not answer to you."

His brows rose as he lifted both hands in a "don't shoot" pose and took a half step back. "I wasn't planning on mentioning you," he said, softening his voice, "unless you decide to spill some state secret that proves irre-sistible." He lowered his arms and gave her a smile that was at once confi-dent and apologetic. "Actually, Sergeant Major, I was hoping we could become allies . . . if not friends. Let's lay down our swords and end the day in peace."

Devorah faltered in the silence that engulfed them. What was wrong with her? If he hadn't thought her ill-mannered and unprofessional, he certainly did now.

She stepped back, wiped her damp hands on her trousers, and shook her head. "I apologize, Captain. I have a temper. Sometimes it gets the best of me."

"Nothing wrong with high spirits." His eyes flashed with something that might had been admiration—or amusement. "But I really must ask, Cohen—can we call it a day? I haven't slept, I'm jet-lagged, and I could use a shower. I'd like nothing better than to find a hotel and get some rest."

"Of course." She gave him a smile and pointed toward the parking lot. "I'll drive you there myself."

Reed spoke little as she drove toward Jerusalem, and she consoled her-self with the knowledge that at least this American didn't babble or conde-scend. He kept his gaze fixed on the horizon and his thoughts to himself, but she found herself wondering why he had immediately assumed she had a husband and child at home. The absence of a wedding ring upon her left hand meant nothing, for most women in the army left their wedding bands at home. A ring could easily be stolen or lost, or it could catch on a weapon and result in disaster.

She glanced again at the clear-cut lines of his profile. Perhaps he thought all women ought to be married. Resting her arm on the car door, she smiled at the thought. If he was a traditionalist, her father would certainly agree with him. He believed a Jewish girl should get married and raise a dozen children, keeping herself to hearth and home and the true faith. A Jewish boy should study Torah, attend a yeshiva, and defend his country. Then he should settle down and raise a large family, observing Shabbat every Friday at sundown and praying throughout the next day.

"What's so funny?"

She erased her smile. "Did I laugh?"

"You're grinning about something." His brittle smile softened slightly. "It would be nice to lighten the atmosphere. Agreed?"

Idly, she tapped the car's roof with the fingers of her left hand. Reed was probably right. If he would be pleasant, she could probably handle this assignment for the duration. So if they were going to be thrust together, they might as well be agreeable.

She shifted her right hand on the steering wheel, then cast him a quick smile. "I was thinking about my father. He is an Orthodox rabbi, very strict, very religious. When we met, you assumed I had a husband and children. My father would like nothing better."

"But you disagree?"

She made a face. "Of course. My mother, of blessed memory, was an Orthodox wife, and I knew I did not want to live as she did. My brother and I were both happy to join the IDF when we turned eighteen. We are both career officers, and we have both disappointed our father."

Reed crossed his arms as his forehead crinkled with thought. "Your father—is he ill? You mentioned a family emergency."

She shrugged slightly. "I'm not sure. He seems fine, but this morning he fainted at the yeshiva. He thought he—" She paused, then backed away from the rest of the story. "Our family doctor says he is fine, but my brother and I are still concerned. It is not like Papa to get sick."

"I seem to recall stories about deep divisions in the Orthodox community about the peace process." Reed relaxed, too, thrusting one arm out the window as she had. He stretched his long legs out as far as he was able then, finding the small sedan a poor fit for his lanky frame, turned sideways in the seat. "How does your father feel about it?"

Devorah checked the rearview mirror, then glanced out at the dusty road. It was late, nearly six o'clock. If they didn't hurry the American would be lucky to find a vacant hotel room.

"My father was concerned, of course," she said, transferring her gaze back to the road ahead. "Many people felt that surrendering the disputed lands was tantamount to devaluing the lives of more than 150 Israeli citizens who died through acts of Arab terrorism. No one could forget that more Israelis died from terrorism in the two years immediately *after* the signing of the Israel-PLO peace accords than in the two preceding years. And some Torah scholars were quick to point out it is not allowed to endanger the life of one Jew today in the hope of a better tomorrow for many Jews."

"So the peace accords have endangered most of the Jews?"

"Undoubtedly."

"And that, Cohen," he said, his voice deepening, "is a point we can agree on. I believe your father and his friends are right."

She looked at him, surprised at the honest compassion in his voice. He was staring out the window, his eyes wide but unseeing, as if his thoughts were a thousand miles away.

With a long, exhausted sigh, Devorah slowed the car on the approach to Jerusalem.

"My sentiments exactly," Reed said, overhearing her sigh. "I'm starving and exhausted. I'd like nothing better than for you to point me toward a hotel and a good restaurant."

"Most hotels have restaurants in them," Devorah answered, slipping into the flow of traffic on a main thoroughfare. "I am sure we can get you settled, then you can eat." She glanced at him and saw that he had pulled a small tour book from his pocket. The sight of the bright yellow book made her laugh—she saw a hundred of them a day down in the Old City of Jerusalem. "So now you are going to play tourist?"

"Just looking for a good hotel," he mumbled. "How about the Seven Arches? It's supposed to have a great view of the Mount of Olives."

"That is fine. Just don't mention it to anyone we meet."

"What's wrong with it?"

"Nothing. It is a perfectly lovely place." She turned and glanced over her shoulder to check the right lane. "But it's built on a desecrated Jewish cemetery. Any Orthodox Jew would be antagonized by the mere mention of the place."

"Then I won't go there."

Surprised, she looked at him. "Why not? Don't worry about me; I won't be offended."

"All the same, I don't want to go there. How about the American Colony Hotel?"

Sighing in exasperation, she worked the gearshift. "Fine. It is lovely. And usually crowded with hundreds of reporters. I will probably see half of my afternoon class in the lobby."

He grinned at her. "Then what do you suggest?"

She thought a moment. "The Mount Zion Hotel is just outside the old walls of Jerusalem. It is quaint—it used to be an ophthalmology hospital."

He chuckled softly and slapped the roof. "Sounds like a winner."

Night had fallen, filling the car with shadows and inky darkness. The dash glowed softly in neon light, and Captain Reed remained silent as she drove, sitting with one arm out the window and the other resting on the seat. She was almost certain he had fallen asleep when his voice cut through the silence: "Why aren't you Orthodox? Or is that too personal a question?"

"No." She blinked in dazed exasperation. "I'm just not. I am Jewish, but I am nonobservant. I believe in God, but not to the extent my father does. I believe God has protected the Jewish people for generations. But we are safe, in our own homeland, and now it is up to us to defend it. My father waits for the Messiah, whom he believes will bring peace and establish a kingdom, but I believe the kingdom has already come. We are here, and we must do the work. God will help us if we help ourselves."

They talked until they reached the hotel, and Devorah was surprised to find that Reed was far easier to talk to in darkness than in daylight. She heard no superiority in his voice now, no cynicism, only frank curiosity.

When they pulled up outside the Mt. Zion Hotel, Captain Reed opened the door, then hesitated before getting out. "Would you like to have a bit of dinner with me?" he asked, his blond hair gleaming in the car's dome light. "It's the least I can do after ruining your day."

She found it impossible not to return his disarming smile. "Thank you, but I ought to go check on my father. And I would like to get an early start in the morning. Now that you have had a quick tour of Lod, why don't we drive out to Hatzerim Air Base, in the southern district? We might as well begin at the outposts and work our way northward."

"Sounds good to me. What time would you like to get started?"

Devorah thought a moment. She ought to stop by her father's house in the morning, but the American probably wouldn't mind a less-than-early start. "Shall I pick you up at nine?"

"I'll be ready." Reed swung his long legs out of the car, stood, then pulled his briefcase and luggage from the backseat.

He paused to lean against the door. "Sure you won't have that dinner?"

"Quite sure, thank you." She waved him away. "I will see you tomorrow."

She turned the wheel and pulled away, pausing long enough at the intersection to glance back. He still stood on the curb, his suitcase in one hand and his briefcase in the other, as if waiting to see that she made it away safely.

She sighed as she turned into the traffic. American men were all the same—guardians of the weak, self-anointed protectors of women. Capt. Michael Reed was no different than the others.

CHAPTER THIRTEEN

Jerusalem
0900 hours
Thursday, October 12

REED WAS STANDING ON THE CURB OUTSIDE THE HOTEL WHEN DEVORAH pulled up. With a wave of greeting, he approached and tossed his briefcase into the Fiat's backseat, then opened the passenger door and slid into the car.

"Good morning," he said, his smile much less frayed than it had been the day before.

Devorah gave him a tentative smile. "I trust you slept well?"

"Thank you, yes, I did. Though my body is not quite sure what time it is, I feel much better today."

She turned the key in the ignition. "Good."

"And your father?"

"He is well today; thank you for asking. He has returned to the yeshiva and seems to be no worse for wear."

She pulled away from the hotel, grateful that the weather showed signs of cooperating with her travel plans. A dazzling white blur of sun stood fixed in the eastern sky, a faultless wide blue curve over the city. A brisk wind would keep the temperatures at a comfortable level, at least until they reached the dry heat of the desert.

"I love this weather," Reed said, resting his arm on the car door. "If I lived here, I'd take my convertible out and just let it eat up the miles."

"I do not think you would." Lifting her chin, she glanced at him and grinned. "You won't see many convertibles over here, and you definitely won't see any military people driving one. First, it is too hot. Second, you would be an easy target—a sitting duck, as you Americans would say. You could be calmly driving along, minding your own business, and suddenly find a rock or a grenade on the seat next to you."

He glanced back at her, his eyes bright with speculation, his smile half sly. "You're right, of course. But do you have to contradict everything I say?"

"I am not contradicting you, Captain." She kept her eyes on the road, lest he see how his superior tone irritated her. "I am just pointing out a few obvious facts."

"Listen, I don't want to be here any more than you do." An unmistakable note of sarcasm filled his voice. "But, like you, I go where I'm told and do what I'm told. That's it. So I'm going to do my duty here. If you have a problem with any part of this assignment, you can go to your CO and beg off."

"It is too late for that." She thumped her hand against the steering wheel, not caring if he saw her irritation. "Yesterday I wanted out. But last night you were almost civil, so I cancelled my classes and told my CO I would see it through."

"To the end?"

"To the *bitter* end." She took a deep breath and squeezed the steering wheel until the urge to strangle him had passed. "So let's just do our jobs, shall we?"

He did not answer for a long moment, and finally Devorah looked over at him. He had turned toward her, crossing his arms across his chest, and one corner of his mouth quirked with humor. For some inexplicable reason, her reaction seemed to amuse him.

"Is something funny, Captain?"

Reed grinned and looked out the window. "I can't believe it, but I think I like you, Cohen. I've never had much use for soldiers who didn't raise a ruckus now and then."

Irked by his confident manner, she cast a sharp glance at him. He was grinning! Rattled by the honesty in his smile, she gripped the steering wheel again and stared at the road ahead as her cheeks burned with a blush. Would this day never end?

They drove in silence for a while, then Reed told her a story about one of his commanding officers during his training days. The story broke through the awkwardness, and they talked of ordinary things as she drove southward toward the Negev Desert base. Reed asked about her brother;

she explained that Asher was attached to a paratroop brigade commanded by Colonel Shiff. A note of pride filled her voice as she explained that the elite unit had been active in the 1956 Sinai Campaign, the conquest of Rafah, and the historic unification of Jerusalem in the 1967 Six-Day War. "In 1973," she added, "Asher's unit was part of a commando raid against Arafat's terrorist headquarters in the heart of Beirut. That was before Asher joined, of course, but today's unit is even more highly trained."

"I've been to Beirut." His voice, which had been so vibrant a moment before, went flat. "In the winter of '82 my SEAL team was sent in to poke at the marines' defenses and see if we could find any weak spots."

Devorah waited, but he did not continue, though there was obviously more to the story. "Did you find them?" she asked after a moment. "Weak spots?"

His features hardened in a stare of disapproval. "We did. We reported the problems, and they ignored us. So we left, and two months later I was promoted out of the SEALs and found myself back in Beirut." He swallowed hard, as if trying to dislodge something stuck in his throat. "I was there when a car bomb exploded at the embassy. My wife died in the blast."

Devorah felt a cold hand pass down her spine. She glanced away, uncomfortable with this private revelation. "I am sorry," she whispered, her voice hoarse with shock. "I remember that terrible time. I had just joined the army and was terrified because we went on alert after the explosion."

She heard herself babbling, then clamped her lips together. The sound of pain had laced his voice, so his wife was not a subject he broached often. He would not want to continue this conversation about Beirut.

They rode in silence for the rest of the journey.

-0100111100-

Michael wasn't sure what compelled him to talk about Janis, but he wondered about it repeatedly as they toured the Hatzerim Air Base. He had never talked about Janis's death with his buddies in the navy, just as he had never talked much about his domestic affairs with his SEAL teammates. Military life was odd that way, especially when a soldier was part of an elite unit that lived and trained together for months at a time. A man naturally felt closer to his comrades than to the wife waiting at home—mainly because he trusted his teammates with his life. Working together as a single-minded unit, literally placing your life in someone else's hands—well, that sort of pressure had a way of binding men together.

Janis never fully understood that, but she accepted it the same way she accepted Michael's desire to spend his free evenings playing pool with his fellow SEALs. Though he often came home with a black eye and bruises, he and his guys never backed down from a poolroom brawl—and never lost one, either. After five years of marriage, Janis seemed to realize that the same guys who watched Michael's back in the pool hall would do the same thing on a mission.

A cold shiver spread over him as he remembered Janis's patient tolerance. The navy had spared no expense preparing him to defy death, but they were helpless—as was he—when it came to protecting Janis.

He cast Devorah a sidelong glance as they walked through the impressive Air Force Museum in the northwest corner of the air base. She hadn't married—had she realized the truth Michael learned too late? Modern warriors couldn't expect to have it both ways. All that happy hyperbole about how a soldier could enjoy a successful military career *and* family evaporated in the scorching light of reality.

The museum was imposing, but Michael was far more interested in the airworthy craft maintained at the base by the Israeli Air Force. Two dozen of the sixty F-16C/Ds Israel had bought from the United States in 1998 were based here, along with fifteen F-15Is. The F-16 was one of the most maneuverable fighters ever built, as tough to bring down as a gnat, but the F-15Is served as the U.S. Air Force's primary air-superiority fighter. Each F-15I was outfitted with LANTIRN—Low Altitude Navigation and Targeting Infrared for Night—pods.

Mentally noting the condition of the Israeli jets, Michael calculated what it would take to launch a full-scale defense against a massive land and air attack rising from the north, east, and south. From what he had already seen, the Israelis were well prepared against the sort of attack they had faced in the past, but they had never confronted an onslaught like the one possibly brewing in Russia.

"Devorah!" A robust and excited voice caught his attention as they exited a hanger. A uniformed paratrooper ran forward, wrapped his arms around Sergeant Major Cohen, and whirled her around in a circle.

Michael lifted a brow. Perhaps he had been too hasty in assuming Cohen had chosen not to marry. This soldier was obviously fond of her.

Michael thrust his hands behind his back, about to retreat and grant the couple a measure of privacy, but the sergeant major's scolding voice stopped him. "Be quiet, Asher, you act as though you have not seen me in a year."

The paratrooper drew back in surprise. "Not here, I haven't. Now I will finally have a chance to show my comrades what a lovely sister I have."

"I'm not here for a social call, Asher. This is business." She pulled out of the man's embrace and tugged at the hem of her jacket, a rush of pink staining her cheek. Michael turned his attention back to the Israeli paratrooper, who met Michael's gaze with a smile that was 20 percent manners and 80 percent challenge.

Keeping her eyes downcast, Devorah gestured toward Michael. "Captain Reed, meet my brother, Asher Cohen."

Asher took off his helmet and tucked it beneath his arm, then extended a broad hand. "Happy to meet you, sir. What brings you to Israel?"

"Routine liaison work, I'm afraid." Michael shook the fellow's hand. "Very dull stuff, actually. Your sister is remarkably patient with me."

"I'm sure she is." Asher looked at his sister with a world of meaning in his eyes. "You did not mention this assignment, Devorah."

The blush on her cheek deepened. "It came up rather suddenly," she said, sounding slightly strangled.

Asher turned to Michael. "How long will you be in Israel, sir?"

"For at least another week," Michael said, switching his briefcase from one hand to the other. "I'm touring all the major military bases, and we've just begun."

"So you'll be here through the Sukkot festival?"

Michael slipped a hand into his pocket and smiled. "Apparently."

"Good." Asher reached out and draped his arm around his sister's shoulders. "You will have to come to my father's house for the feast of Sukkot. We would love to have you as our guest."

Glancing at Devorah, Michael saw his surprise mirrored in her eyes. "Thank you, Asher, but I wouldn't want to intrude."

"It is impossible to intrude at festival time. It is a *mitzvot* to extend hospitality to guests. You will sit with us in my father's *sukkah* and share in our time of rejoicing. You might find it an interesting experience."

Michael wasn't certain what a *mitzvot* or a *sukkah* was, but he had the feeling a refusal might be considered a serious breach of etiquette. Given that his appearance in Israel had already offended the sergeant major, perhaps it would be wise to accept.

He nodded slowly. "You'll have to be patient with me. This will be my first Sukkot festival."

"You will enjoy it," Asher assured him. The paratrooper turned to his sister. "You will pick him up before sundown tomorrow, right? I will meet you and Papa at the house."

The sergeant major's eyes showed white all around, like a panicked horse, but she nodded dumbly. Asher bent to give her a quick peck on the cheek, then turned and moved away with a loose-boned, easy gait.

Hiding a smile, Michael turned and pretended to study the tidy row of jets parked on the airfield. He would never have imagined the sergeant major could be left speechless with surprise.

CHAPTER FOURTEEN

Paris
1330 hours

VLADIMIR GOGOL PRESSED THE FINE LINEN NAPKIN TO HIS LIPS AND SMILED AT his host, Adrian Romulus. A quartet of tuxedoed waiters was busily clearing the table, while a string quartet played Mozart in a corner of the cavernous dining hall.

"May I compliment you on your choice of chef." Vladimir nodded toward Romulus, who sat next to him, at the head of the long table. "I do not think I have ever enjoyed a more delicious meal."

Romulus smiled and shifted his posture with an indolent, tomcat grace. "That is one of the benefits of living outside Paris, General. Not only can I enjoy the beauty of an intelligent city, but its fine cuisine is mine to savor any time I wish."

Vladimir smiled, then leaned back as a waiter approached to take his dessert plate. A fragrant cup of coffee steamed on the table before him, and he lifted it to his lips, surveying the host gathered around Romulus's table.

He was quietly thrilled that not one representative had refused his invitation. Though Romulus was serving as host, everyone present knew that Vladimir had instigated and would control this meeting.

He replaced his coffee cup and folded his hands, studying the men who would join him to change the world. Many of the leaders present wore kaffiyehs on their heads; others went bareheaded. Vladimir wore his military uniform, as did Gen. Adam Archer, the former American now sworn to aid Adrian Romulus and the European Union. Others, the politicians and religious leaders, wore the clothing and insignia befitting their positions. But no matter how different their personalities and roles, all of them—emissaries from Iran, Iraq, Afghanistan, Ethiopia, Sudan, Libya,

Austria, Germany, and Turkey—had come to discuss the problem of Israel.

When the last dish had been cleared, Romulus stood. The string quartet fell silent and discreetly disappeared; the waiters slipped like shadows from the room. Another of Romulus's men, Elijah Reis, stood and moved to his employer's side. The reason became clear when Romulus welcomed his guests and Reis acted as interpreter, translating his employer's words into fluent Arabic.

"Thank you, gentlemen, for joining me here tonight." As Reis interpreted, the lights in the chamber slowly brightened, casting the dark-haired Romulus in an almost unearthly glow. He was a tall man, wide-shouldered and athletic-looking, with an air of authority and the appearance of one who demanded instant obedience. "I know you are all men of considerable importance, with busy schedules and demanding lives. But the time has come to settle an old score. We should not wait a moment longer. We cannot tolerate the arrogance of the Zionist imperialists for one more year."

Every man at the table shifted slightly to give Romulus his full attention. From the corner of his eye, Vladimir saw several of the Arabs nodding agreement.

Romulus leaned forward, bracing himself against the table. "I have invited you here today on behalf of Gen. Vladimir Vasilievich Gogol, whom you have already trusted to train your men. Listen to him now, my friends, and commit your hearts to him. I believe you will find him to be a most capable visionary."

Vladimir inclined his head in acknowledgement, then stood while Romulus resumed his seat. Looking down the table, Vladimir saw over a dozen eager and expectant faces. This meeting was merely a formality; by sending their troops to Pushkina, these men had already agreed to join him in principle. Tonight they would place their signatures on a document and join him in history.

"Comrades," he began, speaking slowly for the sake of the interpreter. "You and I know that the so-called State of Israel has been a thorn in the flesh of the Palestinian people for countless generations. Even though the Israelis have agreed to vacate the disputed territories of Gaza, the West Bank, the Golan Heights, and East Jerusalem, from the testimony of many witnesses we know that continued Israeli occupation continues to severely affect Palestinians' quality of life. As a point of illustration, Israel controls the principal aquifer under the West Bank, as well as most of the water sources supplying Palestinians in Gaza. Israelis have unlimited access to water all year round, at prices far below those paid by Palestinians. Israeli settlers in the surrounding areas have unlimited supplies of water and are estimated to consume five times as much as Palestinians. Many maintain the wasteful luxury of a swimming pool, even during times when Palestinians face severe water shortages. It has been estimated that the three thousand Israeli interlopers still living in the Gaza Strip use 75 percent of the available ground water, while the one million Palestinians in the area use less than 25 percent."

"If I may speak." Gen. Kamal Jawhar al-Nadir, the military leader of Sudan, lifted his hand, drawing the group's attention. Reis translated the general's comment into English, and Vladimir nodded, granting the man permission to take the floor.

Al-Nadir, a barrel-chested man who did not look capable of any pleasant emotion, stood at his place. "We have been most concerned about the barbarous practices enacted by the Israeli General Security Service. As many as fifteen hundred Palestinians each year are still being interrogated and confined by Israeli intelligence. This is an injustice, and it must stop."

President Dismas Rabi, head of the Council of People's Representatives in Ethiopia, stood and waited for the interpreter before speaking: "I would like to add my voice to my brother's. Serious economic and social problems exist in the area as well. Witnesses have told us that employment opportunities in Gaza are nonexistent and the economic situation is very bad. Palestinian vegetables and flowers are allowed to wilt or spoil by the side of the road while the Israelis waste precious time on the pretext of security checks. Since Gaza has no seaport or airport, our Palestinian brothers are at the mercy of the Israelis. Israel is directly responsible for this situation, which has led to serious social polarization between the rich and poor."

The Libyan head of state, Qasim al-Musa, did not wait to be recognized, but barged into the conversation, his dark eyes gleaming with resentment. "Even though the Israelis have withdrawn their police from these disputed areas, the problems persist. They have gone ahead with the building of a new Jewish settlement in the south of Arab East Jerusalem. Their settlers have not left their homes. Their children still fill the schools, depriving Palestinian children of their right to health, education, expression, and play. This is a clear contravention of the Convention on the Rights of the Child."

The German chancellor, Otto von Hirsch, pounded the table with his fist, making the candelabrum jump. "It is very clear that illegal Jewish settlers will continue to colonize the Palestinian territories unless Israel is stopped. For years, Israel has encouraged Jews from around the world to emigrate and settle on Arab lands. Collective punishment, blockades, the desecration of holy Muslim sites, and arbitrary murders of innocent civilians are a flagrant violation of international law and the Fourth Geneva Convention. It is time we did something about it."

"That, my friends," Vladimir said, standing again, "is precisely why we are gathered here today. In a moment we shall adjourn to the next room and sign a resolution that will change the course of human history. We will submit this resolution to the United Nations Security Council, and the council will have no choice but to order enforcement action. Israel has not honored the terms of the peace accord; the Palestinian areas are still occupied by Israeli forces."

"What about the Americans?" General al-Nadir barked out the question. "All five permanent members of the Security Council must support the resolution, and the Americans have long been blind to Israel's injustices."

Romulus tapped his spoon against the side of his water goblet, attracting the group's attention. "Do not worry about the Americans." A smile crawled to his lips and curved itself like a snake. "When the time comes, they will do the right thing."

Taking charge with quiet assurance, Vladimir leaned upon the table and looked from man to man. "You hate the Jews for your reasons; I hate them for reasons of my own. But trust me, friends, after Jerusalem is ours and Israel is destroyed, the entire world will look upon the remaining Jews with abhorrence and hatred. Today we shall set in motion a chain of events that will result in the total destruction of Israel. We will rid the world of this repugnant race for all time!"

His eyes roved over the circle of men, coming to rest upon the interpreter's face. Vladimir caught his breath—Romulus's imposing interpreter,

Elijah Reis, was almost certainly Jewish, but he translated Vladimir's words without any display of emotion. After an uneasy moment, Vladimir exhaled. Apparently Reis knew his people were doomed and had pledged his allegiance elsewhere.

Yasin Diya al-din, representing the Palestinian Liberation Organization, stood and looked at Vladimir with tears in his eyes. "We are all candidates for holy martyrdom. In memory of the noble and brave holy martyrs Abu Iyad, Abu Al-Hol, Abu Muhammad, and Abu Jihad, we will say with complete faith, loudly and clearly, that the song of the martyrs is etched in the path of Palestine. The Israelis are determined to destroy the Dome of the Rock and Al-Aksa Mosque on the Temple Mount and rebuild Solomon's temple, but we will not permit it." He wiped the tears from his eyes and squinted back down the table. "I envy the martyrs and hope to become one of them . . . and I am honored to be among you, my friends."

Vladimir cleared his throat, uncomfortable as always with the intrusion of religion into politics. The Muslims insisted upon seeing every battle as a holy war and every soldier as a martyr, but he was far more pragmatic. It was enough to know that Israel's defeat would open the way to the Mediterranean, and a complete victory would ensure the flow of Arabian oil to Moscow for years to come. Most importantly, once Russian troops occupied the Middle East, Russia would control the flow of oil upon which the rest of the world depended.

"To victory, gentlemen." He reached for the closest thing at hand, his coffee cup, and flushed with delight when the others smiled and lifted their cups in a spontaneous toast.

-0100111100-

When the last representative had signed the treaty of cooperation and resolution against Israel, Romulus tugged on Vladimir's sleeve and pulled him into a private corner of the drawing room. "The training is progressing?" he asked, his eyes gleaming black and dangerous in the candlelight.

"All is well," Vladimir assured him. "My officers tell me that what the Arabs lack in military discipline, they compensate for in enthusiasm. They are willing soldiers and hard workers."

"Very good." Romulus answered without looking at Vladimir. His eyes, alive with calculation, watched the others mingling throughout the room.

Vladimir waited in the silence, gathering his courage for a question. "Are you certain, Mr. President, that the American ambassador to the United Nations will support our resolution?"

One of Romulus's dark brows arched mischievously. "Do not worry about the Americans, General. The coming election has thoroughly tied President Stedman's hands. I have invested a great deal in his opponent, and even if Blackstone does not win the election, he will prevent the Americans from interfering. You could bomb Tel Aviv tomorrow, and the Americans would do nothing more than waggle a scolding finger at you."

Romulus's grin flashed briefly, dazzling against his olive skin, and Vladimir smiled back, feeling obscurely comforted. "Now go and enjoy yourself. This is a time for celebration." Romulus placed his hand on Vladimir's shoulder and gently prodded him toward the center of the room. "Tell them that the Russian fleet will depart for the Mediterranean in nine weeks."

Buoyed by Romulus's confidence, Vladimir marched into the room and greeted his new allies.

CHAPTER FIFTEEN

Moscow
1642 hours

ALANNA SAT ON THE SOFA AND LIFTED THE CIGARETTE SLOWLY TO HER LIPS. SHE drew heavily on it, making the tip glow, then flicked the ashes into a teacup and slowly exhaled.

She hated smoking. She gave it up years before coming to Russia, but last night she had thought she'd go mad, so she slipped the butler an extra hundred rubles for a pack of foul-tasting Russian cigarettes. The lighting, the smoking, the flicking gave her something to do, a means of discharging the anxiety that had been building ever since yesterday's disastrous dinner.

She stood and crossed one arm across her waist, then tasted her cigarette again. Daniel had warned her that Gogol was anti-Semitic, and he'd also warned her not to take her relationship with Gogol too far. She had ignored both warnings, and now she felt as though the slightest breath of wind would bring this fragile house of cards down upon her head.

She turned and paced back the way she'd come, then glanced at the wall separating the living room from the kitchen. The laptop was hidden there, but the maid was still cleaning up after yesterday's festive gathering. She desperately needed to talk to Daniel, to share her panic with someone, but she couldn't do anything until the maid finished her work and left the suite.

"Madame Ivanova?" The maid stood in the doorway now, her head bowed, her shoulders slumped. She extended a hand dotted with age spots toward the windows. "You want I should clean the windows?"

"No, no, you've done enough." Alanna ground the foul cigarette into the teacup and forced a smile. "Why don't you go home now?"

The wizened maid nodded, then reached for the teacup, the skin hanging loosely from her arm.

That's me in thirty years if I don't get out of this place. The thought skittered across Alanna's mind like a panicked mouse. If Vladimir finds out I'm Jewish, if he finds out about Daniel, I'll be sent to some Siberian prison and I'll never see home again.

On an impulse born of mindless terror, she took the teacup from the maid's hand, replaced it with a fistful of rubles, and sent the woman out the door.

Five minutes later, she stood at the kitchen counter, typing a hurried message to Daniel:

D:

    I think I need help. Last night, for the first time, I saw Gogol's anti-Semitism, and it wasn't a pretty sight. I'm frightened, and I don't know what to do. I was so terrified yesterday that I wept purely out of terror, but he thought my tears were due to the fact that he was leaving . . . he thought I would miss him. He's in Paris today, at a meeting with Romulus, and I'm not sure when he'll return.

    Help me, Daniel. He likes me a lot, but I don't think he cares enough to overlook the fact that my mother was Jewish.

    A.

She clicked Send and waited for the modem to dial out, then lit another cigarette and blew a long stream of smoke toward the ceiling. She'd have to stop smoking by the end of the day. Gogol would have a fit if he came back and found her reeking of smoke and nicotine.

Fortunately, Daniel replied almost immediately.

A:

    Get out now. Take the laptop and pack a bag, then take a taxi to the nearest Metro station. Ride the subway to Planernaya, the end of the northwest line. Get off and walk to the train station one block north. I will have a first-class ticket for you reserved in the name of Laura Ivanova. It's a quiet, three-day journey to London, and you can contact me from there. We will fly you home from Heathrow.

    D.

Alanna studied the message and immediately saw the wisdom in Daniel's plan. If she left Moscow by plane, Gogol would check the airports and find her trail. He would never dream she had fled by rail, safely tucked into a private first-class sleeping car.

She committed the details to memory, then wrapped up the laptop and lay it in the bottom of a shopping bag. Moving with the swift, jerky movements of a panicked animal, she thrust all the cleaning supplies back into the sink cabinet and closed the doors, then went to her bedroom and pulled out two changes of clothing. These went into the shopping bag, too, covering the computer. From the bathroom she grabbed a toiletries case and filled it with her toothbrush, hairbrush, and toothpaste.

Whirling in confusion, she caught a glimpse of her reflection in the mirror. Her eyes were wide, her skin pale, and golden strands of hair were flying around her head as if a bolt of electricity had zapped her. Muttering under her breath, she dropped the shopping bag and unpinned the knot that held her hair, then brushed it and smoothed every strand back into place.

Satisfied that she looked like any other privileged Russian woman out for a shopping excursion, she pulled her coat from the hall closet, picked up her shopping bag, and opened the front door.

Her heart congealed into a small lump of terror when she saw the two guards. She stared at them, sheer black fright sweeping through her, and managed to utter the only phrase that came to mind: *"Dobry den,* good afternoon."

The guards turned. "Good afternoon, Madame Ivanova," one of them answered, his smile not at all unpleasant.

Alanna nodded numbly, then closed the door and stood in the silence. What had happened? Had Gogol discovered the secret phone line? The computer? Her heritage?

Her legs broke free of their nightmare paralysis, and she moved across the foyer, the heels of her boots clapping against the marble like gunshots. Lowering her shopping bag to the glass-topped table in the living room, she sank into the chair and tried to corral her racing thoughts.

Gogol hadn't mentioned the guards, but he had never left her alone in Moscow before, either. Perhaps this was just a precaution, another manifestation of his overprotective nature. After all, the guard had looked at her with friendliness, not hostility. So either he was trying to charm her, or he knew she was the general's woman.

She lowered her head into her hands and kneaded her temples. Why had she stopped at the threshold? She had been surprised, of course, but they might interpret her action as guilt. They might even tell Gogol that she had been about to run away, but they prevented it. If they were just here to guard the hotel suite, they might have let her go without saying a word.

She pounded the chair cushion, overcome with frustration and regret. Had she blown her one chance to leave?

No. Surely not. All she had to do was go out there and act like she knew what she was doing. Long ago she had learned that confidence, or at least the *appearance* of confidence, could cover a swarm of insecurities.

Gripping her shopping bag, she stood, buttoned the top button on her coat, and approached the door again. This time she stepped out, locked the door behind her, and gave the guards a determined smile. "*Dos vidaniya,*" she said, taking a step down the carpeted hall. "I will see you later."

One of the guards snapped to attention beside her door; the other took a step forward. "Excuse me, Madame." He nodded decisively. "I am to go with you whenever you go out. It is the general's wish."

"It is?" Smiling, Alanna reached up and touched her hair. "The general said nothing to me of this, and I happen to know he is out of the country. So who gave you this order?"

"Colonel Petrov, Madame." The guard stared at her with deadly concentration. "He is carrying out the general's orders."

"I see." Alanna hesitated, then gave the guard a wintry smile. "Well, I was going out for a few personal things, but I think I would rather shop for those things with the general. But if you have a telephone number for Colonel Petrov, I would like to have it."

A deep line of worry appeared between the guard's eyes, but he produced a slip of paper and proceeded to print a number upon it. When he had finished, he handed it to Alanna, who slipped it into her pocket. Her fingers trembled as she struggled to slip her key into the lock. The guard who had spoken stepped forward to help and opened the door with a flourish.

"Thank you." Alanna put out her hand and did not smile until she held the key again. "Good afternoon, gentlemen. I shall leave you to your duty."

Back inside the suite, Alanna secured the deadbolt, then went to the kitchen and emptied the shopping bag on the floor, tossing her clothing out of the way until she found the laptop. She plugged in the power and crawled beneath the sink to access the hidden phone line, then tapped out a frantic message:

> D:
>
> Have just discovered that I'm under guard. I can't leave the hotel without an armed escort, so am in a holding pattern.
> Please advise.
> A.

While she waited, she found the pack of cigarettes and lit another one as the laptop went through its paces. She had smoked three before Daniel responded.

> Hang in there, Texas. We'll leave the ticket for you at the train station, so get there when you can. We'll be praying for you.
> D.

Alanna stared at the message, then managed a choking laugh. They were *praying* for her? A lot of good that would do! She hadn't prayed since the night she knelt in her footed jammies and begged God to bring her daddy back.

No—if she found her way out of this gilded cage, it would be by her own wiles and subterfuge. She'd used feminine charms to get into Gogol's world, so she'd use the same weapons to get out.

Sighing with weariness, she unplugged the computer, tucked it back in its hiding place, then carried the shopping bag and her clothing to the bedroom. She'd keep a few clothes in the bag, just in case, and if Vladimir remarked upon them, she'd make up some excuse about having to return a few items at the GUM.

She'd find a way out of this . . . and she'd keep her cool. If Gogol hadn't discovered her heritage by now, he likely never would.

-0100111100-

Alanna woke the next morning to the sound of silence. The clock on the nightstand told her that she had slept past ten, so she wrapped her robe about her and walked to the window. There was no sound from outside the hotel, but the air had the peculiar muffled quality that came with snow—and nearly a foot of the stuff covered the ledge outside her window.

She shivered slightly and moved to the kitchen, then flipped the switch for the electric coffeemaker. A small television sat in a corner of the counter, another gift from Gogol, and she turned it on merely to hear the sound of another human voice. As the coffeemaker gurgled and spat, she poured herself a glass of juice and leaned against the counter, her gaze drifting to the television screen.

A puzzling assortment of images flashed on the screen while a newscaster spoke in tense, clipped tones. Alanna saw the exterior of a hospital, then a long corridor, where several nurses embraced and sobbed quietly. The camera cut away to a shot of an elderly woman in a hospital bed, her glazed eyes open and her mouth slack, then the camera focused on a man in a suit who explained something in a weary, resigned voice. Another man's head abruptly filled the screen, his eyes blazing with anger as he shouted at the cameraman.

Perplexed, she moved closer, leaning on the counter as she watched. The camera switched to a reporter, who stood in the snow and spoke into a microphone, then gestured over his shoulder toward a Moscow bank. Alanna leaned closer, recognizing the building. That bank was right around the block! What in the world had happened?

The sound of sirens bled into the air around the newscaster, then the camera wavered as if the cameraman were running. Alanna saw uniformed policemen, armed with clubs and rifles, and a group of people whom they herded like cattle. A man, woman, and child walked at the back of the group, and as the woman slipped on the ice-covered road her face turned toward the camera.

It was Rochel Benjamin.

Alanna stared wordlessly at the camera, her heart pounding. The man bent to help Rochel, and Alanna recognized Ari's sharp features. The little boy, then, had to be sweet Ethan.

Alanna pressed her hand over her mouth, muting a scream of frustration. What had happened? What was this roundup, and what could the Benjamin family possibly have to do with those people in the hospital?

She sat for a long moment and stared at the television, waiting for some clue that would help her put the pieces together, but she couldn't make sense of the newscaster's fluent explanation. Feeling anxious and irritable, she moved to the coffeepot, poured herself a cup, and suddenly realized she knew someone who could provide her with an answer.

Petrov. She had intended to call him today anyway, to ask about the guards at her door.

Without wasting a moment, she went to the foyer and pulled the slip of paper with his phone number from her coat pocket, then picked up the kitchen phone and punched in the number. The number must have rung in some military installation, for Alanna spoke to several people before she could make herself clear. Finally she heard the colonel's smooth voice on the other end of the line.

"Colonel Petrov, I am so glad to finally reach you."

"It is my pleasure to speak with you, Madame Ivanova," he said, his voice courteous but slightly patronizing. "Is there a problem?"

"I just wanted to ask," Alanna curled the phone cord around her wrist, "about the guards at my door. Was that your idea?"

His laughter had a sharp edge. "Mine? No, Madame. The general insisted that we protect you. He was most concerned when he heard about the criminals in the hotel."

Anxiety spurted through her. "Criminals? At the Hotel Metropol?"

"Yes, Madame. There is no need to worry; we have arrested them. But the general insisted that you be kept safe."

Alanna's gaze darted toward the television. "I hope you will forgive me for taking up so much of your time, but there was something on television this morning I could not understand. Something about a hospital and people being taken away in trucks—"

"Yes, I know. All of Moscow has been shocked by the sad story. We discovered that a group of businessmen owned a power company that serviced the Ustinsky Hospital. Because the hospital fell behind in its utility payments, the company shut off the hospital's electricity. Forty minutes later, three patients were dead, and the hospital staff could do nothing."

Alanna's throat ached with sorrow. "That's terrible. Such things would never happen in—well, I've never heard of such a thing."

"Such greed and callousness is uncommon even in Russia."

"Did they turn the power back on?"

"Yes, but only after we arrested the company owners. As I suspected, most of them were Jews."

Alanna opened her mouth, but could not speak. She felt as though she had swallowed a large, cold object that pressed uncomfortably against her breastbone.

"Madame?" Petrov paused. "Is there anything else?"

"Just this," she gasped, finding her breath. "Do you know when Vladimir will return? I would like to prepare something special for him."

"Tomorrow morning, I should think." He hesitated, then added in a lower tone, "If you need anything, you have but to call. I would come immediately."

"Thank you, but that won't be necessary." Alanna hung up, realizing that her voice, like her nerves, was in tatters.

Thirty minutes later, she was dressed and on her way out the door. Two different guards stood in the hall, and as she sailed away one of them automatically followed her. She said nothing when he entered the elevator with her, and they rode down together, each of them staring at the other's reflection in the polished brass doors.

Go ahead, follow me and see what I do. Her eyes, cold and distant in the brass, challenged his. *At this moment, I don't care.*

When the brass doors opened, she braced her shoulders and moved away, zigzagging between noisy tourists in the lobby. She found the curved corridor and followed it without hesitation, then paused at the threshold of the bookstore.

The store was open. She drew a deep breath and nearly laughed in relief. She must have been mistaken, or the grainy television had distorted the images of the people getting into the truck.

"Ethan," she called, moving quietly through the book tables. She glanced over her shoulder. The guard still followed, but at a discreet distance. "Ethan." She lifted her voice, calling the boy as she had earlier this week, when she had stopped in to buy *Uncle Tom's Cabin.* They had played a quick game of hide-and-seek among the bookstacks, and the little fellow had charmed her into buying him a sweet. She bent down, peering beneath the tables to see if he was hiding from her now.

"Can I help you, Madame?"

A pair of thick, stocking-covered legs intersected Alanna's path. She straightened and stared into the iron face of a Russian woman she had never seen before.

"I was, ah, looking for the little boy who works here." Alanna glanced toward the cashier's table. Two strangers stood there, boxing a mountain of books.

"The shop is under new management." The woman's eyes were as unfriendly as her voice. "Can I help you find a book?"

Alanna looked around, noticing for the first time that the English stacks had been moved. "Um . . . yes. Do you have any English editions?"

The woman chuckled with a dry and cynical sound. "Of course not. We will carry only Russian authors, only books that promote the glory and prestige of Russia."

"I see." Alanna answered, but her heart refused to believe what her mind told her. This couldn't be happening, not at the dawn of the twenty-first century. Pogroms and book banning and anti-Semitism were abhorrent practices that should have vanished with Hitler and Stalin.

She measured the Russian woman with a cool, appraising look, then nodded slowly. "Thank you," she murmured, before turning on her heel to walk away.

After leaving her silent bodyguard at the door of the suite, she moved back to the kitchen and sent a message to Daniel, pouring out her heart about her virtual imprisonment, the signs of an impending pogrom, and the injustice done to her friends, the Benjamins.

She finished her note in a flurry of keystrokes:

> I am quite certain they are innocent of these ridiculous charges, but the unstable condition of the Russian economy has provided an opportunity for Jews to be used as scapegoats. Advise me, Daniel, please.

Within ten minutes she had received his answer:

When another Jewish girl found herself imprisoned in a political leader's palace, she mourned her fate. But her uncle counseled her with these words: "Who knows but that you have come to royal position for such a time as this?"

I cannot reveal the future for you, Texas. But, until you can escape, you might be of use to many people. God has a purpose for you, too.

Lauren and I are praying that you find it.

D.

Alanna remained in a dark mood for the rest of the day. Daniel's religious comments made no impression on her mind or heart, and she couldn't begin to see herself as some sort of heroic figure. She had ventured into this situation thinking that she might be able to do a good deed for America and pick up some exciting stories for her grandkids, but she would never have grandchildren if she didn't leave Russia soon.

At eight o'clock, she bathed and then dressed for bed, steeling herself for tomorrow's meeting with Vladimir. Perhaps he would dismiss the guards upon his return, and she could slip away while he slept. In the meantime, she would tidy up and make him think she had been anxiously awaiting his return.

She was transferring a bouquet of flowers from the dining room to the darkened kitchen when she looked up and saw a man's shadow in the foyer. Gasping, she dropped the bouquet. The crystal vase shattered, scattering glass and roses and water droplets over the tiled kitchen floor, but the man advanced confidently toward her, mindless of the shards beneath his boots. "Alanna, my darling, forgive me. I did not mean to frighten you."

Alanna shivered as Vladimir drew her into his arms. She should have known he would come immediately to see her, but she hadn't expected him until tomorrow. And the secure laptop, her most dangerous secret, still lay on the kitchen counter. The computer would be in plain sight if Vladimir turned on the light.

"Vladimir!" She pressed her trembling hands to his cheeks and stepped backward, drawing him into the light of the dining room. "I did not expect you back so soon. Colonel Petrov said—"

"You have spoken to Petrov in my absence?" He smiled, but a jealous light gleamed in the lucid depths of his eyes.

Alanna's breath seemed to have solidified in her throat. "Only once, love. I—I asked him about the guards and when you would return. I wanted to prepare a special welcome for you."

"I am glad to hear it." He smiled, but the suspicious light in his eyes did not dim. "I can take a great many faults in a woman. I can excuse ignorance, pettiness, foolishness, and even laziness. But not disloyalty."

"Vladimir." Alanna kept a smile on her lips like a label on a bottle, hiding her fear. "Have you ever known me to be any of those things?"

"Some would say you are foolish for loving an old man when you could win a younger fellow like Petrov."

He peered at her intently, and Alanna hoped with everything in her heart that this outburst was rooted in simple masculine jealousy. She could handle a jealous man.

She pulled the length of her hair over one shoulder and stroked it, then gave him a tremulous smile. "Why would I want Petrov when I could have you? I care nothing for colonels. I am a general's lady."

He digested her answer in silence, then raked her with a fiercely possessive look. "Then I am here and ready for my welcome. Best of all, I have great news and a great many presents for you."

"Have you? You're so good to me." She forced a light laugh. "I have missed you so much." She kissed him and stepped back, pulling him through the dining room.

Vladimir's hand wound tightly in her hair, snapping her head back. "Ah, my little czarina, what a feisty one you are!" he whispered, his voice low and tense. "I wish you could have been by my side to see history in the making. I would have liked my associates to see you, too, for not one of those men will have as exquisite a treasure resting in his arms tonight."

Unable to make sense of his words, Alanna caught her breath. What was he talking about?

Suddenly, he released her and took a half step back, his boots crunching the glass on the kitchen tile.

She tried to smile, but the corners of her mouth only wobbled precariously. "Surely you're not leaving me already?"

He gestured over his shoulder toward the wine rack by the pantry. "I am going to get a bottle and two glasses. We should drink a toast to the future."

"Not yet, Vladimir." Her heart had risen to her throat, but she caught his hands, then lifted them to her lips. "Later, darling."

Her eyes filled with real tears, and at the sight of them he stepped forward and lifted her into his arms. "I had no idea," he murmured, nuzzling her ear. "Like all men, I dared to dream you might be fond of me, but I could not allow myself to believe you truly cared."

Wrapping her arms about his neck, she buried her face in his shoulder. Though she could hide the anxiety in her eyes, she could not stop herself from trembling as fearful images rose in her mind. Would he be holding her now if he knew she was Jewish? Would he kiss her if he knew she was reporting his movements to an American?

"Poor darling," Vladimir whispered, his breath burning her ear. "I am home, and all is well. You must be brave for me and not carry on when I have to leave you."

"I am trying to be brave." She croaked out the words. "I am trying so very hard."

"You will succeed," he said, carrying her out of the dining room. "You and I will be examples for the Russian people."

-0100111100-

An hour later, Vladimir lay dozing on the sofa under a cashmere coverlet. Alanna pulled her wrap around her shoulders and slipped from her place, grateful that he had been tired enough to fall asleep. In her soft slippers, she padded through the dining room and into the kitchen, pausing at the threshold where the light switch hung on the wall.

If she flipped the switch, the light would reach into the foyer and the living room beyond and might disturb Vladimir. Better, then, to work in darkness.

She moved through the kitchen with a gliding step, trying to push aside the shards of glass as she moved. She found the computer, fumbled for the cord leading to the electric outlet, then quickly pulled it out. She wrapped the cord into a ball and thrust it into the plastic wrap, then hurriedly shoved the wrapping over the laptop.

As quickly as she could, she opened the kitchen cupboard, moved a couple of bottles, and slid the computer inside. She'd replace it behind the disguised panel after Vladimir had gone.

She was squatting on toes of her slippers when she heard the click of a lamp. As light from the living room bled into the kitchen, the glass shards on the floor sparkled like diamonds.

"Alanna?"

Panic like she'd never known before welled in her throat. Moving swiftly, she laid the cleaning bottles inside the cabinet, then gently closed the doors. Completely mindless of the glass on the floor, she tiptoed to the wine rack and pulled out a bottle, wincing when a sharp sliver of glass cut through the bottom of her slipper and sliced the tender arch of her foot. Her fingers trembled as she reached for the cabinet where she kept the goblets.

Suddenly the kitchen bloomed with light. Vladimir stood in the doorway, a pistol in his hand, an angry look of steely resolve on his face. "What are you doing?"

She felt as if a hand had closed around her throat. Her voice came out in a squeak of fear. "I was . . . getting the wine you wanted."

Vladimir's eyes shifted, took in the glass, the bottle in her hand, the pool of water and spilled flowers on her floor. "Why didn't you turn on the light?"

"I was afraid I'd wake you. You were so tired from your trip."

His eyes narrowed. "You are trembling, Alanna. You have never trembled at the thought of waking me."

"Vladimir, I—" She winced in real pain. "If I'm trembling, it's because I'm in agony. I cut my foot on the glass."

He regarded her quizzically for a long moment, then set the gun on a table in the foyer. "I thought it was a burglar." He held out his hand. "Come," he said, apparently not willing to trust his stockinged feet on the floor. "Come and let me tell you how a leader of Russia rewards such devotion."

With prickles of cold dread crawling along her back, Alanna left the wine bottle on the cupboard and gingerly stepped forward until she reached the carpet. Then Vladimir lifted her again, making quiet tsking sounds as he carried her to a chair.

"Do you see how I am bowing before you now?" he asked, kneeling at her feet. He lifted her foot, slipped off the slipper, and frowned as his fingertip brushed what felt like a dagger in her flesh. "All of Mother Russia will soon be kneeling before you, darling. Russia's glory will be restored before the end of this year."

He was staring at her foot, attempting to pull the shard from the soft skin. Alanna pressed her hand over her mouth as a sludge of nausea oozed back and forth in her belly. Had he gone mad? For a moment she had been convinced he was ready and willing to kill her, yet the eyes he lifted now shone with brilliance that could have sprung from ambition or desire, or even love.

"Be still, darling, I know you are in pain," he whispered, pulling the bloody shard from her foot. "Your love drives you to sacrifice for me. I shall reward you, and the people of Russia shall revere you. Do not be afraid, Alanna. Nothing can harm you as long as you are mine."

Overcome by confused thoughts and feelings, Alanna covered her face with her hands and yielded to the compulsive sobs that shook her.

CHAPTER SIXTEEN

District of Columbia
2200 hours

ALONE IN THE FAMILY QUARTERS OF THE WHITE HOUSE WITH ONLY HIS DOG (A sorry substitute for family, but the only White House resident Sam fully trusted), Sam Stedman draped one arm over his favorite chair and stroked the mastiff's silky ears as he watched a videotape of Bill Blackstone's recent campaign through the South. Blackstone was speaking to a crowd at a nursing home in Florida and had just told a group of World War II vets that theirs had been the last great war. "Americans should not ever have to police the world again," he proclaimed to a mob of applauding senior citizens. "Your grandchildren are responsible to defend these fifty states and no one else! We shall solve our own problems, defend our own borders, and supply our own enterprises. America first, last, and always!"

The elderly patriots ate it up, and so did the news reporter. As he complimented Blackstone's appearance, the camera swung over the crowd, lingering for a moment on a row of dignitaries standing on the platform.

Sam's heart thumped against his rib cage when he recognized the tall man looming directly behind Blackstone. Adrian Romulus himself, as smug and self-contained as ever, stood in the line of VIPs behind the Democratic candidate.

Hate beat a bitter rhythm in Sam's heart as he stared at the face of his enemy. Though he couldn't prove it, he knew Romulus had been responsible for Victoria's death. The man had virtually held the country hostage while Sam lay in a drug-induced coma, and only Daniel Prentice's genius had saved Sam—and the country—from certain domination.

The camera zoomed in on Blackstone, but all Sam could see were Romulus's eyes . . . gloating, sinister, knowing eyes.

"You'll get yours," Sam muttered, slowly pulling himself upright in the chair. The dog, sensing trouble, lifted her head with a sudden low woof, her ears pricked to attention. Sam kept his gaze fastened to the television screen. "If it takes my last breath, Romulus, I'll see that you get everything you deserve."

Chapter Seventeen

Jerusalem
1635 hours
Friday, October 13

THE LATE AFTERNOON AIR WAS WARM AND BURNISHED WITH SUNLIGHT. MICHAEL paced outside the entrance of the Mount Zion Hotel, a little surprised at how quickly the city of Jerusalem could shut down as it prepared for the Sabbath. Though sunset was yet a few hours away, most of the shops on the boulevard had already drawn their blinds and locked their doors.

Devorah had warned him they would not accomplish much on Friday, for not only would the Sabbath begin at sundown, but sundown also marked the beginning of Sukkot, one of the three most important religious festivals in the Jewish year. For the next eight days, life in Jerusalem would slow to an almost motionless crawl. Even the military bases, hospitals, and emergency agencies would operate with skeleton crews.

They had spent the morning together, conducting a preliminary inspection of an air base in Beersheba, and she brought him back to the hotel for lunch. A glint of humor shone in her eyes as she dropped him off. "If I were you," she told him, "I would not wear my uniform tonight. Dress comfortably, of course, but leave off the stars and bars."

Michael hesitated before getting out of the car. "Does your father have something against Americans?"

"He appreciates all your country has done for ours," she said, absently brushing a windblown curl from her forehead. "But he lives in a spiritual world, Captain, not a military one. I've found it easier to respect his little quirks."

Michael had actually been relieved to shed his uniform and leave his briefcase in the hotel room. He now wore tan Dockers and a knit polo shirt, and he stood hatless in the rising wind. With his hands in his pockets, he squinted down the Bethlehem road toward the Jaffa Gate, hoping to catch a glimpse of Devorah's blue sedan. Trouble was, all the cars looked alike here—compact and fast.

The Fiat zipped up to the curb and beeped before he recognized the woman behind the wheel. "Captain!" Devorah peered out at him from beneath a scarf and a pair of sunglasses. "How nice to find you waiting."

Michael opened the door and lowered himself into the passenger seat, then folded his long legs into the small space. "If the navy has taught me anything, it's punctuality. Actually, I think you are about two minutes late."

She looked in the rearview mirror before pulling away from the curb. "You Americans are always complaining," she said, but there was no irritation in her voice.

Michael grinned and braced his arm on the car door. He would never have expected to find a mischievous streak in Sergeant Major Cohen's personality, but experience had taught him that many people underwent a subtle personality change when they stepped out of uniform. Frogger, one of the craziest, most daring men in SEAL Six, looked like a Caspar Milquetoast until he put on tiger striped camouflage and picked up an MP10. Dressed in combat gear, he became a man you wouldn't want to run into in a dark alley.

Devorah slammed her foot to the gas and peeled out of the hotel driveway. Michael grinned, enjoying the change in the attractive woman at his side. She wore a long dress of dark brown material, but the white scarf tied around her head and throat emphasized the golden tones of her skin. The wind blew a curl from beneath the winding scarf, and Michael couldn't resist the impulse to reach out and gently nudge it back into place.

"Captain Reed," she glanced at him, a faint smile appearing at the corner of her mouth, "I should warn you that my father is *very* Orthodox. Do you have any idea what that means?"

Michael shrugged slightly. "He's religious. If he's like all the other Orthodox men I've seen around Jerusalem, he wears a black hat and dark clothes—and of course he wears a beard and those long curls in front of his ears."

Her head tipped in a barely discernable nod. "The *payos*. Yes, you are right, but earlocks and beards are external things. Do you know anything about what he believes?"

Michael searched his memory. He had studied Arab-Israeli relations for years. He could have charted the history of terrorist attacks and wars since Israel's founding in 1948, but he had never had a reason to study Judaism as a religion. He had known few Jews in his lifetime and had only worked with one or two in the course of his career. The Jewish people he had known were like Devorah—quiet about their beliefs and largely unobservant. They certainly would have little in common with a rabbi with earlocks.

He gave her a rueful smile. "I'm afraid I don't know much about Judaism," he confessed. "I know your people revere what I would call the Old Testament. I know the Jews are still waiting for the Messiah."

"I haven't time enough to give you a complete synopsis of Jewish beliefs." Devorah turned the car into a section of western Jerusalem Michael had never visited, then tapped on the steering wheel to emphasize her words. "But let me warn you of a few things. First, you must be careful never to touch me— or any Jewish woman, for that matter. Touching is forbidden between unmarried men and women."

Michael lifted a brow. "Not even a handshake?"

"Not in my father's presence." She paused a moment to let her words sink in, then gave him an apologetic smile. "This must seem terribly unsophisticated to you, but there is beauty in the old laws. They are what kept us alive as a people."

Michael shifted in his seat, realizing that his innocent touch a moment ago must have instigated her comments. "I have no problem with your rules, Sergeant Major."

"Please call me Devorah. We are off duty."

"Then you must call me Michael."

A light smoldered in her gold-flecked eyes as she grinned at him. "I will try."

They rode in silence for a moment more, past shuttered stone houses and courtyards that looked at least a hundred years old. Michael had the impression they had turned off a twenty-first-century road and somehow traveled back to medieval times. The streets here were narrow and cobbled, the houses crowded close together, their sloping roofs running into each other at odd angles.

He reined in his gaze and looked at Devorah as she slowed the car, then he pointed to the pager she wore on her belt. "If you're off duty, why are you saddled with that?"

Alarm filled her eyes. "Saddled with what?"

"The beeper."

"Oh, that." She laughed. "I often forget it is there. Every member of the IDF wears a pager, Captain. Even off duty, we remain in a high state of readiness, twenty-four hours a day. It is just something we have grown accustomed to."

Michael transferred his gaze back to the neighborhood outside his window. He couldn't imagine defending a country smaller than New Jersey with a standing army of only 150,000 troops. Even if Israel called in all her reserves, her army would only number 400,000—an infinitesimal figure compared to the potential armies of the Arab nations. At last count, intelligence reports estimated that the Russo-Arab alliance *could* field an army of over twelve million.

Devorah hadn't mentioned another fact Michael was privy to—it would take forty-eight hours for the IDF to mobilize the Israeli army, including reserves. A hostile fighter could fly across all of Israel, from the Jordan to the Mediterranean, within four *minutes* while traveling only at subsonic speed. And a single enemy fighter formation could carry more ordnance than the combined warheads of the thirty-nine Scud missiles Saddam Hussein fired at Israeli population centers during the Gulf War.

He looked at the peaceful neighborhood around him and shook his head. All this could be blasted to powder in less time than it would take Israel to make all those pagers vibrate. Sometimes he thought only a miracle had thus far prevented the nation's obliteration.

"Anything else I should know about Judaism?" he asked, looking at her. "I wouldn't want to offend your father on our first date."

"This is definitely not a date," she responded, her voice light. "And I believe you will be fine. Father is not an ogre; he is a respected and intelligent man. He was born an American." She stole a glance at his face. "Forgive me if this question seems intrusive, but are you a Christian?"

"Born-again and baptized," Michael joked, nodding. "I grew up in a Baptist church and had graduated to usher by the time I was eighteen."

The corner of her mouth drooped in a wry smile. "I wouldn't know about any of that. Just don't argue with my father and don't try to convert him. He won't be converted, and if you argue, you will lose."

Michael's tension level rose a few percentage points. "Is this really a good idea? Perhaps your father would rather you not bring a Baptist home for dinner."

"My father is a generous and kind man." Devorah turned the wheel, expertly navigating a sloping road crowded with black-coated men who spilled off the sidewalk. "But you must remember that our people have suffered greatly in the name of Christ. The Crusades gave European Christians license to rob, pillage, and murder Jews on the way to and from Jerusalem. Even Hitler called himself a Christian—"

"I certainly would not consider Hitler a Christian," Michael interrupted, laughing to cover his annoyance. "I don't know any church who would claim him as a member."

Devorah lifted one shoulder in a shrug. "What else are we to think? He graduated from a Christian school. As a boy, he wanted to become a priest. And the Catholic Church scrambled to secure and retain his favor." Her voice softened. "Hitler claimed he was doing the will of God when he murdered six million Jews."

"But surely you don't believe —" Michael bit off the rest of his sentence. How could he understand what she felt? He couldn't deny that her people had been persecuted for centuries. He knew very little about what the Jews believed, but he knew about the European ghettos in which they were forced to live, the Holocaust, and the prejudice that *still* existed in Europe and America. Many of his coworkers, intelligent and otherwise reasonable people, believed the Jews controlled everything from television and Hollywood to international banking systems.

"I'll be careful," he told her, resting his hand on the back of her bucket seat. "I'll treat your father with the respect due a five-star general."

The glow of her smile warmed him even in the chilly afternoon air. "The analogy is more apt than you know. He is a *kohein,* a priest directly descended from Aaron, the brother of Moses. In military terms, he is rather like a five-star rabbi."

Michael looked out on the street again. The crowds were growing thinner as the sun dipped lower in the west. Men and women were scurrying into their homes, children running in from play. And beside nearly every house, he noticed for the first time that a small tentlike structure had been erected.

"What's that?" He nodded toward one of the tents.

Devorah whipped the car into an empty space on the road before a stone house. "That is a *sukkah,* and it is where we will eat tonight," she said, glancing up as she turned off the ignition. "Each family erects a sukkah for the Feast of Tabernacles, to remind us of our wandering in the desert. Even as we rejoice, the sukkah's temporary structure reminds us how precarious and fragile life can be."

Michael looked at the flimsy structure and noticed how it swayed in the rising breeze. Not only was life fragile, he wanted to add, but so were nations. At the moment, Israel's existence seemed as tentative as the delicate sukkah standing beside the house. One strong northern wind might blow it all away.

-0100111100-

If he had not known that Baram Cohen was a high-ranking member of the religious hierarchy, Michael thought he would have deduced that within ten minutes of meeting the rabbi. Rabbi Cohen was a compact, well-built, bright-eyed man whose hand responded to Michael's tentative handshake with strength and vigor. His handsome face seemed kindled with a sort of supernatural refinement, and the dark eyes that looked out above an untrimmed dark beard were identical to Devorah's.

"Welcome to our home." The rabbi did not release Michael's hand immediately, but pulled him into the front room, which served as a parlor. He studied Michael's face with his enigmatic gaze for a long moment, then released Michael's hand. "I have heard much about you, Captain Reed. Good things, mostly."

Michael looked for Devorah, about to ask what in the world she had told her father, but she had disappeared. He dropped his gaze before the rabbi's steady stare, not certain how to respond. "Thank you for the invitation." He kept his gaze lowered in respect, then sighed in relief when Devorah's brother stepped into the room. "Shalom, Asher. It is good to see you again."

Asher shook Michael's hand as well, then reached into his pocket and pulled out a bit of white satin. "For you," he said, a thoughtful smile curving his mouth as he placed the satin into Michael's hand.

Michael stared at the object for a moment, then realization struck. It was a cap, just like the ones Asher and the rabbi were wearing. He plucked at the folded cloth, opened it, and eased the circle of fabric onto his head. A small hairpin had been clipped onto the fabric, and after fumbling with it a moment, Michael managed to pin the skullcap in place.

The rabbi watched, smiling. "The yarmulke becomes you," he said simply, turning toward a side door. "Now let us go to the sukkah. The hour grows late."

Michael followed the rabbi and Asher outside. The tentlike sukkah had been erected against the house. The stone wall of the house served as one side of the structure, while faded fabric hung from a series of wooden poles to form the roof and three additional walls. Michael thought some of the sukkahs he had seen on the drive had been assembled of PVC pipe and waterproof canvas, but Rabbi Cohen's sukkah was constructed of real wood and silky fabric faded from many years of use.

A table stood in the center of the shelter, with four chairs surrounding it. The rabbi moved to a chair at the end of the table while Michael took the seat across from Asher. A moment later, Devorah emerged from the kitchen with a tray in her hands. On the tray Michael saw candlesticks, matches, and a golden loaf of braided bread. Several other covered dishes already stood on the table, and Michael idly wondered when the sergeant major had found time to cook.

"It is time, Devorah." The rabbi's voice held a trace of reproach. "The Sabbath draws near."

Nodding, Devorah lowered the tray to the table, then moved to the empty chair facing her father. Quickly she drew out a match and lit the candles, then stepped back and covered her eyes with her hands. In a low, throaty voice she recited a melodic Hebrew prayer, and Michael felt himself being caught up in the beauty of it.

"*Baruch ata, Adonai Eloheinu, melech haolam, asher kideshanu bemitsvotav vetsivanu lehadlik ner shel Shabbat.* Blessed is the Lord our God, Ruler of the universe, who hallows us with his mitzvot and commands us to kindle the lights of Shabbat."

As Devorah sank into her chair, Rabbi Cohen stood, lifting his hands.

With his eyes alert and focused upon Asher, he said, "*Ye simecha Elohim ke-Efrayim vechi-Menasheh*. May God inspire you to live in the tradition of Ephraim and Manasseh, who carried forward the life of our people."

He then shifted slightly and looked at Devorah. "*Yesimech Elohim ke-Sara, Rivka, Rachel, ve-Lea*. May God inspire you to live in the tradition of Sarah and Rebekah, Rachel and Leah, who carried forward the life of our people."

The rabbi turned again, and this time he smiled at Michael. "*Yevarechecha Adonai veyishmerecha, yaer Adonai panav eleicha viychuneka, yisa Adonai panav eleicha veyasem lecha shalom*. The Lord bless you and keep you; the Lord look kindly upon you and be gracious to you; the Lord bestow his favor upon you and give you peace. Amen."

Michael nodded silently in gratitude as the blessing went on. Though much of it was in Hebrew and the rabbi did not always remember to translate, he could hear a deep undercurrent of reverence and conviction in the rabbi's prayers. Devorah and Asher both responded in Hebrew, then the rabbi lifted the loaf of bread, which he called challah, and broke it, distributing a portion to each person at the table. Finally, he ended with another prayer, and Michael caught a word he recognized: *sukkah*.

"Blessed is the Lord our God, Ruler of the universe, who hallows us with his mitzvot and commands us to celebrate in the sukkah," the rabbi finished, smiling at Michael. "Eat, and let us enjoy this festive meal."

Devorah acted as hostess, passing dishes and overseeing the table. The soft candles lit the space with a radiant glow as the sun faded and disappeared behind a row of houses. The golden atmosphere of the sukkah seemed to wrap around Michael like a warm blanket.

"This meal is delicious," he said, his stomach rumbling in appreciation of the succulent roast beef. "But when did you have time to prepare it?"

"Unfortunately, I didn't." Two bright spots of color appeared in Devorah's cheeks. "When the housekeeper cannot come, Papa gets his meals from a kosher deli in Jerusalem. He understands that my job does not allow me to do . . . many traditional things."

"But I also understand that my Devorah will not hold this job forever." The rabbi's face was smooth with secrets. "She will marry, and then she will be happy to be what HaShem, blessed be he, intends her to be."

Devorah gave Michael a pained smile. "It is forbidden to disturb the serenity of the Shabbat table with argument," she said, lowering her voice. "Keep that in mind, will you?"

If the rabbi overheard his daughter's comment, he gave no indication of it. "What brings you to Israel, Captain Reed?" he asked, cutting his meat.

Five-star rabbi or not, Michael decided to stick with his cover story. "I'm acting as a liaison for the National Security Agency," he answered, setting down his knife and fork. "Your daughter has been kind enough to serve as my escort. We are visiting several military bases—just to see that all is well."

"Does America not know all about our military bases?" The rabbi lifted a dark brow. "Must you come over and see for yourself how we are doing?"

Michael curled his hand around his water glass. "It's a routine mission, Rabbi. We just want to know how we can help keep the IDF strong."

The rabbi's mouth twisted into a cynical smile. "Something tells me you are a master of understatement, Captain Reed. You have your secrets; we have ours. All is as it should be, and I will not pry into your work." He paused to slice another piece of beef, then shot Michael an inquisitive look. "Have you family at home in America? A wife? Children?"

Michael gripped the water goblet more firmly. "I am a widower."

"I am very sorry."

"Thank you. But my wife died many years ago."

"Some sorrows remain with us for a lifetime."

"Indeed." Michael sipped from his water glass, then remembered his manners. "I'm sorry, sir, that you have been sick." He raised his eyes to find the rabbi watching him. "I hope you are feeling better."

Annoyance struggled with indignation on the rabbi's lined face as he stared at his daughter. "I was not sick."

Michael glanced at Devorah. A furious blush glowed on her cheekbones as she passed a bowl of mixed vegetables to her brother. Apparently father and daughter did not agree on the subject of the rabbi's health, but since argument was forbidden at the Shabbat table . . .

"Abba," she said, her throaty voice simmering with an unspoken warning, "Captain Reed may be interested in attending the synagogue with us tonight. He has never seen a Sukkot service."

"No?" The rabbi took a piece of beef from his fork and chewed thoughtfully, then swallowed. "Then you absolutely must join us tonight. It is a service of celebration."

Michael silently smiled his thanks, then met Asher's gaze. The young man's eyes stirred with interest, Michael thought, and more than a little pity.

-0100111100-

What is he thinking?

Devorah tilted her head, straining to see past the woman on her left. Michael sat with her father and brother in the men's section, his blond hair and clean-cut features shining like a beacon amid a sea of dark heads, prayer shawls, and beards.

Was he sorry he had accepted Asher's invitation to dinner? Was he bored? Confused? She had only mentioned the Sukkot service to chasten him for tactlessly mentioning her father's illness; she had never imagined her father would insist upon his attendance. She lowered her gaze and stared at her hands, folded now around the *etrog,* a yellow citrus fruit, and *lulav,* a bundle of palm and myrtle branches. She should have known to expect the unexpected. Lately her father had been anything but predictable.

She peeked at the men's section again and glared at her brother's profile. Asher was an impulsive fool, overly generous and completely thoughtless. He hadn't even considered how Michael Reed would react to the Sukkot service, to the bearded men who would lift their brows and send questioning glances in her father's direction. They would not understand why Rabbi Cohen would bring a *goyim* to their Sukkot service, especially one as unschooled as Captain Reed.

"Let Israel now say that his mercy endureth forever," the cantor recited, waving the green lulav. "Let the house of Aaron now say that his mercy endureth forever."

"Let them now that fear the LORD say his mercy endureth forever," the congregation responded. The air filled with a gentle swishing sound as the participants waved the lulav in the four directions: north, south, east, and west, then waved the fragrant etrog in one hand while holding the lulav in the other. "The LORD is on my side; I will not fear: what can man do unto me?"

Following the traditional ritual, Devorah pitched her voice to blend with those of the women around her and solemnly wished she could forsake her religion as easily as she had forsaken the things of childhood. These gestures seemed empty, like vestiges of a crutch her people had depended upon during the times of suffering. This waving of citrus fruit and palm branches must seem terribly ridiculous to Michael Reed, who had probably grown up in a staid, serious church where no one ever bowed or danced or wept for the coming of the Messiah.

She was snapped back to her surroundings by the sound of the cantor's nasal voice. "It is better to trust in the LORD than to put confidence in man," he continued. "It is better to trust in the LORD than to put confidence in princes. All nations compassed me about: but in the name of the LORD will I destroy them."

"They compassed me about like bees," Devorah murmured with the rest of the congregation, her eyes seeking Michael's blond head, "they are quenched as the fire of thorns: for in the name of the LORD I will destroy them."

An almost palpable hush fell over the synagogue as her father pulled himself from the rows of men and ascended the lectern. With his prayer shawl framing his face, he recited the rest of the psalm from memory. Devorah closed her eyes as his melodious voice filled the hall. A lump rose in her throat. She could not explain why her father's sincere belief tugged at her soul, but in that moment she knew she could never entirely forsake the faith of her forefathers . . . of her father. She had already distanced herself as far as she could without breaking his heart beyond repair.

"The stone which the builders refused," he recited, his deep voice resonating in the spacious chamber, "is become the head stone of the corner. This is the LORD's doing, it is marvellous in our eyes."

Devorah closed her eyes and thumbed away a tear that slipped from beneath her eyelid. Coming with him to services, serving as hostess at his Shabbat meals, and observing the rituals in his presence—these small concessions were the least she could do to atone for all the ways she had already disappointed her father.

-01001111OO-

Years before Michael had learned that one of the keys to successful intelligence work was learning to blend in with the surroundings. Try as he might, though, he didn't think he'd ever be able to blend into the congregation of an Orthodox synagogue. Though there were other blond and fair-complexioned men in the crowd, Michael had the feeling he was the only one who couldn't read Hebrew, follow the printed program, or wave his bundle of palm branches in sync with the others.

He was almost relieved when he heard the quiet thrumming sound of Asher's vibrating pager. Asher glanced down immediately, looked at the code on the screen, then switched the pager off and slipped from the row. Without hesitation Michael followed, noticing that two other men also left their seats. All the other men continued praying, their eyes either closed or focused on their prayer books.

Devorah had joined them by the time they reached the small foyer that led to the street. "What is it?" Michael asked, looking from brother to sister. An air of suppressed excitement surrounded both of them like an electric field. Michael recognized the signs of tension immediately; he had worn their taut looks on his own face. "What's happening?"

"I've got to make a call," Asher said, a grim look fixed to his mouth as he led the way to the parking lot. Michael saw only a handful of cars; most of the congregates had chosen to walk because driving was a violation of the Sabbath.

Devorah carried a cell phone in her purse and had already punched in a number by the time they reached the car. She listened for a moment, then murmured something in Hebrew, and disconnected the call. "There's been an incident," she said, her brown eyes sparking as she looked at her brother. "Call your CO. I would imagine you'll be asked to report to your base."

"Let me guess," Michael said, sliding his hands into his trouser pockets. "The incident is at the Knesset."

Her brown eyes suddenly blazed into his. "Why would you say that?"

"Something we picked up at the NSA—a series of radio transmissions from Echelon. Among a lot of other things, the word *Knesset* was mentioned."

She stared at him for a long moment, her eyes open and questioning, then she shook her head slightly. "I've been asked to report to the scene. You can either return to the service—"

"I'll go with you."

An odd mingling of wariness and amusement filled her eyes. "If you were a civilian, I'd definitely recommend that you stay here. But, after getting to know you, I can see why you'd be more at ease in a terrorist situation than in a synagogue."

Michael didn't hesitate. "Let's go," he said, opening the car door.

CHAPTER EIGHTEEN

1956 hours

THE SABBATH OFFICIALLY CEASED TO EXIST, MICHAEL REALIZED, WHEN NATIONAL security was at stake. Asher dropped him and Devorah at the rabbi's house, where they jumped into her Fiat and drove toward a modern part of the city known as Kiryat Wolfson. Michael recognized the ribbed concrete Knesset building, the home of Israel's parliament, as they pulled up. More than two dozen military and police vehicles were already on the scene. Bright lights flooded the area, and men swarmed over the grounds as if they had never heard the Sabbath was supposed to be a day of rest.

Devorah left the car in an empty lot and strode confidently into the mayhem. She paused outside a large command vehicle, flashed her badge at a guard, and was allowed to step inside. After a moment, she came back out, her eyes like black holes in her pale face.

"Apparently a group of terrorists has taken several members of Parliament hostage," she explained, leading Michael away from the command post. "They overpowered the guards just after a Parliament meeting had been dismissed."

Michael lengthened his step and turned to cut her off, halting her resolute path across the parking lot. "How many hostages?"

She stopped in midstep, a look of intense, clear light pouring through her eyes. "This is an Israeli operation, Captain. You have no duties here."

"But I have an interest. And so do you."

She showed her teeth in a tight expression that was not a smile. "I've received my orders. I am to keep you out of harm's way."

Michael stepped back, stung. "You're kidding."

A swift shadow of anger swept across her face. "I wish I weren't. I am capable of far more than baby-sitting."

Michael bit back an oath and turned from her, then raked his hand through his hair. She had a right to feel irritated, and so did he. He had come to this God-forsaken land to insure Israel's national security, and now, when it counted, the Israelis were politely and firmly pushing him away.

He kicked at a rock on the ground, sending it scrabbling across the asphalt, then clenched his fists. Israel's special ops teams were good, among the best in the world. He ought to leave them to do their jobs, but he had never been the type to walk away from a fight when he could do something to win it. And he could win this one. With President Stedman's approval, he could get a few special toys the Israelis could use to safely pry those terrorists out of the building.

He whirled around to face Devorah. "I want to speak to your commanding officer."

She shot him a cold look. "That would be a direct violation of my orders. I am to take you to Lod, where you'll be safely out of danger."

"Don't be stubborn!" Rancor sharpened his voice, and suddenly his hands were on her slender shoulders. "Take me to your CO, and now, Sergeant Major. I outrank you, and I've just given you an order."

Her nostrils flared with fury, but she turned on her heel and led the way back to the command post, leaving him to trail in her wake. Within a moment she flashed her badge again, and Michael followed her into the armored vehicle.

Inside the enclosed space, two lieutenants sat at a table and huddled around an Apple PowerBook laptop with an attached whip antenna. One of the men looked up and frowned as Michael entered; another stood and addressed Devorah. "What's the meaning of this, Sergeant Major?"

"Captain Reed insisted on speaking to you." Devorah's voice was tight and clipped.

"Don't fault her; I'm afraid I pulled rank on the sergeant major." Michael took a step closer and nodded to the officer with the most bars on his uniform. "I'd like to offer my assistance in this situation."

The lieutenant, a short, muscular-looking man with a pockmarked face, nodded brusquely. "Thank you, Captain, but we have things under control."

"How many hostages are there?"

The officer pressed his lips together, obviously unwilling to reveal sensitive information.

"Perhaps it would help," Michael ventured, "if I spoke to your prime minister. I can place him in direct contact with President Stedman, who will assure him that I am here to help, not interfere. You won't be violating any national secrets by talking with me; I know all about your Sayeret team; I even know about your top-secret Mista'aravim and Ya'Ma'M. But I also have access to weapons that might give you the edge in this situation."

The thin line of the lieutenant's mouth clamped tight for a moment, then his thick throat bobbed once as he swallowed. "Thirty hostages. Twenty are members of Parliament; the others are aides, secretaries, and office personnel. The minister of the interior and the deputy prime minister are among the captives, and that information is top secret. Two security guards are already dead."

Michael bent over the table and glanced at the laptop. The screen displayed a black and white diagram, and it didn't take a genius to figure out what the officers were studying.

"These are the building blueprints?" When the men did not answer, he looked up and gave them a grim smile. "If I can't help, gentlemen, I will back off and leave you to your work. But what if I tell you that this night's assault could not only end with all hostages safe, but also with several terrorists in custody?" He paused, letting the question echo in the silence. Counterterrorist teams had to be quick and ruthless, which meant that few terrorists ever survived the violent assaults. But if one or two could be safely extracted and questioned in custody, the Israelis could gather information that would prove valuable in the months to come.

The younger lieutenant pushed his glasses further up his nose and pointed to a line on the diagram. "The hostages are being held in the second-floor government room, on the same floor as the entrance. The terrorists have given us until 2300 hours to answer their demands. We have a hostage negotiator talking to them now by phone, trying to stall them. We will send in Sayeret and catch them by surprise."

"You storm the building, and you'll sign your hostages' death warrants." Michael's gaze fell to the blueprints on the computer screen. "This is a rather odd design," he remarked, reaching out to adjust the angle of the screen. "The building entrance is located on the second floor?"

"An afterthought," the other officer said, crossing his arms. "The original plan called for the entrance to be located on the lower level of the southern side, but that area was within range of Jordanian artillery in the West Bank before the Six-Day War. So the blueprints were amended."

With his finger, Michael traced a blue line running alongside the government room. "This interior wall is constructed of—what? Plaster? Dry wall?"

"Plaster and steel beams. The exterior wall is shielded concrete block."

"And do we know how many terrorists have joined the party? Have we any idea who they are or what they want?"

An uneasy silence prevailed, and Michael's patience vanished in a rush of frustration. "Gentlemen," he fixed the senior officer in a steely gaze, "some very influential lives are at stake at this moment. I believe I can help you, but I will need your cooperation and a full briefing on the situation. So either brief me or call for someone who can. I'm quite sure those people in the Parliament building would want you to act speedily."

Still uncommunicative, the senior officer picked up a radio and brought it to his mouth, averting his eyes as he barked several orders in Hebrew. As he waited for a response, Michael watched Devorah's face. When a voice on the radio responded, he saw a gleam of interest enter her eyes . . . and he knew he had won.

"We counted eight terrorists before they cut the power to the video cameras," the lieutenant said, his brows slanting in a frown as he set the radio on the table and turned his dark gaze upon Michael. "We are assuming they are affiliated with the PLO or Hamas. In the guise of a delegation of Israeli Arabs with an appointment to meet with an Arabic member of the Knesset, they entered the building as a session of Parliament prepared to break for Shabbat and Sukkot. Two guards and a tour guide were killed instantly as the intruders overran the staircase. At gunpoint, they herded everyone still inside the building into the government office. An hour ago they released two government officials, both elderly men, with a list of their demands. If we have not met them by 2300 hours, they say they will kill all the hostages."

Michael checked his watch. Eight o'clock, so they had less than three hours before people would begin to die. "How are they armed?"

"Nine millimeter Spectre M-4s, we think," the officer said, his brows furrowing, "and grenades. We have video footage of the initial assault."

"May I see it?"

Without answering, the officer turned and picked up a remote control on the table. A small monitor mounted on a shelf on the opposite wall clicked on, and a red light glared from the video player beneath it. Michael watched the grainy black-and-white image and saw two uniformed guards stationed at a security checkpoint. The guards' heads bobbed once or twice, perhaps they were laughing or talking. And why not? Parliament had just dismissed, the day was nearly done.

A pair of men entered the picture, dressed in the long robes favored by many of the desert-dwelling Arab Bedouin. Michael scratched his chin. The robes would have immediately drawn his attention if he was standing guard, but he couldn't blame the sentries for their lack of suspicion. One saw all sorts of people and costumes on the streets of Jerusalem.

One of the delegates suddenly pulled a dark submachine gun from beneath his robe and dispatched the sentries with quick, neat double taps. The two guards fell silently, struck down before they even had a chance to react. Immediately, a host of other robed men came forward, a similar gun in each man's hand.

He stiffened in his seat. "Stop the tape, please."

The officer clicked the remote and looked at Michael.

"About fourteen inches long, and they didn't pull a safety or cocking lever," Michael murmured, talking more to himself than to his companions as he stared at the frozen image of the gun. "That fits the Spectre M-4, but how did they get it past the metal detectors?"

The Israeli lieutenant tilted his brow, looking at him uncertainly. "I beg your pardon?"

Michael pointed toward the screen. "This can't be your only security checkpoint. There have to be metal detectors at the main entrance, right? So how did these guys get through without setting off every alarm in the building?"

The lieutenant's forehead knit in puzzlement.

Michael looked at Devorah, wondering if she followed his train of thought. "The Russians have been experimenting with weapons formed of lignostone, a compressed wood product originally developed in Holland for fuel." He reached up and tapped the gun on the screen. "Lignostone would explain how these guns slipped through the first security checkpoint. The most recent intel we've received from Russia, however, said they have yet to distribute lignostone weapons to their troops." He turned back to the Israelis. "Anybody got any ideas about how a wooden SMG could turn up in the hands of an Arab terrorist?"

Devorah crossed her arms and stared up at the video monitor. "How do we know they are Arab terrorists?"

"They've made the typical Arab demands," the officer snapped. "They want the prime minister to authorize the release of all Arabs imprisoned for crimes against Israeli citizens. But most of these prisoners are guilty of murder—they are not political prisoners."

"They don't shoot like terrorists," Devorah pointed out. "Terrorists let loose with a hail of bullets. These men were neat and quick—and on target. Like trained commandos."

Michael leaned forward on the table. "She's absolutely right. These demands could be nothing but a ruse. So why break into the Knesset?"

The officer lifted one shoulder in a defiant shrug. "It is not for me to reason why, Captain. My job is to get those people out alive."

Michael turned when Devorah spoke again. "Perhaps they intended to make hostages of the entire parliamentary assembly. They might have succeeded, if the session had not ended early for Sukkot. What better way to shake a nation to its core than by wiping out the government in one sudden swoop?"

The thought froze in Michael's brain. What better way, indeed, particularly on the eve of an eight-day religious festival? If Devorah was right, these terrorists would not release their captives no matter what the Israelis did. They were only grandstanding now, biding their time in hopes of attracting media attention, attempting to get the most bang for their buck when they chose to die with their hostages. Michael had seen it before, in Beirut.

"What would you do?" he asked Devorah.

She opened her mouth to speak, but the lieutenant cut her off. "We are preparing to infiltrate the building," he said, pointing to the blueprint on the computer screen. "In less than one hour, we will send men in here—" he tapped the screen—"here, and here. We estimate that we may suffer a

30 percent casualty rate, but my superiors believe that is an acceptable number—"

"Wait, please." Michael sank to the edge of a bench seat and brought his hand to his chin, his thoughts racing. "You say they have grenades?"

"Yes. One of the released hostages gave us that information."

"OK. So they have grenades. If experience teaches us anything, it's that they will not be afraid to use them. Even if you use flash-bang grenades and incapacitate the terrs for fifteen seconds when you rush the room, reflex alone is enough to make one of those guys trigger a grenade. If you storm the building, you will lose most of the hostages and many of your men."

His eyes shifted from one Israeli officer to the other. "Let me contact my superiors, and I'll see if I can help. I believe I can find a way to free the hostages without any losses. While I'm working, have your negotiator promise the terrorists media attention, and I guarantee they'll be willing to keep talking. I think we can resolve this situation without losing a single man."

The Israeli lieutenant regarded Michael with somber curiosity. "We want to rush the building before the deadline. If we wait for you, we will lose the element of surprise."

"Please." Michael clenched and unclenched his fist. "We'll give them a surprise, but I can't do anything if you continue to let time slip through our fingers. Speak to your CO and let me have that computer. We have no time to waste."

Frowning, the lieutenant in charge picked up the radio.

Two minutes later, Michael sent a message to GWJ@prenticetech.com:

Daniel:

We have an urgent situation at the Knesset. At least thirty hostages, many of whom are members of the Parliament. A dozen terrorists with a nonsensical demand. Probably a suicide mission of the highest order. Will need authorization from SS to initiate a rescue using every capability at my disposal. I have several ideas but will need permission to proceed.

Michael

He clicked Send, then settled back and closed his eyes. His thoughts drifted toward the synagogue, where Rabbi Cohen and so many others had just finished praying for the safety of Israel. *Heavenly Father, this would be a good time to honor those prayers . . .*

He felt Devorah's gaze upon him before he opened his eyes. They were alone in the back of the command vehicle, in a small room not much larger than the closet in his apartment. A single dim bulb burned overhead and fluctuated slightly with the growl of the diesel generator powering the vehicle.

"For a moment, I thought you were praying," she remarked, the faint beginnings of a smile on her lips.

"For a moment, I was." He closed the laptop and looked around the windowless space. Across the street, less than a hundred yards away, more than thirty hostages were sweating in their expensive suits, counting the moments until they died. Surely they knew the situation was no ordinary political ploy. The PLO had never struck the Knesset, and Michael doubted they would ever attempt anything so grandiose. The international reper-cussions would be too great.

"I think you are right," he said softly, looking at Devorah. "They wanted the entire Parliament. And they would have caught every repre-sentative, like fish in a net, if not for the holiday."

"If their plan had worked, we'd be looking at a pile of rubble now." Devorah's eyes turned automatically to the wall facing the Parliament building. "They wouldn't have waited for us to gather. Now they are only stalling for time, trying to milk the situation for publicity."

"They can have the publicity—it won't help their cause." Michael opened the computer again and stared at the blank screen, hoping Daniel wasn't napping or taking a walk or doing whatever he did for relaxation. "I don't want terrorists winning a victory. Violence only begets more violence."

He set the computer on his knees, then turned his hands over and looked down at his scarred palms. He hadn't done counterterrorism work since leaving SEAL Six, though he had stayed abreast of all the latest developments in strategy and weapons. He would have loved to call in his old SEAL team, now known as DEVGRU, but they required four hours notice before deployment. SEAL Team Three, however, maintained a small forward-deployed unit in Germany, and Michael would be grateful for as many of those men as he could get within the next ninety minutes.

A tremor of mingled fear and anticipation shot through Michael when the laptop on his knees chimed. His hand trembled as it moved over the keyboard, then a response filled the screen:

> Capt. Michael Reed—
> Your message relayed through a secure source. Use whatever U.S. resources necessary to secure the situation. And God be with you.
> President Samuel Stedman

Michael blinked at the screen, then turned the computer so Devorah could read it, too. "That's it," he said, breaking the connection and snapping the laptop shut. He stood and moved toward the front of the vehicle. "If the lieutenant can keep the terrorists calm for two hours, I'll get those people out."

"I want to help."

He turned so suddenly she nearly bumped into him. "You don't have to," he said, looking down at her. "This has nothing to do with your obligation to me. Go home; be with your family."

"You are forgetting I'm in spec ops, just like you." She looked up at him, her eyes smoldering with fire. "You yourself told me that all attachés are primarily intelligence gatherers. You came here wanting to inspect our preparation, and it's only fair that I should see yours. I'm staying, Captain."

"This isn't intelligence gathering. This is a dangerous mission—"

"And I am a highly trained CT team leader. If you hadn't barged in, Lieutenant Shiff might have assigned me to the assault team. I *want* to be on the assault team."

Michael considered arguing further, but he didn't have time. He had already learned Devorah Cohen could be uncommonly stubborn when she chose to be, so if she wanted to volunteer for terrorist target practice . . . "Suit yourself," he said, leading the way out.

CHAPTER NINETEEN

2032 hours

AMAZED AND SHAKEN, DEVORAH STOOD BACK AND WATCHED MICHAEL REED take control. His message from President Stedman had to be forwarded to the prime minister's office, approved, verified, and authorized through the Israeli chain of command. Within fifteen minutes, the order came down through the chief of the general staff himself: Capt. Michael Reed was to be granted full operations authority for ninety minutes. If he could not resolve the situation by 2245 hours, the Sayeret Mat'kal team was free to continue with its plan to liberate the Knesset hostages. And while Reed prepared, Sayeret sharpshooters were to remain in place around the building to maintain the perimeter.

Devorah shadowed Reed, supplying information when asked, observing when left alone. The captain placed a SatFone call to the chief of naval operations at the Pentagon, where it was only one o'clock on a lazy Friday afternoon. Apparently Reed's name carried some weight, for the CNO returned his call almost immediately. Reed asked for the forward deployment of as many men from SEAL Team Three as could be dispatched within twenty minutes; he also asked for several weapons Devorah had never heard of. The men and supplies were to be flown by jet from Germany to the Jerusalem airport, from which an Israeli helicopter would ferry the men and weapons to a rendezvous point at the base of a hill south of the Knesset. The rendezvous was set for 2210, only 85 minutes away. "I'll lead the team myself," Reed told the CNO in closing.

When he hung up the SatFone, Devorah stared at him in astonishment. "With all due respect, Captain," she lifted her chin, "why would you want to lead the assault team? Wouldn't the mission be better served if you coordinated the team's movements from the command post?"

The grooves beside his mouth deepened into a smug, confident smile. "What's wrong, Sergeant Major? Don't you think I'm capable of overseeing this operation?"

"Overseeing it from the command post, yes. But you have worked behind a desk for . . . how many years now?"

"Some things you never forget, Cohen, and one of them is that SEAL commanders lead from the front, not the rear." The determination in his eyes froze into a blue as cold as glacier ice, though his lips stayed curved in a smile. "Don't worry about my fitness. I've kept up with my training, and I can still shoot as well as the young guys." He straightened and squared his shoulders. "I scarcely think my years behind a desk will matter tonight."

Devorah lifted her hands and backed away, unwilling to argue. Navy SEAL shooters were legendary; it was said they could put three quick rounds in a human head at fifty meters about as fast as their brains could form the thought. But her team could shoot, too.

"Fine." She looked Reed squarely in the eye. "But some of my men and I will come with you."

Reed shook his head. "I'm not inserting a blasted army into that building. I want an eight-man squad, no more, just two fire teams. I'm sure I'll get the men I need from SEAL Three."

"Twenty minutes isn't much advance warning. You'll be lucky to get two men. Besides, this is Israel, Captain. This is an Israeli operation—and you have already said I could be on the team."

His golden brows drew downward in a frown. "I was humoring you, Sergeant Major. For security reasons, your people will have to stay away. We will be working with classified weapons, and I'm not authorized to give access—"

"All the more reason for us to come along." Devorah felt her mouth twist into a cynical smile. "We have shown you our secrets, Captain; it is time for you to reveal some of yours." He opened his mouth as if he would argue, but Devorah lifted a hand and cut him off. "We haven't time for discussion, Reed. I am going to see if I can find us some camouflage gear. I will meet you at the rendezvous point in an hour. I hope your SEALs will have arrived by then."

She moved past him, knowing he couldn't afford to shut her out. If the

SEAL Three operators were more than twenty minutes from the airport, none of them would make it to Jerusalem tonight.

-0100111100-

At 2200 hours, Devorah heard over the radio that four men from SEAL Three had arrived at the airport. She slammed a magazine into the Uzi and leaped out of the armored vehicle that had arrived to support the assault, then jogged toward the command post where Reed and the Sayeret lieutenants were still sketching out details.

She moved more slowly than usual, burdened by thirty pounds of equipment. A bulletproof vest lay under her flame-retardant overalls, and over the overalls she wore a load-bearing tactical vest holding extra ammo clips, a flashlight, a first-aid kit, a pair of flash-bang grenades, and a radio digitized with an encryption system so only the assault team members could pick up each other's transmissions. A holster with a pistol and ammo lay strapped to her thigh, and her Uzi hung from a sling that wound around her neck and over her shoulder.

"Since only four SEALs are en route," she panted, climbing heavily into the vehicle, "you're going to need two more operators." She looked directly at Reed. "I'd like to recommend Berger and Navron—they're both excellent shots."

Reed glanced at Lieutenant Shiff, who nodded slowly.

"Berger and Navron it is," Reed said, standing. Devorah blinked at the sight of him, caught off guard by the transformation. He wore tiger-stripe black fatigues and black boots. A pair of leather gloves hung half out of his vest pocket, and a pair of night vision goggles dangled from a strap. He carried the same weapons she did, but instead of a Nomex balaclava hood, he wore a black knitted cap that blended perfectly with his blacked-out face.

He grinned when he caught her staring at the cap. "What's the matter, Cohen? Don't like my headgear? Sorry, but I've never been fond of those tight hoods."

He removed the cap and tossed it onto the table, then picked up a headset and fitted it over his skull. After securing the headset with the tight cap, he wriggled the radio earpiece into his ear, then adjusted the filament microphone so it sat just below his lower lip. Devorah knew that every word he said would be transmitted to the command post, so if things went badly, Lieutenants Shiff and Mofaz would hear it live. She didn't find much comfort in the thought.

"Twenty-two o-five hundred hours," Mofaz called, staring at his watch. "Five minutes until rendezvous."

Devorah jerked her head toward the door. "Navron and Berger are outside. They're ready."

Michael flashed her a grin. "Then let's rock and roll."

A black MD530 "Little Bird" helicopter touched down at precisely 2210 hours, and Devorah joined Reed, Navron, and Berger as they climbed into the open doors. The rotors whirled overhead, chopping the air in a dull rhythm as Reed greeted the four Navy SEALs and made quick introductions, then explained how the operation would go down. The SEALS wore expressions of grim determination as they listened, respecting Reed's orders as if he'd led them for years.

Devorah leaned back against a mesh barricade, impressed. Reed must have really earned those four bars if he commanded instant respect from these guys. Like her, they were dressed in black and armed to the teeth, their wide eyes shining with the bold audacity that adrenaline produces in true warriors.

While the Israelis carried Uzis, the Americans held Heckler & Koch MP10s in their leather slings. She knew the state-of-the-art submachine guns featured single, semiauto, three-round burst and automatic positions. A detachable "aiming projector" scope created a narrow beam of intense light along the line of fire, enabling the shooter to hit targets of about four inches in diameter—the average width of a human forehead—from a distance of seventy-five meters.

She brought her Uzi a little closer to her chest. No operator in her right mind would want to change weapons going into an assault, but she wouldn't mind an opportunity to play around with the Americans' guns for a while.

As Reed continued his explanations, Berger and Navron listened silently, though they and Devorah knew they were along more for backup than to actually play a role in this drama. The leader of SEAL Three, a lieutenant named Dickerson, nodded as Reed explained the layout of the building and what they knew of the terrorists inside.

"We're going to keep this operation simple," Reed said, shouting to be heard above the rotors' rhythmic whopping. "We don't know who might be watching around the perimeter, and we'd like to get this situation resolved before the media gets wind of it. The IDF promised full media coverage, but it was all a bluff—just something to keep the tangos happy for a couple of hours."

His blue eyes locked on Dickerson. "Did you bring the thermal guns?"

Dickerson grinned, his white teeth shining through the darkness. "Roger that, Captain. Everything you asked for. Best of all, Miles, Webb, and Phillips here are certified to use them. You've got yourself a group of regular Jedi."

"Perfect." Reed pulled a folded sheet of paper from his vest and spread it on the floor. As if he could read the captain's mind, Dickerson pulled a flashlight from his vest and illuminated the area. Devorah looked down and saw that Reed had sketched a rough map of the second floor where the hostages were being held.

"We're going to insert through the roof," Reed said, glancing up. He looked at Devorah and her teammates. "I hope you have strong leather gloves. This will be a fast-rope drop, so nothing but your hands will see you safely down."

Devorah drew a deep breath and forbade herself to tremble. Fast-roping was not her favorite means of insertion, but everyone in her unit had gone through the training. It required dropping two operators simultaneously, one from each side of the chopper, without any safety hooks or belts. The sensation reminded Devorah of sliding down a fireman's pole. If done correctly, an operator's gloves would be chafed and almost smoking by the time he or she hit the ground. If done incorrectly, the operator would be dead.

She met Reed's gaze without hesitation. "We can handle it."

"Good." Reed nodded. "We're going to move in fast, before they can hear the chopper and send a man to the roof—we wouldn't want to be dangling targets for some tango to pick off at his leisure. Dickerson and I will ride on the skids and drop as soon as we're forty feet above the roof. The rest of you peel off in ten second intervals." His eyes roved over the group. "Berger, you go last, opposite Cohen."

Devorah lowered her eyes, grateful that the black face paint hid the extent of her embarrassment. Being female, she'd been paired with the smallest man. It was a logical, sensible decision, for the chopper had to be balanced during the fast drop, but Reed's comment seemed to imply that he didn't think a woman—or the Israelis—were capable of performing at his level.

A tart reply rose to her lips, but she bit it back. She knew all about the chauvinism that ran rampant in the elite American corps. The four women who made it through Delta Force training in the early '80s left after their male counterparts hounded them out. The five female operators who now served in Delta were assigned to an intelligence detachment known as the "Funny Platoon." At least they were allowed to serve as spies, infiltrating countries to recon targets for their male counterparts.

"Once down, we're going to blow the rooftop door and move out in teams of four," Reed was explaining now, one hand on the map. "Remember—speed, surprise, violence of action. That's what we're after." He nodded toward the Israelis. "Berger, Navron, Miles, and Webb will advance to the double doors at the main entry." He paused and looked up, a trickle of perspiration shining on his brow. So—the Captain was not quite as confident as his manner appeared.

"The government room is on the same floor as the entrance, but four of you will go downstairs and surveil the rooms below. Miles and Webb will use infrared to be certain the tangos have not moved any of the hostages. Navron and Berger will cut the power to all areas *except* the government room. You'll find the circuit breakers here." He pointed to a small X marked on the map. "Flip all the breakers but the one in the second bank, top right-hand corner. I want to blind any tangos in the hallway, but I don't want the hostages or their guards alerted to our presence. I also want those breakers flipped two minutes after we hit the roof."

Berger let out a long, low whistle, but Reed's request didn't seem to phase the SEALs.

"What about infrared?" Dickerson asked. "We could pinpoint the hostages' location from outside the building."

Reed shook his head. "According to the blueprints, the exterior walls are shielded. Infrared won't penetrate the building, so we won't be able to take any readings until we get inside." He flashed a rueful smile. "Sorry I couldn't do better, guys. Those of you on the stairs will be moving targets for any sniper on the lower floor, so be careful and proceed with caution. After you've flipped the circuit breakers and cleared the area, come up and join us on the second floor."

Miles set his jaw. "Roger that."

Reed gave Berger and Navron a mischievous smile. "If you make it up to the second floor, gentlemen, you'll be treated to a demonstration of our new toys. Of course, we're going to have to kill you afterward."

Though Berger smiled a little uncertainly, he nodded in approval. Navron looked at Devorah and mouthed a question: "He is joking—right?"

"Cohen, Dickerson, and Phillips—you three will come with me to this west wall." Reed tapped the map again. "We'll move through the hallway in a Congo line, and you'll take defensive positions outside the government room." He grinned. "The other side of the wall features a painting of the Sea of Galilee, a busy surface that will disguise our activities while we work."

Reed looked up and glanced at the squad. "Any questions?" When no one spoke, he nodded and tapped the chopper pilot's shoulder. "Let's move out."

Devorah clutched her Uzi and stared at the floor, certain that fear radiated from her like a halo around the moon. From the corner of her eye she watched Reed and Dickerson pull on their gloves, then toss out the heavy British ropes used for a fast-rope insertion. The soft, twisted nylon lines uncoiled and fell from the chopper, then swayed gently from their hooks as the chopper moved up and into position.

Dickerson and Reed caught the lines and lowered themselves to the skids, each man leaning his entire body weight on the ropes as the Knesset's rooftop came into view. Forty feet above the roof, the chopper hovered while Reed and Dickerson stepped back, positioning the ropes between their boots, then kicked themselves free of the skid and dropped out of sight. Devorah stood, mentally counting to ten between the others' descents, then finally grasped the rope herself, caught Berger's eye, and stepped out into nothingness.

The pebbled gray rooftop seemed to rise at an alarming rate, and the night air struck her face like a cold slap. Then, suddenly, she was on the ground, her hands warm from the friction of the rope. Without wasting a moment, she tossed the rope free, snatched the Uzi in both hands, and followed the others, who were moving like shadows through a maze of air vents and hulking air-conditioning units. Dickerson had already blown the access door by the time she arrived, so she and Berger slipped down the metal stairs as silently as they could.

Inexplicably, her thoughts drifted to her father, who would still be sitting in the synagogue, lifting his prayers for Israel's safety among the nations. For half an instant she wondered if he would think to pray for her, then she remembered that very few people in Jerusalem knew anything about the situation. If all went well, they would never need to know of it.

Moving with the grace and skill of trained dancers, the members of the assault team broke off and moved to their assigned positions. Devorah doggedly followed Reed, Dickerson, and Phillips, then paused in the service hallway and waited for Berger and Navron to cut the lights. She let the Uzi rest in its sling as she pulled her NV goggles from her vest and fitted them over her balaclava hood. Holding the eyepiece over her forehead, she looked up at a bank of fluorescent lights in the ceiling. Almost immediately, the lights went out.

She pulled the NV goggles over her face then gripped the Uzi, blinking as her eyes grew accustomed to the oscilloscope-green tint that now illuminated the hallway. Reed held up his hand and lifted two fingers, his sign for the Congo line formation. Devorah knew it well—all counterterrorist teams were drilled in several standard approaches to hostile spaces. Each team member had to know whether to go right or left, to shoot low or high. Without a plan and a pattern, operators could end up shooting each other.

They moved into the hallway, assumed their high/low positions, and froze, each operator scanning the space. Devorah saw no movement, only emptiness. Reed lifted his hand again, pointed in the direction of the government room, then drew an *S* in the air. He wanted to enter this hallway in the snake pattern, one man following another. It was risky for the point man, but safer for the others . . . and Reed was taking the point. She felt her heart rate increase as they swept down the dark hallway.

A score of questions rose to her brain as she followed Phillips and glanced over her shoulder every five steps to be sure no tangos moved behind them. What if one of the terrorists decided to step out in search of a restroom? What if one of the hostages tried something desperate and accidentally set off a grenade? She knew what to expect from professional soldiers, but terrorists didn't play by the rules and hostages were hopelessly unpredictable.

Thirty feet shy of the doors leading into the government room, Michael stopped and pumped his fist twice. Dickerson stepped forward and aimed an infrared scope toward the corridor ahead. From studying the blueprints Devorah knew they were outside a storage room. The government room and the hostages lay at least twenty-five feet further down the hall. She glanced down and saw movement on the infrared screen, faint red blips surrounded by a fuzzy white aura.

"So far, so good," Reed whispered, shifting his sniper rifle from one hand to the other. "The hallway appears clear."

"Wait." Devorah leaned forward and pointed toward another blip, one moving westward and located farther north than the others. "Who is that?"

Dickerson flashed an appreciative smile. "A lookout, no doubt. Caught in the dark, and as suspicious as a navy wife by now. He'll be expecting us."

Michael glanced at Dickerson. "Can you take him out when he turns the corner? Silently—we can't alert the others."

"Piece of cake." Dickerson handed the infrared scope to Devorah, then straightened and pulled his suppressed submachine gun from its sling. Devorah heard the click of the MP10's safety as he flicked it downward to full fire.

On the scope, the blip changed direction. It was now moving southward, straight toward them. Devorah looked up and could see movement in the green-tinted night beyond. A man crept there, a SMG in his arms.

"Now, Dickerson." Reed's voice was a jolt of energy, sending the lieutenant two steps forward. Devorah heard a soft double tap—*pfft pfft*—then a sound like a bag of potatoes falling to the floor. She looked up and squinted through the darkness. The man in the distance had fallen.

The lieutenant's southern drawl interrupted her thoughts. "Clear to advance, Captain."

Without another word, Reed gestured to Dickerson, sending him to the north end of the hallway to secure that position, then he motioned Devorah and Phillips forward. When they were still ten feet from the entrance doors, Reed looked at Devorah and held up the flat of his hand, indicating that he wanted her to hold her position and make certain no tangos approached from the southern hallway.

She nodded and turned to face the corner they had just rounded, crouching in a firing position as Reed and Phillips moved toward the double entrance doors to the government room. Though she kept one eye on the hallway she had been assigned, she couldn't help being fascinated by Reed and Phillips.

Silently, Reed stepped up to the wall separating him from the hostages and pulled out an electronic device that led him to a hollow spot in the plaster wall. Satisfied, he nodded to Phillips, who stepped forward with a black drill.

Devorah watched in silence as the noiseless drill whirred, sending a thin plume of plaster smoke into the air. After a moment, Phillips stepped back while Reed approached the hole and extended his hand. Like a nurse supplying a surgeon, Phillips pulled a slender ten-inch rod from his tactical vest and snapped it against the captain's gloved palm.

Reed slipped the tube into the drilled hole, then fastened a wire to the end of the cylinder. Phillips produced a small black monitor, which Reed connected to the wire. He then knelt down and focused on the monitor's screen, and, as an afterthought, looked up and gestured to Devorah.

She cast a quick glance over the empty hallway, then rose from her crouch and crept forward, peering over Reed's shoulder. Like a tiny television, the screen displayed the interior of the room. She could see all thirty hostages, some in chairs, some bound and sitting around the circular table—and five gunmen, each carrying an automatic weapon. The most agitated man, apparently the leader, also carried a grenade in his clenched first.

"A fisheye lens," Dickerson whispered, grinning up at her. "Neat gadget, huh?"

Devorah didn't answer but stepped back to reassume her position. It was a wonderful spy device, but the IDF had similar tools. And what was the point? Reed had promised to end the situation without casualties, but so far he hadn't done anything the IDF counterterrorist team wouldn't have done. Though there were only five terrorists inside the room, any attempt to rush the doors would certainly result in an explosion. The leader wouldn't hesitate to trigger the grenade.

As if he had read her mind, Michael tapped the screen and spoke in a rough whisper. "What sort of grenade is that?"

Dickerson leaned closer and squinted at the jerky image. "It looks like a Swiss HG 85 electronic fragmentation hand grenade—they're nasty little beasties. They'll bring down anything within one hundred meters of the detonation point."

"Trigger?"

"A self-destruct button. Right on top, within easy reach."

Devorah shifted her gaze back to the hallway and felt fear burn the back of her throat as something moved in the emerald darkness. Her finger covered the Uzi's trigger, ready to fire . . . then Reed's voice scraped like sandpaper across her ears. "Roger that, Miles. We've got you in sight, so come on down."

Moving in a single line, Miles, Berger, and Navron crept down the hallway toward the government room. As Navron and Miles moved toward Reed, Berger knelt at Devorah's side.

"Where's Webb?" She was almost afraid to ask.

Berger leaned closer, the narcotic scent of his tobacco assaulting her nostrils. "Left him to guard the stairs. We took out two tangos on the first floor."

Devorah exhaled in relief. Eight tangos in, three dead, five in the government room. All terrorists present and accounted for.

Silently, Reed pointed to Devorah, Navron, and Berger, then gestured toward three spots in the wall and made a twisting gesture, as if he were turning a doorknob. Devorah nodded, understanding that he wanted mouse holes blown in the wall. She released her Uzi, allowing it to dangle on the sling, and pulled a handful of Primacord from a pocket in her tactical vest. Moving to the wall, she stuck the explosive to the wall in a rectangular shape, then pushed a blasting cap into the upper right corner. She worked quickly, determined to observe everything going on around her.

Murmuring into the radio microphone, Reed called for Dickerson, who jogged back without a sound. Then, by pointing to his men and touching the monitor, Reed assigned each of the four SEALs to one of the terrorists on the screen. Understanding his silent signals, the operators nodded and moved along the wall, each man keeping a wary eye on the video display as the terrorists paced back and forth in the room.

"We'll get them." Michael looked at Devorah, mouthing the words, but she understood him as clearly as if he had shouted in her ear. What she didn't understand was how they were supposed to incapacitate these men while on the other side of a wall the leader held a grenade within killing distance of thirty of Israel's most influential political leaders.

Gripping the detonator control in her left hand, she grabbed the grip of her Uzi and brought it up to point at the ceiling, then backed ten feet away from the wall. She checked her watch: 2232. Fear blew down the back of her neck when she realized they had been in the building fifteen minutes. Terrorists with any training whatsoever would require sentries to check in frequently, and these madmen were certain to expect a radio report from the dead guy in the hall or the two lookouts on the first floor. More important, the Sayeret, *her* people, were preparing to storm the building at 2245. If Reed and his men didn't hurry, they might all end up in the rubble of the Knesset.

From their backpacks, the SEALs pulled weapons she had never seen before. They were shaped like rifles, but with narrow barrels, scarcely wider than a pencil. Each man flipped a switch, activating some sort of mechanism that lit the shooter's face with a green glow. Adjusting her position, Devorah stared at the closest man, Miles, and saw that this weapon featured a small infrared screen, enabling the shooter to discern thermal body images through the wall. By comparing the moving infrared blips with the video screen, each man was able to distinguish between his assigned target and the others in the room.

Devorah blinked in wonderment. She had no idea what these men were doing, but this was not the time or place to ask. She would take mental notes and pass them on to the intelligence community later. Though the Americans were usually generous with their technology, they had not offered to share anything like this.

The four SEALs, each operator still tracking the movements of his assigned enemy, waited for Reed's signal. He stood and lifted his hand, looked right and left to check his men's preparation, then brought his hand down in an abrupt movement.

Devorah flinched as a sharp crackling sound filled the air. Twenty seconds passed, then she heard sounds of distress from the room beyond. She cradled her weapon and aimed it toward the wall where she had planted the charges. She cut a quick look to the video screen and saw that four of the terrorists, all but the leader, had dropped their weapons and fallen to the floor. The agitated leader's face had darkened with anger, the hand with the grenade flailing in frustration.

Michael raised the sniper rifle, then jerked his head, urging Devorah and her men forward. "Blow the holes," he commanded, his voice filled with a quiet menace all the more intimidating for its control. "I'll take out the leader."

Devorah pressed the button on the detonator, then turned her head as the section of wall imploded, sending a cloud of white dust and smoke into the air. Her feet carried her forward and through the opening, and she fell to one knee, covering the fallen tangos with her weapon, while the grenade-wielding leader stepped forward, his eyes blazing, his hand lifted defiantly.

"Drop your weapon!" he called in Arabic, his face a glowering mask of rage. "Drop your weapon or—"

Before he could complete his sentence, a single shot cracked and a faintly pink cloud bloomed around the terrorist's head. Carried by momentum alone, the man spun in a slow circle, then buckled at the knees and collapsed on the ground. The shiny grenade slipped from his hand and rolled over the carpet, landing only a few inches from Michael Reed's boots.

Devorah took a wincing breath, then exhaled slowly. The device had not been triggered. It couldn't have been; Reed's shot had gone through the control centers of the brain, instantly killing all motor function.

"Clear!" The call came from the men scattered through the room. "Clear!" "All clear!"

"Sergeant Major." Reed wore a crooked smile when he turned to face her. "Why do you look so surprised? I told you we could handle this with no casualties—well, almost none."

Her heart seemed to have stopped dead when the grenade rolled toward him, and it now resumed beating much faster than usual, as if to make up for lost time. "What took you so long?" she stammered, staring at the grenade.

"Must have been all those years behind a desk," he answered, his voice dry.

Reed moved past her, back out into the hall, as Devorah lifted her NV goggles and stared at the chaos in the room. The other four terrorists lay on the floor, their faces as pale as death, their khaki shirts and trousers mottled with sweat. The hostages were clapping, shouting, embracing in a sea of relief. One man came toward her, chanting Hebrew words of blessing as he drew her into his arms and patted her on the back.

Devorah smiled numbly, quietly accepted the man's thanks, then slipped back out into the hall. Reed was facing the wall and talking to the command post on the radio, telling the Sayeret to stand down and send an ambulance. The situation had been resolved. Four terrorists were safely in custody for questioning, and all thirty hostages and eight assault team members were alive and well.

Just like he'd said they would be.

-01001111OO-

Michael thanked the members of the SEAL Team Three, made each of them promise to look him up if they came through Fort Meade, then stood back as the Little Bird lifted off and swung away into the night sky. The operation had been a complete success, and tomorrow the Israelis would thank him.

But the victory had not been won without cost. Even if only a skeleton story were reported in the press, by tomorrow morning the world would know that American soldiers had been brought in to help resolve the situation. While the Israeli lieutenants in the command post were plenty grateful to have their necks rescued by American SEALs, the higher-ups might not feel so appreciative. And Sam Stedman, still facing a tough political battle at the polls, would undoubtedly come under fire for authorizing the use of American troops.

The weapons were another touchy subject. The thermal guns they had used to immobilize the four terrorists were still classified. The concept of a thermal weapon—one which could raise an enemy's body temperature to a ripping 106 degrees—had been on the drawing board for years, but few people outside SpecWar forces knew a prototype had actually been developed and tested. Yet tonight he had displayed the gun and its capabilities before several Israelis, including Devorah, who would undoubtedly want to know more.

He wasn't surprised when she offered to drive him back to his hotel after their after action review. "I can take a taxi," he offered, gesturing at the still-crowded street. "It's late, and you're probably exhausted."

"My father will know Asher and I left the synagogue." She looked up and gave him a tired smile. "And I think he would like to hear about what happened tonight. You began the evening with his hospitality—why don't you end it with him as well?"

Michael fell silent, torn between common sense and an inexplicable desire to please a woman who had proven her mettle in the last hour. He had often privately wondered how a woman would perform as a member of an assault team, and tonight he had seen that Devorah Cohen, at least, could pull her weight.

He nodded slowly. "I'll come, if only for another piece of that delicious challah." He gestured toward the street. "But I think you'd do a fine job of telling the story."

"You'll tell it better." A secretive smile softened her lips as they began to walk. "And I can't wait to hear all the details."

-0100111100-

The windows in the rabbi's house were dark, but Devorah assured him her father would still be awake. "The lamps are controlled by a timer, since turning them on and off would violate the Sabbath," she explained as she led the way up the cobblestone walk. "He would usually be asleep by this hour, but I'm sure he's still awake. He doesn't rest when there is trouble afoot."

As Devorah rapped softly upon the door, Michael slipped his hands into his trouser pockets and shivered slightly in the chilly air. The adrenaline that had flooded his body was ebbing away, leaving him feeling drained and empty.

The golden glow of a streetlight illuminated the porch and shone upon a small silver container that had been mounted at eye level beside the door. Leaning closer, Michael could see a piece of rolled parchment visible through a tiny glass window in the center of the receptacle.

Devorah saw him studying the container. "It's a mezuzah," she explained, folding her arms. "The parchment is inscribed with a portion of the Scripture."

Michael nodded slowly as a memory rose in his tired brain. "'Write them on the doorframes of your houses and on your gates,'" he quoted.

"Exactly." She smiled in approval. "'Tie them as symbols on your hands and bind them on your foreheads'—that's why you see men praying with tefillin bound to their arms and foreheads." She sighed softly. "My people take the Law of Moses quite literally."

The door opened, and the streetlight gilded Rabbi Cohen's solemn features. He had a diplomat's face, Michael thought, almost anything could have been going on behind that facade of patient reserve, but a note of relief echoed in his one-word welcome: "Devorah."

Her mouth curved with tender affection. "I am well, Abba. I thought you might like to know what happened tonight."

As calmly as if he were accustomed to receiving visitors at midnight, the rabbi opened the door further and gestured toward the front room. Devorah moved easily through the dark foyer, but Michael paused a moment, letting his eyes become accustomed to the gray streetlight that seeped through the thin curtains at the front window. When he was certain he could move without tripping over furniture, he made his way to the couch.

He heard the creak of the rabbi's chair and knew the man waited to hear the story. Devorah, who had vanished into the black confines of a wing chair in a shadowed corner of the room, remained silent, waiting for Michael to begin.

Michael told the story in stark and simple terms, offering no details despite Devorah's broad hints. "By using a special weapon," he shot a gimlet glance toward Devorah's chair, "we incapacitated the terrorists. The Parliament leaders have been released unharmed, and the four surviving terrorists are in custody."

Through the gray gloom Michael saw the rabbi gently stroke his beard. "A great tragedy," he finally said, a weight of sadness in his deep voice. "The Master of the universe, blessed be he, must grieve when such things occur in his city, on his Shabbat."

He turned to Devorah. "And your brother? Was he involved in this?" As father and daughter conversed, Michael leaned back on the sofa and reviewed the evening. Terrorism, by definition, was an unpredictable and dangerous business, but several pieces of this scenario did not fit. These particular tangos were either complete idiots or they had missed their mark by a matter of minutes. And why had they attacked a huge building like the Knesset with only eight men? Only professionals would dare assault a high-profile target with such a small team. What had they hoped to accomplish?

Devorah and her father were speaking in Hebrew now, and the melodic lilt of their voices combined with the darkness to increase Michael's exhaustion. His back ached between his shoulder blades, a sure sign of the tension he'd barely noticed earlier. He sighed, rubbing the back of his neck with his hand, massaging away the weight of leadership.

Samuel Stedman had asked him to investigate an impending threat to Israel's national security, and Michael couldn't help but wonder if his investigation and the tangos at the Knesset were somehow linked. The terrorists had been carrying top-of-the-line SMGs made of lignostone, and under their Arab robes they had worn European clothing. The leader had worn a beard, common among the Arabs, but he could have grown one in preparation for this attack. And the Echelon information had contained the word *Knesset*.

A seam of fatigue opened in Michael's mind as he tried to fit the pieces together. He shook his head, realizing he needed three things before his brain would function properly—he needed rest, he needed food, and he needed to talk to Daniel Prentice. Wherever Daniel was, he needed to know what had happened tonight. Maybe he could help Michael solve the puzzle.

-0100111100-

Two hours later, Michael sat at the desk in his hotel room, his laptop open before him, the screen flickering faintly. Daniel had just sent a long and disturbing report, and Michael's tired brain was still grappling with the implications.

His mission was about to change, and his relationship with Sergeant Major Cohen would have to change with it. Daniel was suggesting that they strike out in another direction, one quite removed from the safe structure of the Israeli military, and Michael wasn't sure that Devorah would be willing to go.

But she had followed him into the Knesset and proved herself a capable operator. Perhaps, if he explained the situation clearly, she would follow him to Belgium as well.

Rousing himself from the numbness that weighed him down, Michael keyed in a quick response to Daniel's latest report:

> D.
>
> I'll talk to the sergeant major soon and will use all the charm in my power to convince her to play along. I'm not sure my charm is what it was twenty years ago, but it will have to do.
>
> I appreciate the update. We'll make good use of the information.
>
> BTW, if you get a chance, can you locate Thomas Freeman, AKA "Shark" for me? If there's some way you can say hi for me without revealing my location, I'd appreciate it. I need to ask him something about a night in Desert Storm.
>
> Get some rest, Daniel. You can save the world tomorrow.
>
> M.

Chapter Twenty

Moscow
2400 hours

VLADIMIR GOGOL SWIVELED HIS OFFICE CHAIR AS SOMEONE RAPPED ON THE door. A thrill of anticipation touched his spine as he called out: "Come."

Petrov entered, his eyes flat and expressionless as he crossed the Oriental carpet that stretched between the double doors and the carved desk. The colonel saluted. "General."

Vladimir returned the salute, half-wishing his aide were not so intent on formalities. He wanted news, and he wanted it now, but Petrov would observe every jot and tittle of military order.

"What news?" He leaned over the desk and pressed his hand to its flat surface. "Tell me, Colonel—what news have you from Dyakonov?"

Petrov went stiffer, if possible, and seemed to stare at a spot on the wall behind Vladimir's head. There was a long, brittle silence, then the man finally spoke: "Dyakonov is dead."

Vladimir sat still, breathing in shallow, quick gasps. The man couldn't be dead. Dyakonov was the best; he and his team had been training for months. They had practiced the assault on a scale model of the Knesset; Vladimir himself had visited the place, noting that the spetsnaz captain had correctly located every doorway, every window, even noting the electrical outlets on the walls.

His gaze rose and locked on Petrov's, then focused with deadly intensity. "How?"

A scarlet flush rose on the colonel's cheekbones. "A series of mistakes. The assembly dismissed early, and many of the government members left before Dyakonov's people were in position. We might have still inflicted extensive damage, for the Israelis were operating by the book, but an

American intruded. A captain named Michael Reed placed a series of calls, and soon a helicopter with other American special warfare operators arrived on the scene. They inserted from the rooftop and somehow managed to creep up behind Dyakonov."

Vladimir uttered a curse. Romulus had promised that the Americans would not interfere. As influential and powerful as the European Union president was, apparently not even he could control the situation in Israel.

Seething with anger and humiliation, Vladimir ran his hand over his head, then let his palm rest at the back of his neck. It could have been over in a day, on a lucky Friday the thirteenth, but again fate had intervened. Israel had more lives than a cursed cat.

He drew a long, quivering breath, mastering the anger that shook him. If not today, he would destroy Israel tomorrow. In the interim, he would continue to seek out their cursed kind in Russia. He would find them, put them on trial for wrongs committed by them and their ancestors, and put an end to the blighted race that had troubled the earth since the dawn of time.

He glanced up at Petrov. "Survivors?"

"Four, sir. All prisoners of the Israelis."

Vladimir drew a deep breath, then exhaled it in an audible rush. "Such a waste. So much money spent on their training, so many hours of work."

Petrov said nothing, but his eyes darkened with resignation.

"Write their families." Vladimir waved the unpleasant matter away. "Tell them that these men gave their lives in defense of glorious Mother Russia. And enclose a check for ten thousand rubles—one check for each family."

Petrov inclined his head without speaking.

"That is all, Colonel."

When Petrov had left the room, Vladimir shook his head in dismay and stared down at his empty desk top. Such a waste. He had been waiting here for news, hoping to fly to Alanna on the wings of rejoicing, but he could not see Alanna tonight. Not in this mood. Not with the stench of despair clinging to his uniform like smoke.

An unpleasant business, this. The mole, of course, would see to it that the four prisoners never talked. Sometime within the next twenty-four hours he would make his way into the secure facility where the others were kept, and he would quietly administer the red suicide pills. Willingly or unwillingly, the four survivors would die for the glory of Mother Russia.

He made mental note to remind Petrov of another important matter. The colonel would have to dispatch another check, this one to a Swiss bank where it would be deposited into the account of Lt. Gabriel Mofaz. The mousy little officer wasn't worth his weight in weeds, but he would be paid . . . until the Jewish problem was forever settled.

Vladimir stood, then walked across the room to the tall window. Snow had begun to fall; it now blew across the courtyard, moving in long, dusty lines, creeping up to the edges of the pavement.

How he hated snow. He had hated its milky whiteness ever since the day he walked into the hospital morgue and found himself searching through photographs of unknown women who had been dumped at the hospital and forgotten. Though he couldn't feel the chill of their flesh, their faded lips told him they were as cold as the snow outside, as dead as the stiff-legged dog he had seen lying in a gutter on a Moscow street.

The old feelings of grief and hate surfaced into his consciousness, pulling at him like a powerful undertow that drew him under against his will. He clenched his fists, then shoved them into his trouser pockets and trembled until the storm of hate blew past.

Vladimir closed his eyes, his mind burning with the memory of his mother's pale, sensitive face, framed by soft blonde hair and lit by eyes as blue as the sky.

"I will avenge you, Mama." He cleared his throat of rumbling phlegm, then pressed his forehead to the window and felt the sting of its icy touch. "Every Jew in the world will pay for what he did to you, for what they did to Mother Russia. All the Jews will pay . . . for all the mothers who have suffered."

The only answer was the mournful call of the winter wind across the courtyard, as lonely as the cry of a lost and wandering spirit.

CHAPTER TWENTY-ONE

Jerusalem
0900 hours
Sunday, October 15

DEVORAH LET THE SABBATH PASS WITHOUT SEEING OR CALLING MICHAEL REED. They both needed time to rest, she realized, and she had promised herself she'd spend the Sabbath with her father as a sort of penance for breaking the Sabbath Friday night. Though he no longer openly chided her for placing her career above her calling as a Jewish woman, she saw rebuke in his eyes every time she appeared in uniform. When she was eighteen and freshly graduated from her year of seminary, he approved of her desire to defend her country. When she chose to make a career out of military service, however, he quietly withdrew his approval. Orthodox Jewish women, he told her, ought to marry and raise children to the glory of the Master of the universe. They were not meant to kill and desecrate the Sabbath.

On Sunday morning, she slipped into her uniform, grabbed a quick breakfast, then drove to the Mount Zion Hotel. When Reed did not answer his phone, she left a message at the desk, explaining that she would meet him at noon to discuss his plans for the coming week.

Part of her hoped he had seen enough. One air base was much like another; and the terrorist incident at the Knesset had demonstrated the extent of IDF counterterrorist abilities—as well as their shortcomings. She suspected that he might ask her to remain silent about the thermal gun he had used to disarm the terrorists, but she couldn't make that promise. He had used those weapons with the full knowledge that he was taking a security risk.

She walked out of the hotel and drove to the base at Lod, then reported to her commander's office. A message had been waiting on her answering machine when she returned to her apartment Saturday evening, and she hadn't been surprised to hear that she was expected to report to the CO's office early on Sunday morning. Only respect for her father and his position had prevented them from asking her to report on the Sabbath.

The corporal on duty escorted her into a room where her captain waited at a laminated table strewn with foam coffee cups and printed reports. She saluted, then relaxed when he invited her to take a seat at the table. The other officer present, Lieutenant Shiff, looked up and gave her a wary smile as she approached.

"This is just a routine inquiry," the captain said, uncapping his pen. "We are pleased with the outcome of the Knesset situation, of course. We only want to understand exactly what transpired."

Devorah glanced up at the large mirror behind the two men. It was a one-way mirror, of course, and though she couldn't see who sat behind it, she had a feeling that the intelligence officials in the opposite room were much less relaxed than the two men conducting this after action review.

"I've already spoken to Lieutenants Shiff and Mofaz," the captain gestured to the officer at his side, "and their reports have been entered into the record. Now I would like to hear your version of the story."

Devorah drew a deep breath and wiped her palms on her skirt. "Where shall I begin?"

The captain gave her a brittle smile. "At the beginning, Sergeant Major."

And so she told of receiving the emergency page at the synagogue, of leaving the service with Captain Reed and her brother. Of telling Asher to report to his base, of Captain Reed's insistence that he might be of service.

"Did Captain Reed seem surprised by the emergency alert?"

"Of course. Although I think he was almost relieved to be excused from the synagogue. He seemed a little lost in the Sukkot service."

Apparently the captain did not find her comment amusing. Without smiling, he urged her to continue.

"At the scene, I reported to the command post. I was ordered to see that Captain Reed remained safely away from danger."

"Yet an hour later Reed was in the thick of the trouble."

"He insisted, sir." She directed her gaze to the lieutenant at the captain's side. "He pushed his way into the command vehicle and convinced

Lieutenant Shiff that he could help. He implied that he would contact the prime minister directly if we did not allow him to participate in the rescue."

The captain thumped the end of his pen on his tablet. "Go on."

Devorah lifted her shoulder in a shrug. "Everything happened quickly after that. Our people planned a shock attack, but Captain Reed insisted that we give him until 2245 before sending in our CT team. He insisted he could resolve the situation with few casualties, while our people estimated a thirty percent loss." She nodded toward Shiff. "It is my opinion, sir, that our leadership acted prudently. Captain Reed did keep his word."

"Did he seem unwilling to let you and your men join the team as well?"

Devorah considered the question for a moment, then shook her head. "He resisted the idea, but only for a moment. He seemed to understand that it was a delicate situation. Four SEALs arrived from Team Three, and I recommended two of my best sharpshooters to complete the team. Reed wanted to send in eight operators."

"Did Captain Reed explain his plan before execution?"

Devorah suppressed a smile. *This* is what they really wanted to know. The long preamble served no other purpose than to warm her up to the important information—they wanted to know how Michael Reed operated and how much information he had shared with her. "Not really, sir. He seemed to be operating on a need-to-know basis. We were dealing with severe time constraints."

The captain eyed her with a calculating expression. "Do you feel that Captain Reed endangered your life at any moment?"

"No, sir, I do not. I felt as safe as one can feel in such an unpredictable situation. The terrorists never even knew we were outside the government room until we had incapacitated all but one."

The captain squinted slightly as his jaw moved to the side. "The means of this incapacitation—had you ever seen one of these 'thermal guns' before?"

"No, sir."

"Did Reed explain the weapon to you—either before or after the incident?"

"Not really, sir. The effects were obvious. When we entered the room, the targeted individuals were unconscious, soaked in sweat, and pale. The weapon obviously disrupted their bodily functions."

Despite his efforts to appear nonchalant, the captain's bright eyes betrayed his eagerness. "Would you be able to draw a detailed picture of this weapon?"

"No, sir. We were wearing NV goggles, and I was busy setting charges to blow a mouse hole. Before and after the weapons' use, the SEAL team operators kept the guns in a covered sling. I did not have an opportunity to examine them."

The captain looked down and scratched a few notes on his tablet, then squinted up at her again. "One other thing, Sergeant Major—in the command post, Captain Reed remarked that he believed the tangos were carrying unique weapons. Did he discuss the significance of those weapons with you?"

"He pointed out that ordinary SMGs would have been intercepted at the metal detectors. He also said that the Russians have been working with a new substance of compressed wood—lignostone, he called it. He was surprised that Arabs would possess such weapons."

"He was assuming, of course," the captain remarked, "that the terrorists were PLO."

"I don't think Captain Reed ever assumes anything." Devorah frowned. "*Were* they PLO?"

"We think they were a renegade Arab group, disenchanted with the peace process." The captain stood and thanked her with a smile. "That's all, Sergeant Major. Please give our regards to your father and our apologies for disturbing the serenity of his Sabbath. You are to continue your work with Captain Reed, following his orders as you would my own. If you have any questions, or if he does anything unusual, please contact me immediately."

In a surge of memory, Reed's own words came back to her: *Everybody knows attachés are used for gathering intelligence. We're just more subtle about spying on our allies than we are our adversaries.*

She stood, saluted, and pivoted toward the door, her mind vibrating with a thousand thoughts.

-0100111100-

"So—did you enjoy your debriefing yesterday?"

Reed buried his smile in his coffee cup, but Devorah heard the teasing tone in his voice. "It was fine, thank you, and we held it this morning, not yesterday. Yesterday was the Sabbath."

He seemed relaxed and casual, not at all worried about her debriefing. He wore civilian clothing, khaki trousers and a blue cotton shirt with the sleeves rolled up to his elbows. The shirt, she noticed, matched his eyes, especially when they were lit with laughter . . . like now.

"Sorry. I sometimes forget these things."

"Don't worry about it. Half the people in Israel pay no attention to these things."

She dropped her eyes to her napkin, feeling suddenly uncomfortable beneath the intensity of his gaze. There was a new quality to his smile, a familiarity that could only have arisen from their shared experience. Such a familiarity could not be good.

"I am supposed to continue my work with you." She looked up and forced herself to meet his eyes. "I was told to obey you as I would obey my own captain."

"How convenient."

Her lips thinned with irritation. "How much longer do you think you'll be in Israel, Captain? I do have my own work, you know. I have classes to teach and operators to train—"

"Actually, I was thinking of postponing the base inspections for a while." He lowered his coffee cup and folded his arms on the edge of the table. "What did they tell you about the men who stormed the Knesset?"

She frowned. "Nothing. Why?"

"Because I know who and what they are." He glanced quickly left and right as if he might be overheard, then leaned closer. "I have a contact— never mind who he is—who was able to access the IDF videotape of the intruders."

"What? How?"

"Never mind that. My contact has identified the ringleader as Uri Dyakonov—does the name mean anything to you?"

Devorah closed her eyes and struggled to remember. The name did ring a distant bell, but why? She had seen it in a printed report, perhaps something from Interpol . . . No, not Interpol. The man wasn't a terrorist— he was military. She snapped her fingers as the name linked with a recollection. "Afghanistan. He led the Russian spetsnaz team that wiped out the entire government in five minutes."

"Very good." He leaned back and grinned at her, obviously impressed. "Christmas Day 1979. Dyakonov and his team took out the Afghan government under the express command of General Vladimir Gogol, who was then working for the general staff's Main Intelligence Directorate."

Devorah stared at him. "What's the connection?" she asked, trying to formulate a link between Afghanistan and Israel. "And why didn't he succeed at the Knesset? A man with Dyakonov's training should not have failed."

Michael shook his head. "The Soviet elite units were once among the best in the world, but Russia's economic crisis has dramatically affected them. Once a man has concluded his service in a spetsnaz unit, he can leave military life and earn a soldier's monthly wages in a day. The best operators haven't remained with their units—they're out working for private security firms or criminal organizations. Only the most gung-ho have stayed in uniform."

"So—did Dyakonov go to work for the PLO?"

Michael snorted softly. "Gung-ho is too mild a word for Dyakonov. The man was a nationalist zealot—he'd give nothing less than all for Mother Russia." Michael's strong and tapered fingers tapped his coffee mug. "There are dozens of spetsnaz units in Russia, but Dyakonov's unit was the crème de la crème, the most secret and the most dangerous. They are trained to act in groups of five to ten people, move autonomously for days at a time, and carry out orders that have nothing to do with military operations. Quite simply, they are trained to search, find, and assassinate . . . on the enemy's territory."

"So—has Dyakonov been training Arab terrorists?"

Michael gripped the cup again, and Devorah saw the muscles of his forearm tighten. Instead of answering, he asked a question: "Did they learn anything from the four men in custody?"

Devorah waved her hand. "My captain said they are members of a splinter Palestinian group disenchanted with the peace process."

"He's wrong. I'd bet my last shekel that all eight of our tangos spent last month in a Russian military training camp called Pushkina. I'd also bet that not one of those men in jail is an Arab . . . or alive at this moment."

She stared at him in total incredulity. "You're going to have to explain yourself, Captain."

"Dyakonov didn't leave his spetsnaz unit; he brought it to Jerusalem."

Michael leaned forward again. "I e-mailed a friend of mine back at the NSA and picked up a few bits of useful information. Russian Military Intelligence controlled Dyakonov's unit. Their teams were trained to destroy the enemy's command and communication posts, operation systems, and—" he lowered his voice—"physically eliminate the opposite side's military and political leadership."

Devorah stared at him, her mind blank with shock.

"We missed something," Michael continued, looking fully into her eyes. "You told me that the Parliament meeting dismissed early because of Sukkot, remember? Dyakonov wasn't after Parliament members alone. Who else would have attended that meeting Friday afternoon?"

Devorah rested her elbow on the table. When she could speak, her voice came out in an uncertain stutter. "The—the other government officials have offices in other parts of the city. The prime minister's office is west of the Knesset, while the minister of defense—" She gasped as the shock of discovery hit her full force. "The meetings of the government are usually held at the prime minister's office," she whispered. "But on days when the members of government are obliged to participate in Parliament meetings, government members convene in the Knesset, where all the ministers have bureaus."

Michael nodded, his mouth tight and grim. "Friday was such a day. If not for Sukkot, all the members of the Israeli government would have been inside the Knesset and at Dyakonov's mercy. He thought of everything a Russian commando would consider—but he forgot to think like a Jew."

A thunderbolt jagged through her. "They'd all be dead." Her voice rasped in her own ears. "They would have killed every last man." Her gaze flew up to his face. "But why? What does Russia have against Israel?"

Uncertainty crept into Michael's expression. "Who knows why the angry finger of the Kremlin pointed in this direction? Things are anything but stable in Moscow. It might have been a test . . . or a diversion."

"A diversion from what?"

He leaned upon the table, one arm extended toward her, the other supporting his head. From a distance, anyone might have supposed them to be lovers . . . but the stirring in Devorah's heart convinced her far more was at stake than the lives of two people.

"Can I trust you, Devorah Cohen?" Reed spoke slowly, as if carefully measuring each word before pronouncing it. "This morning—what did you tell them about the thermal guns?"

Devorah felt her cheeks blaze as though they had been seared by a candle flame, but she refused to tear her gaze from his. "I answered their questions truthfully. I told them I couldn't see the guns in the dark . . . and that you didn't explain them."

He watched her through glittering eyes that were both admiring and accusing. "So you gave them no more and no less than your duty demanded. Obviously," his voice dropped to a deeper pitch, "you did not paint me as an enemy of Israel, or I'd be on my way home."

"What should I have told them?" She clenched her hands under the table, resisting the creeping uneasiness at the bottom of her heart. "If you are not an ally of Israel, Captain Reed, I will not cooperate with you. If you have any regard for me at all, you will not force me into a difficult situation."

His face creased into a sudden smile. "I can assure you I'm not a spy— no more than any other attaché, in any case. But I do need to know if I can share information with you . . . and not have it appear on the front page of the *Jerusalem Post* within two days."

She looked away, picked up her spoon, and idly dropped a teaspoon of sugar into her tea. He was encroaching upon forbidden territory, and yet she could not find it within her heart to tell him to back off. She was a career officer in the IDF, as committed to Israel as to her own family, and any significant information she learned should be immediately reported to her commanding officer. Yet there was something about Michael Reed . . . and he certainly seemed to trust her. Her captain had deliberately ignored her question about the terrorists' identity, yet Michael had freely shared information about Dyakonov and his intentions.

"You can trust me not to run to the *Post*." She rested her chin on her hand, her mouth curving in a bemused smile. "And you can trust me to protect a fellow spec warrior. If it is necessary to keep a confidence in order to protect you, Captain Reed, you can trust me to keep quiet . . . for as long as you are here."

"Diplomacy, beauty, *and* brains." He shifted in his chair, regarding her with amusement as he signaled for the check. "Will you come for a drive with me, Sergeant Major? I'd like to explain my entire reason for coming to Israel and how I think it ties into what happened at the Knesset Friday night. There are some other new developments I'd like to tell you about, too." He hesitated. "I suppose we can take your Fiat—it's not likely to be bugged, is it?"

She stiffened in shock. "You think my car might be bugged?"

"One can never be too careful." He pulled a handful of shekels from his wallet, placed them on the table, then stood and gallantly gestured toward the exit. "Shall we go?"

CHAPTER TWENTY-TWO

The White House
0932 hours

SAM STEDMAN HAD JUST OPENED VICTORIA'S BIBLE WHEN HE HEARD A RESOUNDING thump on the curved door leading into the Oval Office. Jack Powell entered without knocking, a fluttering newspaper in his hand. Frowning, Sam looked out and saw a Secret Service agent standing in the doorway, his arms uplifted and an I'm-sorry expression on his face. Powell didn't have an appointment, but these days he didn't seem to think he needed one.

"Have you seen this?" Jack dropped a copy of the *Washington Post* over the Bible, then thumped the headline with his thick index finger. "How did this happen, Sam? What were you thinking?"

Sam pinched the bridge of his nose as he read the headline: U.S. Uses Navy SEALs and Top-Secret Weapons to Oust Terrorists from Knesset.

"Ouch." He lowered his hand and looked wearily at his chief of staff. "Not much we can do about it now, I suppose."

Jack sank into the guest chair across from the desk and slapped the armrest in frustration. "What in the world possessed you, Sam? You know William Blackstone is going to eat this up. He's been hoping something like this would happen. Now, a few weeks before the election, he's caught us."

Sam tented his hands. "How'd the word get out?"

Jack used his knuckle to wipe small sparkles of sweat off his upper lip. "Who knows? Probably half of Jerusalem saw the SEALs land outside the Knesset. And I hear there's a pirated copy of a surveillance videotape playing on the Internet. It's grainy and dark, but you can see our guys shooting through the wall with whatever that thermal thing is." His gray eyes darkened as he held Sam's gaze. "How could you do it, Mr. President? The Israelis accepted your help, then turned around and stabbed you in the back by releasing that videotape. Blackstone will use it to destroy us; you've got to know that."

"I don't know any such thing." Sam's lower lip trembled as he returned Jack's glare. "Someone released the tape—OK, but that could have been anyone from a custodian to a foreign agent. Daniel Prentice taught me that few things are truly secure these days. We can't lay the blame for this leak on the IDF."

"But you sent a SEAL team into a public place!"

Sam's mood veered sharply to anger. "I could do no less! The Israelis are our allies, and they needed our help."

Powell pressed his lips together, then drew a deep breath, his long nose pinched and white with resentful rage. "The media might learn that Michael Reed was at the scene. If the interest level in the story remains high, they'll dig until they uncover every detail."

Sam shrugged. "He is participating in a routine liaison mission. He happened upon the situation by chance."

"An Israeli paper is already reporting that an American led the team."

"Then let's call the man a hero and get back to work." Sam reached out and cupped his hand around his coffee mug, then flipped the revolting newspaper off the Bible. "This won't hurt us, Jack, unless we let it. If Reed's involvement reaches our press, issue a statement praising Reed for his bravery, then assure our people it was a one-time action and nothing more. For once in your life, fight the lies with truth, then stand back and let it blow over."

Powell stood and lifted the newspaper from the desk. "Blackstone's going to hit us hard with this. By sunset he'll be saying we want to reinstate the draft and send eighteen-year-olds to fight in the Middle East."

Sam struggled to maintain an even, patient tone. "Just tell the truth, Jack, and let the American people sort it out. They usually do."

As the chief of staff walked away, Sam took a sip from his coffee mug, then lifted his hand. "And Jack—next time, don't throw your newspapers on my desk. I'd rather read Victoria's Bible than the *Washington Compost* any time."

CHAPTER TWENTY-THREE

Moscow
1745 hours

AS THE TINNY RADIO HUMMED WITH THE ANNOYING AND FALSELY CHEERFUL rhythms of Russian pop music, Alanna's heart seemed to keep pace with the thumping sounds of the bass drum. Vladimir had just left the hotel suite in a dark mood again, and the worm of anxiety that had been needling her heart slithered lower to writhe in her stomach.

Something was not right. Though life inside her gilded suite seemed to glide on as usual, she could feel darkness descending, growing deeper and denser as the autumn days grew shorter. She saw it in the freezing blue eyes of the Russian couple who had taken over the bookstore; she saw it in the boarded windows of the small synagogue that stood across from *Revolutsii Ploschad,* or Revolution Square. Each evening the television newscasts featured more people being loaded into trucks and taken away, and Alanna didn't need to understand Russian to know they were Jews. The city that had once comforted and thrilled her was now filled with foreboding, its buildings casting grim shadows across her path, the walls of Red Square gleaming darkly, as if painted with dried blood.

Winter was coming and drawing some unspeakable horror in its wake.

Alanna checked her watch, then moved to the window and pressed her hands to the chilly glass. Twenty floors below, Vladimir and his entourage moved from the curb into the black limousine, then the car nudged into the traffic and moved toward the Kremlin.

She had time.

She ran to the front door and shot the deadbolts home, first one, then the other, not caring if the guards heard the sound. Scurrying to the kitchen, she knocked the bottles of cleaner aside, then pulled the laptop from its hiding place and ripped away the plastic. With trembling fingers she plugged in the modem and the power, then set the computer on the counter and typed in the familiar address.

She tabbed down and hesitated at the subject line. What could she say? *Help, I want out?* She had not yet found an opportunity to escape. She had concluded that for the moment she was safer remaining where she was than trying to run.

Her fingers hovered over the keys as she searched for words to describe the premonition that had invaded her hotel suite. How could she describe these foreboding feelings to a thoroughly practical man like Daniel Prentice? She could say that in the last few days Vladimir seemed absorbed and distant, that lately he looked more like a lion scenting the breeze than the doting lover she had come to know. Would Daniel realize the significance of these observations, or would he think her a foolish female with an overactive imagination?

The keyboard made a ghostly clatter in the silence of the kitchen as she typed:

> I'm worried. Vladimir seems preoccupied. He has been in a bad mood lately, but he won't say what's troubling him. He says a woman shouldn't be bothered with such things. He is gone now to prepare for a meeting with a group of foreign officials, and I am to appear later tonight at his side. He is planning something, but I have no idea what.
>
> Outside, the city is in turmoil. I am in a quiet place, but the television newscasts are filled with reports of Jews being taken away in large white vans. It looks like a purge, though I cannot imagine what crimes could possibly be attributed to these people. A lovely Jewish family disappeared from my hotel and their shop has been given to others.
>
> If they are purging Moscow of Jews, I'm frightened, Daniel. Am I safe?

She pressed Send, then stared at the keyboard and nibbled on the edge of her nails. She had not tried to contact Daniel since the night Vladimir had frightened her into breaking the crystal vase, but she could not continue in this uncertainty much longer.

She turned to the refrigerator and pulled out a pitcher of orange juice, an unbelievable luxury Vladimir delighted in obtaining for her. She poured a glass and drank it mechanically, her eyes fixed to the computer screen. *Please, please respond. Tell me what to do.*

She jumped when the computer beeped softly, then grimaced at her own skittishness. Setting her glass in the sink, she moved to the laptop and retrieved the message.

> Greetings, Texas.
>
> Do not fear for your personal safety. We altered your national ID records, as well as your mother's. If anyone checks, your mother was Elizabeth Harris, your grandmother Edna Williams. Your secret should be safe.
>
> I understand that you do not know the agenda of G's meeting. But has he mentioned anything about a timeline? Is he operating on a schedule? Most important—has he done anything at all unusual in the last few days?
>
> We are still praying for you.

Alanna nervously tapped the keys as Daniel's questions echoed in the stillness of her mind. Vladimir never told her anything, so she was practically useless as an informant. She should never have allowed herself to be seduced by the position, privilege, and power of an important man. But unless he went away and took his men with him, she did not see how she could escape.

Those thoughts brought others in their wake as she typed her answer:

> G. is an erratic man; one day is never quite like another. As to timing, he will only tell me that things will be dramatically different for us after the first of the year.
>
> Please, Daniel, you've got to get me out of here before then. Whatever he's planning, I know it can't be good. My skin crawls to think of it, and lately there's been a dark edge to his moods that I can't seem to lift no matter what I do.
>
> Thanks for the prayers. I never had much use for prayer myself, but right now I'll take all the help I can get.
>
> Don't forget about me, Daniel. I can be patient, but I can feel an angry storm brewing, and Gogol is at its center. God help anyone who gets caught in the vortex.

CHAPTER TWENTY-FOUR

Jerusalem
1650 hours

MICHAEL ASKED DEVORAH TO DRIVE TO A SAFE PLACE WHERE THEY COULD NOT be spied upon, and for a moment her mind went blank. Like all Israeli soldiers, she was sensitive to the threat of public places, but Michael seemed to be more paranoid than even the most suspicious Israeli soldier. She finally turned onto the road that would lead them deep into Me'a She'arim, home to her father and a community of other Orthodox Jews.

Michael chuckled when he realized where she was taking him. "Are you sure your father won't mind you bringing me here?" He flashed a blond brow in her direction. "He may not feel as hospitable toward me in the light of day."

"My father is at the yeshiva." Devorah glanced at him from the corner of her eye. "But his housekeeper will be present. We will be properly chaperoned, if that's what's worrying you."

"I'm not in the least worried." Michael cast a paranoid glance out the window as he spoke. "I just want to be out of range from your military intelligence types."

"Then you will be safe in my father's house." She turned onto Etyopya Street, then parked before the small stone house and led Michael through the front door. After calling a greeting to her father's surprised housekeeper, Devorah motioned Michael toward the dining room and asked Rivka for something cool to drink. Eager to be of use, the housekeeper hurried away.

Standing beside the table, Michael watched the housekeeper go with concern in his eyes. "Aren't you worried about her overhearing?"

"Rivka is almost completely deaf," Devorah answered, sinking into a chair. "She will watch us, but she will not hear. Your secrets will remain safe."

Michael took the seat across from her, then pulled a laptop computer and a manila folder from his attaché case. "My contact," he said, patting the computer as if it were alive. "I call him Daniel."

"Like the prophet?"

He gave her a lopsided smile as he opened the machine and powered it on. "You could say that."

When the machine finished booting, he typed in a command, then looked up and caught her eye. "You didn't ask what I did yesterday, so I'll tell you—as long as you understand that this information cannot be shared until we confirm it. My friend Daniel is a genius, but sometimes he operates on instinct and conviction, not fact."

"He is an American?"

"Yes, but he does not work for the government. He does, however, communicate with President Stedman. Stedman trusts Daniel, and so do I. He hasn't failed me yet."

He turned the computer to face her, and Devorah frowned as she studied the image on the screen. She was staring at a photograph of a soldier, a compact man with startling blue eyes, European features, a determined expression, and more decorations on his uniform than she could decipher.

"A German?"

"A Russian. That is Vladimir Vasilievich Gogol, Russia's minister of defense and the man who sent Dyakonov to take out the Afghan government in 1979. Daniel believes, as do I, that two days ago Gogol sent Dyakonov to Jerusalem to eliminate the Israeli government."

"Why would a Russian general want to destroy Israel?"

Michael folded his arms on the table. "Because Russian President Chapaev is weeks, perhaps only days, away from death. Everyone in Moscow knows Gogol is running the country and has been for months. Three days ago, Gogol convened a covert meeting with the leading Arab powers and convinced them to sign a treaty of cooperation and a resolution against Israel. I have not seen the document, but Daniel is certain it will soon be debated in the UN Security Council. If Gogol and his allies can force a Security Council vote on the resolution, the United Nations may authorize sending troops against Israel."

"And this resolution censures Israel for—what?" Devorah spoke calmly, but with that eerie sense of detachment that comes with an awareness of impending disaster. She knew the answer, but she needed to hear Michael say the words.

"Israel's unwillingness to vacate the disputed territories. The UN will insist that Israel surrender the military bases in the West Bank."

"My country cannot survive without those bases. We've already given up so much; any more would be suicide. Without the West Bank, an enemy could cut our nation in half in a matter of hours with only a tank assault—"

"I know. Gogol knows it, too. He will move against Israel no matter what Israel does."

Reed's words fell into the silence with the weight of stones in still water. Devorah stared at the man on the computer screen as a chilly black silence surrounded them.

"Why?" The pulsing knot within her demanded an answer. "Israel is a small country. We could not possibly defend ourselves against an attack of combined Russian and Arab troops."

Michael reached out and probably would have taken her hand had she not pulled it away. "Each nation has its own reasons," he said, a light bitterness in his voice. "The Muslim countries see the destruction of Israel as a spiritual and moral imperative. Russia needs Arab oil if she is going to regain her status as a superpower. And Gogol is the personification of ambition. He also hates the Jews."

Michael pulled a bound report from the manila folder and slid it across the table. After opening the cover, Devorah found herself staring at a dossier on Gogol.

"Vladimir Gogol, age 58, was born in Moscow, in the very shadow of the Kremlin," Michael said, summing up the information on the page before her. "A former commander of the Russian special forces in Afghanistan, he spent the '80s cementing the Russo-Iraqi political alliance. He wooed Saddam Hussein with guns and anthrax and promises to keep the UN inspection teams off Hussein's back. In return, he was promoted from Russian foreign minister to minister of defense. Now he is running the country during Chapaev's illness and is poised to take control if and when the president dies." The cold edge of irony filled Reed's voice.

"Chapaev is not an obstacle. When Gogol is ready, the president of Russia will suffer a sudden heart attack or some other illness, and Gogol will be elected to stand in his place. There's no doubt, Gogol is firmly in control."

"Personality?" Devorah murmured.

"Pragmatic, determined, intensely logical and decisive. He believes he can achieve the impossible, and he has done everything he has set out to do—thus far. He loves to move mountains—and he has moved more than a few in his lifetime."

"Weaknesses?"

"Only one we know of—he has a susceptibility to beautiful American blondes, the classic Grace Kelly type. Believe it or not, he has an American mistress, whom he appears to treat with kindness. He keeps her tucked away in a Moscow hotel suite, and he spoils her rotten. When we first heard rumors that Gogol was attempting to buy a sizeable diamond, we thought he intended to give the stone to his lady friend."

Devorah dropped the dossier to the table. "You've lost me, Captain. We were talking about war and Russia, so why are we talking now about diamonds and women?"

Michael's hand fell upon the computer. "Daniel has a contact in Brussels, a man loosely affiliated with the worldwide diamond syndicate. A Russian military officer known to be working for Gogol has been making discreet inquiries about a flawless diamond of at least two hundred carats. He is offering three to five million euros for a suitable stone."

Devorah's mouth dropped open. "That's unbelievable. The Russian economy is so weak, I'm surprised anyone in the military has access to that kind of money."

A tinge of sadness colored Michael's eyes as he leaned toward her. "Have you heard, Devorah, about the persecution of Jews in Moscow? Daniel tells me that Jews are being rounded up and taken away in vans, much like they were in Stalin's Russia. If they are convicted of whatever trumped-up charges are brought against them, their property is confiscated by the government—Gogol's government." He shot her a twisted smile. "Are you beginning to see how Gogol could be financing the purchase of this diamond?"

Devorah closed her eyes as the terrifying realization washed over her. Scenes from Nazi Germany and Stalin's Russia played on the backs of her eyelids, sepia-toned images of weeping women, gray-bearded men in prayer shawls, small children clinging to their parents' hands as they were pulled away and forced into prison work camps.

Reed's voice broke into her thoughts. "We need to find out what's happening in Russia. We must know if Gogol is the mysterious diamond buyer and what he intends to do with the stone. Heads of state, even *wealthy* heads of state, don't usually flaunt diamonds of that size and quality, so it's possible Gogol is planning to use the diamond for some technological purpose. Diamonds are now used in space flight, supercomputers, x-ray detectors—the list is endless. Gogol could even be developing a new kind of laser weapon that might require a diamond of that size."

She stared at him in amazement. "You're talking as if you expect me to have some interest in this."

"You ought to be very interested." He pulled the laptop toward him and typed in another command, then turned the screen so she could see the document on the screen. "This information came from Daniel just yesterday. It's a dossier on Devorah Cohen, a sergeant major in the Israeli Defense Forces, age 35. Father is Baram Cohen, rabbi and teacher at the Toldot Aharon Yeshiva in Jerusalem, brother is Asher Cohen, a lieutenant in the Israeli Air Force."

Devorah thrust out her hand. "May I see that?"

Michael turned, blocking her grasp. "Here's the really interesting part—Devorah's uncle is Oskar Cohen, a diamond dealer in Brussels, Belgium, with residences in Antwerp, London, and Jerusalem. Oskar Cohen has a daughter, Lila, who works in the Brussels diamond syndicate. Your cousin is married to Gavriel Greenberg, who works with her. Together they handle over fifty million dollars per year in diamond sales."

He looked at her, his eyes wide and questioning, waiting for her to— what?

Nervously she moistened her dry lips. "You want my cousin to help you find a diamond for Gogol?"

"No, I want you to help. We don't want to involve civilians, but you and I could infiltrate the diamond market and handle the sale." He leaned toward her, his eyes bright with the stimulation of anticipation. "We will go to Brussels, where you will take your cousin's place and meet the Russian who wants to buy the raw diamond. You will be friendly, you will ask questions, and together we just might learn what Gogol intends to do with the stone."

Wholly taken aback by his suggestion, Devorah pressed her fingertips to her mouth and stared at him. "What if my cousins don't have a raw diamond that size?"

"We don't need a real stone. The Russian is not a diamond expert; he won't know a man-made stone from the real thing. Daniel feels certain the man can be convinced to have the stone cut in Brussels. Your cousins will retain possession of the stone while it is being cut. If the payment does not come through, nothing is lost."

"They don't expect to be paid?"

"No. As you know, these business dealings are always conducted on a handshake and a word of honor. Once your cousins heard about the purge underway in Moscow, they decided they had no qualms about substituting a synthetic stone."

Devorah's breath caught in her lungs. "Are you quite certain this Daniel can be trusted? We could be walking into a trap. And I would not want to risk the lives of civilians—"

"Your relatives are devoted to Israel . . . and they understand that this is important. Don't you see?" Reed's face darkened with a host of unreadable emotions. "We suspect this diamond has something to do with Gogol's overriding ambition to restore Russia to superpower status. That same ambition has driven him to forge an agreement with the Muslim nations. In exchange for Russia's armies and Gogol's help in defeating Israel, his allies will grant him oil and cold, hard cash—enough to buy real international power."

Devorah leaned back in her chair, trying to put her confused thoughts in order. This Daniel certainly seemed well connected, for the information on Dyakonov and the Russians had been right on. If Michael spoke the truth, her cousins had already agreed to participate in a risky operation for the sake of Israel. Could she agree to do less?

Her thoughts shifted toward her military obligation. Her captain had given her permission to obey Michael, and she could see nothing in this situation that might damage Israel's national security. If anything, she would be helping uncover a dangerous force that might threaten them in the near future.

She took a deep breath and forced herself to face the undeniable facts. Michael was not proposing some dangerous assassin's mission. She would merely go to Brussels, negotiate the sale of a diamond, and make polite small talk during the exchange. The assault on the Knesset had been a far more hazardous operation.

"Do I need to inform my superiors?" she asked, looking down at her hands on the tabletop. "Should I tell my father?"

"Daniel will take care of your superiors," Michael answered, his voice a little unsteady. "And I suppose you may tell your father that we are taking an official trip to Brussels. But say no more than that."

She nodded slowly, then looked up to meet his gaze. "What happened to you, Captain Reed? When we first met, I gathered the impression that you wanted nothing more than to do your job and go home. Now you want to go to Brussels."

His pupils widened slightly, as if the question had caught him by surprise. "I am only trying to do my job." A betraying flush darkened his throat, then his mouth curved in a cocky grin. "Maybe it's the challenge that appeals to me. Gogol threw down the gauntlet when he sent Dyakonov to Jerusalem, and I'd like to—I'd like *Israel* to respond and knock the Russian off his feet. But we can't surprise him unless we know exactly what he has in mind." His smile softened as he lowered his voice. "I'm up to my neck in this situation now, Devorah, and I'm not the type to bug out in the middle of a fight. I want to see this thing through."

Devorah looked away. His answer made sense, for Michael Reed was a soldier through and through, his motives rooted in pure military machismo. Whatever had caused her to think that he might be staying because of *her*?

She shook the foolish idea out of her head and met his eyes. "When do we leave?"

"Tomorrow morning would be best. I'll arrange everything." Reed closed his laptop, then stood and gathered his reports. "Wear civilian clothes, by the way. Neither of us can be in uniform after we leave Tel Aviv."

"All right. You can pick me up here. I'd like to tell my father good-bye before we go." Devorah gave him a plastic smile and stood, wondering how she would tell her father she was about to go to Belgium—unescorted— with an American soldier.

Chapter Twenty-five

0938 hours
Monday, October 16

THE NEXT MORNING, MICHAEL HUDDLED IN THE CAB FOR A LONG MINUTE outside Rabbi Cohen's house, staring at the fat and milky white raindrops in the headlights. The weather seemed an ominous sign, and he hoped Devorah and her father weren't superstitious about such things.

He stared out his window, past long, wavering runnels on the glass. A light came on in the rabbi's house, and he could see a broad shadow behind the sheer drapes. Someone was watching and waiting.

"Be right back," he told the cabby, then he hunched into his trench coat and sprinted across the lawn to the rabbi's front door. Devorah opened it a moment later, a suitcase in her hand. She was not smiling.

"Come in, please," she said, her voice rough. "My father would like to speak with you before we go."

Michael stepped into the foyer and turned down his collar, wondering if he should leave his wet coat in the hallway. He didn't have to wonder long, for Devorah tugged on his sleeve and pulled him forward, virtually dragging him into the dining room where the table was still strewn with breakfast dishes. Asher sat in one chair, an uncertain smile on his face, and a somber Rabbi Cohen sat in another.

"*Boker tov*, good morning, Captain." Asher lifted his gaze from the table and stood to offer his hand.

Michael accepted the handshake and the smile but knew this was no time for small talk. His hunch proved reliable a moment later when the rabbi looked up and gestured to his son. "Asher, take the umbrella and walk Devorah to the taxi."

Asher dropped his napkin on the table, then nodded at Michael and moved to do his father's bidding. Michael turned in time to catch the forlorn look on Devorah's face, then she moved down the hallway and out of sight.

The abrupt slam of the front door sounded like a death knell in Michael's ears. He turned to the rabbi and managed a twisted smile. "She will be safe, sir. This is not a high-risk mission."

Michael saw a flash of teeth in the rabbi's dark beard. "I do not fear outside dangers, Captain Reed. The Master of the universe, blessed be he, will watch over my Devorah."

The rabbi fell silent, and Michael could feel the weight of his gaze, as dark and powerful as the sea. "Is there something else?"

"Just this." The rabbi folded his hands. "I have seen the way you look at her. You admire her, yes?"

Feeling like a sixteen-year-old about to take a girl out for the first time, Michael shifted uncomfortably. "She is an unusual woman. Very talented, intelligent, and brave."

"She is a true daughter of Israel. And she will have no life apart from her people." A tremor passed over the rabbi's face as a spasm of grief knit his brows. "Do you understand?"

Michael lifted a hand in a defensive posture. "I can assure you, sir, I have no plans to pull your daughter away from her family. I respect you and your beliefs."

"I know this is true." The rabbi smiled, but with a distracted, inward look, as though he was listening to some voice only he could hear. "But the heart is deceitful and desperately wicked, who can know it? I trust you to guard my daughter, but I would urge you to guard your heart as well."

The rabbi lifted a hand and murmured a blessing in Hebrew, then sent Michael out the door.

–0100111100–

"Would you like something to read, monsieur?"

The pink-cheeked flight attendant stopped by Michael's seat and offered a selection of periodicals. Caught a little off guard by the offer, Michael withdrew a Belgian news magazine and thanked the woman with a smile.

Devorah reached out, her hand brushing Michael's arm as she tapped the glossy cover. "If we're lucky, we might catch a glimpse of this guy on this trip. Who knows? A friend of mine went to New York and actually saw Donald Trump getting into a cab on Sixth Avenue."

Michael stared at the magazine, noticing for the first time that the cover featured a profile shot of Adrian Romulus, president of the European Union's Council of Ministers. Since the Council headquartered in Brussels, Romulus undoubtedly spent a great deal of time in the city.

"I don't know that *lucky* is the word I'd use to describe an encounter with Romulus." Michael held the magazine up and frowned at the picture. "Most of the people I know don't trust the man."

Devorah shrugged and folded her hands over her seat belt. "I don't really know much about him. Unless he begins to instigate acts of terrorism, I'm perfectly content to leave him alone. I've never been terribly interested in European politics."

"Maybe you should broaden your horizons." Michael flipped through the magazine and turned to the article on Romulus.

As the plane backed out of the gate and the flight attendant began her emergency instructions, he skimmed the first paragraphs. According to the writer for the Belgian *Newsday,* Adrian Romulus had rescued Europe from the verge of financial collapse in the wake of the Year 2000 Crisis. Now that Europe had coalesced and economic markets had stabilized, he wanted to turn the world's attention to spiritual matters. "Man is more than intellect and emotion," he told the writer for *Newsday.* "He is also spirit. For too long we have celebrated our intelligence and indulged in pleasure. Now it is time we focused on spirit and discovered the divine flame burning bright within each man, woman, and child."

Michael nudged Devorah with his elbow. "Did you know that Romulus is planning a worldwide convocation of religious leaders next summer."

Her disinterest showed in her face. "Really?"

Michael referred back to the article. "Yeah. The meeting will be held in Rome on July 29. They are expecting over five thousand religious leaders from all different faiths."

Her mouth took on an unpleasant twist. "Well, I hope they aren't expecting my father and his crew. It doesn't sound like their kind of party."

Michael consulted a list printed in a sidebar. "Judaism will be represented, though. This article lists three prominent rabbis who have already endorsed the meeting."

Devorah sniffed. "Reformed Jews, no doubt."

Michael suppressed the urge to chuckle. "What is this attitude? I thought nonobservant Jews were below your disdain. Why should you care what they do?"

"You can't help caring about something that is completely and forever a part of you." Her words came out hoarse, as if forced through a tight throat. "You must understand, Michael—I was reared in the *Chareidi,* the ultraorthodox community. My education, through school and my year of seminary, was markedly Jewish. Even Jewish women are expected to have an extensive knowledge of practical Jewish law and a solid grasp on basic Jewish philosophy. While my brother and his friends were studying Talmud, I was pouring over *Tanach,* Jewish Scripture. I think it's fair to say that any girl who graduates from the Orthodox school system knows more about Torah than the average non-Orthodox rabbi."

Michael turned in the seat and stared at her, struggling to conquer his involuntary reactions to the gentle, confused look on her face. She was like no woman he had ever met—bright and beautiful, warm and engaging when she chose to be, yet consistently aloof, almost unearthly.

As the plane taxied down the runway, his mind fluttered back to a movie he'd taken Janis to see years before. The film had portrayed the story of a woman who entered a convent and spent seventeen years systematically suppressing every human desire. When the nun could no longer handle the supernatural struggle and left the convent, she had difficulty learning how to be human again—how to make small talk, how to make change in a market, how to relate to men. In some ways, Devorah was like that nun—a woman in the world, but not really of it.

He let the magazine fall to his lap as the jet climbed through the clouds, then he reached out and gently brushed a dark curl from Devorah's shoulder. "For a woman who has left the world of Orthodox Judaism, you certainly speak with a lot of conviction."

She looked down, the fringe of her lashes casting shadows on her cheeks. "I haven't left it," she whispered, her hands twisting in her lap. "I've only set it aside to concentrate on my work. My father doesn't understand how fragile the State of Israel is—and how important it is that we defend our country. He cannot see that the situation grows more desperate with each passing day. Without our military bases in the Golan Heights and the West Bank, Israel cannot defend itself with conventional weapons."

"Perhaps," Michael spoke in as gentle a tone as he could manage, "your father expects someone else to defend the nation."

Her eyes flew open. "The Americans? We cannot count on you. Your Congress has always given too little, too late. They routinely condemn us for military strikes we are forced to make in order to insure our safety—"

"Hold on, calm down." Michael lowered his voice so the people around them wouldn't hear. "I wasn't talking about the United States. I was talking about God."

Her eyes widened for an instant, then narrowed as she gave him a glare hot enough to sear his eyebrows. "Right. And the Messiah is scheduled to hold a press conference on the Mount of Olives next week. He will set all things in order—no more suffering, no more anti-Semitism, no more evil. I've got my front row seat reserved." She flushed to the roots of her hair. "My father and people like him live on another plane, Michael. I've seen enough suffering to know all the prayers in the world aren't going to change things."

Her eyes darkened like angry thunderclouds as her hands clenched in her lap. "When I was twenty-four and serving in the border police, my unit was called to Nablus, the largest Arab city in the West Bank. The Palestinians there had been throwing rocks and fire bombs at innocent people going about their business, and it was our job to stop the violence. I had been trained to fight against tanks and grenades, but I found myself opening fire on rabble-rousers who would not return to their homes."

Her voice fell to a rough whisper. "That wasn't the worst of it. Not only were we killing children, but we were killing ourselves, our own souls. The first time I saw a man whose face was swollen after a beating, I was horrified. The second time, I felt numb. The third time, I felt nothing. I thought I would be a good soldier, that these things would not bother me, until the day I obeyed a command to open fire upon a group who were throwing fire bombs at an Israeli girls' school. When the smoke cleared, I discovered that we had shot and injured three twelve-year-olds."

"You can't beat yourself up for that." Michael spoke with quiet firmness.

"Your job is to protect your people, no matter who opposes you. It's sad that your enemy chose to send children against you, but would you rather see innocent Israeli children die? War is never fair. We don't have to like what we do; we just have to do it. Kill or be killed—it's really that simple, Devorah."

She looked up at him, her mouth as pale as her cheeks. "That's when I asked to be assigned to the counterterrorism unit. As part of the Sayeret, I knew I would be fighting evil . . . not children."

Michael remained silent, allowing the talk of the other passengers to wrap around them. He, too, knew the horrors of war, but he had never had to face the particular nightmare of shooting at a child. Understanding the difficult moral position in which IDF soldiers had found themselves, his heart welled with compassion.

Silent still, he reached out and placed his hand over Devorah's. For a moment her hand lay motionless beneath his, then she lowered her other hand over his.

"Thank you." The words were scarcely more than a breath, but gratitude shone from her wide, dark eyes.

Michael squeezed her hand, hoping the yearning that showed in her face was not as apparent in his own. He lowered his gaze, not certain how to proceed, and the photograph of Adrian Romulus caught his eye.

"Who knows?" He lightened his voice and removed his hand to pick up the magazine. "Perhaps Romulus and his cohorts will solve all the world's problems next summer. You and I can give up our jobs—maybe move to the country and take up farming."

"I can't imagine you on a farm." A smile ruffled her mouth as she took the magazine and flipped through the glossy pages. "And I can't believe mankind will find the answers to its problems in religion."

She found the Romulus profile and stopped to skim it. After a long moment, her brows drew together in an angry frown.

"What's wrong?"

"Romulus's conference is to convene on Sunday, July 29." She tossed the magazine into Michael's lap, then paused to pick up her attaché case.

"So?"

She held up a finger, urging patience, then pulled a small calendar from her case and flipped through the pages. Her brow creased with worry when she found the page she was seeking. "That date is *Tish-ah Be-Av*." She looked up and gave him a bleak, tight-lipped smile. "The ninth day of Av, a traditional day of Jewish mourning."

He stared at her, baffled. "Why is that significant?"

"The Bible tells us that on the ninth of Av, in 587 before the Common Era, the Babylonians destroyed the first temple. Generations later, on the same date, the Romans destroyed the second temple. The ninth of Av is also the date when Spain expelled 400,000 Jews in 1492."

Michael shifted in his chair. "But those things don't have anything to do with Romulus. And you've already said that Orthodox Jews won't attend this convocation, so there's no conflict—"

"It doesn't matter." She set her chin in a stubborn line. "The leading rabbis will see this event as an evil omen. Anything significant that occurs on the ninth of Av will be seen as a portent for destruction and sorrow for the Jewish people."

Michael scratched his chin and looked away, not knowing how to reply. What had happened to the levelheaded young woman he had come to know? One moment she was telling him about the necessity of defending Israel through military strength, in the next she was wide-eyed with apprehension about a date on a religious calendar.

Michael smiled, ruefully accepting the truth: Her father the rabbi cast a longer shadow than Devorah Cohen realized.

-0100111100-

At least, Michael thought when they walked through the gate, they wouldn't have to guess which of the people waiting in the lounge were Devorah's cousins. Amid the flurry of embraces, exuberant greetings, and waving welcome signs, two men and a woman stood like somber statues. The woman wore a shoulder-length brunette wig, attractively styled but obviously false, and both men wore beards, black hats, and the distinctive black coats of Orthodox Jews. The fringes of gray prayer shawls extended beneath the hems of their coats.

Like the unerring needle on a compass, Devorah turned toward the trio.

"Your cousins?" Michael asked, keeping his voice low.

"Gavriel and Lila," she said, nodding slightly as she caught the woman's eye. "I do not recognize the man with them."

A moment later the two women were embracing. Michael introduced himself and shook Gavriel's hand, then stepped back as the young man introduced the stranger. "Captain Reed," he said, his voice formal and restrained, "this is Rabbi Yacov Witzun. He contacted us and expressed an interest in meeting you."

Michael glanced at Devorah as a warning spasm of alarm rippled through him. "You knew we were coming?" he asked, uncertainly extending his hand toward the aged rabbi.

"It is my very great pleasure to meet you." The rabbi took Michael's hand in both his own and nodded slightly. "We have a mutual friend."

Michael withdrew his hand and shrugged to hide his confusion. "I wasn't aware that anyone knew about our trip."

Kindness shone from the rabbi's dark eyes. "My friend is called Daniel. He told me how to reach the Greenbergs and how to contact you."

Michael grinned as the light of understanding dawned. Apparently Daniel had contacts everywhere. "Are you—" He paused, casting about for words that would not reveal too much in a public place. "Are you going to help us in this business?"

Laugh lines radiated from the corners of Witzun's eyes as he smiled. "Indeed I am. I am going to pray. And I will be available to answer any questions you might have."

Lila linked her arm through Devorah's. "We should be going, Husband," she said, her dark gaze flying to her husband's face. "We can talk in the car."

"Yes." Gavriel nodded in what looked like relief, then gestured toward the corridor where a mob of passengers streamed to and from various gates. "After you, Rabbi."

Twenty minutes later, all five of them had crowded into Gavriel's black BMW. Lila rode up front beside her husband, while Michael, Devorah, and the rabbi shoehorned themselves into the backseat. The rabbi, Michael noticed, allowed Devorah to enter first, then slid to the center of the seat, effectively acting as a barrier between them. Did he do it on purpose?

"I didn't know Daniel knew anyone in Belgium," Michael began as soon as the car moved into the traffic outside the international airport. "But by now I shouldn't be surprised by anything Daniel does."

The rabbi looked at Michael with a smile hidden in his eyes. "I met Daniel last year, when he was in Brussels working with Adrian Romulus and the Council of Ministers. He came to my apartment, and we exchanged a few words. Daniel was not a believer then."

Michael stared at the rabbi in a paralysis of astonishment. Daniel had become a believer in Christ in the months since his work for Adrian Romulus, but surely this was not what the rabbi meant.

"Daniel," Michael lifted a brow, "was not a believer . . . in what, exactly?"

"In Romulus, may his name be blotted out. I tried to tell him that Romulus is the next Hitler, but Daniel would not listen. Now, however, he believes."

Michael turned away, carefully cloaking his confusion. He wanted to see Devorah's reaction to the rabbi's comment, but Witzun sat between them, an impassable barrier.

For some moments they rode in silence through the suburb of Zaventem, then Gavriel exited the freeway and slanted the car onto another road. "Devorah has spoken to me and outlined your plan," Gavriel said, catching Michael's eye in the rearview mirror. "And though we do not necessarily approve of subterfuge, we understand that such things are sometimes necessary. The arrangements have all been made. We have procured a synthetic stone of two hundred carats, and the Russian buyer is scheduled to appear tomorrow morning at eleven o'clock. He has spoken to Lila on the phone, but he has never seen her."

The rabbi lifted his hand. "Let the matter rest, Gavriel. We will talk tonight after dinner, but for now, let us consider how the Master of the universe will bring his will to pass. Who knows but that these things may be the final sufferings before the arrival of our *Moshiach?* The Messiah is coming, and he will possess advantages, superiority, and honor to a greater degree than all the kings that have ever existed, as was prophesied by all the prophets, from Moses, peace be upon him, till Malachi, may he rest in peace. The Messiah, the Prince of Peace, will establish his kingdom, and of it there shall be no end . . ."

As the rabbi's voice droned on, Michael leaned into the car's upholstery and watched the outskirts of Brussels slide by, content to ponder the perplexing events of the last hour.

-0100111100-

They dined that night on beef and vegetables in the cozy kitchen of the Greenbergs' house. Lila Greenberg seemed to eat on the run; she sprang up every time one of the men looked around the table or needed something from the kitchen.

As they ate, Michael studied the young couple. Gavriel Greenberg was a pleasant-looking man, with smooth pale skin stretched over high cheekbones, a dark brown beard and earlocks, and slightly protruding coffee-brown eyes. He did not speak much during dinner, and Michael wondered if his reticence sprang from natural shyness or the fact that a learned rabbi was sharing their evening meal.

Lila was a lovely girl, probably six or seven years younger than her headstrong cousin. She had Devorah's dark eyes and sharp nose, but there the resemblance ended. Devorah possessed the sable beauty of a deadly panther, while Lila seemed an unstylish, soft little woman. The heavy wig that covered her hair for modesty's sake seemed to compress her small frame, shadowing her eyes and capping her natural exuberance.

No matter how hard he tried to resist, Michael felt his gaze being drawn to Devorah. She ate quietly, respecting her cousins' beliefs, and didn't contradict Michael even once. The light from the candles bathed her smooth skin in a golden glow, and twice he had to press his hand to his thigh to restrain himself from reaching out and stroking one of her wayward curls. Though she always looked attractive, she shone with an ethereal beauty in the subdued atmosphere, and Michael knew he would have found himself in real trouble if they had been alone.

When the meal ended, the rabbi led them in a song of thanksgiving. Michael sat silently and listened with appreciation. These people might not approve of him or his relationship with their cousin, yet they had welcomed him to their home and their table. He knew Americans who wouldn't open their homes to an outsider as easily.

The rabbi closed his eyes at the end of the song, murmured a prayer in Hebrew, then pressed his hands to the tablecloth and gave Gavriel a reassuring smile. As if this was a cue, Lila and Devorah rose from their places and began to remove the dishes from the dinner table. Michael slid his chair back, ready to offer his help, but Devorah caught his eye and gently shook her head.

When the last dish had been cleared from the table, the women resumed their places. As Lila sank into her seat, Gavriel cleared his throat and looked directly at Michael. "I was a little hesitant to take part in this," he began, one corner of his mouth twisting. "But I would do anything for Israel. The rabbi assures me that this Russian has valuable and important information."

"Ordinarily," Lila lifted her chin to meet Michael's gaze, "a buyer outside the diamond trade would not be admitted to one of our offices, much less be allowed to view a diamond and negotiate a price. Only the world's most influential diamond dealers are allowed to purchase diamonds at what are known as sights, but we will make an exception in this case."

Gavriel nodded. "Three months ago, a Russian by the name of Oleg Petrov contacted my father-in-law's London office with an unusual request. He is searching for an uncut diamond of at least two hundred carats and offering to pay three million euros."

Michael had heard this much of the story from Daniel, so he nodded at Gavriel. "I understand you are planning to offer him a fake stone."

Gavriel fingered the edge of his beard. "A synthetic stone, yes. My conscience has troubled me on this account, for I have never defrauded a customer. But the offer of three million euros seems suspect. The Russian economy is weak; the nation can barely feed itself, so how can they afford such a stone? Furthermore, it is our feeling that selling a genuine diamond to the Russian leadership would be tantamount to selling ancient scrolls to an arsonist. Though we are not certain what this Oleg Petrov plans for the diamond, we are not certain he can be trusted."

"Can any Russian be trusted?" Lila said, each word a splinter of ice.

Michael lifted a brow. Lila had scarcely spoken all evening, and her vehement suspicion caught him off guard.

The rabbi lifted his hand and looked in Michael's direction. "We have heard about the current purge in Moscow, Captain Reed. Though we are saddened by such grievous news, we are not shocked. The Russians have been killing Jews for centuries. They killed over a hundred thousand as their troops mobilized for World War I."

"On Tish-ah Be-Av," Devorah whispered, catching Michael's eye. "The ninth day of Av."

Rabbi Witzun shot Michael a penetrating look. "The Russian nation has been persecuting Jews since the time of the czars. The word *pogrom,* referring to the massacre of a helpless people, rose from the Russian language. Less than fifty years ago, Joseph Stalin, may his name be forever blotted out, planned to exterminate the Jews in Russia. He arrested nine Moscow doctors, six of whom were Jewish, and falsely charged them with plans to murder Soviet leaders. He planned to publicly hang them in Moscow and then incite the public to three days of rioting against the Jews. Like Haman of old, Stalin wanted nothing less than the complete extermination of our people. He told the assembled Politburo that he would round up the Jews of Russia and exile them to Siberia, but two-thirds of the captives would never arrive. His men would kill them en route and blame their deaths on the angry Russian people."

The rabbi paused and drew a shuddering breath. "Only the almighty hand of the Creator, blessed be he, saved the sons of Abraham, Isaac, and Jacob. Stalin suffered a stroke only days before the doctors were to have been murdered. One month later, *Pravda* announced that the nine doctors had been declared innocent and released."

"Of course," Gavriel added, "that is not to say we mistrust all Russians, no more than we believe all Arabs are intent upon Israel's destruction. But the country itself has not been kind to the Jews, and we suspect Oleg Petrov is acting as a representative of the Russian government. For that reason alone, I cannot trust him."

"We are breaking every rule to accommodate this Petrov." Lila's mouth spread into a thin-lipped smile. "Never before have we allowed a stranger to negotiate a sighting. If not for the rabbi's persuasion, we would not agree to this."

Rabbi Witzun's expression softened into one of fond reminiscence. "And I would not agree if not for Daniel. I believe he is right. This ruse is not terribly dangerous, not a moral problem. Tomorrow we shall meet this Russian and give him the false stone. And if the Master of the universe, blessed be his name, is pleased, all will be well with us."

Chapter Twenty-six

1037 hours
Tuesday, October 17

A COLD LUMP GREW IN DEVORAH'S STOMACH AS SHE SAT IN THE BACKSEAT OF THE BMW. Reed was waiting on the curb outside his hotel when she, Lila, and Gavriel arrived to pick him up, but not even the sight of his confident smile could stem the chilly tendrils of apprehension spreading through her body.

As they drove to the diamond exchange, or *bourse*, Gavriel assured Devorah that Oleg Petrov did not know what Lila Greenberg looked like. "The Russian was referred to us by my father's office," he said, carefully negotiating the winding streets, "and he arranged his appointment by telephone. We have not seen him; he has not seen us."

Devorah tugged on the bangs of the wig she now wore, a necessary part of every married Orthodox woman's wardrobe. "Don't worry about me, Gavriel," she said, glancing at Michael. "And you need not fear for yourself, either. I'm certain we shall discover all we need to know."

The bourse was located in the Marolles, an older, fading sector of Brussels. "We do not cater to the tourist trade," Gabriel explained as he parked in an alley between two brick buildings. "The people who need us know where to find us."

Devorah was surprised to see that only a simple brass plaque announced the bourse's address—21 Rue de la Samaritaine. A plush, carpeted lobby beyond the front doors muffled their footsteps as they entered the building. A security camera high on the wall monitored the second door.

Loosening the scarf at his neck, Gavriel nodded at the camera, and a moment later a buzzer sounded. He caught the doorknob and pulled the door open, waiting for the others to pass.

The bourse was housed in a long and narrow room. A weighing station occupied the far end, and at least a dozen tables were arranged down the length of the building, perpendicular to floor-to-ceiling windows in the north wall. "So open," she marveled, blinking in the bright light flooding the room.

Lila nodded as she slipped out of her coat. "Northern light is the best for examining diamonds. A diamond glows in bright sunlight."

Trading had already begun by the time they arrived. Devorah had heard much about the diamond business, but she had never had an opportunity to visit a bourse. As Reed chatted with Gavriel in low tones, she stood in the center of the room and silently observed the routine.

Once a visitor had announced himself in the foyer, a plain-clothes guard escorted him into the main viewing room. The client was assigned to one of the sellers, who sat patiently behind a fluorescent lamp at a small table. Once the buyer and seller had greeted each other, another plain-clothes guard brought out a little wooden box and set it on the table before the buyer.

"Each box contains diamonds specially selected for each buyer," Lila explained, following Devorah's gaze. "We know what sort of business each man does, whether high-end or low, whether he wants quality or quantity in his purchase. He is free to accept or reject the box we offer him—but if he rejects his box, he may not be invited to the bourse again." She jerked her head in an emphatic nod, the heavy sheaf of her wig's bangs flopping into her eyes. Automatically, she brushed the hair away and continued, "We don't put up with foolishness. We are serious about our work, and so are our buyers."

At one table near Devorah, a potbellied balding man pressed a loupe to his eye and shouted something in French while holding a diamond in a pair of silver tweezers. Lila's tight expression relaxed into a smile. "He's complaining," she whispered, pulling Devorah away from the table. "That's a good sign. Next he will tell David to get Gavriel on the phone so he can complain. Gavriel will listen, and then he will name our final price." She nodded confidently. "He will buy that stone."

As Lila moved away to take a phone call, Devorah shifted her gaze to another table, where a business deal had apparently been concluded. The buyer and seller, both men, stood and shook hands, then the seller said, "*Mazel U'Bracha.*" The buyer scooped the diamonds into a small felt pouch, slipped them into his inner coat pocket, and went out the door wearing a satisfied smile.

Devorah turned around and saw Reed standing behind her. "*Mazel U'Bracha?*" he asked.

"With luck and a blessing." She smiled. "It is tradition. Even non-Jews say it to conclude a deal." She lifted her hand. "Come with me. I think Gavriel is ready to set up our table."

Reed followed her to the empty table where Gavriel stood. Devorah sank into the empty chair, adjusted the small lamp at her right hand, and smoothed the wrinkles from the velvet-covered foam cushion. While Gavriel murmured a prayer in Hebrew, she grinned up at Reed, trying to disguise her nervousness. "Tell me this could be fun."

"Lila will ring you when the Russian arrives," Gavriel said, a no-nonsense expression on his face as he pointed to the phone at Devorah's left. "You, Captain Reed, will come out of the vault with the stone in a wooden box. You will bring it directly to Devorah, then step back and wait. Do not speak—your accent would arouse suspicion in a moment."

Reed stared in surprise. "I have an accent?"

Devorah rolled her eyes, momentarily enjoying the upper hand. "A thick one. Believe me, Gavriel is right. Be silent and watch."

"When you have shown him the stone," Gavriel continued, transferring his gaze to Devorah, "ask if he would like to have one of our cutters shape it for him. From his answer, we may be able to determine the stone's purpose."

"What is a reasonable figure if he wants to have it cut?" Reed asked.

Gavriel folded his arms. "For up to two hundred pieces—tell him ten thousand euros. If he wants it cut into one perfect stone, the price would be a hundred thousand. But after quoting those prices, offer to do the cutting for half that amount. I do not want anyone else to see that stone—they would know he had been cheated and would tell him so in an instant."

Devorah nodded. "I understand."

Reed looked down at her. "Seal the deal and pronounce the blessing—but don't forget to try to find out everything you can."

"Roger that." She smoothed her skirt, wishing Reed would leave her alone to center her thoughts, but he merely locked his hands behind his back and looked expectantly toward the front door. Finally she caught his eye and gestured toward the small office across from the weighing station. "Shouldn't you be getting to your post, Captain? I believe that is where the security monitor is located. From there you can have the first glimpse of our visitor."

A wry but indulgent glint appeared in his eye, then he walked away. Devorah slowly exhaled as he left, then drew a deep breath and steeled herself for the operation to follow.

It would be simple, Reed had promised. Nothing could go wrong.

-0100111100-

Suppressing a smile, Michael left Devorah at her table and moved to the small office across from the weighing station. Lila buzzed him through the locked door, and once inside he saw that one office wall was completely taken up by a steel vault, its wide door now open. Peering inside, Michael saw that the vault was lined with shelves, upon which a series of wooden boxes stood in careful order and velveteen pouches bulged with treasure.

A desk occupied the opposite office wall, and a security guard—this one in uniform—sat at a console watching a row of monitors. Michael noticed that security cameras not only monitored the entrance, but the examination areas as well. A ceiling camera caught every movement of the buyers and sellers seated at the velvet-covered tables.

Gavriel sat at another desk, a phone at his left hand and a cluttered pile of papers at his right. "The high cost of doing business today," he said, jerking his thumb toward the bank of security monitors. "In my father's day these things were not necessary. But the world is changing."

"Everything is changing," Michael murmured, his eyes following a streak of movement on one of the monitors. A man and woman entered the front doors and announced themselves over the intercom. From her small desk outside the vault, Lila rang one of the guards in the outer room, and a moment later an escort led the couple in and seated them at one of the trading tables.

All the tables were filled now except Devorah's. Michael glanced at his watch. The Russian's appointment was for 11:00. According to his watch, the man was already three minutes late.

He turned to Gavriel. "What if he doesn't come?"

The younger man shrugged. "Who am I to say what will happen? He will call again or go elsewhere. These things are out of my control."

A bright slash of light crossed the foyer monitor, and Michael refocused his attention on it. Two men stood outside the locked double doors. One of them was wearing an ordinary wool coat and dark trousers, not a military uniform. But the sight of the first man's companion gave Michael pause—the second man wore the dark hat, coat, and beard of an Orthodox Jew.

"Gavriel," he whispered, his voice tense and urgent.

The diamond broker looked up, then frowned at the monitor. "This is not good," he murmured, rising from his chair.

"Why would he bring someone with him? Why a Jew?"

Gavriel crossed his arms and stared at the monitor with a look that said his brain was working hard at a new set of problems. "There is only one reason. The Russian knows nothing about diamonds, so he has brought an expert."

Michael felt his heart leap uncomfortably into the back of his throat as Gavriel pushed past him into the vault. "An expert?" Michael asked, following. "But you are showing him a worthless stone."

"Not if I can help it." Gavriel's hands fluttered over the boxes and caressed the felt bags, considering the heft of each through the fabric. "We would be exposed in an instant."

Michael clenched his fists, growing more uncomfortable by the minute. They had broken one of the first rules of combat and underestimated their enemy. Unless they came up with an answer, their careful plan would be worthless. "Do you have a stone of that size?" he asked, hearing a note of anxiety in his voice.

Gavriel gave him a narrow, glinting glance, then turned to Lila, who sat at her desk with a desperate expression on her face. "We will see what we can find. Meanwhile, Wife, send an escort to let them in. We cannot arouse suspicion by holding them in the lobby."

Michael glanced up at the monitors while Lila picked up the phone to ring one of the waiting guards. Soon the Russian and the Jew would be seated at Devorah's table.

"I should warn Devorah," Michael said, moving toward the door. "She can create a diversion to stall them."

"It will do no good." Gavriel stood motionless in the middle of the vault, his hands hanging limply at his side. "I have no stone that size. We have only the synthetic diamond. It will have to do."

Michael's mind refused to accept the merchant's words. "Surely you have something close. A stone of one hundred carats? Eighty?"

"Nothing." Sighing, Gavriel moved toward his desk, then picked up the phone.

Michael clenched his fist and grasped at a last hope. "Are you calling London? Will they be able to send a genuine stone?"

Gavriel shook his head. "I am calling the rabbi. If we ever needed prayer and inspiration, it is now."

-0100111100-

Devorah took a deep breath and stood as the guard helped the visitors shed their coats, then escorted the two gentlemen to her table. A tide of goose-flesh had rippled up each arm when she saw that a Jew accompanied the Russian, but now she lifted her head with confidence and greeted them with a smile. Reed and Gavriel would have seen both men on the security monitor. They would do something to prevent disaster.

"*Bon jour*, Monsieur Petrov," she said, then noted the Russian's frown.

"Please, Madame Greenberg," he said, removing his hat, "unless you speak Russian, may we converse in English? I am not fluent in French."

"Of course." She gestured toward the empty chair before her, then motioned for the escort to fetch another for the second man. "I am pleased to meet you at last. We have found a superlative stone, and I believe it meets your specifications."

The Russian had an erect posture, a square chin, and a wide mouth which tipped in a faint smile. "Excellent. Madame, I would like you to meet Benjamin Wildenstein, a jeweler and dealer in diamonds." The Russian sat and crossed his legs. His companion, a man of about her father's age, took his seat with grave dignity, then proceeded to examine Devorah's face with considerable absorption.

After a moment he flicked a basilisk glance at the Russian, then returned his gaze to Devorah and softly asked a question in Hebrew. "You are married, my daughter?"

A flush of guilt colored Devorah's cheeks. He'd seen the wig, of course, which every Orthodox wife wore as a sign of modesty and submission. But she wore no wedding ring, and Devorah suspected he had also noted a most unorthodox flash of rebellion in her eyes.

Girding herself with resolve, she forced her gaze to remain locked with Wildenstein's. "No," she answered in Hebrew. "I am not married."

He leaned back, nodding slightly, then rested both hands on the top of his cane and allowed his gaze to drift off to safer territory.

"Well?" The Russian thumped the table and looked around. "Where is it? I am most anxious to see this diamond."

"One moment, sir." Deliberately slowing her breaths to keep her hands from shaking, Devorah reached for the phone, then halted when she saw movement from the corner of her eye. Reed stepped out of the office, a wooden box in his hand. She exhaled slowly as he came forward and placed the box on the table with an almost ceremonial air.

He retreated a few steps, then locked his hands behind his back, watching from a safe distance. Devorah stared at the box, her heart pounding hard enough to be heard a yard away.

"Do not fear," the old man whispered, speaking in Hebrew again.

"Speak English," Petrov snapped, his blue eyes flashing as he glared at the older man. "And open the box. I am on a schedule."

Devorah forced her fingers to move. She unlatched the hook, then lifted the hinged lid. Resting inside on a bed of ruby-colored velvet lay an oval stone about an inch wide, three-quarters of an inch deep, and one and a half inches long.

"It is 208.30 carats," she said, reading from a small slip of paper attached to the side of the box. "The color is very good."

Petrov picked up the stone, tossed it into the air, and caught it in his palm, then nodded as if that ridiculous exercise meant something to him. He then handed the stone to Wildenstein.

The jeweler pulled a loupe from his pocket, fitted it to his eye, and picked up the stone. Devorah felt her stomach sway as he held it to the light.

"Well?" Petrov crossed his booted ankle across his knee. "Will it make a perfect diamond or not?"

"It is clear white, with no yellow and no obvious imperfections," the old man said, squinting at the stone. "The grain is right for an oval, if that is what you wish."

"It is."

Recognizing a perfect opportunity, Devorah moistened her dry lips and smiled at the Russian. "Such a lovely stone! I was hoping you would not want to carve it up into several small pieces."

Petrov folded his hands and regarded her with a lurking smile. "I am not at liberty, Madame, to discuss my employer's intentions."

The old man took the loupe from his eye, then lifted a bushy brow in Devorah's direction. "I believe, sir," he said, slowly shifting his gaze to meet the Russian's, "you would be wise to purchase this stone."

Devorah felt the lump in her throat dissolve in relief. Wildenstein had to know the stone was synthetic, but as long as he was willing to participate in this little charade . . .

Petrov lifted his chin and boldly met Devorah's gaze. "What is the price?"

"Four point five million euros."

"Too much! I am authorized to give you two."

"Three point five million." With a slight smile of defiance, she added, "Not a euro less."

The Russian paused, pretended to consider the offer, then inclined his head in agreement. "Done. You will have a certified check within a week."

With trembling fingers, Devorah wrapped the counterfeit stone in white tissue paper from the desk drawer. "Would you like for us to arrange to have it cut? Some of the best diamond cutters in the world live in Brussels, and we are authorized to provide you with a substantial discount. The usual price for cutting a stone this size would be 100,000 euros, but one of our cutters will do the job for half that amount."

Petrov's smile held only a shadow of its former warmth. "I have been told that the best cutters are in New York, Antwerp, and Tel Aviv. With all due respect, Madame, I believe I will take the stone to Antwerp."

Devorah glanced at the jeweler as sheer black fright swept through her. If Petrov took the stone to anyone else, he would soon know they had deceived him. And then, depending upon what kind of man he was, he might return to take some sort of vengeance upon her cousins and even the jeweler Benjamin Wildenstein.

"Monsieur Wildenstein," she gave the older man a careful smile as she slipped the stone into a felt bag, "I am certain you can convince Monsieur Petrov that our Brussels cutters are skilled. They are more than qualified to create the stone he desires . . . for whatever purpose he chooses."

Wildenstein opened his mouth as if he would respond, but the Russian cut him off with a sharp laugh. "I am done with Brussels," he said, his eyes snapping with maliciousness as he stood and took the stone from Devorah's hand. "I only came here because this bourse was highly recommended by the London syndicate. But I commend you on your persistence, Madame."

"In case you change your mind," Devorah pulled a slip of paper from her pocket and scribbled a name on it, "contact this man. Yacov Witzun has many contacts in the diamond community, and he will be able to help you."

Petrov frowned, but at the last moment he took the paper and thrust it into his pocket. Devorah stood and murmured the traditional blessing. "*Mazel U'Bracha*." The Russian ignored the wish for blessing and luck, but Wildenstein whispered the words with her, his sparkling black eyes sinking into nets of wrinkles as he smiled.

Michael stepped forward to escort Petrov to the door, and Devorah hurried out from behind the table, ostensibly to help the older man into his coat. "Why?" she murmured in Hebrew as she plucked his coat from the wall hook where he had deposited it.

Watching him, Devorah saw something like bitterness enter his lined face. "What would make a daughter of Israel disguise herself before a Russian?" he asked, turning to shrug into his coat. "Only danger. And I did not lie. The stone is as perfect as a man-made stone can be." He lifted his chin and sent a smile over the fur collar of his heavy coat. "Do not worry about me, daughter. The Creator of the world, blessed be he, will guard my footsteps in the days ahead. I am an old man and cannot be held responsible if my eye leads me to make a mistake."

Devorah stepped back and clasped her hands together. "*Mazel U'Bracha*," she repeated, and never had she whispered the benediction with more feeling.

Chapter Twenty-seven

Moscow
0900 hours
Wednesday, October 18

Cushioned against a mound of velveteen pillows, Alanna sat before the fireplace and held her hands to the roaring blaze. A sullen gray cloud, heavily pregnant with snow, hung outside the windows, rattling the glass as the wind sent breaths of frigid air through the suite.

She shivered as a chilly draft touched her shoulders. Vladimir lay on the sofa, surrounded by his morning newspapers, the cordless telephone by his side. He had awakened early in a state of unusual anticipation and seemed content to remain in her suite, but Alanna had no idea what had excited him so.

The phone rang, shattering the stillness, and Vladimir immediately picked it up. He spoke in Russian, but Alanna had little trouble following his conversation. Fed by a daily diet of Russian soap operas and news telecasts, her comprehension of the language had improved remarkably.

He paused to listen to the caller, then snapped, "So you have it?"

Alanna stole a glance over her shoulder. The worried lines that had etched his face last night lifted, and a blush of pleasure rose to his cheeks. "Do not delay," he said, seeming to stare at the place where his bare toes traced a pattern in the wool carpet. "Find a man in Brussels; we haven't time to travel the world for a cutter. Find a Jew to do the job—those people have a knack for these things."

He paused a moment more, then shifted his gaze toward Alanna. Embarrassed to be caught spying, she blew him a quick kiss and turned back to the fire, lifting her hands to the crackling blaze. She could hear just as well from this position, and Vladimir could not see a telltale flash of comprehension in her eyes.

"Don't worry about the check." Vladimir lowered his voice. "Soon there will not be enough Jews left in the world to care about such things."

The phone thumped on the carpet; the newspaper rustled again. After a long, edgy minute, Alanna folded her legs under her gown and hugged her knees. "Is everything all right, Vladimir?" she called in English, injecting a wheedling note of worry in her voice. "Are you going to leave me again?"

The paper crackled as Vladimir lowered it and peered at her over the edge. "Not yet, my dear. When all is ready, I will go away just once more, then all our partings will be at an end. All of the pieces are falling into place."

She smiled at him over her shoulder, then turned back to the fire and rested her head on her bent knees. Her smile faded as she recalled his comment about the Jews.

She had to tell Daniel. She couldn't tell him much, for she had no idea what Vladimir was planning, but he never did anything by half-measures. If he wanted to rid the world of Jews, he would do it—quickly and thoroughly.

She opened her mouth wide in a pretend yawn, tapped at her lips, then pulled herself up off the floor and padded to the kitchen. She'd make Vladimir his coffee, brush his uniform, and suggest that he go out for a breath of fresh air. If all went well, he might leave the suite within the hour and give her an opportunity to contact Daniel.

−0100111100−

Less than twenty-four hours after Petrov left the bourse, Daniel contacted Michael with news that the Russians were in a hurry and might have the stone cut in Brussels after all. He suggested that Michael and Devorah remain in Brussels for at least a week, in case Petrov decided to contact the bourse or Rabbi Witzun. Until he did, Daniel added, the diamond exchange might do well to double their guard and perhaps the Greenbergs should take a room in a nearby hotel. If Petrov discovered he had been given a relatively worthless stone, he might decide to personally take his revenge.

"I've done some checking," Daniel wrote in his e-mail. "Colonel Oleg Petrov is Vladimir Gogol's executive officer and most trusted confidant. Not only has he personally overseen the purge of Jews in Moscow, but he is believed to be responsible for the deaths of more than a hundred people who have resisted Gogol's reforms. Take him seriously, Michael, and keep those people in Brussels out of harm's way."

Michael immediately spoke to Gavriel and insisted that the diamond merchant and his wife take his room at the hotel. He then called Rabbi Witzun, and that generous soul insisted that Devorah and Michael stay at his apartment until the situation resolved. "My home is not large, but you are welcome to share it," the rabbi told Michael. "And we shall talk of many things while we wait for the Russian to either call us or kill us."

He barked a short laugh, but Michael couldn't see the humor in his statement. After hanging up the phone, he and Devorah left the bourse and moved their bags to the rabbi's home, a small, dusty space located on the fifth floor of a sprawling complex on the Rue Blaes. The apartment itself looked more like a library than a home, for pine shelving lined the walls and groaned under the weight of myriad books. A solid oak table, laden with a candelabrum and more books, dominated the front room. Behind the small kitchen, Michael found two bedrooms. The rabbi insisted that Devorah take the largest. He and Michael would share a second room furnished with two cots.

Two days later, Michael felt as though the book-lined walls of the apartment were closing in on him. They'd been waiting for some sign of action or threat from Petrov, yet the Russian had not made a single appearance or phone call. Michael didn't know if the man was drunk, dead, or on his way back to Moscow.

He picked up yet another book, saw that it was written in Hebrew, and set it back in its place. The rabbi indulged in an obvious love affair with rare and ancient volumes, but most of them were written in languages Michael couldn't understand.

Devorah, however, sat curled up in a wing chair next to the oak table with a book in her lap. She had begun to examine the rabbi's library soon after their arrival, and she had skimmed through book after book, often looking up with a thoughtful expression. Occasionally she asked the rabbi a question in Hebrew, then debated with him as energetically as she argued with Michael. Michael knew he ought to be relieved that someone else was shouldering the weight of her emphatic opinions, but after a while he began to miss the sharp sting of her comments.

He stared out the small curtained window, unable to read and growing more uneasy with every passing hour. What if Petrov decided to take
the stone to another jeweler? What if he had lost the paper with Rabbi
Witzun's name? He could be at another diamond cutter's office this
minute, his face flaming as he realized he had been deceived by an old man
and a young woman . . . both Jewish.

The heavy ring of the telephone startled him. Michael drew himself up
and swallowed to bring his heart down from his throat. The rabbi moved
toward the phone, then lifted it to his ear and murmured a soft word of
greeting. He listened intently, then answered in English. "Yes, I would be
happy to consider the job. Bring the stone to 93745 Rue Blaes, apartment
5-D. Four o'clock, please."

Witzun hung up the phone and stared at Michael, his dark eyes shooting sparks in all directions. "The Russian is coming."

Michael's blood was suddenly swimming in adrenaline. "Great! I was
afraid he'd gone elsewhere."

Devorah lowered her book. "What do you suppose he's been doing for
the past two days?"

Michael clasped his hands, wishing he and Devorah weren't alone in
this mission. They could have used some good intelligence operators to
shadow Petrov over the past forty-eight hours. Resigning himself to reality, he gave Devorah a rueful grin. "He could have been anywhere. Don't
forget—the European Union is headquartered here. He could have been
visiting officials on behalf of his boss, even meeting with Adrian
Romulus. Or maybe he was just enjoying the nightlife and sleeping during the day."

Devorah sat back in her chair, a frown puckering the skin between her
dark eyes. "Well, now it's time to move. Are we ready?"

Michael rested his elbows on his knees, then looked up and regarded
the rabbi with a smile. "What do you think, Rabbi? Are you ready to play
the part of a diamond cutter?"

The rabbi's somber face lit with mischief. "I have been looking forward
to it," he said, grinning like a boy with a box of matches.

Devorah tossed her book on the table and moved toward the phone.
"I'll call Gavriel."

"Good." Michael rubbed his hand over his jaw, hearing the rasp of three days' stubbled growth. If he didn't get back to the real world soon, he'd have a beard as thick as the rabbi's.

In the two days of waiting, they had formed a careful plan. Now he stood and walked to the side of the table, reviewing the plan for the rabbi's sake. "Devorah and I will hide ourselves in the bedrooms, Rabbi, while you talk to Petrov. Take the stone, ask for a hundred thousand euros, let him talk you down to fifty thousand, but no less. If he seems talkative, ask for more information about the diamond's purpose."

The unanswered question had remained uppermost in all of their minds. At the bourse they had learned only that the stone would be kept in one piece and cut into an oval. Though that information seemed to indicate the diamond wouldn't be cut up for use in supercomputers or x-ray machines, at least a hundred other possible uses remained. Daniel had written that he was particularly worried about emergent technology with telecommunications and laser weaponry.

"Don't worry, Rabbi." Devorah held the phone away from her ear as she dialed Gavriel's number. "Michael and I will be ready. If something goes wrong, we'll protect you."

The rabbi lifted his hands. "What could possibly go wrong?"

−0100111100−

By half past three, Gavriel Greenberg had transformed the rabbi's oak table into a professional diamond cutter's workspace. A Diamondlite, a special lamp that provided an artificial light equivalent to northern exposure on a clear day, sat at one end of the table, behind several diamond cutter's tools.

"Should I be cutting a stone when the Russian arrives?" the rabbi asked Gavriel.

"Do whatever you like," the diamond merchant answered, grinning. "You are an artist and therefore allowed to be eccentric."

And so, when a knock sounded at precisely four o'clock, Rabbi Yacov Witzun was sitting in his chair reading one of his dusty books. Michael stood and watched through a narrow crack between the bedroom door and the doorframe, his stomach clenched tight, his hand itching for the reassuring heft of his H&K USP .45. Below him, on the floor, Devorah crouched in a ready position, her empty hands pressed to her thighs, her gaze glued to the same opening he studied. They were both trained warriors, but neither of them had brought a gun to Brussels, not wanting to risk detection on a commercial flight. Now Michael wished they had tested the rules.

They watched the rabbi disappear after he stood to answer the door, then Petrov's nasal voice filled the room. "Good afternoon. You are the diamond cutter Witzun?"

"I am Witzun."

The rabbi moved back into their range of vision and resumed his seat. Petrov stood beside him, facing the bedrooms, and pulled the small felt bag from a pocket in his coat. Michael nodded in approval as the rabbi unwrapped the tissue paper with a careless, diffident air. Gavriel had warned him that a professional would not be impressed with the stone's size or quality—cutters handled rare and beautiful stones every month.

The rabbi examined the stone under the Diamondlite, then lay it on the velour-covered table without a word.

"Isn't it beautiful?" the Russian asked.

The rabbi lifted one shoulder in a shrug. "I have seen better."

Michael grinned as the Russian released a soft word that sounded like a curse. Petrov's square jaw tensed visibly. "Is it appropriate for an oval?"

"You want an oval?" The rabbi pretended surprise. "Why not a rectangle or a square? I could cut two beautiful squares from this stone. Or I could cut four rectangles, so you could make four times as many women happy."

"It has to be an oval." The Russian's response held a note of impatience. "*One* flawless oval, cut to absolute perfection. And it has to be finished by the first of the year." Petrov thrust his hands behind his back. "My employer insists upon it."

The rabbi shrugged again. "It would be helpful if I knew what the stone will be used for. Will it adorn a lovely lady's neck . . . or, heaven forbid, reflect its glory in some dull laboratory or museum?"

A thin smile crawled to Petrov's lips. "You do not need to bother your brain with such things, old man. Cut the stone, and work quickly. Do your best and you will be rewarded."

Sighing dramatically, Witzun fitted a loupe to his eye, then picked up the stone and squinted at it. "I shall only need four weeks. I will cut you an oval . . . for one hundred thousand euros."

Michael heard a soft hiss as Petrov drew in his breath through his teeth. "I was told you would do it for thirty thousand."

The rabbi lowered the stone to the table and removed the loupe from his eye. A melancholy frown flitted across his features. "Fifty thousand is my lowest price. After all, I am an artist."

The Russian's lips puckered with annoyance, then he nodded. "Very well. I will call for the stone on December first. Make sure it is ready."

The rabbi said nothing as the Russian turned and walked away but picked up his book and ignored the stone on the table. After a moment, Michael heard the slam of the front door.

"Wonderful, Rabbi!" he called when Witzun looked toward the bedroom. Michael waited for Devorah to stand, then he opened the door. While Devorah moved to congratulate the rabbi, Michael walked to the window to follow the Russian's departure.

"You are a born actor," she said, resting her hand on the back of Witzun's chair. She picked up the synthetic stone and stared at it under the Diamondlite. "You almost had me believing this thing was real."

"We pulled it off, yes?" the rabbi said, turning to look at Michael.

"It appears so, Rabbi," Michael said, lifting the edge of the curtain as he watched Petrov exit the building. He waited until the Russian slid into a waiting cab, then dropped the curtain and looked at his companions. "I'm beginning to have second thoughts about our plan. I know we had planned to have the rabbi give Petrov a cut synthetic stone when he returns in four weeks, but what if he does the same thing he did at the bourse? If he brings another jeweler, we will be placing you in danger, Rabbi. Petrov is a cold-blooded murderer, and something tells me he does not intend to pay anything for the cutting of that stone."

He looked at the rabbi, whose smile had vanished, wiped away by astonishment.

"Rabbi is there some place you could go for a few months? I hate to ask this of you, but you will not be safe if you remain here."

"Come to Israel, Rav Witzun." Devorah slipped into another chair at the table. She rested her chin in her hand and looked at the rabbi with affection in her eyes. "Come to Israel and live in Me'a She'arim. You will be welcome there, and you will be appreciated. My father would love to meet you, and the yeshiva is always looking for good teachers."

Joy suffused the rabbi's lined features as he looked at Devorah. "I have always wanted to live and die in Israel." He uttered the words in a hoarse whisper, as though they were too unrealistic to speak in a normal voice. "I never thought I would have the chance. There were too many things keeping me here—my children, my books, my studies—"

"What is keeping you here now?" She lay her hand on the table next to the rabbi's, and Michael knew she was resisting the impulse to bestow a fond touch. "Your children are grown. We can pack up your books so they'll journey with you, and you can study in the Holy Land, in the shadow of the Temple Mount."

She looked up at Michael. "I will call my father, who will make arrangements to move the rabbi to Jerusalem. He has done his people a very great service."

"We will have time to settle things here," Michael added, looking around the room. "Petrov won't be back until December. While we're getting the rabbi ready to move, I'd like to do a bit of looking around and see if I can't discover what connections General Gogol might have here."

The rabbi smiled, his eyes gleaming in the brightness of the Diamondlite. "What did I do to deserve such good friends?"

"Kindness always begets kindness, and HaShem is always faithful," Devorah murmured. She turned to Michael. "So, we confirmed Gogol wants an oval. One perfect stone—but whatever for?"

"That's still a mystery," Michael admitted.

"I have something to show you," Witzun said, his eyes sparkling as he turned a page in the open book on the table before him. "Since I was waiting for a Russian, I decided to read about Russia. Look what I discovered."

Michael leaned forward. The book was written in French, but the black-and-white photograph on the page needed no translation. He recognized the austere features of Nicholas II, the last czar, and the pale face of Alexandra, Nicholas's wife and empress. The photo was a formal shot; the ill-fated rulers sat stiffly upon their thrones, surrounded by their somber children.

Michael crossed his arms and shifted his weight, unable to see anything significant in the picture. Devorah, however, drew in her breath in an audible gasp. "I see!" she whispered, an unmistakable thread of excitement in her voice.

The rabbi smiled in appreciation of her quick understanding. "Can this be the reason our Russian wants a similar stone?"

Suddenly Michael's mind blew open. Alexandra Romanov, the foolish woman who ultimately led her country to the brink of the Russian Revolution, stared at the camera beneath a heavily jeweled tiara. Resting in the center of the beautiful crown was a huge oval diamond.

Devorah jabbed at the photograph with her fingernail. "Is it possible that our man Gogol wants to create another tiara? Whatever happened to this one?"

"It would be easy enough to investigate," the rabbi said. "The Romanov crown jewels—or what remains of them—have been carefully catalogued. Most reside in museums throughout the world, but quite a few of Russia's treasures are locked in the State Armory in Moscow."

Devorah's gaze flew to meet Michael's. "What interest would Gogol have in a tiara?"

The rabbi tugged at his beard. "Perhaps he intends to present his country with a crown, a symbol, in order to elevate his reputation among the people."

"Perhaps," Michael added, imposing order on the whirling thoughts in his brain, "he wants to elevate *himself.* We have always assumed he would arrange to have himself elected president once Chapaev resigns or dies, but—"

"Perhaps," Devorah interrupted, her eyes darkening as she stared at the photograph, "he doesn't want to be president—he wants to be *czar,* and this crown is for whomever he selects as the next czarina." Her extraordinary eyes widened as she stared at Michael. "He wants to restore the monarchy—which would require another Russian revolution."

Michael stared at the photograph, mesmerized by the possibility that they had stumbled upon the truth.

Chapter Twenty-eight

District of Columbia
2330 hours
Tuesday, November 7

THE CLOCK OVER THE FIREPLACE MANTLE SLOWLY CHIMED THE HALF-HOUR AS
Samuel Stedman, forty-third president of the United States, swiveled his
chair to face the wide windows overlooking the darkened White House
lawn. The metallic clang of the clock rattled against his nerves, scraped at
ribbons of guilt and regret for things he might have done differently.

The polls had closed, and Sam had not won a second term. Right now,
Bill Blackstone stood in a crowded ballroom of the Los Angeles Hyatt, one
hand uplifted in victory, the other wrapped around his anorexic wife. In
less than eleven weeks, Blackstone would be sitting in this office, in this
chair, and Electra Zane would be brushing her teeth at the same sink
Victoria had used.

Sam looked away from the window, his vision gloomily colored with
the thought of the useless woman who would walk and talk and dress in
the rooms where Victoria had lived. Strange, how at this moment the
image of Electra Zane disturbed him far more than thoughts of her husband. The people had *chosen* her husband, but the woman who came with
the presidential package wasn't worthy to sit at Victoria's graceful desk in
the East Wing.

He lowered his head into his hand, knowing that the burning rock of
disappointment in the pit of his gut wasn't going away . . . not for a long,
long time. Up until 10:00 P.M. they had been hopeful, but within minutes
after the polls on the West Coast closed, the computers revealed that Texas
voters had granted Blackstone a solid victory. And if *Texas,* a solid, southern, traditional state, could vote for Blackstone . . .

At 10:30 P.M., Sam had gathered his closest people about him. He shook their hands and thanked them for their hard work, then went out to face the cameras. After a short concession speech, he stepped into the presidential limo and let the driver whisk him away from the crowds.

He had wanted to be home, in his office. But it would not be home much longer.

Could he have changed things? Part of his brain wanted to believe he could have, that if he had approved a different series of campaign ads or selected a different campaign manager—but those were only incidentals. Never before in American history had two candidates been more sharply divided, and the people had made their opinions clear. They did not want tradition and responsibility. They wanted to turn the national attention inward, to adopt an adolescent self-centeredness and shed international obligations. Like grown children who return to the family homestead after finding the adult world a difficult place, America wanted to return to its youth and irresponsibility, leaving others to rule the risk-laden world stage.

He swiveled his chair again, ran his hand over the polished surface of his desk, glanced down into the small space where John-John Kennedy used to hide during games of hide-and-seek with JFK. The rich scent of lemon furniture polish rose from the wood, mingling with the heady scents of red roses, white carnations, and blue irises—the bouquet Francine had brought in this morning in anticipation of victory.

The scent of the flowers provoked the first tears. He hadn't breathed in that scent since Victoria's funeral, when the White House had practically reeked of roses and the sharp tang of tropical plants. Sitting motionless at his desk, Sam breathed in the sickly sweet smell and heard his heart break. It was a small, sharp sound, like the snapping of a twig underfoot.

He stared at his reflection in the polished wood and felt the touch of cold hands upon his heart, slowly twisting the life from it. Bill Blackstone and his cronies would soon control this room, this government, this beloved, misguided country. People from all fifty states would follow Blackstone into an era of license, tossing traditional values and ethics aside as easily as they disposed of plastic cutlery and aluminum soft drink cans. Virtue and honor and duty—thousands of Americans had died for those ideals on the shores of Normandy, in the jungles of Vietnam, and in the burning sands of the Middle East. But those ideals and those Americans meant nothing to Blackstone or the giddy group that would ride his coat-tails into power.

Would the country even realize what they were rejecting? Sam wasn't foolish enough to think he was any great treasure, but he stood for qualities that had fallen into public disfavor. He represented the old days, when truth and honor were more valuable than gold, and a man's reputation was the most precious thing he could own. He stood for responsibility, for truth and right in a world gone wrong—and the voters had just demonstrated how out of touch he really was.

Overcome with loss, Samuel Stedman lowered his head into his hands and wept for what might have been.

CHAPTER TWENTY-NINE

Brussels
0615 hours
Wednesday, November 8

MICHAEL AWAKENED AS IF SLAPPED FROM SLEEP BY AN INVISIBLE HAND. THE GRAY light of dawn seeped from the edges of the window blind, and across the room, the rabbi still snored softly on his cot. Michael turned onto his stomach and punched his pillow, but a current of energy pulsed through his mind, assuring him that sleep would be impossible.

He rose from his cot, took a moment to stretch, then slipped into a pair of jeans he'd tossed over a chair. Leaving the rabbi asleep, he crept out of the room, then walked silently through the kitchen, not wanting to make any noise that might alarm Devorah. She had been up late the night before, plowing through books on the Romanov dynasty and Russian history.

The rabbi joked that he had no sooner packed his books than Devorah unpacked them, but over the past few days her research had illuminated one of their suspicions. The huge diamond in the center of the Romanov tiara had disappeared during the revolution of 1917. The jeweled body of the crown remained in the Moscow State Armory, but the fabulous center diamond had undoubtedly been cut into a dozen smaller stones and sold on the black market. Devorah was convinced Gogol sought a diamond to replace the missing stone from the czarina's tiara.

Yawning, Michael moved past the cardboard boxes stacked on the floor, then pushed aside the heavy curtains at the front window. Outside, the lights of Brussels shone like diamonds in the twilight, and a police car prowled the Rue de Blaes. Within an hour, Brussels would fully awaken.

Raking his hair out of his eyes, he slipped into a chair at the oak table and reached for his laptop. He punched the power on and yawned again as the screen flickered to life, then he reached for a knitted afghan and tossed it over his bare shoulders. Despite the steady hiss of the steam radiator against the wall, the apartment was chilly.

Hunching forward like an old woman under her shawl, Michael waited for his modem to check for e-mail, then he lifted his chin as a message from Daniel filled the screen:

Michael:
   This is a dark day, buddy. Have you seen the papers? Stedman lost the election.
   Lauren and I are still in mourning.
   Later,
   D.

Michael stared blankly at the screen, then brought his fist down on the oak table, not even feeling the impact. How could this have happened? Were the American people really so foolish? How could they prefer a California playboy to a man who had literally given everything he held dear in the service of his country?

He shivered from a cold that had nothing to do with the chill in the apartment, then drew the afghan closer around him. He wanted to awaken Devorah and share this terrible news, but she wouldn't understand. Though she often spoke of Stedman with respect, she didn't know the man. She had never seen his eyes burn with compassion for Israel or heard the intensity of his voice when he spoke of America's future.

And Stedman hadn't trusted *her* with the task of safeguarding national interests in the face of a Russian-Arab military coalition. He had trusted Michael.

Michael swallowed hard as a sharp pang of sorrow pierced his heart. What was he supposed to do now? He was in Brussels on Stedman's behalf; for the last month he'd been working to fulfill Stedman's orders. What would become of those orders when William Blackstone took office?

Michael knew Blackstone wouldn't allow him to continue his mission. He'd be called home immediately, he and any other American servicemen working in the Middle East. The Sixth Fleet would be pulled out of the

Mediterranean, and the Americans stationed at NATO bases brought home, probably with great hurrahs and celebration.

But Blackstone was not president yet.

Michael leaned toward the laptop and began to type, letting the afghan fall from his shoulders. He addressed an e-mail to the president, then routed it through Daniel's secure ISP.

Dear Mr. President:

Words cannot convey the sorrow I'm feeling at this moment. But you should know, sir, that we are making progress here. Our base inspections have been postponed, as seemed prudent after the Knesset situation, but we are gaining new insight into the man who seems to be heading the Russian charge.

Unless directed otherwise, sir, I will continue to work at the task you sent me to perform. We are not finished yet. We shall keep up the fight and remain vigilant.

Sincerely,

Capt. Michael Reed

He encrypted the message with Daniel's code, then sent it off with a series of double clicks. Daniel would make certain Stedman received it.

Leaning back in his chair, Michael wrapped the afghan about his shoulders again, then looked toward the brightening window. The newspaper outside the door undoubtedly told the full story of the election, but it would be written in French. Even if it included an English translation, Michael knew he wouldn't have the heart to read it.

-0100111100-

Michael, Devorah, and Rabbi Witzun left Brussels two weeks after the American election. The rabbi took an apartment in the Orthodox section of old Jerusalem, not far from where Devorah's father lived. Michael stopped to check on the rabbi the day after their arrival, and Witzun seemed blissfully happy. "The Master of the universe has blessed me above all I could ask," he told Michael. "I am awaiting his pleasure with great joy."

Now that the Knesset hostage situation lay safely buried in history,

Michael and Devorah planned to continue their work of inspecting the Israeli military bases. Though Michael still operated under the pretense that his visit was nothing more than an ordinary liaison mission, he was certain the entire world now knew that Russia and a host of Arab nations were preparing for war. Though the Russian ambassador to the United Nations insisted that the Russian military was merely engaged in training operations, any country with a spy satellite could see that Russia had begun to mobilize her troops. Furthermore, any thinking person with access to a newspaper knew that Russia and her Arab allies had presented a resolution against Israel to the UN Security Council. The debate was raging hotly among the fifteen-member council, and the resolution would be put to a vote after every member nation had been presented with an opportunity to speak.

Michael felt a sourness rise from the pit of his stomach when he picked up a *Jerusalem Post* in the hotel lobby and read the list of current Security Council members. Most of the nine rotating members were traditionally Muslim countries and would be certain to vote in support of Russia's resolution against Israel. A resolution to order military enforcement action could not proceed, however, if vetoed by any one of the five permanent Security Council members—Russia, the United Kingdom, France, China, or the United States. As he folded his paper, Michael prayed that at least the American ambassador would have the strength to resist Russia's resolution.

Devorah picked him up outside the hotel. From the way her mouth flattened into a grim line when she saw the paper tucked under his arm, Michael knew she had read the same article. They spoke little as she drove to the Palmachim Air Base, situated in central Israel.

Michael knew that Palmachim was Israel's main helicopter base. A row of AH-64 Apaches, Hughes Defenders, and AH-1 Cobras stood in an orderly row on the flight line, well-maintained and on alert. A corps of Sikorsky and Bell choppers stood ready to transport troops and equipment if needed in an assault, medevac, or rescue mission.

"You're not writing anything in your notebook," Devorah remarked as they exited the last hangar and moved toward the parking lot.

"I don't need to." Michael turned away, hiding a thick swallow in his throat. What was the point? Israel's days were numbered and so were

Samuel Stedman's. Michael was only going through the motions here, fulfilling a promise made long before the growling Russian bear began to arouse his neighbors.

"I forgot." Devorah lightened her voice, as if deliberately choosing to ignore the ominous cloud that loomed over them. "I keep reminding myself that you have a photographic memory."

He stopped suddenly and turned to face her. "It's not photographic, but it's pretty darned good."

The wind whipped past them, roaring like the blood in Michael's ears. Devorah held his gaze while she reached up and pulled the windblown curls from her face. "So tell me what you'll remember, Michael. What memories will you take with you when you leave Israel?"

She had to raise her voice to be heard over the wind, but Michael could hear the gentleness in her words. "What will I remember?" He locked his hands behind his back as his gaze traveled over her face and searched her eyes. "I'll remember the way you're always tucking those curls behind your ear. And I'll remember that crazy broken turn signal in your car and the way you bite your lower lip when you disagree with me but don't want to speak up."

"But I always speak up." Her cheeks colored under his gaze. "You used to complain that I argued too much."

"I don't complain any more. And I don't think you enjoy arguing like you used to." They stood in the silence for a long moment, not speaking, not touching. An absurd thought ricocheted through his brain—if this were a movie, at this moment a symphony of violins would swell with the sighing wind as he drew her into his arms and kissed away the obstacles between them.

But this was real life. With an effort, Michael wrenched himself away from his unexplainable preoccupation with her arresting face. He gestured toward the car. "We'd best be going."

She answered in a broken whisper: "Roger that."

—0100111100—

Back at the hotel, Michael found an e-mail message from Daniel waiting on his computer:

Michael:

Can you be available for an on-line chat tonight? I've decided to call together some principals so we can learn from each other. Don't worry about security—we'll be encrypted. Meet us tonight at 3 p.m. EST—that'll be ten o'clock for you. Just link to the following URL and wait for us: http://ftpprenticetech.net/scramble/romperroom.

I guarantee you an interesting night.

BTW . . . Thomas Freeman, AKA "Shark" is one tough man to run down. But he says to tell you hello and to remind you that you owe him a favor. Says he was ready to throw himself on a shell one night when it landed near your camp in the desert, but the thing didn't explode . . . Should I follow up?

—D.

Michael stared at the computer screen, too surprised to do more than grunt at Daniel's news. So, Shark had seen a shell in that desert camp. So, if in the dream Janis was telling the truth . . .

He lifted his eyes to the ceiling, wondering just what God wanted of him. Though his reputation as a special operations man was nearly spotless, he wasn't exactly in the miracle business.

Settling back down to the task at hand, Michael typed a quick response and promised to be on-line at the appointed time, then exited his e-mail program and opened his word processor. He stared again at the report he'd been trying to write. Though the base inspections were now pointless, in Brussels he had realized that the Israelis desperately needed ASAT, anti-satellite technology. Unfortunately, not even the United States had fully implemented an ASAT program, despite the fact that the U.S. victory in Desert Storm was largely due to knowledge gleaned from satellite technology. While Saddam Hussein operated blindly, the Allied forces could see Iraqi troop movements via satellite. Iraq had no spy satellites, and Russia and France, who might have sold satellite imagery to Saddam, had complied with an American request to stop selling pictures of the Middle East.

But now Russia had firmly allied itself with Iraq and the other Arab nations, and Michael worried that Israel would greatly suffer for it. At least thirty countries now owned or operated orbiting satellites, many of which could be used for both civilian and military purposes. Any of

Israel's traditional enemies could purchase imagery from those revolving "eyes in the sky," virtually detailing any and all Israeli troop movements. But if Israel had the capability of intercepting and/or destroying hostile satellites, she would be able to reinforce her safety.

He placed his fingertips on the keys and struggled against a wave of frustration. Blackstone and the incoming political crew might never even read this report, much less give it any credence. But NSA file reports never died, and this one might be picked up by a congressman or senator who would wield the power to make a difference.

"In any future conflict, Israel must expect its adversaries to have spies in the sky," he wrote. "An ASAT program will be essential to protect IDF forces, counter hostile satellites, and achieve control of overhead space. In short, the United States should prepare to offer Israel an ASAT program, ASAP."

The phone rang in the middle of his thought, and Michael reached for it. "Yes?"

It was Devorah, wanting to know if he'd had dinner.

A sudden inspiration seized him as he considered her invitation. Why not invite her to sit in on Daniel's chat? He trusted her implicitly, and she might be able to add valuable insights to the conversation.

"No, I haven't," he said, pushing his laptop aside. "Are you cooking?"

He could almost see her blush. "It won't be anything fancy. But yes, I thought I might manage a couple of steaks. It's about time you visited my home."

Michael reached for a pencil. "Give me the address, and I'll hire a car and drive over. But be forewarned—it might be a late night."

She caught her breath in an audible gasp. "I don't know what you have in mind, Reed, but I have an early morning tomorrow."

"It's not what you think. Daniel's throwing an on-line party at ten o'clock, and I'd like you to go with me. I think you'll find it very interesting."

"Count me in," she said, her voice firm. "I would not miss it."

-0100111100-

Devorah lived in Ramla, a thoroughly modern city not far from the Lod Air Base and only a thirty-minute drive from Jerusalem. Michael enjoyed the drive. A brilliant sunset blazoned the western sky with shades of gold and crimson that contrasted exquisitely with the deepening azure of the view from the car's rear window.

A mezuzah hung on the doorpost outside Devorah's apartment, and as Michael waited for her to answer his knock he wondered if she or her father had placed it there. She was a thoroughly odd contradiction. To the world she appeared to be a modern female and capable soldier, but at times the veneer cracked and he could see traces of the devoutly Orthodox woman at the core of her being.

She opened the door, her face flushed and smiling. "Come in," she said, leading the way through a foyer as neat and uncluttered as her military personality. "The steaks are thawed, but I didn't want to put them under the broiler until you arrived."

Michael followed her through the hallway and glanced through an archway at the living room—an extremely functional space marked with bright splashes of color where she had tossed red and yellow pillows on the blue sofa. Framed photographs of Asher and her father stood on the table, along with a stack of leather-bound books.

She caught him glancing at the books. "Those belong to Rav Witzun," she said, motioning for him to follow her into the kitchen. "He's been quite generous with his library. I've never read so many interesting things."

Michael stepped into a large kitchen, decorated in cheerful shades of red and white. Apple wallpaper lined the walls; a red and white checked tablecloth covered the small table. The bright room suited her.

He set his laptop on the table, then sank into a chair. "How is the rabbi adjusting to Jerusalem?"

"Like a fish taking to water." She pulled two raw steaks from the refrigerator, then set them on a broiling pan. "He and my father spent the morning together. For three hours they debated the meaning of an obscure passage from the Talmud. They seem to deserve each other."

She bent to place the steaks in the oven, then glanced at him over her shoulder. "I hope you like steak. I didn't even ask."

"I like anything." Leisurely, he leaned back and stretched his long legs beneath the table. "A home-cooked meal sounds really great. I had almost forgotten that yesterday was Thanksgiving, and—well, that's a big holiday at home. Lots of food—turkey and cranberries and dressing."

She came toward him and leaned on the counter, compassion flickering in her eyes. "I'm sorry. If I had known you were homesick, I'd have done my best to find a turkey."

"Don't worry about it." He shrugged her concern away. "When I had a family, it was a big deal, but it's not so big anymore. My folks are gone, and the only family I have left is the navy." He swallowed against an unexpected constriction in his throat. "At this moment, the dearest people in the world to me are you and the rabbi. Funny, how living with people for a few weeks can draw you close."

"Yes . . . it's funny." Her eyes clouded for a moment with hazy sadness, then she pushed herself off the counter and moved to the sink. "Let me get the salad ready. Why don't you go into the living room and see if you can find a CD you like. I'll do the food; you handle the music."

By all means, let's keep busy. "Aye aye, Sergeant Major." Michael snapped a sharp salute, then moved into the living room to do her bidding.

-0100111100-

They had just finished clearing the kitchen dishes when the alarm on Michael's watch sounded. "We've got ten minutes," he said, picking up his laptop. "Can you point me toward your phone line? I'll get this thing set up and ready to go."

Wordlessly, Devorah pointed toward the kitchen phone. While she wiped the counter, he booted the laptop, logged onto the Web, then clicked on the URL Daniel had provided.

The Web page was unremarkable; it featured the logo of Prentice Technologies above an animated GIF of twinkling lights that spelled *Romper Room*. From the corner of his eye, Michael saw Devorah pick up a towel and dry her hands.

"That's cute," she said, peering over his shoulder. "But what's Romper Room?"

"An old American kids TV show." Michael scratched his jaw as he stared at the screen. "I barely remember it, but I know it was on right before *Captain Kangaroo.*"

Devorah tossed the towel on the edge of the sink, then pulled up a chair and sat next to Michael. At precisely 10:00 P.M., the Prentice Technologies logo began to scramble before their eyes.

"Amazing," Devorah said, leaning close enough for him to smell her perfume.

Against his better judgment, Michael reached up and lightly fingered a loose tendril of hair on her cheek. "I'll have to tell Daniel you're here."

Her earnest eyes sought his. "I'm sure he'd appreciate that."

Michael grinned as a tinny strain of music played over the speakers. An instant later, a cartoonish Dudley DoRight character filled the screen, then shrank to a smaller size, the head ridiculously large compared to the pencil-thin body. Behind the first character, Michael could see a row of cartoon character icons, each labeled with a name and a city.

The music stopped, and a cartoon balloon materialized above Dudley's head. A word appeared and filled the balloon. "Greetings."

Devorah stared at the screen with an expression of amused wonder. "Is this guy serious?"

"Oh yeah."

The balloon filled again, with a liquid stream of words that lingered a moment, then disappeared as another phrase took its place. "Thanks for joining us tonight. I suppose I should introduce all of you to each other."

The Dudley DoRight cartoon character pivoted and pointed toward the first icon, a bearded figure that reminded Michael of Colonel Sanders of Kentucky Fried Chicken fame. "Joining us from the U.S. is Sam."

Obeying a hunch, Michael typed "Welcome, Sam," then grinned when the words appeared in a balloon over Beetle Bailey's head.

Devorah laughed and pointed to the picture of the freckle-faced soldier with a cap on his head. "That's you?"

"I guess so." Michael rested his chin in his hand and grinned at the screen. The icon who had presented his words was identified as "Mike, in transit."

Devorah laughed as the others followed Michael's example and typed greetings. Dudley DoRight lifted his hands in mock horror. "Hold on, buckaroos, we're not ready to chat willy-nilly just yet. Let me finish the introductions."

Dudley pointed toward the second icon, a scratchy representation of a girl who resembled Lucy from the Peanuts comic strip. "This is Alanna, from Moscow. She's a little nervous."

The Alanna character lowered her eyelids in a demure pose, then her balloon filled: "Hello. I'm so glad to know I'm not alone."

"Next, we have Mike, who never knows where he'll be tomorrow," Dudley said, gesturing toward Beetle Bailey. Michael lifted a brow, grateful that Daniel hadn't given away his position. All of these descriptions and locations, in fact, were extremely vague. Though Michael strongly suspected that Sam might be Samuel Stedman himself, he had no way of knowing if Daniel had convinced the president of the United States to join in an on-line cartoon chat.

"Hey," Michael typed, "I have a guest with me tonight. I've told you about her, and she's eager to listen in."

Dudley's head zoomed toward the screen, blocking everyone else from view. "Would that be Debbie the cheerleader?"

"It would."

"Cool."

Dudley shrank back down to size and went on to introduce two other characters, Eli from Israel, and Jacob from Brussels. Daniel had chosen a grinning bulldog to represent Eli and a smiling Fred Flintstone to represent Jacob.

Devorah pointed toward Fred Flintstone. "Do you think Jacob could be Rav Witzun? We know the rabbi was in touch with Daniel in Brussels."

"Could be." Michael leaned back and rubbed his jaw, wondering how Daniel had managed to fashion this little fraternity. He glanced at Devorah. "Any idea who Eli is?"

She bit her lower lip. "Could be anyone—someone in the military, or even in the prime minister's cabinet." She snorted softly. "For all I know, it could be the prime minister himself."

"If it was safe for us to know, Daniel would have given us a clue."

Calling upon the magic of computer codes and cyberspace, Dudley DoRight waved his arm and the scene changed to a conference room. The animated cartoon characters were now seated around a large table, and Michael grinned in disbelief when he saw that they were blinking and nodding their heads just as real people might. He pointed to the screen when he realized that a new character had joined the group. The nameplate on the table before her read, *Deb, Mike's friend.*

Devorah giggled. "That's me? Who in the world am I supposed to be?"

Michael's mouth twitched with amusement. "If memory serves me correctly, he's drawn you as Little Orphan Annie. And with your curly hair, it isn't a bad likeness."

He threw up his hands and leaned away from her, certain she would throw a punch, but the activity on the computer screen drew their attention. Dudley folded his stick-figure arms and nodded toward the bulldog, the contact in Israel. "Eli, why don't we start with you? Tell the others what you've been telling me."

Every cartoon head turned toward the bulldog, who stood and leaned his paws on the roughly sketched conference table. "Intelligence confirms that the Russian army is mobilizing. The Russian navy has spent the last six months refurbishing the fleet at ports in the Black Sea, and infantry troops have begun to move southward from Moscow. Already there are reports of Russian troops bivouacking in the Caucasus Mountains."

"What does it mean?" The Alanna character spoke up, her cartoon balloon flooding with words. "The Russian people know nothing of this. Though we hear much about the purge of Jews taking place in Moscow, there have been no reports of war, and nothing in the newspapers . . . but I read only the English translation."

Michael propped his elbow on the table and rested his chin in his palm, trying to imagine whom Daniel had enlisted in Moscow. Was Alanna an American news correspondent? The ambassador's wife? A missionary?

"May I speak?" The Jacob character, wearing Fred Flintstone's saber-tooth tiger tunic, stood to address the group. "I know nothing of troop movements or the military, but I do know the ancient writings."

"That's Rabbi Witzun," Devorah announced, crossing her arms as she leaned back in her chair. "Who else could it be?"

Michael's mouth quirked with a wry smile. "Almost any rabbi in Europe. They all know the ancient writings."

"*I* know the ancient writings," Devorah countered, tugging on a rebellious dark curl. "And I'd wager my last shekel that we're listening to Rav Witzun."

The Jacob character continued: "The ancient writings foretell that Gog, a man, and Magog, a country, will invade the beloved land on the 24th day of Kislev, the anniversary of the laying of the foundation of the second temple. The Master of the universe, blessed be he, has already redeemed Jerusalem twice on that date. On the 24th day of the ninth month in 165 B.C.E. my people repulsed Antiochus Epiphanes, the Syrian who murdered more than 40,000 Jews and desecrated the holy temple."

Jacob turned his head to address those at the other end of the table. "On that date in 1917, after the Turks had held Jerusalem for 400 years, the Allied Expeditionary force approached the Holy City. The commander of that Allied force sent biplanes circling over the city, while his men dropped leaflets that read 'Flee Jerusalem.' Unknown to him, a Muslim prophecy had predicted they would not lose Jerusalem until a prophet of Allah told them to go. The Englishman who signed the leaflet was the First Viscount Allenby, a British field marshal. When the Muslims saw his name—Allen-by, or Allah-man, on the warning leaflet, they panicked and fled the city. The British never had to fire a shot. All this happened to fulfill the prophet Isaiah's words: 'The Lord Almighty will hover over Jerusalem as a bird hovers around its nest. He will defend and save the city; he will pass over it and rescue it.'"

"I've never heard that story," Michael whispered, his thoughts fiercely concentrated. "That's amazing."

"I believe," wrote Jacob, words furiously filling his balloon, "that the prophet Haggai has clearly revealed that God will deliver Jerusalem once again on the 24th day of Kislev. If any army comes against the beautiful city—Russian or Arab or European—God will intervene. On the 24th day of the 9th month, the Creator of the universe, blessed be he, will deliver his holy city."

Michael cocked an eyebrow at Devorah. "What is the twenty-fourth day of the ninth month on the English calendar?"

Devorah thought for a moment. "This year it will be December 21, the day before Chanukah."

"If this rabbi is correct—" Michael let out a long, low whistle—"that's less than four weeks away."

Devorah stared at the computer screen, her deep-brown eyes large and surrounded by dark shadows. "If that is the day God is supposed to *deliver* Israel, an attack could begin at any time." She looked at Michael, and some of the tension left her face. "*If* the rabbi is right. I'm not sure I place much faith in the ancient writings."

Michael turned back to the screen. Daniel believed in the ancient writings. Even now Dudley DoRight's balloon was flowing with almost poetic language: "'I will make known my holy name among my people Israel. I will no longer let my holy name be profaned, and the nations will know that I the Lord am the Holy One in Israel. It is coming! It will surely take place, declares the Sovereign Lord. This is the day I have spoken of.'"

Devorah looked at Michael, her brows slanting a question. "May I?"

"Be my guest. After all, you're seated at the table, too."

Devorah pulled the laptop closer and hit the question mark key. Instantly a balloon appeared above Little Orphan Annie's head.

Devorah bit her lip and began to type: "Friends—I respect all of you and your opinions. But if the full truth be known, the ancient writings also foretell that Israel's enemy will be ruled by a king, Armillus, who will be born from a union between Satan and the stone statue of a girl in Rome. Can this possibly be true? Of course not. So we should tread carefully, sorting fact from fable, and reality from religious rhetoric."

Jacob, or Fred Flintstone, leapt to his feet. "Twenty-five centuries ago, the Book of Zerubbabel refers to a false messiah by the name Armillus, also known by the name Romulus. I believe this man is Adrian Romulus, president of the European Union.

"Buckle your seat belt," Michael murmured, as several of the other characters lifted their hands, waiting for permission to speak. "It's going to be a bumpy night."

Dudley DoRight grinned on the computer screen, and for an instant Michael thought he could almost see a resemblance to the man he had met years before. Dudley's balloon filled as Daniel began to type: "After much study, I am certain, my friends, that the allied nations the Bible describes will shortly come against Israel. I have heard rumors that Adrian Romulus—no matter what his origin—has at least given tacit approval for this attack. The allied troops will be led by Vladimir Vasilievich Gogol, high commander of Russia's armies. If Scripture is true, and I believe it is, many nations will be allied with him, and Israel cannot stand against the advancing horde unless God himself delivers his people."

The conference room vanished, and the screen filled with a three-dimensional map of the Middle East. A small revolving star of David marked the location of Jerusalem, and a solid red star, directly to the north, pinpointed Moscow.

Daniel's parting words scrolled across the bottom of the screen. "Pray with me for the peace of Jerusalem, friends. My prayers and thoughts will be with each of you in the days ahead."

-0100111100-

Though Michael wasn't willing to accept all of Daniel's apocalyptic predictions, in the days that followed he often felt a dire sense of foreboding. He filed his report about the Israeli need for ASAT technology with his NSA superiors and sent a copy to the White House, knowing that the NSA would bury it and Stedman was virtually powerless. He and Devorah continued to visit and inspect military bases despite the fact that Daniel apparently believed Israel's preparation would mean little in the face of God's prophetic plan.

They visited the Jerusalem airport, Hertzlia Airfield, and Sde Dov Airport in Tel Aviv. They devoted an entire week to an inspection of Ramat David Air Base in northern Israel, and Michael noted with approval that all airmen at this base wore flight crew uniforms without rank insignia. Although all flight personnel proudly wore their squadron patches, not a single uniform exhibited any stars, bars, or wings. If one of these fliers were shot down, the enemy would not be able to tell if they had captured a colonel pilot or a sergeant flight engineer.

Though the Israeli Air Force would undoubtedly play a huge role in defending the country from a border attack, Michael knew the coastline was also vulnerable. He and Devorah devoted two weeks to inspecting the Israeli naval bases—Ashdod and Haifa on the Mediterranean, Eilat on the Gulf of Aqaba. At Haifa, Michael met several operators who were part of Flotilla Thirteen, the Israeli Navy's counterpart to the American SEALs. One of the commandos was quick to point out that though the Israeli Navy was small, during the Yom Kippur War of '73 it sank eight Arab FFLs and destroyed or evaded over seventy Arab Soviet-supplied SS-N-2 Styx missiles without losing a single Israeli vessel.

Michael couldn't help but be impressed with the pride and honor exhibited by nearly every member of the Israeli Defense Forces. They were driven, not by the latent patriotism or opportunism that prompted most Americans to serve in the armed forces, but by sheer necessity. Tiny Israel was surrounded on three sides by nations that either were or had been antagonistic, and she could not afford to drop her guard for one moment.

He and Devorah stood inside a new Elisra ECM/ESM electronic warfare suite on board a *Sa'ar V* and watched a demonstration of the new Israeli-designed Typhoon naval gun system. The gun, mounted on a patrol boat, employed a 25mm cannon and could be fired by remote control, thus reducing the risk to seamen manning it. With the added capabilities of the new Dolphin submarines and *Eilat/Sa'ar V* missile corvettes, Michael believed the Israeli Navy would confront her enemies with a remarkable demonstration of strength. But could she beat them back? If pressed, he would have answered no.

On every base, Michael noticed a subtle rise in tension. By the end of November the IDF was holding regular drills; on weekends the reservists reported for special training. In commanders' offices, lights burned twenty-four hours a day and empty coffee cups proliferated upon tables strewn with maps and field reports, yet life as usual continued on the streets of Jerusalem.

Michael marveled at the calm pace of life around him. Though intelligence reports indicated that the Russians were continuing to mobilize their troops, the average Israeli citizen seemed indifferent to the menace in the north. Michael had to remind himself that these people had not only lived through the constant threat of terrorism, but also Desert Storm, when Saddam Hussein rained Scud missiles upon them and the peril of biological or chemical weapons was an inescapable reality. As a people, the Israelis had grown used to the specter of annihilation.

By the beginning of December, the United Nations Security Council debate over Israel's continued military presence in the disputed territories had grown into a raging furor. While the Arab nations launched diatribe after diatribe against Israel for maintaining its military bases in the West Bank, the UN ambassador from Spain challenged the Russian representative with a series of harsh questions: "What does Israel possess that you could possibly want? Are you planning to invade the land for citrus fruits and vegetables? Your land is more productive than hers and nearly one thousand times as large!"

The representative from the United Kingdom lodged a rather gentle diplomatic protest, and the American ambassador to the United Nations,

Julia Chittendon, scolded Russia and the Arab nations for mobilizing their troops.

But on December 8, when the Security Council voted on the resolution to send troops against Israel to enforce the peace treaty and evacuate the disputed territories, all nine rotating members and the United Kingdom, France, China, and Russia voted in favor. Doubtless bowing to pressure from the incoming Blackstone administration, the American ambassador abstained. The resolution passed.

That night, Michael sat in a vinyl chair on the balcony of his hotel room and watched the city lights of Jerusalem begin to twinkle in the pinkish glow of the setting sun. His laptop sat on the small table next to him, and from the screen Daniel's last message shone in the faint light of the display:

> By now you've heard, of course. President Sam personally called Julia Chittendon, but she wouldn't listen. She's thinking now of Blackstone.
>
> Ezekiel saw it clearly. He wrote: "Sheba and Dedan and the merchants of Tarshish and all her villages will say to you, 'Have you come to plunder? Have you gathered your hordes to loot, to carry off silver and gold, to take away livestock and goods and to seize much plunder?'"
>
> The prophet called it, Michael. The other nations went through the motions of chiding Gog and Magog, but they cannot stop him. Time is growing short.

A breeze blew past Michael, bringing with it unintelligible voices from an overhead balcony. More shaken by the day's events than he cared to admit, he folded his hands on his bent knee and scanned the horizon. Ever since coming to Israel, he had hoped that something would change—Stedman would work a miracle in Congress or Daniel would pull another computer virus out of his bag of tricks and do something to stymie the Russian-Arab armies. But apparently no one could stop the storm blowing toward Israel from the north.

Daniel Prentice's prophetic ramblings seemed less incredible every day.

Far over the horizon, bright arteries of lightning pulsed in the sky, followed by a low throb of thunder. A thin ribbon of sweat wandered down Michael's back. A voice in his head whispered that he ought to feel honored to know he was Samuel Stedman's only hope in the Middle East, apparently the only military operative still working for Israel's safety. Though less than six weeks remained in Stedman's term, the president had not ordered him home. Michael interpreted the silence to mean that he was to continue acting on Stedman's behalf. He had no idea what he would be able to do if the Russians decided to move, but as long as he remained in Israel, he would do what he could. When Blackstone was inaugurated, Michael would almost certainly be recalled immediately.

Somewhere overhead a jetliner whispered through the cloudy sky. Looking up, Michael stared at the low clouds and thought of home. Those same clouds, hovering over a Maryland horizon, would bring snow, just as snow brought Christmas and fir trees, hot chocolate and mittens.

He bent his head, knowing that people at home were thinking more of Christmas and shopping than of Israel and the looming threat of war. Though there wasn't a Christmas tree or stocking to be found in Old Jerusalem, the Palestinians who occupied Bethlehem were delighted by the hordes of religious pilgrims who would soon flood the ancient shrines and fill their coffers with American dollars and Israeli shekels. The spirit of capitalism thrived even under the shadow of war.

But not even the thought of Christmas and Aunt Margo's pumpkin pie could entice Michael home this year. Devorah had told him that the latest intelligence reports showed continued Russian-Arab troop movement through the Caucasus, and Muslim revolutionaries were demonstrating on the streets in support of claiming Jerusalem for their own capital. Yasir Arafat's bizarre claims, scoffed at in years past, now seemed prophetic.

With a shiver of vivid recollection, Michael recalled seeing a 1998 video clip recorded by Palestinian Television. Standing before a cheering crowd, Arafat had proclaimed, "The battle for Jerusalem is a battle of life or death, life or death, life or death!" The mob erupted with shouts and the chattering sound of ululation, a sea of uplifted fists and rifles enforcing his prediction.

Soon, a nation's life or death would be decided on the sloping mountains of the Golan Heights, the geographic invasion route into Israel since biblical days. Asher Cohen would be among the men defending the nation, Rabbi Cohen and Rabbi Witzun would be among those praying for it. And Devorah . . .

Michael swallowed hard and wrapped his arms about himself. He had not intended to feel anything for Devorah but friendship and camaraderie. He had never considered himself a romantic man, and he didn't know what to do with the slender delicate thread that had formed between them and entwined their lives.

He closed his eyes and studied the memory of his last love. He and Janis had married soon after high school. While he served his country, their lives were a hopscotch quilt of days spent together and days spent apart. He had truly loved Janis, but with a feeling based upon affection and the exuberance of youth. That love would have deepened with the arrival of their child and the passage of time. If not for the bombing in Lebanon, he might have retired from the military and gone into the insurance business with Janis's father, carving out a quiet life in Roanoke, Virginia.

But God had allowed a tragedy . . . and Michael had remained in the military, surrendering himself completely to the job of hunting men. As a SEAL he had learned to shoot and scoot, to kill tangos without hesitation and move out before he had time to think about the death he was leaving behind. Even at the NSA, he had learned to remain detached from his work. He did his job and moved on when the job was done.

A cynical inner voice whispered that he should move on now. Why not? The United Nations had voted. Just as George Bush obtained UN approval to use American troops to force Iraq out of Kuwait, Gogol had just obtained the UN's blessing to use Russian and Arab troops to drive Israel out of the disputed territories. For the sake of her own survival, Israel would resist with every means in her power, possibly including nuclear weapons. This pleasant Jerusalem mountaintop might soon become a scorched wasteland . . . unless Daniel was right and God really cared about what happened to these contentious people.

Pensively, Michael looked out into the gathering darkness. He could go home, file his last report, congratulate the president on a brave attempt, and go to Aunt Margo's house for Christmas. Samuel Stedman would certainly understand, and Daniel would agree that Michael had done his job. But if he left now, he'd sacrifice precious weeks with Devorah.

He'd be leaving part of his soul behind if he left her now. She understood him. As part of the IDF's counterterrorist team, she had learned to live with the thrill of terror, to calm her heartbeat and wait for the striking moment. Like him, she had tasted fear, savored it, learned to use it. She had experienced that plane of heightened emotion only professional soldiers and daredevils ever reach, and she understood him like no other woman he had ever met.

He breathed deep and felt a stab of memory, a broken remnant of the dream he'd had before coming to Israel. He smiled, thinking about Janis and what she had said about his trip. *God saved you because he loves you, Michael. He's always had a plan for you, and the greatest part is yet to come.*

Was falling in love with Devorah Cohen part of God's plan? Michael knew her father wouldn't think so. And if he were supposed to accomplish some great thing in Israel, he still had no idea what it might be. Then again, perhaps a man's subconscious mind always imagined great things for him.

He snorted softly and rubbed his hand over his jaw. General Gogol's subconscious had certainly conjured up a grandiose and ambitious vision. Two weeks before, upon Russian President Chapaev's sudden death, Gogol had made the leap from minister of defense to president, overwhelmingly elected by the 178-member Council of the Federation and the 450-member State Duma. As powerful as Gogol's new position was, Michael suspected the wily general had far greater ambitions yet to fulfill.

"What's your secret, Gogol?" he murmured, resting his chin in his hand as the shades of night fell around him. "You make conquering the world look so easy."

Chapter Thirty

Moscow
2000 hours
Saturday, December 9

INSIDE THE CRENELATED WALLS OF THE KREMLIN, VLADIMIR STEPPED AWAY FROM the window of his new home, smoothed a wrinkle from his tuxedo shirt, and smiled at his reflection in the window. He and Alanna had been living inside the Presidium of the Supreme Soviet of Russia for nearly a week, yet still he sometimes wanted to pinch himself. Chapaev's removal had gone as planned; the old man had been so weak for so long that the people scarcely noticed his carefully scheduled demise. Still, Gogol insisted upon holding an elaborate state funeral inside the Cathedral of the Assumption. Long lines of mourners passed before the ebony casket, pausing long enough for the world's television cameras to note that Gogol's Russia would continue to honor the fallen ones of previous eras.

He drew a deep breath and thrust his hands behind his back, glorying in the grandeur of the mansion he intended to occupy until the end of his days. He had already planted his spies among the Duma and the Council; when he had eliminated the cancer of Israel once and for all, they would exalt his name to the skies. He would restore Russia to its deserved place as supreme among the nations. He would show them all that he was not just another man, another *president,* but one who deserved the title *Czar of all the Russias.*

He paused as yet another black limo pulled up outside the window. He had invited only a select group of influential people to be his guests this night, for this was a private, most special occasion. He lifted his head in satisfaction as he recognized the couple alighting from the car—American ambassador Horace Nance and his wife, Irene.

Vladimir pursed his mouth in resignation. Though he was not pleased

with the obstinate posture the Americans had taken during the recent
United Nations debate, at least their ambassador had not voted against his
resolution. He could forgive their abstention, particularly since Alanna
counted Irene Nance as a friend.

He lifted his hand and snapped his fingers, catching the attention of a
guard at the door. "See that all the guests are assembled in the ballroom,"
he told the man, pausing to adjust his white tie in the reflective window-
pane. "I will go find Madame Ivanova. The moment we enter the ballroom,
the orchestra is to play the national anthem."

The guard nodded stiffly. "Yes, Mr. President."

Vladimir found Alanna in her dressing room, as pale and beautiful in
this silver gown as she had been on the night he first saw her. He entered
softly and ran his hands over her bare arms, then smiled when he felt her
shiver. She looked up, her wide blue eyes meeting his in the mirror. "Am I
late, sweetheart?"

"It is time." He caught her hand and helped her from the vanity stool,
then carefully linked her arm through his. What an elegant beauty she was!
The dull politicians and ambassadors assembled in the hall would be
speechless with surprise at his announcement, but they would understand
his reasoning once they looked at his treasure. Alanna Ivanova possessed
an ideal sort of beauty, pure light and brightness. Her loveliness, combined
with his strength, would produce children fit for the throne of Russia,
kings deserving to rule the world.

"I should probably warn you, my love," he whispered as he led her out
of her dressing room, "but the group downstairs is rather small—only one
hundred people. These are the men who will be closest to me in the days
ahead; they are the ones who should know just how important you are to
me. That is why I invited them tonight."

She looked up, her blue eyes filled with shifting stars. "Is there something special about tonight?"

"Of course." He patted her hand. "Tonight is the night I announce our
impending marriage. After all, the president of Russia certainly should be
married to the love of his life."

He heard her quick intake of breath. "Married?"

"Of course, darling." He kept walking, pulling her through the ornate
outer chamber. "We will have a small wedding next Wednesday, nothing to

attract undue attention. A simple wedding now, a glorious coronation later. How would that please you?"

It was a simple question, but her head jerked up as though he had stabbed her with it. "Vladimir, you can't mean—" Her luminous eyes widened in astonishment. "I thought you were just joking, all this time—"

"I never joke, darling. I mean every word I say." He turned to face her and took both her hands in his own. "When I have returned from the battlefront, Russia will change. The people are hungry for a strong leader, and I am ready to lead. Already I have planted the seeds of revolution. The land is being plowed, the stones removed and purged, the land tilled for growth. A new and fertile nation will rise from the broken soil, and Russia will be stronger than ever before. And you and I, love, will reign as czar and czarina over all the Russias."

Her eyes were as wide and blank as the windowpanes, as though the shock of surprise had shooed her wits away. A little alarmed, he reached up and cupped her cheek with one hand. "Alanna? Darling, you must look happy tonight. I know this may not be what you expected of your life, but destiny has brought us together. Your life is now entwined with mine."

Her mouth curved in a bland smile. "Of course, Vladimir. Whatever you say."

"You are a good girl." Vladimir pressed a kiss to her round cheek, then linked her arm through his again and led her out to meet their guests.

-010011100-

Alanna couldn't speak. Vladimir was leading her down a wide, carpeted hallway, yet his quick steps were no match for her pounding heart. All she could feel was anxiety like a balloon in her chest, swelling and swelling until it would surely burst.

Married! How could she marry him? She couldn't. She was already a prisoner, now locked even more securely within the thick walls of the Kremlin itself, but at least she had remained free in her own eyes, in the eyes of the law, in the eyes of God. But if she married him, she'd be his wife, his partner, his . . . *czarina?*

The fears that had been lapping at her subconscious suddenly crested and crashed. Gogol was a madman, a bloodthirsty tyrant, and she'd been so blind! Daniel had tried to warn her, Mrs. Nance had told her not to get too close, but she had allowed Gogol to woo her with luxuries and power and influence. What price would she pay for her foolishness? He was talking about *revolution.*

She bit her lip, resisting the urge to scream as panic rioted within her. Revolutions were wrought in blood; kings and queens and their innocent children were murdered solely for political reasons, and those who toyed with political power almost always paid a dear price. She hadn't meant for it to go this far! She had been waiting, obeying Daniel, hoping she could slip away when Vladimir left Moscow to join the Russian troops. If they were married, he would never let her get away.

She pressed her hand to her mouth, stifling a cry, and felt her fear intensify when Col. Oleg Petrov suddenly came around the corner.

"Mr. President." He snapped a salute and bowed. "I am glad I have caught you."

"Can it wait, Colonel?" Vladimir pressed his free hand over Alanna's, silently urging her to be patient. "We are on our way to join a very important party."

"It is news of Brussels, sir."

Vladimir's jaw tensed, and when he spoke again, he spoke in Russian. Alanna looked away, pretending not to understand, but an oddly primitive warning sounded in her brain.

Petrov spoke in Russian, too, in clipped sentences and staccato cadences. "The diamond cutter—we can't find him anywhere, and we've been searching for nearly two weeks. No one in Brussels knows where he has gone."

"The people at the bourse are bound to know."

"They say they do not—indeed, I can't find a single diamond merchant in the entire syndicate who has heard of a cutter called Yacov Witzun. He and the diamond are both missing."

Two deep red patches appeared on Vladimir's cheekbones, as though someone had slapped him on each side of his face. A stream of curses spewed from his mouth as his fist pounded the air, then he glared at Petrov. "Those filthy Jews are in league with one another! Of course they know who he is! They know *where* he is! They have conspired to mock the glory of Mother Russia!"

Petrov blanched. "At least we have not lost the money. We have not paid the bourse."

"Still, it is a matter of honor! Those Jews pride themselves on their integrity, and an agreed-upon sale is binding. They are doing this to mock me, and they will pay for this in blood." Breathless with rage, Vladimir lifted his arm again, and Alanna took a hasty half step back. His anger resonated through the hallway, and the power of it frightened her.

Petrov turned slightly and lowered his voice, murmuring words that were obviously designed to console or appease. Alanna shivered in the silence, fighting hard against the tears she refused to let fall. If she lost control now, all would be lost. Her only hope at escaping this nightmare was to find help and keep Vladimir under her power.

At last Vladimir drew a long breath, controlling the fury that had taken him. He reached out and took Alanna's arm again, then looked at Petrov, radiating disapproval. "Find another stone, another cutter, another bourse. See if you can find a diamond broker who is not a Jew! And do not worry yourself about the Jews in Brussels. We will take care of them and their kind . . . very soon."

He clenched his fist and squared his shoulders, somehow managing to tamp down his anger, but he was still breathing raggedly when he smiled down at Alanna. "A bit of bad news, love, but nothing to worry us. Shall we continue?"

He led her down the red-carpeted stairs, then swept her through the gilded arch that led to the ballroom. An orchestra began to play the stately Russian national anthem as they appeared in the doorway, and a sea of tuxedoed and sequined guests burst into polite applause. Alanna looked around the crowd, as dazed as a deer caught in a hunter's spotlight, until her gaze fell upon a familiar face: Mrs. Irene Nance.

Somehow, the kindly face of the ambassador's wife supported Alanna through the nightmare of Vladimir's announcement and an endless chorus of congratulations.

After an hour woven of eternity, Vladimir released her to mingle with the women while he joined the men. Alanna smiled stiffly at Russian wives until she thought her face would break, then she found Mrs. Nance and pulled the woman into a recessed window nook. "You've got to help me," she whispered, casting a false smile over Irene's shoulder as she waved to a couple watching her from the dance floor. "I can't marry him. I didn't even know what he was planning until tonight."

Mrs. Nance's brows nearly met her hairline. "Oh, dear. I thought—we thought—well, never mind what we thought."

A tide of uncertainty washed through the woman's eyes, and Alanna was certain Mrs. Nance saw the same dark currents in her own. "Please, Mrs. Nance, you've got to help me. If I could get to the embassy, you could help me get back home, couldn't you?"

The sharp look in Irene's eyes pierced Alanna's soul. "We assumed you had fallen in love with him. When time passed and you continued to see him—"

"I've been a virtual prisoner for months." Alanna nodded pointedly toward the guards stationed at each entrance. "I'll admit that I took things too far, but I was lonely and—well, selfish. But when Vladimir instigated the purge, I knew how dangerous he really was. By then I couldn't get away. Daniel was going to try and help me—"

"You're still in touch with Daniel?"

"Yes. I'd have gone crazy without him and Lauren." She paused to smile at another couple, a heavyset man and his wife who were staring at her with frank curiosity.

She lowered her gaze and met Mrs. Nance's eyes. "Please. I'm in over my head, and I don't know how to get out."

A tremor touched Mrs. Nance's smooth, elegant face. "I'll help you if I can, dear. But I think it's time you turned to someone more powerful than me."

Alanna nodded. "I'm trying. But Daniel's not here, and I don't know what he can do from a distance—"

"I wasn't talking about Daniel. I was talking about God."

Alanna snapped her mouth shut, stunned by the woman's answer. *God?* What did God have to do with anything?

"Darling!"

Vladimir's voice broke into her reverie, and she could only nod at the ambassador's wife. "I will try to help if I can," Mrs. Nance whispered, patting Alanna's hand as Vladimir approached. "And you can always talk to Daniel and Lauren. They know that God is orchestrating this situation. He cares about you, Alanna."

She stared, speechless, as Mrs. Nance glided away and Vladimir took her place.

-0100111100-

While Vladimir snored on the pillow next to her, Alanna stared at the domed ceiling and wondered how many other Russian presidents had slept in this room. The Presidium was huge, with over a dozen chambers that could function as bedrooms, but Vladimir had chosen this, the grandest one, for her. Tonight he had told her that in just three days, after their wedding, it would be hers for life.

She turned her head. Asleep, the taut skin of his face had slackened against the pillow, and he looked strangely old. His hand, thick and powerful, lay pressed against his pillow, while the other stretched across the sheet as if reaching for her.

She slid away from him, slipping silently across the satin sheets until her toes touched the cold floor. A crystal nightlight burned above her bureau, and the luminescent numerals of the clock glowed through the darkness: 3:53.

She stood and reached for her robe, then shivered as she knotted the belt around her waist. She had no idea what time zone Daniel and Lauren Prentice were living in, if they were awake or asleep. But she knew she desperately needed to talk to them.

Leaving Vladimir asleep, she tiptoed to the outer room. Several boxes of her personal belongings lay stacked along the wall, and her laptop computer lay hidden inside one of them. She hadn't used it since the move, not trusting the phone lines in this public government building, but perhaps no one would suspect a single encrypted call.

She lifted the laptop from the box, pushed away the torn plastic wrapping, and untangled the telephone and power lines. A silvery rectangle of moonlight streamed in through the tall window between the two sofas, lighting the coffee table but leaving the wall in darkness. She ran her hand along the plastered surface, then sighed in relief when she found a pair of outlets. Working quickly, she plugged in the computer and the modem, then sank to the floor in front of the sofa and tapped the power on.

Almost too late, she remembered that the computer would beep as the operating system booted up. She grabbed a pillow and held it over the machine, muffling the sharp sound, then let the pillow fall to the floor. She clicked on a series of keys, activating Daniel's encryption program, then sent a query:

> Hello? Anyone up and awake? I need to talk.
> Texas.

She nearly jumped out of her skin when the computer beeped with a reply. Her heart thumped painfully in her chest as she looked toward the open doorway that led to the bedroom, but nothing stirred in the darkness beyond. He still slept.

She looked down at the computer and saw Lauren's reply:

> Hi, Texas. Daniel's asleep, but I'm here. How can I help?
> L.

Alanna's fingers flew over the keys, keeping pace with the erratic rhythm of her pulse.

> I really wanted to talk, Lauren, but I can't have this thing beeping every time you post a message. V. is in the next room asleep, and we're no longer living at the hotel. He's moved us to the Presidium, and I'm scared to death. He wants to marry me, in just three days. I don't see how I can, but I don't see how I can get out, either. Help!

She clicked the Send key, then picked up the sofa pillow, ready to smother any sound the computer might make. To her surprise, the computer didn't beep, nor did Lauren send an answering e-mail. Instead, a small window opened at the bottom of the screen, and Lauren's words filled a text box in an easy, conversational pace.

"Why don't we do it this way? Daniel's figured out how we can chat in real time. It's an encrypted program, so you don't have to worry about being picked up."

Alanna pressed her hand to her chest and sighed as her pulse began to slow. Operating on instinct, she moved the cursor to the text box, clicked, and began to type a reply: "Thank you, Lauren. I am going crazy here. What am I supposed to do? I thought I could slip away when Vladimir goes to lead the army, but if I'm married, I'll never be able to get away. If the security around me is tight now, I shudder to think what it will be like if I am the Russian president's wife."

"Do you know when he is leaving to join the army?"

"No, but the wedding is set for next Wednesday, so he'll be in Moscow at least until then. He won't give me details about the military operation. He just keeps saying it's a routine operation to force the Israelis to keep the terms of their peace accords. More frightening, he keeps insisting that things will be different when it's over. I never knew *how* different until tonight. He actually thinks he can convince the legislative houses to name him *czar!*"

"Daniel has a friend who suspected as much. Gogol is more dangerous than most people believe. But he will meet the end he deserves, Alanna. Scripture tells us he will not survive this military advance against Israel. You must have faith. Deliverance is coming."

A shock wave slapped at Alanna. She would never have believed it possible that a woman as bright and beautiful as Lauren Prentice would use the Bible for foretelling the future—just as she couldn't believe Gogol was mentioned in it.

She shook off Lauren's absurd comment and continued her previous train of thought. "I've never felt more uncertain of the future. What if Gogol's government falls out of favor? I've read too much Russian history to think everything's going to be OK. Rival governments tend to take a dim view of the competition's family members. If Gogol dies, his grieving widow, me, will pay the price for everyone he has offended during his rise to power. I want out, but I don't know how to get out. Security is even tighter at the Presidium than it was at the hotel."

"I'm thinking. OK, here's an idea. Why don't you just tell Gogol the truth? Tell him you don't want to marry him. Tell him you're not suited for political life or that you miss America too much. Tell him you've had second thoughts."

"You don't tell Gogol anything he doesn't want to hear. Trust me. Tonight his top aide told him something about a diamond they couldn't find, and I thought Vladimir was going to take the guy's head off."

"You could always tell him the truth, about who you are. About your mother."

Alanna stared at the computer screen, not certain she had read the words correctly. Had Lauren lost her mind? She knew about the purge against the Jews in Russia, about Vladimir's anti-Semitism. "I can't, Lauren. He'd never forgive me. He loves me, I think, but he loves his own ideals more. And his hatred of the Jews is irrational. It springs from some place inside him I've never reached."

The screen remained blank for a moment, then another thread appeared: "Alanna, have you ever considered the possibility that God brought you to this place for a reason? Daniel and I prayed long and hard about approaching you all those months ago, and we've been praying for you ever since. We really believe God has his hand on your life, that he wants to draw you close to him."

Alanna groaned and raked her hand through her hair. Was God the life preserver people routinely tossed to drowning women? Tonight Mrs. Nance had uttered the same sentiments, but Alanna still couldn't see how drawing close to God was going to get her away from Vladimir Gogol.

"I don't mean to be disrespectful, Lauren, but God and I aren't really on speaking terms. I haven't even thought about him since I was a little kid in Sunday school. So I'd rather come up with a realistic way I can get out of Moscow. I was thinking that I could go out with my bodyguard tomorrow and visit the American embassy. They'd have to grant me sanctuary, right? Of course, I don't know how I'd get from the embassy to the airport, but if I stayed long enough, there's always a chance Vladimir will forget me."

She knew that idea was hopeless even as she typed the words. Elephants never forgot, and Gogol never forgave. She'd shrivel up and die in the American embassy before he would call off his spies and allow her to go home.

"I have an idea, Alanna, and I hope you'll try it. God promises to draw close to us if we draw close to him, and one way to do that is through fasting and prayer. For the next three days, I'm going to abstain from food so I can pray for you with no distractions. You can do the same, if you like, and together we will beg God to show you what you should do. Everything I have seen in my life has taught me to trust God for all I cannot see. I have faith. You can find faith, too."

Alanna stared at the screen, her mind a crazy mixture of hope and fear. Going to God with an empty stomach was supposed to produce what—a miracle? She tapped her fingers on the keys. Maybe the idea wasn't as ludicrous as it sounded. She certainly wouldn't have much of an appetite in the next few days. She could always tell Vladimir she was experiencing pre-wedding jitters.

"OK, Lauren. I'll pray. For courage and a way out. And I'll try to check my e-mail when I can, but I can't leave the computer plugged in here. I don't know who's monitoring the phone lines."

"That's fine, A. Daniel and I will be praying that God will show you a way home. And remember, dear, a wise man once said, 'Unless there is within us that which is above us, we shall soon yield to that which is about us.' Look up to God, dear one. He will lift you up."

Alanna shut down the program and unplugged the modem, then stared for a long moment at the darkened screen. She had never gone without food in her life, not even during the days of her college poverty. Since childhood, she had never prayed for anything more substantial than help on an unexpected pop quiz.

She didn't know what prayer would accomplish, but she had just agreed to stake her life on it.

Chapter Thirty-one

1100 hours
Wednesday, December 13

"You look beautiful, Madame."

Alanna stared at her reflection in the mirror and automatically reached up to adjust the edge of the lace veil framing her face. The servant was only being polite, for the mirror clearly revealed the smudges of fatigue under her eyes and the lines of strain bracketing her mouth. For three days she had lived in dread of this hour, for three days she had done her best to think about God and what he might have wanted to do with her life. And even as her stomach shriveled and her energy depleted, Alanna's soul cried out for meaning and found . . . memories. Of childhood Sunday mornings spent in a small wooden church, of stories and songs that had nothing to do with her present situation.

She and the servant were standing inside a small stone room, one of many in the Cathedral of the Annunciation, the smallest of the three churches inside the Kremlin walls. She was wearing an elegant white satin gown, trimmed at the cuffs and neck with white Russian sable. She had pulled her hair back into a severe bun, but the veil softened her appearance. Vladimir, who had just left the room, had kissed her cheek and told her she made a beautiful bride.

He and a priest stood now in the sanctuary outside, waiting for Colonel Petrov, who was to act as a witness to the service that would join them in the bonds of holy matrimony. Alanna's mouth twisted at the thought. The word *bonds* would certainly apply to matrimony with Vladimir, but there was nothing *holy* about it.

Over the past three days, while Vladimir had huddled with Petrov and other commanders of his army, she had struggled to recall the things she had learned as a child in Sunday school. The first day of her fast she could remember nothing more than the fact that they had listened to stories enacted on a flannelgraph. By the second day, she was able to recall snatches of a story she had learned, a tale about three Hebrew boys who had been tossed into a fiery furnace because they would not bow down to an idol, and how God had sent Jesus himself to spare them from the flames. By the third day of her fast, when her body so yearned for food that even ice cubes seemed to take on a distinctive taste, she could remember the doughy scent of the Sunday school teacher's paste and the little snub-nosed scissors they used to cut out pictures of those brave Jewish boys. A song she had not thought of in years came back to her, ruffling through her mind like wind on the River Moskva: *Jesus loves me, this I know* . . .

The little servant stepped back and bobbed her head, presenting the mirror with a thin, starved-looking face, dominated by faded blue eyes. "Are you ready, Madame?"

Alanna turned from the mirror. "I think we are waiting for Colonel Petrov."

The woman nodded and clasped her hands. "I could go see if he has arrived—"

"Wait." Alanna put out her hand, unwilling to be left alone. She lowered her hand and gave the woman a timid smile. "Are you a Christian?"

A tiny flicker of shock widened the woman's eyes. "Madame?"

"A Christian." Alanna flung up her hand and gestured at the elaborate religious paintings on the walls around them. "A follower of Christ."

The woman retreated from Alanna's gaze and tried on a smile that seemed a size too small. "Yes, Madame. I am."

Alanna nodded slowly. So even here, in the heart of Moscow and the heart of the Kremlin, Christianity still existed. Though the Soviets had tried to stamp it out, people stubbornly continued to believe in miracles, in a God who rescued men from fiery furnaces.

A note of wistfulness stole into the woman's expression. "And you, Madame Ivanova? Do you belong to the Lord?"

The gentle question snapped at Alanna's conscience, making her flinch. She closed her eyes, her thoughts filtering back to the days when she had visited a sunlit classroom with wooden floors, small chairs, and a flannelgraph on an easel. The teacher, a woman with soft, wrinkled hands, had told them that the same Jesus who saved Shadrach, Meshach, and Abednego would come into their hearts to stay. All they had to do was ask and believe, and he would keep his promise.

Alanna had lifted her hand, she had bowed her head and prayed. And afterwards she had felt a warm glow flow through her, a sensation more comforting than her daddy's arms and her mother's lap.

Daniel and I prayed long and hard about approaching you. . . . We really believe God has His hand on your life, that He wants to draw you close to Him.

Alanna sank slowly into a chair, heedless of her gown and veil. The Holy Spirit of God had entered her heart that day in childhood, when she had willingly placed her life in his hands. But somewhere along the way she took her eyes off him. She stopped going to church, stopped praying, even stopped remembering.

But God had not forgotten her. He had led her to Daniel and Lauren and to this moment—but for what?

"I'm trying to have faith," she whispered, staring at her empty hands. "But it's not easy."

"Madame, may I tell you a story?"

Alanna looked up, surprised by the request. "Of course."

The woman's blue eyes softened. "I have heard it said that England's King George once had a dream. In the vision, he asked the angel who stood at the gate of the new year for a light, so he could tread safely into the unknown."

She paused, her eyes brimming with tenderness. "The angel replied, 'Go out into the darkness and put your hand into the hand of God. That shall be to you better than light and safer than a known way.'" She reached out and touched Alanna's arm, her hand trembling with eagerness. "That is all the faith you need, Madame. Just enough to place your hand in God's."

Alanna closed her eyes and considered the woman's words. Vladimir would say that faith was nothing but an illogical belief in the improbable, but he believed in nothing greater than himself. She had once felt the love of God, and she had seen how he worked in the lives of men and women . . .

A loud booming sound echoed through the spacious chamber outside, and the servant rose to peer into the hall. "Madame! The colonel has arrived, and the president is gesturing for you!"

Moving on wooden legs, Alanna allowed herself to be pulled up, then accepted the bouquet of white roses pressed into her hand. Fussing and clucking, the servant opened the door and stepped back to fluff the full skirt of the wedding gown as Alanna moved through the doorway and into the narthex.

On cue, the organist began to play a stately processional. Alanna hesitated for a moment, then dropped her bouquet to her side. She could not marry Vladimir Gogol. She would speak to him face to face and tell him she had been wrong all along. She could not give him her life when years before she had given it to another.

The aisle, flanked by empty wooden pews, stretched out before her like a crimson highway and ended at the altar. An extravagantly robed priest stood directly before the Communion railing, and beside him, in full uniform, Gogol waited. He held his hands clasped before him in an expectant pose, but one corner of his mouth dipped with frustration as Colonel Petrov and another officer hurried forward from a side door.

"Mr. President, I must speak with you." The brim of a hat hid Petrov's face, but the splinters of ice in his voice were tipped with poison.

Alanna heard the menace in his tone. For a fleeting instant she wondered what had upset him, then she strode forward. In her careless forward rush the rose bouquet slapped against a pew; she glanced back and saw a carnage of petals strewn over the ruby-red carpeting. Impulsively, she tossed the bouquet onto an empty seat and grabbed up the fullness of her gown in order to quicken her pace.

Gogol's eyes widened at this display of haste, then his expression clouded in anger as he turned to face the colonel. "What is it, Petrov? Surely this can wait!"

"No, sir," Petrov answered, and Alanna felt the heat of the colonel's gaze as she hurried down the aisle. "We did a Web search, sir, hoping to complete a biography on this woman."

Taking a deep, unsteady breath, Alanna took the final two steps, then stood before Petrov and Gogol. She felt an instinctive stab of fear as Petrov pulled a folded sheet of paper from his coat pocket and brandished it before Gogol's eyes. "This is a page of Holocaust survivors, General. This woman's name is among those listed."

Alanna struggled to steady her erratic pulse. "That's crazy. I'm not a Holocaust survivor. I'd have to be at least sixty years old!"

Vladimir took the page, then pulled his glasses from his pocket and studied it for a moment. He glanced at her face once, as if her picture were somehow imprinted on the page, then lowered the paper and calmly removed his glasses. "The page is a listing of Holocaust survivors and their descendants." He threw the words at her like stones. "You are listed as being the daughter of Esther Honig and the granddaughter of Holocaust survivor Ethan Honig."

Alanna stared at the floor, feeling as though her breath had been cut off. The priest, obviously uncomfortable, stepped back, leaving them alone in the heavy silence.

"Can you tell me this is a lie?"

Alanna closed her eyes. She could tell him anything—but why should she? Lying would only deplete the last of her self-respect. She had lied to him for months, and with each false smile she had sunk more deeply into the quagmire of evil and hostility surrounding him.

God, help me.

Petrov edged forward, his blue eyes widening in accusation. "We also found a computer in her things. There are encrypted message files on the hard drive. She has been communicating with someone."

The muscles in Gogol's face tightened into a mask of rage. Alanna took an involuntary step backward, then clenched her fist in the fullness of her skirt.

"Is this true?" He gave her a killing look. "With whom have you been talking?"

"No one you know." Her capacity for panic had reached its limits, and her emotions veered crazily from fear to fury. "And yes, it is all true. My mother was Jewish, my grandfather a survivor. Jews will always be survivors, Vladimir, because you cannot destroy what God has chosen!"

"It cannot be." He spoke in a taut voice, his eyes black and dazzling with fury. "I could not have loved a Jew!"

She lifted her head and met his accusing eyes without flinching. "No, you could not. You could not love anyone, Vladimir. You love only yourself and your dreams of glory, but those dreams will die very soon. God Himself will destroy you when you move against Israel. It is written in the Bible, therefore it must be true."

Triumph flooded through her when he winced at her words, but she knew she would not have the upper hand for long. She turned to walk back down the aisle.

"Alanna! Stop!"

She lifted her head and studied the slanting sunbeams from the windows. They fell upon the floor, bathing the pews and carpeted aisle in a brilliant white light. "Jesus loves me, this I know," she whispered under her breath, fixing her gaze upon the narthex. "For the Bible tells me so."

She heard the gun slide from a leather holster, heard the click of a safety being drawn back. "Alanna! Stop where you are!"

"Little ones to him belong."

Two shots sounded in the same second, and immediately a dull kind of pressure knocked against Alanna's rib cage. Surprised, she looked down at the snowy expanse of her dress and saw a brilliant red spot, darker in the center, like a radiant rose unfurling before her eyes, so she took another step, pain rising inside her like a wave, breaking, sending streamers of agony in every direction, and the white mountain of her wedding dress moved with her, swishing in the stillness, while the sharp odor of carbon wafted through the nave and reached her nostrils, so she brought her hand up to her face, and the movement sent tiny jabs of sharper pain whipping through her arm, and she noted with surprise that the white satin sleeve was torn, the snowy sable flecked with crimson splashes of blood.

She clamped her jaws together, felt her breath come hard through her nose with a faint whistling sound. Taking another step, she drew a ragged breath and sang another phrase of the little song, as clear in her memory now as it had been on that Sunday in childhood: "They are weak, but he is strong."

Another shot sent a shaft of pure white pain ripping through her chest. Alanna halted, pressed her hand to her heart, then lifted it and stared at her wet palm. She tried to take a breath and couldn't. Something was pressing against her chest, but that wouldn't stop her from finishing the song, from victory, because God had called her, God had kept her, and God would welcome her home. Shadrach, Meshach, and Abednego had spoken the truth to a pagan king, and so had she; she had told Gogol that God would destroy him, and he would, because God always kept His word and His promises and always preserved his people no matter who came against them, just as he always gathered in the souls that belonged to him . . .

The floor rushed toward her. Alanna felt the carpet against her cheek, smelled its musty odor, saw a single rose petal before her eyes, and it was white, as pure as the light from the windows, as perfect as the place where she'd find herself when she opened her eyes again.

Yes, Jesus loves me.

Chapter Thirty-two

From: D. Prentice <GWJ@prenticetech.com>
To: Michael Reed <MReed@dnsa.osd.mil>
Date: Friday, December 15, 2000 7:15 p.m.
Subject: Alanna James Ivanova

Dear Michael:

We would be naive to think we could mount a war against evil without experiencing casualties. Lauren and I were saddened to hear that Alanna James Ivanova, whom you knew as "Alanna from Moscow" died this week. According to the report given to Irene Nance, the American ambassador's wife, Alanna died in her sleep from an undiagnosed heart defect. Because she was the widow of a Russian citizen, she was buried quietly and, from all accounts, quickly.

Alanna was a brave soul. We shall miss her.

D.

Chapter Thirty-three

Jerusalem
0915 hours
Tuesday, December 19

AS THE DAYS OF DECEMBER SLOWLY TICKED BY WITHOUT INCIDENT, MICHAEL felt some of the tension ease out of his neck and shoulders. The Russian troops were still advancing, several of the Arab nations had begun to mobilize, and a contingent of UN troops had landed in Lebanon and set up peacekeeping bases along the southern border. But such movements, he knew, were mere posturing in the grim ballet of war. If Israel decided to close even one of the disputed military bases, or if any of the advancing armies tired of shadowboxing, the entire situation could dissolve and the advancing armies would turn homeward.

Michael skimmed the daily IDF intelligence reports with grim satisfaction. Despite their histrionics and hyperbole, the Arab armies were unlikely to rush into the theater of war, no matter how well the Russians had trained them. In four other wars Israel had managed to defeat them against all odds, and the experience had left the Arabs undeniably skittish.

Michael had lived and worked under the cloud of impending war before, and he knew it could be weeks, even months, before the storm either broke or blew away. Daniel stood by his prediction of December 21 as the date when God would deliver Israel, but when December 19 dawned without an enemy in sight, Michael took a moment to send a quick e-mail to his friend: "Hey, buddy: Two days out, and all is quiet here. I think you got your years mixed up!"

He found himself humming a Christmas carol as he dressed. Because he knew Devorah would want to be with her family at Chanukah, he had planned a festive brunch at his hotel. She was supposed to meet him at ten for a quick bite before they left for the air base at Uvda.

She was waiting in the lobby when he came downstairs.

"You're early." He resisted the urge to kiss her cheek.

She shrugged. "I picked up my files at the base and decided to read them later. Besides," she said, grinning, "I am starving."

Michael slipped the waiter a generous tip and asked for one of the tables out in the sunny courtyard. After the waiter seated them, Michael whisked two small objects out of his coat pocket—a four-inch Christmas tree and a five-inch menorah, complete with tiny candles. Grinning, he set them in the center of the linen-covered table.

For once she was speechless. "You are insane," she whispered, the light of appreciation glowing in her eyes.

Michael folded his hands and leaned toward her. "All quiet on the northern front this morning?"

"Nothing has changed." She unfolded her napkin and dropped it into her lap, then reached out to touch the tiny bristles on the Christmas tree. Her smile relaxed as she looked up at him. "I've always wanted to decorate a tree, you know. But my father would faint if I even suggested such a thing."

"Lots of interfaith families in America celebrate both holidays." Michael took pains to keep his voice light. "They have a tree and a menorah and treat each holiday as special. After all, the dates do run together."

She gave him a warning look that put an immediate damper on his rising spirits. "I don't think I like the way this conversation is going."

He swallowed his disappointment and looked out at the street, where scores of shoppers moved up and down the sidewalk in a restless throng. "Then we'll talk about something else."

"That's probably best."

Michael didn't answer but let the silence stretch between them. Long ago he had learned that all you had to do to make someone talk was stop talking yourself—most people were so uncomfortable with silence that they naturally babbled to fill the emptiness. But Devorah was at ease with quiet and with him, so she wrapped her fingers around her water goblet and joined him in watching the street.

While Devorah ordered, Michael kept his eyes on the ebbing tide of street traffic and struggled to get a handle on his emotions. He had never intended to feel this way about an Israeli woman—he had never thought he'd feel this way again. But Devorah had crept into the empty places of his heart and filled them with her brightness. The thought of leaving Israel without her filled him with despair.

He found himself following the timber of her voice as she asked the waiter about a dish on the menu. Michael deliberately focused his gaze outward, watching a young man who struggled to pedal a bicycle against the steep slope of the street. Two bulging bags hung over the bicycle's back wheel, and the man stood on the pedals, forcing his weight to push the bike up the hill. Despite the cool air, sweat streamed down the man's temple and into his dark beard, darkening the red scarf tied at his neck.

For no reason at all, the man on the bike turned his head and caught Michael's eye. While Michael watched with an eerie sense of déjà vu, the line of the man's mouth curved, a sudden twitch in the darkly bearded face, and the hair on the back of Michael's neck rose with premonition. Prodded by some long-buried instinct, he rose from his chair as the cyclist turned the handlebars and darted across the road, bringing a car to a screeching halt. The young man careened through a crowded marketplace where women and tourists gathered around open-air booths, then he turned again and sent a gleeful smile winging across the street . . . toward Michael.

His heart contracted like a squeezed fist.

"May I take your order, sir?"

Michael lifted his hand, and in that instant the market exploded. Michael flinched, then pushed the scrambling waiter aside in an effort to reach Devorah, but she had already ducked beneath the table. Michael slipped to the ground and used the low brick courtyard railing for cover. Dust and debris rained down through air filled with smoke and sound.

Michael's ears rang from the concussion of the explosion, but after a moment he crawled under the table and reached out to Devorah.

"Are you all right?" he asked, anxiously searching her face for lacerations.

With her hands braced on the concrete flooring, Devorah nodded. "I'm fine. What was that?"

Michael peered out over the tabletop and scanned the carnage in the marketplace. "I think it was a bicyclist. I saw this guy ride by just before the explosion, and he grinned at me like he knew I knew what he was about to do."

The words had scarcely left his mouth when another boom echoed from a different part of the city. Devorah's eyes widened further, then the pager at her waist emitted a dull throbbing sound.

She glanced at her belt. "It's 101—the emergency signal. I have to return to the base."

"I'll go with you."

Michael took her arm and led her out of the pandemonium, then sprinted with her to her car.

Twenty minutes later, they stood in a briefing room outside the ground corps commander's office. "The PLO has apparently orchestrated strikes in every city," the major general told them. Droplets of sweat ran down his pale face, but his eyes glinted with determination. "We believe this is a diversion for the troops amassed on our northern, eastern, and southern borders. We are sending police and reservists to combat the terrorist strikes while our active duty personnel remain on full alert at their bases. The air force has already sent up E-2C Hawkeyes to assess the developing situation."

Devorah caught Michael's eye and mouthed three words: "It has begun."

Chapter Thirty-four

District of Columbia
0800 hours

STANDING IN THE VERMEIL ROOM, SAMUEL STEDMAN LACED HIS HANDS BEHIND his back and smiled at a group of sixth graders who had come to sing carols before the White House Christmas tree. Victoria had always insisted upon placing the tree in this room, where the portraits of six serene first ladies brought a touch of personality to the austere surroundings.

One of the sixth graders caught Sam's eye, and he smiled, remembering how Jessica had looked at that age. Elementary and middle school had passed too quickly; he had been on the road with political campaigns during her concerts, athletic events, and school parties. He would give anything to relive those years.

"*O Christmas Tree, O Christmas Tree, how lovely are your branches.*"

Sam steered his thoughts away from painful memories and forced himself to smile at the children. They were from a small school in Maryland and had probably sold dozens of cookies and brownies to raise the money for this trip to Washington. For their sakes, he needed to honestly enjoy their singing.

Jack Powell stepped into the room, nodded at one of the group's chaperones, then strode across the carpet, ignoring the choir director. Sam felt his smile freeze—Jack was either being uncommonly rude, or a true disaster had just occurred.

Jack came forward, caught Sam's arm, and leaned in. "Word from Israel, Mr. President." His voice dissolved in a thready whisper. "The invasion has begun."

Sam felt a cold panic start somewhere between his shoulder blades and prickle down his spine. He had hoped—oh, how he had hoped—that the

Russians would wait until he left office. Then he could sit in the solitude of his North Carolina cabin and call down curses upon Blackstone until his throat ached. But now he would have to act. He was still president of the United States.

Sam leaned forward, grateful that the children were still singing. Perhaps the sound of their music would drown out the pounding beat of his heart. "Assemble the members of my Cabinet and the National Security Council. We will meet in an hour. First, though, I will need some time alone in my office."

Powell nodded and stalked out of the room, and Sam forced himself to casually tap his foot to the gentle rhythm of the children's song. He'd listen to one more selection, then he'd thank them and send them home.

Chapter Thirty-five

Jerusalem
1510 hours

Alone in his office at the yeshiva, Baram Cohen closed the door and adjusted the venetian blinds that covered the window facing the outer hallway. The window to the street he left open, and through the panes he heard the sound of gunshots in the distance, like the thin crack of breaking sticks. These were the sounds of terrorists doing their best to strike fear in the hearts of God's people. Earlier he had heard explosions and felt the brick building tremble as it shuddered in sympathy for the city.

The yeshiva had sent its students home to brace for whatever evil was approaching. The halls now echoed with silence broken only by the occasional sound from outside and priestly prayers.

Closing his eyes, Baram pulled his prayer shawl over his head, then lifted his hands and began the ritual chant of his afternoon prayers. He had just completed *Ashrei* when a cloud shadowed the yeshiva, filling the small room with a cold, almost palpable darkness.

Baram fell silent as the wings of shadowy foreboding brushed his spirit. Now frigid air swept across the backs of his legs, and his scalp tingled beneath his prayer shawl. An evil presence seemed to fill the room with the reeking stench of an animal's breath.

Icy fear twisted around Baram's heart as he closed his eyes and lifted his thoughts to the Creator of the universe. "Master of the world who was king before any form was created," he prayed, his voice hoarse, "He is One, and there is no second to compare to him or be his equal. He is my God and my living Redeemer, and the Rock of my fate in times of distress. He is my banner and He is a refuge for me, my portion on the day I cry out."

Another explosion rocked the city, this one quite close. Baram clenched his fists as the crackling roar faded, then held his breath during the silent moment between the blast and the screams that would follow. "Into your hand I entrust my spirit," he whispered, hearing a note halfway between disbelief and pleading in his voice. "When I sleep and when I wake, HaShem is with me and I am not afraid."

He lowered his head, knowing with pulse-pounding certainty that the time had come. The great sages had predicted the birth pangs of the anointed one; they had foretold the *Ikvot Meshicha,* the terrible time just before the Messiah appears. Baram himself had noted the increase in pride, wars, poverty, foolishness, and lack of respect for elders and righteous men. His own children had departed from the true path, preferring to walk with those who would establish a secular Jewish state and not *Eretz Yisroel,* the promised kingdom of God.

"Now I understand," he said, bowing his head as tears welled within his eyes, "why the ancient ones prayed, 'Let the Messiah come, but at a time when I will not see him.' We have suffered through the ages, but it is not enough. I will praise you, HaShem, but first I will bow my head with sorrow for the things that must come."

CHAPTER THIRTY-SIX

From: Michael Reed <Mreed@dnsa.osd.mil>
To: President Samuel Stedman <GWJ@prenticetech.com>
Date: Tuesday, December 19, 2000 7:04 p.m.
Subject: Attack Commencement
Dear Mr. President:

As I am certain you know, the allied Russian-Arab attack commenced with the shelling of Bet She'an at 1500 hours. The IDF ground forces were anticipating a strike and responded in kind, and the air defense forces thus far have kept the invaders outside Israel's borders. The situation is being exacerbated, however, by PLO strikes within cities. We have not had a moment's rest since the terrorist strikes began at 1000 hours, Jerusalem time.

Please, sir. I know the situation is difficult, but we could use any help you can authorize. I will continue with my efforts to aid IDF officials unless directed otherwise.

Thank you, sir, for any help you can give.

Capt. Michael Reed

SAMUEL STEDMAN STARED AT THE MESSAGE FORWARDED FROM DANIEL PRENTICE, then turned away with a feeling of shame, as though he had abandoned someone drowning. What could he do?

Jack Powell sat across from him, a copy of Reed's message in his hand. "I can't believe you've kept him over there." A critical tone lined Powell's voice. "After that fiasco at the Knesset, I thought you'd bring him home."

"Reed did what he had to do to save those people. I'd send him again if I had to."

"And you'd pay for it again, too."

Sam ignored the comment. Powell had convinced himself that the brouhaha over American involvement at the Knesset situation had turned the entire campaign in Blackstone's favor, but Sam knew better. He'd lost because the American people had been duped. While Blackstone and the pundits turned a blind eye to blatant anti-Semitism in the United Nations, Sam had quietly been trying to help Israel in a tangible way. The world was preparing to grab that tiny nation by the throat while Blackstone and the UN choked America with a string of lies.

Powell leaned into the lamplight, which accented the lines of heart-sickness and weariness on his face. "Sam, it's over. I know you have a soft spot in your heart for Israel, but the American people would have a fit if you authorized a military strike on those Russian troops. You'd be committing us to World War III."

Sam clenched his mouth tighter. "The War Powers Act allows me to commit troops for sixty days without congressional authorization."

"You don't have sixty days left. If you sent our people over, Blackstone would pull those troops back ten minutes after he's sworn in. You would have risked our national security, spent millions to mobilize a peacetime army, and for what? So they can go over there and trade blows with the Russians for a couple of weeks? Forget it, Sam. You can't do this—especially at Christmas. You can't expect America's mothers to get behind the idea of sending their boys overseas during the holidays."

"What about America's Jewish mothers?" Sam's voice coagulated with sarcasm. "They aren't celebrating Christmas."

"They don't want their sons killed, either. Listen, Sam—America's Jews don't see themselves as part of Israel. If they believed in Zionism, they'd have emigrated long ago. They're Americans, and they don't want to go to war, not for anybody." A shadow of annoyance crossed Powell's face. "Sam, we've already done a lot. America has been Israel's best friend. We've sold them weapons and technology and satellites. We've provided foreign aid packages paid for with billions of American tax dollars. And I'm telling you straight—unless you want to go down in history as a president who left office in a cloud of shame, you'll let Israel take care of herself this time. We can't afford to lose the ground we've gained in our relations with the Russians, and we don't dare risk our access to Arab oil."

Silence, thick as fog, wrapped itself around them. Sam stared past his chief of staff for a long moment. "I could order the Sixth Fleet to move closer. Not to engage the enemy, but merely to intimidate."

Powell gave him a black look. "The Russian fleet is in the Mediterranean. You think they are going to understand that we're just bluffing? It's too great a risk, sir. They might fire on us, and if a single American boy dies, you'll be vilified in every paper from here to Kalamazoo. Blackstone has sold our people on the concept of peace and safety and cast you as a war-mongering wolf. You can't risk sending our people in."

"I could send in Reed's old SEAL team, DevGroup. Maybe they could take out the Russian leadership."

"Yeah, look at how successful we were at taking out Saddam Hussein." Powell winced in phony remorse. "Look, if we can't get to Saddam, what makes you think we could get to Gogol? If he's smart, he's traveling right in the thick of things. Short of dropping a platoon right on top of him, there's no way we could get to him—and we have no way of knowing where he is. And a single CT team won't make a dent in that invasion force. Our latest figures indicate that at least four million troops have gathered around Israel. And Israel's maximum force, with reservists, is what? Five hundred thousand?" Jack shook his head. "I'm sorry, Sam, but those are terrible odds. We can't get involved."

Sam ran his hand over the polished surface of his desk. How had other presidents handled similar situations? JFK had been a veteran, and he talked tough during the Cuban Missile Crisis. Not much action, but big results. Clinton, however, sent cruise missiles into Iraq, ordered air strikes in Bosnia, conducted military operations in Somalia, and threatened to invade Haiti. Lots of action—but few results.

Sam glanced up at the bust of Franklin D. Roosevelt on the far bookcase. Roosevelt had governed a land bent upon isolationism during the start of World War II. During his presidency Italy conquered Ethiopia while Hitler invaded Poland and threatened Britain and France. Roosevelt didn't commit American troops, though, until after the bombing of Pearl Harbor.

"There are six days until Christmas, sir." Powell's voice was quiet and subdued. "And thirty-two days left in your presidency. Don't do this. Don't go down in history as the president who gave us World War III for Christmas."

"Thank you, Jack." Sam hauled his gaze from Roosevelt to his chief of staff as a memory surfaced in his mind. "I appreciate your concern . . . and your opinions."

Powell placed his hand on the armrest of the chair as if to push himself up, then hesitated. "Sir? Have we resolved this issue?"

"I have." He lifted his chin and met Powell's gaze. "When Franklin D. Roosevelt was faced with a similar situation, he instituted the Lend-Lease Act. He didn't send men, but he gave weapons and aid to any country whose defense was considered vital to the United States. More than thirty-five governments received our help."

"Sir, Israel's defense is not vital to the United States."

His courage and determination like a rock inside him, Sam looked at Powell. "Indeed it is. We have shared many of our military secrets with Israel. On that basis alone, I would be justified in sending weapons and planes to aid in her defense."

Powell rubbed at his jaw. "So you're absolutely determined to do this?"

"I am. It might take me a few hours, but I'm going to give the Israelis everything I can. I'll start by authorizing any requests Michael Reed might make on Israel's behalf. He's over there—and I'm going to use him."

Jack smiled, but the customary expression of good humor was missing from the depths of his eyes, replaced by a weary resignation. "Well, then. I hope your Christmas is merry, Mr. President."

"It will be, Jack. Merry Christmas to you, too."

-0100111100-

When Jack had gone, Sam moved to the small study off the Oval Office, sat at his desk, and pressed his finger to the laptop's touchpad, bringing the screen to life. As he had suspected, messages from Daniel Prentice and Michael Reed were waiting.

The president skimmed Daniel's letter, another collection of scripture verses and cryptic comments, then he brought up Reed's message.

Dear Mr. President:

   As ordered, sir, I have assessed the situation and would like to request that you send as many Sentinel air defense radar systems as possible, armed with AMRAAM and Stinger missiles. I understand that the Fourth Infantry at Fort Hood has tested an updated version that is suitable for air transport and quick insertion.

In addition, we could use any and all trained F-22 Raptor pilots. Though the Israeli Air Force is skilled and capable, their F-16s are no match against the Russian Sukhoi S-37s. I would be honored to oversee the transport and insertion of these systems and pilots.

I will be awaiting your response.

Sam stared at the screen, then automatically tabbed back to Daniel's letter: "This is what the Sovereign Lord says," Daniel had written, "In that day, when my people Israel are living in safety, will you not take notice of it? You will come from your place in the far north, you and many nations with you, all of them riding on horses, a great horde, a mighty army. You will advance against my people Israel like a cloud that covers the land. . . . This is what will happen in that day: When Gog attacks the land of Israel, my hot anger will be aroused, declares the Sovereign Lord."

Cold, clear reality swept over Sam in a terrible wave. It had happened. Just as Daniel and Ezekiel and Victoria had predicted. A prophetic scene from the Bible was playing out before his eyes.

But what could he do about it? If the Scriptures were true, God himself would deliver Israel. The Almighty certainly didn't need Sam Stedman or the United States to lend a helping hand.

But . . . Michael Reed was waiting for help. And Russian jet fighters were flying over Israeli airspace. People were dying even in this prelude to all-out invasion.

Sam looked at the computer and read Daniel's final comment: "The Lord said to Abraham, 'I will bless those who bless you, and whoever curses you I will curse.'"

He picked up the phone and pressed the speed dial button for Frank Howard, secretary of defense. He would have the Joint Chiefs put together an aid package, complete with Sentinel batteries, Advanced Medium Range Air-to-Air Missiles, and any F-22 Raptor pilots who would volunteer to spend a few days honing their skills against the Russian Sukhois. The Joint Chiefs would choke on the idea, particularly since the F-22s weren't even scheduled to enter service until November 2004, but Sam knew there were a dozen of those planes waiting in a top-secret Nevada hangar. Might as well put them to good use.

He settled back in his chair and clenched his jaw as he brought the phone to his ear. This might not be the most popular decision he would ever make as president, but without a doubt it was the most right.

CHAPTER THIRTY-SEVEN

Tel Aviv
1100 hours
Wednesday, December 20

STARING BLANKLY AT A BANK OF COMPUTER MONITORS, MICHAEL SHIFTED HIS focus and caught sight of his reflection in the glass. The stubble of his unshaven chin shimmered above the latest reports from the ground-based radar system, and weariness showed in the drooping slope of his shoulders. He pushed away from the desk, then reached for his coffee cup and found it empty.

He sat in the war room, an underground, shielded bunker beneath IDF headquarters outside Tel Aviv. The situation room was state-of-the-art. Three huge screens covered the front wall, and a virtual army of computers linked the screens with IDF ground troop commanders, the E-2C Hawkeye aircraft, and the chief of the general staff's office.

Michael sighed, rubbed the back of his neck, then crumpled his empty coffee cup and tossed it toward an overflowing trash can. The well-equipped facility was able to sustain a full staff for up to ten days—the maximum number of days, Michael estimated, that Israel could sustain a war. Since the sirens began to sound twenty-four hours ago, every able-bodied reservist had reported to his post, which meant that most Israeli businesses ground to a halt. If the Russians and Arabs never escalated the battle further than this steady shelling, Israel might not be destroyed militarily, but she'd be devastated economically.

The room was staffed with junior action officers who scurried to and fro and with commanders who sat on molded plastic chairs and smoked, drank coffee, and occasionally yelled at the computer screens. Behind the bank of computers and the men who fretted at them stood a row of long tables, topped with a mélange of paper cups, black intelligence binders, and ashtrays. Above the table, several wall-mounted speakers occasionally squawked with field reports.

Michael covered his eyes with his hand and rubbed his forehead, then lifted his eyelids and tried to focus on the door. Devorah stood in the doorway, and the sight of her was like a tonic to his weary brain. She paused at a desk to give a sheaf of papers to a commander, then looked up, caught Michael's eye, and smiled.

In the hours since the terrorist bombings that had heralded the advance of the Russo-Arab armies, Israel had flown sortie after sortie, dropping ordnance upon the tank columns and pounding the assembled troops as far north as coastal Syria. But on they came, hundreds of thousands of Russians and Arabs, setting their guns on the sloping hills of the Golan Heights and pointing them toward sleepy little towns in northern Israel. Already there were reports of enemy troops moving into the West Bank, where Israeli citizens were being forced to surrender or flee for their lives. Though the Israeli Air Force had mounted a valiant defense against the encroaching armies, squadrons of Russian MiGs and Sukhoi-37s kept the slower, less-agile F-16s at bay.

Michael had received a reply from President Stedman at 0700 hours. Six F-22 Raptors, piloted by America's best and brightest, were en route, as was a C-130 Hercules transport carrying eight Sentinel batteries, complete with crews and armed with AMRAAM missiles. The Sentinels would be welcome, for unlike the Patriot batteries, the Sentinels were automated defense weapons. Once delivered to a site, they could be turned on and left to monitor the skies. When they detected electromagnetic energy on a preset frequency, they automatically launched weapons that would seek out the transmitter—most likely the radar on an enemy fighter or incoming missile.

Michael studied the map on his desk and plotted positions for the Sentinel batteries. Israel was virtually surrounded on all sides. Reports from Israel's southern borders indicated that while Egypt had not joined in this attack, she had opened her borders to the armies of Libya and Sudan. Both of those nations had troops bivouacked along the Egyptian border, ready to push through the desert and invade from the south. Syria and Jordan lined Israel's eastern borders; Russians and Lebanese nationals guarded the north. And the Russian fleet filled the Mediterranean, blockading the Israeli ports.

Jerusalem, for generations a divided city, had been forced into a state of siege two hours after the shelling began. Michael studied Devorah's face as she approached, searching for signs of apprehension. He knew she was worried about her father.

She plucked at his sleeve, then knelt beside his chair. "I've just heard," she whispered, lowering her gaze, "that my father is safe. As one of the Kohein, he was picked up and taken to safety shortly after the advance began."

"That's good news."

Her answering smile was a little twisted. "I suppose. I hear they had to forcibly remove him from the yeshiva." She looked up, and he saw that her eyes were damp with pain. "Many of the Jews will refuse to abandon the old city. They will remain in their homes even if shells begin to fall on their heads."

Michael held up his hand and turned as the fax machine beside him rang, then began to spit out a series of images. He'd called in a favor to Tom Ormond, a former marine lieutenant colonel who worked special ops assistance in a basement room two stories beneath NSA headquarters at Fort Meade. After receiving Michael's call, Ormond had scrambled an SR-71 spy plane, whose cameras snapped shots of Jerusalem and the surrounding area from 85,000 feet. At that height, the plane was invisible to anyone on the ground.

Tom had promised to fax the spy shots ASAP and provide full imagery—photos from one of the KH-11 spy satellites—in a few hours. Michael felt good about getting the reconnaissance shots, but the knowledge that Gogol also had access to recon photos rankled. If he had filed his ASAT report a few months earlier, President Stedman might have convinced Congress to sell the technology to Israel. Then they could disable any spy satellites that snooped too close.

He pulled the last photo from the fax machine and spread it on a desk with the others. Devorah leaned over the pictures, then stepped back to avoid blocking the light.

"Look here." Michael pointed to several areas inside the West Bank where enemy activity was clearly visible. "They dropped troops into these positions, probably through HAHO insertion. They flew at a high altitude over Jordanian airspace and let their men just drift down, probably covering between twenty-five to fifty miles in the descent. That's why your radar didn't alert you to the transport planes."

"If that was their plan," Devorah said, her dark eyes studying the photos, "then we're looking at recon units. The first wave will come tomorrow."

Major General Ilan Halutz, deputy chief of the general staff, approached the desk where Michael had spread the photos. "Are these the latest shots?" His eyes roved over the photographs. Michael knew the Israeli intelligence division was studying photos in another office, but these were as recent as anything the deputy chief would see for hours.

He nodded. "Yes, sir. Their recon units are in position, and the first wave is bound to advance within the next twenty-four hours—probably at first light tomorrow."

The general's mouth was tight with distress, his eyes slightly shiny. "Rear Admiral Amidor has reported that the Mediterranean is bristling with Russian warships. We've also picked up traces of submarines in the area." He turned slightly, clasped his hands behind his back, and rocked forward as he studied the map mounted on the north wall. "They are goading us," he said, speaking to anyone who would listen. "They want us to fire our nuclear weapons. If we do, we'll be condemned by the rest of the world. We'll be exterminated here, and our names will go down in history as those who chose to rain nuclear devastation upon the Middle East."

The general turned to Michael, his brows pulling into an affronted frown. "Can you tell me why they want this land, Captain? It will be worthless, contaminated once they begin firing biological or nuclear weapons. And it is just a tiny strip of earth."

Not certain how he should answer, Michael glanced at Devorah. General Halutz's question was almost certainly meant to be rhetorical, yet it brought a hushed silence to the situation room.

"I think, sir," Michael finally dared to answer, "that the battle has little to do with territory. I have a friend, a man I respect, who believes this is first and foremost a spiritual battle."

The general smiled without humor. "Perhaps your friend is right. A few months ago the Arabs demanded land for peace, and we gave it to them. Even though no other country has ever surrendered territory it captured during a defensive war, we returned the Golan Heights and the West

Bank—land bought with the blood of thousands of young Israeli soldiers. Of course we kept our military bases in place, and of course the Israelis who lived there remained, just as the Arabs who live in Israel's lands are not forced to move with the shifting of political tides. We gave them what they wanted, control of the land, and now they repay us with warfare. Now they taunt us, waiting for us to fire a nuclear weapon, because then they will have an excuse to erase Israel from the face of the earth."

"You know that won't happen." Michael spoke with more conviction than he felt. "The State of Israel was founded by God himself."

The general smiled benignly, as if dealing with an idealistic child. "There are some who say we acted too soon when we founded this nation. They say we should have waited for the Messiah."

For no reason he could name, the general's attitude of weary resignation lifted the hairs on the back of Michael's neck. It was almost as if the IDF had already decided the situation was hopeless . . .

The Samson Option.

He felt an icy finger touch him, just at the base of his spine. "Tell me, sir, that it isn't over." Michael tried to keep the stunned disbelief out of his voice, but patently failed. He stepped closer and spoke so none of the others would hear. "Tell me you haven't already decided to exercise the Samson Option. Help is on the way. President Stedman has agreed to my request; the fighters and Sentinels will be here in a matter of hours."

The general stood very still, his eyes narrowing. "Can so little do anything against so many? We will do what we must do. We will not go willingly into the concentration camps again. We will not allow our little ones to be taken captive, our elders to be victimized."

Michael took a deep breath and felt the bands of tightness in his chest. "Think of the rest of the world, General. Think of the United States, who has been your ally. Consider what will happen to her if you launch a nuclear strike."

An aura of melancholy radiated from the general's narrow features like some dark nebula, but he did not respond. In a wave of desperation, Michael reached out and grasped the general's upper arm, then leaned forward to whisper in the man's ear: "Surely you know about the Dead Hand."

The general's fear was visible—his eyes wide and dark, his skin waxy and pale.

Michael felt the wings of tragedy brush lightly past him. "General, you don't want to launch nuclear weapons. They are only shelling the borders; they have not yet hit us hard. And help is on the way."

"It is only the first wave. At dawn they will come at us with full strength, and we will not be able to hold them for long."

"But you can wait, General. Israel has allies; she has hope. Who knows what dawn's first light will bring?" A memory opened before him as if a curtain had been ripped aside. "General," he turned, holding the man's gaze with desperate intensity, "I don't know much about the ancient writings of your rabbis, but I do know that men wiser than I believe God will deliver Israel tomorrow, on the twenty-fourth day of the ninth month. It was written nearly three thousand years ago, and here we are, standing on the brink of God's promise."

Major General Halutz's lined face showed no more than mild interest, but his eyes were alert in their caves of bone. "Why, Captain Reed," he said, a slight tinge of ridicule in his voice, "I had no idea that American officers based military decisions upon ancient religious texts."

Michael stiffened, momentarily abashed. "They don't, sir, as a rule. But if I had a choice between using nuclear weapons and waiting upon God, I would wait."

The deputy chief of staff did not answer but gazed at the computer screens with chilling intentness for a long moment, then nodded at Michael and moved away.

-0100111100-

Devorah did not speak until she and Michael found a quiet corner in an abandoned office. Michael sank into a steel-and-vinyl chair before an empty desk, then rubbed a hand over his face, scrubbing roughly as though he could wipe away all feeling.

She leaned against the desk and looked down at Michael. "Are you going to tell me?" She folded her arms, noticing the way the muscle of his jaw clenched as he stared at the floor. "I heard what you told the General. What is this Dead Hand?"

"The Samson Option." He sounded as if he were strangling on a repressed epithet. "If Daniel is wrong, tomorrow your people will use nuclear weapons to defend themselves. If you do, the entire world will pay the price—and so will all the Jews, even those living outside Israel."

She turned his answer over in her mind and struggled to make sense of it. All morning she had concentrated on pushing aside her personal worries about her father and brother, and now Michael was telling her he was worried about the entire *world?* When had the world ever cared about what happened to the Jews?

"The world did not care when Hitler murdered six million Jews," she said, prodding him. "Why should the world be involved if we defend ourselves against the Russians and Arabs?"

His eyes narrowed. "How can you say that? The United States alone lost over 400,000 servicemen in World War II. We gave the best we had to stop Hitler."

"We gave six million." She spoke softly, but with iron in her voice. "Today there are just over five and one half million Jews living in Israel. Your General Gogol could kill every man, woman, and child in this country and still fall short of Hitler's accomplishment. The United States did too little, too late for the six million who died sixty years ago—"

"We are trying to help."

"By doing what? Sending a few weapons?" She paused and let the weight of her words fall into the silence between them. "Oh, I know your president has promised to send us some newfangled toys, but this struggle may not last long enough for his help to make a difference. So all America has given us . . . is you."

He lifted his chin, defiance pouring from his burning blue eyes. "We have stood by Israel for years. We have given you billions in military aid. We have shared our technological secrets. We have sold you Phantom fighters and antimissile technology—" He lifted his hand, then slowly clenched his fist and dropped his gaze. "But what does it matter? The Dead Hand will even the score. America will pay for what she has not done."

Leaning forward, Devorah placed both hands on his shoulders and lowered her head to meet his eyes. "Tell me, Michael," she whispered. "What is this Dead Hand, and why do you look as if it spells the end of the world?"

"Because it could." Lines of concentration deepened along his brows and under his eyes as he looked past her. "The Dead Hand is a Russian doomsday system designed to automatically initiate a retaliatory nuclear launch process in the case of nuclear strikes against Russian cities or bases. We first learned about it in 1995."

Releasing him, Devorah leaned back and listened with a vague sense of unreality.

"According to a story leaked from Russian intelligence, the Dead Hand system was invented in the late 1970s, at the height of the Cold War. In case the Soviet leadership was ever destroyed by an American nuclear strike, the doomsday system, or Dead Hand, would automatically fire nuclear weapons at pretargeted American cities."

"That's insane." The words slipped from Devorah's lips before she could stop them. "First of all, the Russians have been desperate to corral and consolidate their nuclear arsenal since the collapse of the Soviet empire, so it's not likely such a system is still in place. And why would they leak that information now instead of during the Cold War? Such a system would only have a deterrent effect if the other side knew it existed."

He smiled at her, his eyes sharp and assessing. "Good question, Sergeant Major. If you thought about it long enough, I'm sure you'd come up with the answer."

"We don't have a lot of time on our hands here."

"Good point." He leaned forward, resting his elbows on his knees. "The story about the Dead Hand is obviously part of General Gogol's disinformation campaign. The system, if it exists at all, wasn't developed during the Cold War, but during the last decade, when Gogol was minister of defense. The reason for the leak is simple—Gogol has provided a likely excuse for Moscow to launch a nuclear attack against the West. If Israel exercises the Samson Option and strikes at Russia with a nuclear weapon, Moscow will fire upon her old enemy, the United States." The Adam's apple in his throat bobbed as he swallowed. "When the dust settles, the nuclear destruction will be blamed upon the Jews . . . and any Jews that survive will be persecuted throughout the world."

Her heart went into sudden shock. "That cannot be true, Michael. No one would seriously blame the Jews for Russian aggression."

Michael took a deep breath. "Our people at the DOD have been familiar with the Dead Hand scenario for the last five years. I thought it would be a nuclear situation in Iraq or North Korea to finally pit us against the

Russians, but Daniel convinced me that Israel would be the flint to spark this fire." Sudden anger rose in his eyes. "This is so aggravating! Here I sit, trained in every aspect of military activity, yet I can't do a blasted thing to help until the transport arrives."

"What else are we to do?" Her voice emerged as an inelegant croak, rusty with swallowed frustration.

Michael's face emptied of expression and locked. Devorah felt the sudden icy silence that surrounded him, then he looked up and gave her a knowing smile. "Come on," he said, standing. "I left my laptop in the situation room."

"Where are we going?"

She heard a trace of laughter in his voice when he answered: "We're going to find the surgeon who may be able to amputate the Dead Hand."

CHAPTER THIRTY-EIGHT

1314 hours

"SERGEANT MAJOR COHEN? I HAVE AN URGENT MESSAGE FOR YOU."

An ensign caught Devorah's attention in the hallway, and Michael hesitated.

"Go ahead. I'll catch up later," she called, taking an envelope from the ensign's hand.

Michael flashed his temporary ID badge before the guard on duty at the Special Operations Division checkpoint, then made his way back to the war room. He had already dialed out on his laptop by the time Devorah joined him. "Are you being deployed?" he asked, glancing toward the unopened message in her hand.

"I have no idea." She slipped her thumbnail under the sealed edge and began to tear the envelope open. "It's probably a report on sniper activity around the base."

She nodded toward the computer on Michael's lap. "Do you think Daniel knows about the Dead Hand?"

"I know he does—he's the one who tipped me off," Michael muttered, watching the computer go through its paces. "I don't doubt that he can hack into the Russian military computers, but what I don't know is if he realizes that we're about two minutes away from nuclear doomsday."

As Devorah watched over his shoulder, Michael typed in a simple note, then clicked the Send key.

Daniel:

Things are getting a little tense here. We're only a few hours from exercising Samson against those Philistines. Is the Dead Hand still connected, or are you counting on Ezekiel's vision to pull us through?

M.

Together they watched the message vanish from the screen, then Michael sat motionless while Devorah took a folded sheet of paper from the envelope and began to read.

The subdued air of the situation room shivered suddenly into bits, the wailing sounds of a siren upsetting generals and ensigns alike. The tenor of the shouted commands changed immediately, and Michael knew the worst had come to pass—the air defense systems had picked up an incoming missile. Only time would reveal whether it was armed with a conventional, biological, or nuclear warhead.

Devorah's gaze flew up at him. "Fourteen minutes," she whispered, following his thoughts. "From the time of radar detection to contact. But the Patriots should bring it down."

"Well." Michael straightened his back while his thoughts roiled. "We could sit here and wait for Daniel to respond." His eyes fell upon the page in her hand. "But something tells me you'd better finish reading that letter."

Devorah sighed heavily, then lifted her shoulders and lifted the letter again. "Arab terrorists are attempting to cut all communications within Israel," she said, her eyes moving from right to left as she scanned the message in Hebrew. "They've cut the road two miles from here. The paratroopers dispatched a chopper to dislodge the tangos, but somehow the terrorists brought it down. They want to know if I can pull together a rescue team to rescue the White Alpha squad—"

She choked back a frightened cry. "Michael—that's Asher's squad! But—with this siren, I don't have time to coordinate my team. My people are all at Lod."

Michael didn't hesitate, not even when the laptop beeped with an incoming message. He closed the laptop and set it on the desk, then took Devorah's arm. "We're a team. Let's go get your brother."

For an instant his words didn't appear to register, then she gave him a grateful nod and moved toward the door. "We have twelve minutes, by my count," she called over her shoulder, moving with long strides. "We've got to get him out and to safety before they seal off the base."

-0100111100-

Michael had met several unique women in his lifetime, but as Devorah steered her little Fiat out of the base parking lot and onto the open road, he thought he'd never met a woman as single-minded as Sgt. Maj. Devorah Cohen. Before leaving the IDF Command Headquarters Building she paused by the armory long enough to grab two Sig Sauer P226 handguns, an extra magazine for each pistol, and two 9mm Uzis. After scribbling her name on a form, she told the duty officer she would also need six gas masks.

The guard shook his head. "Sorry, but under an alert I can only distribute one mask per person."

"But we're on a rescue mission—"

Michael squeezed her hand, cutting her off. It would do no good to argue. The paratroopers should have masks aboard their helicopter, and they didn't have time to debate the issue. For once, she didn't argue, but gathered the weapons and handed one of each to Michael, then led the way out of the building.

Now Michael braced himself against the car door and tested the submachine gun's firing mechanism. Satisfied that it would function, he checked to see that the thirty-round magazine was full, then slid it into the proper port on the bottom of the weapon. After working the bolt back to the safe position, he placed the Uzi beside Devorah. He was checking his SMG when she pulled the Fiat off the road and onto the sandy shoulder.

"They've got the road blocked just ahead, beyond that rise." She took the handgun he offered and shoved it into the waistband of her slacks, then lifted the Uzi and cradled it as naturally as a mother carried her child. Like a cat scenting the breeze, she lifted her head and pointed toward the sandy hill. "See that gray cloud at two o'clock? That's got to be the crash site. Let's get in and get those guys out."

Michael caught her arm. "We can't both go; there isn't time. One of us will have to go in on foot and clear the area, while the other drives in from behind. Then we can load survivors in the car and drive back to the base." He glanced at his watch. "We have only seven minutes. It took us three minutes to drive here."

She pressed her lips together, but he knew she wouldn't waste time arguing. "I'll take the point."

"No. You've got the keys, lady. You've got to drive."

Before she could argue, he stepped out of the car and sprinted across the sand, his mind racing ahead as he contemplated the enemy. If the

Palestinians were attempting to cut all the main roads, it was possible they had left only two or three men at this checkpoint—but Devorah would need the road to make good time on their run back to the base. No way could they haul injured guys through the sand in that small car.

He knelt in a patch of scrub, pressing his chest and arms into the earth, willing the sand to stick to his sweaty skin and provide a small measure of camouflage. As a SEAL he had trained long and hard for counterterrorist operations, but he had never had to come up with a plan and implement it in less time than it usually took him to get dressed in the morning.

He lifted his upper body on his arms, raised his head, and looked through a shrubby bush at the scene beyond. Three men with machine guns stood on the road, laughing as they sprayed random fire over the glimmering asphalt. A burned-out car sat beside the road, its paint peeling black and scabrous. One hundred yards beyond the tangos on the road, a MD530 helicopter lay like a discarded child's toy, its bubble windscreen shattered. Glass glistened on the sand, and three bodies lay on the ground outside the wreck. One paratrooper, Michael noted grimly, remained inside, still strapped to the pilot's seat. The man had to be dead, or the tangos would have dragged him out with the others.

Two terrorists paced between the smoking chopper and the three inert bodies. One of them carried an assault rifle with a bayonet attached, and Michael's eyes narrowed when the tango whirled and thrust the bayonet into an injured soldier's thigh. The man screamed and curled around the pain, lifting his head high enough for Michael to make the ID: Asher Cohen.

Michael steeled himself to the necessity at hand and flipped off the safety. And then, without further thought, he stood and ran forward in a zigzag crouch, spraying fire in a careful pattern—double taps to each tango at the helicopter, dropping them like stones. The goons on the road responded with wild sprays of machine gun fire as he raced toward the abandoned car. Crouching behind the heavy engine block, Michael rose up, caught the startled tangos in his sights, and rhythmically took them out in measured double taps, one by one by one.

He had just dropped the third man when the Fiat roared up on the sand behind him. Leaving the engine running, Devorah raced from the vehicle and ran to Asher. "He's alive," she said, placing her fingers beside the carotid artery in his neck. With an ease any SEAL would have envied, she eased her shoulders under her brother's arm and lifted him, then balanced him on her back as she held his arms and walked back to the car with her head down.

Michael checked the others—and noted that though their flesh was still warm, both were dead. The first bore bayonet wounds in his legs, arms, and chest. Michael guessed the tangos had been planning to torture Asher Cohen in the same way before finally killing him.

He leaned into the helicopter, checking for any other survivors, but saw none. He glanced at his watch—four minutes remaining. He turned, then ducked reflexively when a spray of bullets slammed into the airframe and ricocheted in the cabin.

The sharp *craaack* of a pistol brought the hail of bullets to a sudden halt. When Michael turned, he saw Devorah crouched behind the Fiat, her left palm supporting the chunky black Sig, her eyes focused on the abandoned car. Michael grimaced when he approached and saw the tango lying in the sand—apparently he had just dinged one of the three Arabs on the road.

"Let's go," Devorah called, sliding into the driver's seat. Asher sat in the back seat, his head lolling sideways against the window. Michael hopped into the passenger seat, then held on for dear life as the little car whipped up dust and spun out onto the highway.

-01001111OO-

"What do you mean, the gates are locked?" Rising up from behind the steering wheel, Devorah thrust her head and shoulders out the open window and stared at the electric gates outside the IDF Command Headquarters Building. The on duty sentry stood behind the gate with his gas mask on and his machine gun ready.

"What is going on here?" Choking on her own words, Devorah sank back into the car and looked at Michael. "He's got to let us in. My brother is hurt."

"Devorah, look around you." Michael squeezed her shoulder, forcing her to acknowledge what she was trying hard to ignore. There were at least a dozen vehicles strewn over the road here, and at least fifty people standing in front of the gate, their hands clinging to the link fence, their faces drawn with entreaty. A few wore gas masks; others carried masks in their arms and cast worried glances toward the blue sky. If not for the daunting roll of concertina wire at the top of the fence, Devorah was certain some of them would have already tested the guard's resolve.

Michael spoke in an oddly gentle tone. "We can't go in—we'll start a riot if we even try. We need to find a shelter where we can take care of your brother."

Devorah glanced at her watch. One minute till contact. She sat without moving, terror lodging in her throat as she stared at the sweeping second hand. "Even if we manage to shoot the missile down," she whispered, pushing the words through her tight throat, "if it's a biological warhead, the contamination will spread. And we only have two masks—"

"We're going to get through this." Michael caught her hand and held it.

As a distinct murmur swept through the crowd outside the gates, Devorah looked up toward the sky. A white trail had appeared in the north, and as it drew nearer, a Patriot missile roared away from the base in a gout of fire. She held her breath as the defensive missile disappeared into the blue, then her hand tightened around Michael's as a gray cloud suddenly blossomed in the deepening sky. Cascading ivory plumes trailed away from the intersection of the two missiles, and a full moment later the dull rumble of an explosion rattled the chain links of the fence.

The crowd outside the gate cheered, but a guard inside picked up a bullhorn and reminded them of a truth Devorah could not forget. "Put on your protective gear," the sentry called, his voice sounding mechanical and strained through his mask. "The 'all clear' has not been given. Please, the danger is not past. You must wear your protective gear or retreat to a protected space."

"Have you a protected space?" Michael asked.

Devorah shook her head. "Every apartment building has one, but tenants are instructed to enter within two minutes of the warning siren. Once everyone is present, the doors are sealed. I couldn't ask them to open it for me—we may be contaminated at any moment."

Michael reached into the space behind her seat and pulled out the two gas masks. "Put this on. I'll put the other one on Asher."

He dropped the mask into Devorah's lap, but she pushed it away. "What about you? I couldn't take your mask."

"You're driving. I can't have you passing out on the road."

As Michael leaned over the seat to slip the second mask over Asher's face, Devorah looked in the rearview mirror and saw her brother's eyelids flutter at Michael's touch—a good sign. When Asher's mask was in place, Michael settled back in his seat and gave her a cocky grin. "I've been vaccinated for just about everything you can think of. So go ahead. Put on your mask and drive us out of here."

Though she wasn't certain she believed him, she slipped on the cumbersome gas mask and started the car. Backing carefully through the shifting crowd, she did a three-point turn and moved out, carefully negotiating the road through the limited visibility of the gas mask. It took an hour to drive a distance she usually covered in half that time, but apparently the threat of incoming missiles had frightened most of the terrorists into hiding. The road between Tel Aviv and Ramla was clear, though they passed several burning cars. Just outside Lydda, someone got off a lucky shot and spiderwebbed the windshield. She accelerated as Michael turned to scan the street, his Uzi in hand.

Once at her apartment, she and Michael carried Asher upstairs. While Michael went back out to bring in the weapons, Devorah tended Asher. He regained consciousness briefly, then smiled through a haze of pain while she cleaned the wound in his thigh. "We'll get you to a hospital first thing in the morning," she told him, her voice sounding thick and muffled through her mask. "Fortunately, the blade missed the artery and only scraped the bone, I think. Now go to sleep, and keep this mask on. I'll check on you in the morning."

Asher didn't speak but closed his eyes and opened them again, signifying his understanding. When she was certain he would sleep, Devorah went downstairs and into the kitchen. Michael stood at the sink with his hands in his pockets, his face turned toward the window. The sun had begun to sink toward the west, and the strong golden rays bathed the kitchen and Michael's strong profile in a radiant glow.

Leaning against the doorframe, Devorah resisted an unexpected wave of hot tears. This man had just saved her and her brother, and now he stood, alone and unprotected, against whatever chemicals or biological organisms might be riding the air currents outside. The apartment building had been strangely silent when they entered, and she knew her neighbors, their children, and even their pets were safely tucked into the protected spaces located near the staircase on each floor. They would not come out until the sirens stopped wailing and the all-clear signal was broadcast on television and radio.

She glanced toward the clock and blinked in amazement when she saw that it was only 3:30. She felt as though she had aged five years in the last three hours.

Michael moved into the living room and turned on the television. Wordlessly, she followed him and lowered herself to the padded arm of her sofa while he flipped through the channels in search of CNN. After finding the cable station, he stepped back and crossed his arms as the pictures and sound filled the living room.

Horror snaked down Devorah's backbone as she watched her worst nightmares flicker across the television screen. The news footage showed Russian troops on the slopes of the Golan Heights and tanks advancing through Syria in long columns. "Israeli bombers have launched preemptive strikes against key military installations in Jordan, Syria, and Lebanon," the newscaster said, his voice stern and utterly impersonal. "In the first twenty-four hours of the 1967 Six-Day War, Israel had destroyed over three hundred enemy aircraft, but the Israeli Air Defense Forces are hopelessly outnumbered by the Russian jets now threatening Israel's borders. Israeli bombers have managed to infiltrate Syrian air defenses in several locations, but nothing has stopped the progress of the mighty Russo-Arab army. United Nations officials, of course, are hoping this assault will force Israel to surrender the Palestinian lands so peace can finally come to the Middle East."

Shots of Israeli bombers flashed on the screen beneath the newscaster's words. Those images were followed by video clips of barefoot, bedraggled Syrian children who wept as buildings burned in the background.

Devorah stared, amazed that the media could cast the IDF in a negative light even as one of the largest armies the world had ever known bore down upon Israel.

The newscaster turned next to political news, profiling several men and women who were rumored to be Cabinet appointees for president-elect William Blackstone.

"That's it?" Devorah didn't know whether to be surprised or relieved.

"Apparently so." Michael punched at the remote and found the local emergency channel, which displayed the bright red and black emergency warning symbol. He muted the sound, then dropped the remote on the sofa and turned to her.

A silence settled upon them, an absence of sound that had an almost physical density. Devorah lowered her eyes as a wave of emotion threatened to pull her under. "I think I should stay in my room, in case Asher needs anything," she said, suddenly grateful for the hot confines of the mask over her face. Michael couldn't see the tears in her eyes and would attribute the thickness of her voice to the mask. "I'll sleep on the floor there tonight. You can raid the refrigerator, help yourself to anything, and sleep on the couch or the floor in the living room, whatever is most comfortable."

A sparkle of sunlight caught his eye as he glanced at her. "Thanks. I'll be fine."

She gestured down the hall. "There's a bathroom—if you'd like to shower. I think you're still wearing a coat of desert sand."

His smile deepened. "I guess I am."

"My computer is by the phone in the kitchen—if you want to try and reach Daniel."

"Thanks."

"Michael?"

"Yes?"

"Thank you."

He gave her a smile that sent her pulses racing. "Aw, shucks, ma'am. 'Tweren't nothing."

She had no idea what his words were supposed to mean, but his tone drew her like a magnet. In a heartbeat, her arms were around his shoulders, her head pressed to his chest. For an instant he stood motionless, as still as a statue, then his hand swept the tangle of curls that spilled from the straps of her awkward mask. She thought, she hoped, she was almost certain he pressed his lips to the top of her head.

"There, now." His tender voice was as intimate as a kiss. "Go take care of your brother. I'll make myself at home here and see you in the morning."

Sniffling, she pulled out of his embrace, then realized that crying and protective gear did not mix. She'd be drowning in her gas mask if she didn't get a hold of herself.

She walked through the kitchen and into the hallway, then turned. He had moved to the kitchen sink and rolled up his sleeves. He was soaping his hands and arms, washing his skin with the diligence of a surgeon scrubbing for surgery.

"I hope I see you in the morning," she whispered, knowing that an unexpected attack in the night could end it all.

She turned and walked slowly toward her bedroom, wondering if any of them would wake to see another day.

Chapter Thirty-nine

Ramla, Israel
0600 hours
Thursday, December 21
The twenty-fourth day of Kislev, 5761

A DULL RUMBLE PENETRATED AND SHOOK THE MISTY WORLD OF DEVORAH'S dream. She clung to the soft darkness as hard as she could, burying her face in her pillow, then swam up into the space between sleeping and waking, knowing that her world had undeniably shifted on its axis.

She sat up in the heavy gray light of her bedroom, felt the soft nubs of her carpet beneath her palms, and heard the stertorous sounds of Asher's breathing. That was all—just the sounds of quiet, punctuated by Asher's snoring breaths. The warning sirens had fallen silent.

She pulled the cumbersome mask from her face, then took a moment to breathe in the clean scents of fresh air.

The world shifted dizzily as the events of the past forty-eight hours came back with a rush. She closed her eyes until it righted itself, then leaned onto her bed and pressed her palm to Asher's forehead. His skin was cool and clammy, thank heaven, not feverish. She lifted the gas mask from his face as well and noticed that his brows lifted in an expression that looked like gratitude.

She felt the corner of her mouth lift in a smile when Asher shifted beneath her touch. He was going to be fine. Just a little rest, a few stitches, and he'd be back to work.

Work! She glanced at the alarm clock, which had begun to jangle and skitter across the nightstand, its hard plastic feet tapping the laminated tabletop like a pair of castanets. In horrified amazement she watched the clock finish its course and drop with a soft *plop* onto the carpet.

She picked up the clock, stunned. She hadn't set the alarm, so why—

She froze at the sound of breaking dishes, then stood and ran for the stairs.

Wearing his trousers, a pair of socks, and a sincerely baffled expression, Michael stood in the kitchen before an open cupboard. "What is it?" she asked, her eyes taking in the rattling pottery on the floor and countertop. "A missile?" Another clattering caught her attention—in the living room, a bookshelf spilled its bounty while a pair of framed photographs danced off the coffee table and shattered on the stone fireplace hearth. Michael swept her laptop computer off the kitchen table and held it, protecting it from the same fate.

Michael looked up, his eyes roving over the shuddering walls and ceiling. "I think this is an earthquake. Look."

He pointed toward the seam between the kitchen wall and ceiling. Stepping forward, Devorah saw that the plaster had cracked—before her eyes, an ugly fissure zigzagged down the wall, creating a gap between the plaster and the surface beneath it. She gripped the kitchen counter as the rumbling began again, stronger this time. The cupboard doors swung on their hinges as if blown by a strong wind; the stove jostled forward while the plumbing groaned beneath the sink.

"I've lived here all my life," she said, lifting her voice to be heard above the noise, "and we've never had an earthquake!"

"Under the table!"

Michael pushed the kitchen chairs out of the way and pulled Devorah under the table just as another stack of dishes slid to the edge of the cupboard and fell, shattering on the edge of the counter and the tile floor.

She clapped her hand over her ears to block the noise. "What about Asher?"

"He'll be fine—as long as the roof holds." Slipping his arms around her, Michael held her tight as the rumbling died away. A moment later, they crawled out from beneath the table and stepped carefully through the broken glass. Devorah took a moment to run upstairs and check her brother— he had slept through the entire thing.

"Don't move," Devorah cautioned as she came back into the kitchen. She tiptoed toward the pantry. "The broom's in here."

While Devorah swept away the mess, Michael plugged in Devorah's laptop and accessed her e-mail program. She had just put the broom away when she heard him shout.

"What?"

"A message from Daniel." He pointed to the computer screen. "I was going to read this yesterday, but we left Tel Aviv in a hurry and the phone lines were tied up last night."

Devorah wiped her dusty hands on a dishtowel as she moved toward the computer. As usual, Daniel's message was relevant and to the point:

Dear Michael and Devorah:

Read Ezekiel 38:18–39:6. You'll find a map of tomorrow's activities. I have a hunch the day will begin with movin' and shakin'.

Oh, and you don't have to worry about the Dead Hand. As of midnight, the Dead Hand is off-line. I inserted a bug into the program that's going to be nibbling at the Russians' programs for some time to come. Might even cause them some problems in the field.

Just doing my little bit for truth and justice. God is going to do the big stuff.

Daniel

Michael looked at Devorah, a gleam of triumph in his eyes. "Daniel sent this yesterday."

Despite the good news, she felt a sudden chill. "How could he know we were going to have an earthquake? What is he, a seismologist?"

"Do you have a copy of the Hebrew Bible? The writings of Ezekiel?"

Devorah nodded, then walked slowly toward the living room. Her books were strewn all over the floor, partially hidden by the collapsed bookshelves. "It'll take me a minute to find what I'm looking for," she called, sobered by the frightening possibility that the writings she had ignored for years might be more relevant than today's newspaper.

She finally found the book she needed under a stack of contemporary novels. She blew the dust from the worn cover then took the volume into the kitchen and handed it to Michael. He opened it, then laughed and handed the book back to her. "You'll have to read it, sweetheart. My Hebrew isn't all it should be."

Blushing, she took the copy of Scriptures and flipped through the pages, from right to left, until she found the writings of the prophet Ezekiel. With a quick intake of breath, she began to translate the passage Daniel had mentioned: "And it shall come to pass at the same time when Gog shall come against the land of Israel, saith the Lord GOD, that my fury shall come up in my face. For in my jealousy and in the fire of my wrath have I spoken, surely in that day there shall be a great shaking in the land of Israel; so that the fishes of the sea, and the fowls of the heaven, and the beasts of the field, and all creeping things that creep upon the earth, and all the men that are upon the face of the earth, shall shake at my presence, and the mountains shall be thrown down, and the steep places shall fall, and every wall shall fall to the ground. And I will call for a sword against him throughout all my mountains, saith the Lord GOD; every man's sword shall be against his brother. And I will plead against him with pestilence and with blood; and I will rain upon him, and upon his bands, and upon the many people that are with him, an overflowing rain, and great hailstones, fire, and brimstone. Then will I magnify myself, and sanctify myself; and I will be known in the eyes of many nations, and they shall know that I am the LORD.

"Therefore, thou son of man, prophesy against Gog, and say, 'Thus saith the Lord GOD; Behold, I am against thee, O Gog, the chief prince of Meshech and Tubal: And I will turn thee back, and leave but the sixth part of thee, and will cause thee to come up from the north parts, and will bring thee upon the mountains of Israel: And I will smite thy bow out of thy left hand, and will cause thine arrows to fall out of thy right hand. Thou shalt fall upon the mountains of Israel, thou, and all thy bands, and the people that is with thee: I will give thee unto the ravenous birds of every sort, and to the beasts of the field to be devoured. Thou shalt fall upon the open field, for I have spoken it, saith the Lord GOD. And I will send a fire on Magog, and among them that dwell carelessly in the isles; and they shall know that I am the LORD.'"

When she had finished reading, Devorah sat in a stunned huddle, the book resting upon her lap.

Michael broke the silence. "God's vengeance has begun."

She winced slightly, as if her flesh had been nipped by an unseen hand. "But—fire and brimstone? Surely we aren't meant to take this *literally*—"

"God's judgment began with an earthquake this morning, on the

twenty-fourth day of the month of Kislev, just as Daniel and the rabbi predicted. And it will continue, just as Ezekiel said, with fire and rain and
plague and men killing one another."

Devorah ran her hand through her hair, her mind whirling. Thoughts
she dared not formulate came welling up, an ugly horde of them. She had
based her life upon the simple belief that God helped those who helped
themselves, but if Michael was right and all these things came to pass, God
didn't need her help. He didn't need any of them—not the Strategic
Defense Command, not the Americans, not the nuclear arsenal. He
wouldn't need *anything* to defend Israel.

She scrambled to her feet and left the book of Scriptures on the table.
"This is all crazy," she said, folding her hands across her chest. "The earthquake is undoubtedly due to an explosion, maybe a bomb or a missile. I
don't know why Gogol and his army didn't blow us off the face of the earth
last night—the defense systems must be holding far better than we thought
they would." She flung out her hands, gesturing to the mess in her kitchen
and the cracked walls. "That's all this is. Reverberations from a missile that
struck near here. Or maybe vibrations from a launch of one of our missiles. They could be launching Patriots from across the street, for all we
know. Or maybe your president sent those F-22s, and we're hearing the
sonic booms from a couple of jets doing mach three—"

"Negative on that," Michael murmured, tapping at the keyboard.
"According to this message from the head of the Joint Chiefs, the weapons
intended for Israel are presently sitting at an Italian air base—grounded by
a nasty weather formation over Israel. They haven't made it in, and they
probably won't, at least not until the weather clears."

"There are still a thousand things that could explain all this. Geological
faults, the bad weather, the sonic booms from all the jet activity—"
Devorah raked her fingers through her hair again, realizing that she was
babbling to cover her confusion.

Michael looked at her, an impudent grin on his face. "So what do we
do now?"

She surveyed the damage to her apartment, then shrugged. "Let's get
Asher to the hospital. Then I'm going back to the base."

Michael grinned and closed the laptop. "Give me a lift?"

As if she had any choice.

Chapter Forty

Tel Aviv
0910 hours

MICHAEL HAD VISITED GENERAL SCHWARZKOPF'S COMMAND HEADQUARTERS during the height of Desert Storm, but never had he seen anything like the scene at the IDF HQ on the morning of December 21. He and Devorah encountered the usual rush of deputies and aides beneath the ever-present cloud of cigarette smoke, but the pervasive grimness that had filled the building yesterday had completely vanished, replaced by an infusion of hope.

He was feeling hopeful himself. He had twisted the truth a bit when he told Devorah he had been vaccinated against almost all the biological agents. He *had* been vaccinated against anthrax, but he was overdue for a booster and he hadn't bothered to stop by the medical office before leaving for Israel. So this morning he had given himself a good, long look in the mirror, hoping he wouldn't see any signs of illness. Thus far, he felt great.

He and Devorah joined a host of other officers waiting to hear news from the situation room. General Almog's aide stood in the doorway and lifted his chin in acknowledgment of their arrival.

"What's happening here, Colonel?" Devorah asked after they threaded their way through the crowd. "We woke up to something that sounded like an earthquake, but I figured it was an explosion."

"It *was* an earthquake." The colonel smiled a grim little grin as he turned sideways to allow an ensign through the doorway. "For a while everything was a mess here, but we're putting things back together, and our defensive batteries have not reported any serious damage. The enemy, however, can't say the same thing."

Michael folded his arms. "What do you mean?"

The officer's face split into a wide grin. "Intel is reporting that the enemy advance is falling apart. A hailstorm pounded the eastern perimeter at 0600 hours, and the Russians are knee-deep in mud. There have even been reports of mudslides on the eastern side of the Golan Heights."

Shock flickered over Devorah's face. "You're joking."

The colonel lifted one shoulder in a shrug. "It *is* the rainy season."

Michael glanced past the colonel at the bank of computer monitors on the wall in the war room, where a series of revolving satellite-supplied images displayed the position of enemy troops. "Can you tell me why the enemy is pulling back from the Lebanese border?"

The colonel turned, his gaze shifting toward the monitors. "Yes— Lebanon. The Russians had fortified that border with rocket launchers loaded with chemical weapons, but the earthquake overturned most of them. Apparently, at least one of the warheads spilled its payload and contaminated the area." The officer's jaw clenched. "We believe those missiles were loaded with BZ—that alone could explain the damage we're now hearing about. Intel is reporting that the enemy troops are disorganized, entire platoons in disarray. There are firefights on every hand—it's pure madness. They are killing each other."

"BZ?" Devorah turned questioning eyes toward Michael. "Does that mean something to you?"

Michael gave her a rueful smile. "Unfortunately, yes. BZ is a glycolate developed in the United States. It's a psychotomimetic agent, inducing psychosis in those it affects. It was designed for sabotage against high-priority limited targets, not for large-scale assaults."

"They're saying those missiles were aimed at Israeli military installations." The colonel drew his lips into a tight smile. "They wanted to incapacitate us, and now look what they've done."

The situation was so absurd Michael began to laugh, though he felt a long way from real humor. The possibility that he might have breathed in a bug was still rattling around in his brain, but—

"God will protect us." Thinking aloud, he looked at Devorah. "Don't you see? The rain, the earthquake, the enemy turning on his brother— Ezekiel foretold every bit of this 2600 years ago. It's all happening, just as the prophet predicted. God is delivering Israel just as he said he would."

Devorah's expression shifted into the surprised look of an operator who has just been dinged by an unseen assailant, then she turned on her heel and retreated through the crowd.

She was running from the truth. Michael couldn't blame her, not really. Until yesterday, he had been reluctant to accept Daniel's assertions, too.

"Are you Mike?" The colonel leaned closer, his face squinched into a question mark. "Do you have a friend named Daniel?"

Michael felt a slow smile spread over his face as something clicked in his brain. "You must be a real *bulldog,* Colonel."

A faint light twinkled in the depths of the man's brown eyes. "Eli Mordechai, and I'm pleased to meet you."

Michael reached out and shook the colonel's hand. "Thank you, sir. Any friend of Daniel's is a friend of mine. Should I assume that you agree with Daniel and believe it will be over soon?"

A bright blush overspread the colonel's face. "I wasn't convinced until Daniel explained the meaning behind his e-mail address. Then the pieces fell into place."

Michael frowned. "GWJ? I'm sorry, but I haven't been able to figure that one out."

The beginning of a smile tipped the corners of Colonel Mordechai's mouth. "Daniel is a Hebrew name, meaning *God will judge.* Daniel has believed that all along. God is the one saving Israel today. There's no other answer for it."

Michael nodded slowly, smiling to himself, then saluted and went in search of Devorah.

CHAPTER FORTY-ONE

Jericho, The West Bank
1024 hours

VLADIMIR GOGOL COULD TASTE THE HATE IN HIS MOUTH—ACID, FOUL AND burning. In a silent fury that spoke louder than words, he stared at the two inept field commanders in the mobile command post. Each of them had lost a platoon this morning when their Arab troops panicked and ran in the hailstorm. For their negligence, each deserved to die.

"You will be executed on my command within the hour." He uttered his judgment with contempt. "Commanders who cannot control their men do not deserve to live. That is all."

Colonel Petrov pulled his pistol and jerked it toward the door. The two men turned and stumbled through the exit. If they begged for their lives, they would do it outside before the firing squad.

Gogol pressed his hand to the bridge of his nose and squeezed while guards led the condemned men away. A sense of anticlimax had weighed upon him since sunrise, a heaviness centering in his chest. Today was to have been the day when their tanks rolled into Jerusalem, but their tanks could not move in the sea of mud that had formed in the heavy rains.

The Americans had a name for this—when everything went wrong, they joked that Mr. Murphy had come to visit. Well, Vladimir thought, lowering his hand, the Americans' Mr. Murphy had not only visited during the early morning hours, but he had brought his brothers and cousins to wreak havoc as well. The trouble began at sunrise—which did not come on schedule because a seemingly impenetrable cloud blocked the light from the rising sun—and continued with failed communications, illness, confusion, and insubordination.

"General." Petrov stood by the SatCom, the receiver pressed to his ear.

"I have Marshall Stolypin on the line, sir. He has urgent news from Moscow."

Vladimir stared in surprise. The SatCom was working? Apparently Mr. Murphy had overlooked one piece of technological equipment.

He moved to the phone. "Marshall Stolypin?"

"General!" Stolypin's voice crackled over the hissing line. "Sir, Moscow is burning, and the Kremlin has been demolished. We have been trying to reach you for an hour—"

A new kind of surprise shook Vladimir's body from toe to scalp, twisting his face. "Impossible! The defense systems would have detected an incoming missile."

"They did not fire, General, and this—well, this destruction is like nothing I have ever seen. Several scientists believe we are being struck by pieces of an asteroid. The skies over Moscow are literally raining fire and brimstone. We heard a sound like thunder, then a dark cloud rolled over the city and devastation began to fall upon us. St. Petersburg is experiencing the same phenomenon, and so are Irkutsk and Kiev, even outposts in Siberia—"

"Quiet." Vladimir uttered the command like a curse. Rage welled in him, black and cold, as horrifying images of a charred and ruined Moscow filled his brain. His beautiful city, the throne of the czars! How could a city that had stood against Napoleon and Hitler be felled in one day? It couldn't—and neither could other leading Russian cities. This was no act of nature—this was a diabolical new sort of weapon, aimed at the crown cities of Mother Russia.

He felt ice spreading through his stomach and gripped the receiver, then turned so Petrov couldn't see the play of emotions across his face. He needed to think. He needed time to plan a response. He had not anticipated that the Israelis would strike so quickly or so forcefully. And this new weapon—a missile that could launch undetected and rain fire and brimstone without warning? Such a weapon could only have come from the nefarious Americans at NASA. Somehow the Americans and Israelis had cooperated in secret and were now congratulating themselves on his defeat.

His strength returned as his heart pumped outrage through his veins. All the treaties, all the talks about disarmament and détente—all lies! But he was not defeated yet.

"Marshall Stolypin," Vladimir turned to face Petrov, whose watery eyes held absolutely no expression, "engage the Dead Hand."

"General." Stolypin's voice echoed with despair. "We tested the system when the attack began. Our automatic weapons systems are off-line; the computers aren't engaging properly. The Dead Hand is completely inoperative."

After a long pause, during which Vladimir fought for self-control, he issued the command. "I am personally placing you in charge of attending to my commands. Send a launch order to every base. Every nuclear missile in a silo is to be fired as soon as possible. Use the preset coordinates; hold nothing back. The Americans and Israelis will pay for what they have done today."

An unnatural silence rolled over the phone line, then Vladimir heard the soft sound of Stolypin's answer. "It shall be done, General."

Vladimir disconnected the call, then stood in the quiet of the mobile command post and took a deep breath. The empty air vibrated, the silence filled with dread.

Petrov was the first to speak. "This action cannot be countermanded. If you launch upon the United States, President Stedman will be forced to respond."

Vladimir fought back the surge of fury that murmured in his ear. "He already has, Petrov. And he has signed America's death warrant."

-0100111100-

Marshall Pavel Stolypin, the officer in charge of Moscow's defense, placed the SatFone back in its receiver and considered the command before him. Each nuclear missile in Russia's armory was aimed at a city in the continental United States. They had no evidence that the United States had anything to do with the terrible calamity befalling Russia, so Gogol's command was madness, especially in this confusion.

A rebellious thought skittered across his brain. Why not ignore the order? Moscow might be ruined, but at least they would not awaken the sleeping giant across the sea. If he launched nuclear missiles at the United States, he would bear the weight of responsibility for unleashing a holocaust . . .

He thought of his wife and three daughters, safe, he hoped, in their dacha in the Lenin Hills. He had been wise enough to tell Anna to keep the girls away from the city until after Gogol's return.

If he obeyed Gogol's order now, would he ever see his beloved girls again?

He reached for the SatFone and lowered his hand to the receiver, feeling the coolness of the hard plastic. One call to each of the top-secret missile installations, a few words murmured into the ear of each commander. The binder containing the activation code words sat on the desk before him. There was nothing to stop him but his conscience . . . and his love for his wife and children.

Pavel's heart skipped a beat when the phone jangled under his hand. He hesitated a moment, his stomach churning, then picked up the receiver. "Yes?"

"Marshall Stolypin?" The voice was Colonel Petrov's, yet it seemed distorted, and an odd coldness settled upon Pavel at the sound of it. This was the sort of fearful voice that could not belong to an officer; it was the voice of a man facing a firing squad.

"Pavel Stolypin, have you given the launch order yet?"

Pavel straightened his shoulders as a spark of hope flared in his breast. Perhaps the general had changed his mind about the nuclear attack. Perhaps Petrov and his men had risen up to relieve Gogol of command. "No, Colonel. There is still time to rescind the order."

The uneasiness without a name returned when Petrov made a soft shushing sound. "I cannot rescind the order. But I would urge you to use caution. Call one base, authorize one set of launches. But do not, I beg you, unleash a full-scale attack."

Was this a test of his loyalty? Pavel lurched around in his chair, half-expecting to see one of Gogol's spies in the shadows behind him. But he was alone, surrounded by useless computers and blank monitors.

"If you love your country," Petrov said, his voice dark and brooding, "trust me. Follow orders since you must, but make *just one call*. There is something strange about this day. We are struggling against forces beyond my comprehension."

A loud hiss abruptly drowned out Petrov's voice. Trembling, Pavel dropped the phone into its cradle, then stared in hypnotized horror at the folder containing the launch codes. Never in his entire career had he been faced with such a dilemma. He had been given an order by General Gogol, yet Colonel Petrov, who knew Gogol better than any man alive, had just urged caution. And Petrov, that unflappable officer, had sounded genuinely terrified.

As a confusing rush of anticipation and dread whirled inside him, Pavel opened the binder, then picked up the phone.

-01001111100-

The news hit the IDF situation room like a shock wave. Someone tuned the satellite to the CNN feed, and Devorah stood silently behind Michael's chair and stared at the television screen. Scores of personnel flooded the room, and in the press of warm bodies she shifted and wondered what else could happen in a single day. First they had heard that the earthquake that rattled Israel had wreaked damage in cities across the world, then a freak hailstorm grounded Israeli and enemy pilots while asteroids pelted Moscow and several other Russian cities. Now the United States had been struck by—what?

"This just in." A CNN reporter abruptly cut into a commercial for Ford trucks. "We've just received word that the United States has come under attack from enemies unknown. We are hearing reports—we cannot confirm yet, but we've heard reports of devastating explosions in New York City and Los Angeles. Witnesses in the surrounding areas are reporting what are described as mushroom clouds over the population centers."

The reporter stared into the camera, his eyes momentarily vacant, his face glistening with tiny pearls of sweat. He pressed his fingertips to the transmitter in his ear, and when he spoke again, his voice was fainter than air. "Ladies and gentlemen, I regret to inform you that New York—" He paused, accepted a sheet of paper from a hand that edged into the screen, then went a shade paler. "New York, Los Angeles, and Washington, D.C., have apparently been struck by nuclear weapons. We will keep you apprised of the situation as soon as we know more. Remain tuned to CNN for continuing—"

The screen suddenly went black. The war room swelled with silence as each man and woman present tried to make sense of what the newscaster was saying.

"Is CNN in New York?" Devorah's voice was raw and ragged.

Michael shook his head. "No, it's in Atlanta. They've struck Atlanta, too. And probably Tampa, Fort Meade, Denver, and San Francisco . . . who knows where else."

He turned and looked up at her, his gaze as remote as the ocean depths. "Gogol may have just been insane enough to think that the fire and brimstone God is raining upon Moscow came from the United States. I may not have a home anymore. I might not have a president. And Daniel, if he was in the States—"

He stood and moved toward the doorway, while Devorah tried to follow. "Where are you going?"

He turned and looked at her, a pinched, uncertain expression on his face. "I'm going to find a quiet place—somewhere I can pray."

Devorah absorbed this answer in silence, then stepped ahead of him and motioned for him to follow.

The closet wasn't much, but it was one of the few unoccupied rooms. Michael leaned against the wall, then slid down it in a crouched position, bowing his head as he rested his folded hands on his bent knees. Not certain what she should do, Devorah knelt on the floor in front of him, keeping one eye on the door.

A change came over Michael's features, a sudden shock of sick realization. "Oh, God," he prayed, his words soft with disbelief, "what are you doing now? How can this be part of your plan to judge Israel's enemies?"

Devorah lowered her head as Michael continued to pray in words that seemed to flow from his heart. Feeling awkward, she glanced at the door, half-hoping that someone would come in and break up the prayer party. But as Michael continued to pray, Devorah found herself listening. His prayers were nothing like her father's. Though both men spoke in sincere tones and with due reverence, Michael used common, heartfelt language as he talked to his God. There was nothing musical or formal or traditional about his words. He spoke in the contrite voice of a man who is begging a favor of a dear friend . . . to whom he hasn't spoken in a long time.

"I confess, Lord, that I haven't been as reliant on you as I should have been. I beg you to look down upon us and remember your people. Israel cries out to you, God, as do I. Defend your people, Lord, and protect those in America who love you as well. Be our strength and defender, God; be our mighty shield."

Devorah stared at him, perplexed. Now his words sounded familiar— almost as though they had sprung from the psalms. She had assumed he would pray to Jesus, but he was praying to a God she recognized, using words and phrases she could understand.

Looking away, she gave herself a stern mental shake. Michael Reed was a Christian, one of those who claimed God was a Trinity, when one of the basic tenets of Judaism proclaimed that HaShem was one, a unity unlike any other possible unity.

An image focused in her thoughts—her father, sitting at the Shabbat table, quizzing her and Asher on the thirteen foundations of Jewish belief. "The twelfth foundation of the *Ramba'm,*" he said, his voice ghostly in her memory, "is the time of the *Moshiach,* the anointed one. There is no king to the Jewish people except from the House of David and the seed of Solomon. We are not to calculate the time of his coming, but we are to believe and be certain that the Messiah will come. He will not be late. He will come at the proper time."

Looking up at the dimpled ceiling tiles, Devorah lifted her thoughts to HaShem. "Surely this is a good time to send the Messiah. For the sake of my father and those who have suffered so much for so long . . ."

She felt the pressure of Michael's gentle squeeze upon her fingers, then lowered her gaze to find him watching her. She blushed, suddenly aware that she had spoken aloud without meaning to.

"Come." Michael stood and helped her to her feet.

"Where are we going?"

"We're going back to the situation room . . . to watch God work. Remember what Ezekiel said? Today is the day when the nations will know that God is the Holy One in Israel." He took a deep breath, then gave her a smile. "I don't know how, but it's all going to work out."

–0100111100–

Alone in his command vehicle, Vladimir Gogol studied the keyboard of his laptop computer and cursed softly. Everything that could go wrong had gone wrong in the space of a few hours, and the reports coming in now only deepened his anger. How could the world's strongest, most trained, and most capable army be defeated by mud, rain, and earth tremors? Those three elements of nature had confounded his positions at sunrise, and the mudslides and collapsed weapons systems had begun a chain of tragic failures that seemed to grow worse by the minute. Not even the reports of several successful missile launches on the United States had improved his mood.

He did not need to look outside his window to know that the weather would not improve in the next few hours. An air of brooding desolation lay over this land, and some cynical part of his brain wondered why the Arabs had ever wanted to claim it. The sun was hiding behind an oppressive blanket of clouds; the light was as weak as yesterday's dreams. Wind, rain, and hail were tossing his men and their weapons like tree branches, first one direction and then the other, and every so often the gloom went nova as a bolt of lightning skittered through the darkened sky. The lightning had already fried several of their communications systems; he hadn't been able to reach the commanders of the other allied units since before dawn.

He heard a commotion outside the door of his vehicle. "Enter!"

Colonel Petrov, his second in command, opened the door and climbed up the stairs, his face pale and wet. He saluted, then began to babble. "Excuse me, General, but we have just received word from the Libyan units deployed along the Egyptian border. A plague has broken out among the troops. The men who are not ill have panicked and run, while Israeli jet fighters have begun to strafe our convoys—"

"Have you gone mad?" Gogol spat out the words contemptuously. "How could they come down with plague?"

"It's the weapons, sir." Fresh misery darkened Petrov's face. "That unit was armed with missiles carrying bubonic plague."

Gogol stared at his aide across a sudden ringing silence. "Impossible. They could not have been exposed. Plague has an incubation period of two or three days. Even if there was an accident in the earthquake this morning, there hasn't been time for anyone to develop symptoms."

"There were no accidents in the Libyan sectors, sir." Petrov's steady gaze burned through Gogol. "The men believe they were exposed en route, as they transported the missiles from our warships. An Egyptian doctor has confirmed the symptoms—it is plague, sir. There is no doubt about it."

Numb with increasing rage, Gogol clenched his fist and pounded the table, then looked away. This felt like a bad dream, like that terrible day when the love of his life had confessed to being a traitor and a Jewess. What was happening to him? He was Vladimir Gogol! He had risen from the pits of obscurity to become the most powerful man in Russia. He had spent years preparing for this day, and his men had trained for months. They had even agreed to train those hotheaded Arabs, who put far more emphasis on zeal and religious causes than on military discipline and procedures.

Trembling, he felt a heat in his chest and belly he recognized as pure rage. Not even Alanna had roused his anger so.

He turned, transferring his gaze to Petrov. "Have the men mount another nuclear missile."

"But, sir—the Israelis have already intercepted three nuclear warheads."

Vladimir looked down at his map, his breath burning in his throat. "Don't target Tel Aviv this time. Set the target coordinates for Jerusalem."

A chilly silence settled over the cabin, and after a moment Gogol turned back to Petrov. The colonel stood stiff and somber in the silence, his mouth tight with mutiny.

"I gave you an order, Colonel."

"Sir—you cannot target Jerusalem. The Arabs will never stand for it. Many of the Jews have already fled the city, and thousands of the remaining inhabitants are Palestinian."

"I *will* target Jerusalem. The Arabs can rebuild their holy mosque— what do I care if it falls? But the Jews won't expect this one. It will slip by their defenses, and when it does—"

"There are others who revere that city. Adrian Romulus speaks often of Jerusalem."

Vladimir closed his eyes as alarm and anger rippled along his spine. Petrov was right. Not only would the Arabs never forgive him for targeting Jerusalem, neither would Adrian Romulus. The stones of that three-thousand-year-old city might be dusty and ancient, but most of the world considered it a holy place. Romulus had often mentioned his love for

Jerusalem, and if at this moment there was a man more powerful than Gogol, it was Romulus.

Vladimir swallowed a hysterical surge of angry laughter. "You are right, of course. Do not send a nuclear weapon to Jerusalem. Send a chemical weapon to Tel Aviv instead—on the new Revenant missile."

Surprise siphoned the blood from Petrov's face. "The Revenant? But, sir, the fiberoptic guidance system has not been tested under these weather conditions. With so much electrical activity in the atmosphere, we cannot be certain it will correctly target—"

"It passed our tests at Pushkina, and it will work now." Vladimir waved aside the colonel's hesitation. "It will fly so low that Israeli radar will not pick it up until it is too late. We will give them a surprise, and we will mount the warhead with . . ."

He paused, considering his options. He wanted instant death, not prolonged illnesses, and none of the biologicals acted quickly enough. Of the nerve agents in his arsenal, VX was the most toxic and fast-acting, but VX was a liquid and dispersed effectively over a relatively small area. But Sarin—that nerve agent could be inhaled, and death occurred in one to ten minutes. The victims of this attack would fall dead before they even knew what had killed them.

"Mount the warhead with Sarin dispersal devices."

Petrov nodded stiffly, saluted, then exited the vehicle to execute Gogol's order.

-0100111100-

Ten minutes later, Vladimir stepped outside the mobile command vehicle, thrust his hands behind his back, and moved toward the ridge where the Revenant missile launcher had been mounted on a wheeled vehicle. Petrov stood beside the truck and snapped to attention as Vladimir approached.

The ground was uneven here, broken by ridges and hollows, and every foot of the surface was strewn with rocky debris. To Vladimir's right rose the jagged precipice known as the Mount of Temptation; behind him, the Jordan valley stretched away like a broad green canvas. He was concerned with the mountains to the west, over which the missile would fly toward Tel Aviv.

Vladimir's eyes took in the missile, the launcher, and his men ready to do their jobs. The Revenant had a range of up to seventy kilometers and used infrared imaging for high-precision targeting by day or night. The images from an infrared camera in the nose of the missile were transmitted through a fiberoptic cable to a firing post miles away, where the images were automatically analyzed, processed, and displayed to the weapon system operator. The operator could send the missile precise guidance instructions via the optical fiber cable.

The Revenant operated unlike any other weapon. Like all missiles, it flew toward predetermined target coordinates, but unlike other missiles, an inflight Revenant relayed a picture of its target and instantly allowed a remote operator to choose the exact moment and point of detonation. It was also capable of dodging missiles from defensive Patriot and Arrow batteries.

Vladimir was going to fly the Revenant right through the wall around the Israeli Defense Headquarters and detonate it in General Yehuda Almog's war room. After that, he'd send another Revenant to the prime minister's office and a third to the Knesset to atone for the botched raid by Dyakonov and his spetsnaz team.

A smile tugged at his lips. The State of Israel would die today.

The rising wind came whipping past him, lifting the beribboned medals on his uniform. He turned to Petrov and let his gaze rove over the assembled men. They would never forget this moment.

"This will show them that we are undeniably superior." He stepped back and surveyed the rocky terrain to the west, land he would soon control. "Are you ready to launch, Colonel?"

"Yes, General." Petrov stepped forward and his eyes met Gogol's. "Will you give the order, sir?"

"I would be honored." Vladimir stepped forward onto a small rise and lifted his chin, allowing the assembled men to see that his face remained full of strength and confident peace despite the morning's setbacks. This moment would fulfill his destiny. He had been born to conquer Israel; fate had chosen him to restore Russia to her former greatness. In an hour, Israel would know Vladimir Gogol was all-powerful. And in the coming weeks, the world would realize that Jews were the root of all evil and deserved the fate he would deal their nation today.

Gogol lifted his hand. "Initiate launch sequence."

The soldier at the firing station tapped on his keyboard, aligning his control panel and high-resolution display with the global positioning system and command, control, communications, and information system interface in the missile. A digitized map of Tel Aviv appeared on the display, with the IDF headquarters outlined in red. The operator adjusted the final impact position to within ten meters of the building's center, then stepped back. Additional target direction would be required only when the missile neared the target.

Petrov and his company released the metal straps holding the missile in its canister, then stepped away from the mobile launcher.

"Launch codes activated, sir. Sixty seconds until launch."

Gogol thrust his hands behind his back and stared at the roiling sky. The men around him remained silent, undoubtedly understanding that this was a highly significant moment. Soon the missile would be away, accelerated by a solid propellant booster to an initial cruising speed of more than 150 meters per second. The turbojet engine would take the missile to the target under control of the guidance system, allowing the operator to determine altitude and missile speed.

History would be made in exactly eight minutes, when this missile flew sixty-five kilometers to Tel Aviv and dispersed deadly Sarin gas in the center of IDF headquarters. In their last ten minutes of life, the Israeli high command would know they could not defeat a superior force.

The quiet sound of humming machinery filled the silence as the mobile platform rose to the correct launch angle. Overhead, a gray cloud churned while the wind blew soft raindrops that spattered upon the launch canister and shone like pearls on the steel gray casing.

"Forty-five seconds," the control operator called, his eyes fixed to the display. Vladimir stared at a landscape bled of all color and felt the earth begin to tremble. A slash of lightning stabbed through the gray cloud overhead, but Vladimir held his position. He would command this launch and ride the hot winds of the afternoon to victory.

Thunder echoed across the empty vista, and lightning stabbed at the ragged fretwork of stone on the cliffs. The vibrations beneath his boots continued, growing in intensity, and for a moment Vladimir wondered if somehow the earth itself had sensed his jubilation. Let the mountains move! Let these rocks fall upon Israel! The moment of victory had come!

A hiss of steam escaped the vents beside the missile fins while the launch platform continued to rise. A glance at the computer telemetry told Vladimir that the correct launch angle was forty-four degrees. The missile's nose slowly continued its upward arc, then vibrated softly as the launch platform settled into its proper place.

"Thirty seconds," the controller said, lifting his head to check the missile's position.

The gusting winds created small whirlwinds of dust and grit that scoured Vladimir's flesh and left him grinding sand between his teeth. He ignored the irritation and kept his gaze fixed on the western horizon. Let a storm come! The Israelis would think he was cowering beneath the bad weather, waiting to fight another day. They would not expect this mortal blow.

Vladimir glanced out at the rocky terrain. A gray tree, leafless and scoured by the wind-driven sand, stood ten meters to the west. As the wild wind hooted, its bare limbs bobbed in agitation, then the tree toppled forward, the crown of its roots rising as the skeletal branches crashed to the earth below.

Vladimir's nerves tensed as a low rumble beneath the earth gave rise to a terrifying roar. The rocky terrain crumbled and cracked, then a massive rock pushed its way out of the earth and jostled the launch platform, lifting the front wheels of the vehicle.

Fear brushed the edge of Vladimir's mind as his men scrambled back. "Stop the launch!" he roared, but the bawling winds snatched his words away. The controller pecked at the firing station keyboard, but the red-rimmed rock kept rising from the earth, lifting the Revenant's nose and distorting the launch angle. The nose of the missile moved to fifty degrees above the horizon, then fifty-five. As dirt and rocks and small trees toppled in the quake, the intruding stone continued to propel the missile upward.

Vladimir felt his throat go dry. If the rocket launched at this angle, it would deviate from its projected path and might be picked up by Israeli radar and destroyed miles away from Tel Aviv. Unlike a nuclear warhead, which could be destroyed without detonation, the Sarin gas would fall *somewhere*, perhaps on his own troops scattered throughout the West Bank.

"Cancel the launch!"

At the command post, the controller shook his head. "General, the system is locked up. The electromagnetic circuits are not responding!"

Petrov broke from the line of observers and ran toward the rocket just as the missile leapt from its launcher. A sheet of dazzling flame poured from the solid fuel rocket motor, blackening the rocky ground and igniting brown bits of shrubbery and desert grass. Screeching in agony, Petrov fell to the ground, a human torch, as the engine accelerated the missile upward too fast for the eye to follow.

Vladimir felt a scream rise in his throat and choked it off. While the scorched ground smoked and a swarm of men surrounded Petrov, he looked toward the intrusive rock that had somehow managed to elevate the Revenant to an astounding ninety degrees.

He stalked to the firing station and shoved the hapless controller aside. After punching in the codes for a ninety-degree launch trajectory, Vladimir noted the results and nodded grimly.

"Can we adjust the angle in flight?" he asked the controller, turning the display so the man could see it.

The soldier's face was dead-white and sheened with a cold sweat. "No, sir." His eyes met Vladimir's. "We could make minor adjustments, but nothing to override the pull of gravity."

Vladimir nodded, then stepped away from the controls.

Perhaps destiny has led me astray. The wry thought made him smile, if only briefly, and dispelled the frisson he had felt at the realization that the missile would fly upward for sixty-five kilometers, then determine it had not reached its target coordinates. A self-destruct circuit would sense the absence of acceleration and explode the missile harmlessly, but the Sarin would be released in the air currents and drift back to earth on the wings of the wind.

-0100111100-

Alone in the mobile command vehicle, Vladimir locked his hands behind his back and paced in the narrow space between his bunk and his desk. He had slipped on his gas mask immediately after entering the vehicle, but now wondered if his action had been wise. His men might panic if they saw him wearing a mask, and he couldn't afford a large-scale uprising. Few of his men even had gas masks, for all intelligence reports indicated that the Israelis had never stored biological or chemical weapons.

He looked out the small window. Which way was the wind blowing? One moment it appeared to move eastward, another moment it seemed to blow west. He would take a chopper and fly away from this ghastly spot, but unless the wind calmed he wouldn't know if he was flying out of the Sarin dispersal area or directly into it.

Irritated at the frightened current moving through him, he lumbered to the front of the mobile command post and took his place behind the wheel. He had never actually driven the armored vehicle, but how difficult could it be?

He patted the dashboard, shoving maps and papers and forms out of the way, then felt an ignition switch in a shallow indentation. He flipped the lever and felt a moment's satisfaction as the engine roared to life. A pair of sentries beyond the tinted windows backed away in surprise as Gogol gripped the wheel and shoved the vehicle into gear.

He had to get away. He would drive out of the area and take a chopper to an allied air base. They would launch another assault tomorrow, and another, as many as it took to rid the earth of the Jews.

Staring through the round circles of the gas mask, he lowered his head and kept his eyes on the rutted road. Bolts of lightning chased each other across the dark sky, as white and jagged as the bones of sun-bleached skeletons. The wind blew at the vehicle, raining sand upon the windshield, while Vladimir inhaled air so hot and wet he felt as though he were breathing through a vinyl-scented towel.

The vehicle bumped heavily over the road, and he crunched the gears, trying to work the sluggish trailer up to speed. The wind blew stronger now, and blowing sand obscured his vision. He pressed down on the brake and leaned forward to squint through the narrow windshield.

The men in his camp were dying. Several lay face down in the sand, others convulsed before his eyes, their hands reaching toward him like claws. The Sarin cloud had descended.

Setting his jaw in determination, Vladimir applied his foot to the accelerator and moved steadily through the gloom. If not for this mask he'd be on the ground, too. Keeping one hand on the wheel, he brought his fingers to the round filter cover at the end of the mask and felt for the reassuring rim of the lifesaving filter.

He couldn't feel it.

Vladimir felt a sudden darkness behind his eyes. He slammed on the brake, a chilly dew forming on his skin as he lifted both hands and clutched at the round protuberance that jutted from the end of his mask. He lifted up the vinyl cover and gouged his thumbnail into the space between the two heavy layers of plastic, seeking the filter's rim . . . and felt nothing.

He'd grabbed a mask without checking its filter . . . so he was breathing the same air as the dying men outside. He sniffled, then noted with professional detachment that he was already experiencing the first symptom of Sarin poisoning.

He wrenched the mask from his head and stared out the window at the empty pewter sky. This was a place of death, a cursed place of ruins and rocks. In a moment the pupils of his eyes would contract and he would have difficulty seeing, in two minutes he would feel as if a tank were sitting on his chest. These symptoms would be followed in rapid succession by nausea and vomiting, cramps and involuntary loss of bodily functions, twitching, jerking, convulsion, coma, and death.

His throat burned already; his mouth felt as dry as sandpaper.

He stumbled out from behind the steering wheel and moved toward the computer on his desk. With trembling fingers he accessed his e-mail program, then typed the first three letters of Romulus's electronic address. Thankfully, the program picked up the thread and filled in the blank spaces.

Vladimir tabbed down to the message area and struggled to type on a keyboard he could no longer clearly see. His fingers seemed to have lost all coordination, however, and a sudden spasm of his chest muscles caught him off guard, pulling him to the floor.

Below his half-finished message, the laptop's cursor blinked patiently:

Kill them all __

CHAPTER FORTY-TWO

Jerusalem
1203 hours
Friday, December 22

WHILE ASHER SNORED IN THE EASY CHAIR, NO LESS THE WORSE FOR HIS experience in the desert, Michael and Devorah sat in the prim parlor of her father's house. The rabbi had not yet returned to Jerusalem, but Devorah had wanted to keep an eye on Asher and check on the condition of her father's house after the earthquake.

Now Michael sat next to her on the sofa watching the television tuned to CNN. Forced to operate out of an affiliated office in Charleston, South Carolina, that network had sent its cameras around the world to survey the damage brought about by the war they were now calling "Gogol's Invasion."

Though few reporters correctly linked the war with God's supernatural deliverance of his people, none could deny the significance of the worldwide earthquake that coincided with the Russian general's advance. Cities around the world had trembled in the earthquake that rumbled beneath Israel at dawn on December 21, and portions of Tokyo, Athens, Rome, Sydney, San Francisco, and Mexico City had been reduced to rubble. Seismologists were still struggling to explain how the quake's shock waves seemed to grow *stronger* as they spread from the epicenter of Jerusalem. "We can only surmise that this was a cataclysmic, extraordinary event," one seismologist told a CNN reporter. "Some religious leaders are saying the source is supernatural, but there has to be a scientific explanation. We just haven't discovered it yet."

As incredible as the earthquake was, the reports of nuclear devastation were far more compelling. According to the latest reports, more than twenty nuclear warheads had been launched at key cities in the United States, including most of the military installations on the East and West Coasts. Most of the nuclear missiles had been detected and successfully intercepted, but New York, Atlanta, Washington D.C., and Los Angeles had had been targeted for multistrike attacks and sustained overwhelming damage.

In those cities, the Federal Emergency Management Agency had stepped in to declare martial law. President Stedman had escaped injury only because he had decided to spend Christmas away from Washington; Vice President John Miller was counted among the known dead. Though the capital had been annihilated, due to the holiday break, every congressional representative had survived.

A flash of wild grief ripped through Michael as he watched the newscasts. With the single exception of Pearl Harbor, no American city had ever been bombed by a foreign power. The horror of nuclear war left him speechless. His eyes filled as he saw burned children screaming, mothers weeping for their dead babies, angry fathers venting their frustration and pain in violence. Michael had grown accustomed to the face of war, but even he had tended to compartmentalize it—war was something that happened to other countries in faraway places. In the constant flow of televised images, he realized how false his assumptions had been.

America *was* vulnerable—more vulnerable than he had realized. And now Americans were suffering even more than the Israelis. God had stepped in to defend his chosen people and his holy city.

Shifting on the sofa, Devorah turned to look at him, her eyes shining moist and her voice husky. "How are you feeling?"

He shook his head and shrugged, unable to find words to convey his thoughts. Daniel Prentice, wherever he was, had been right about everything, though he had taken his cues from a couple of prophets who had been dead for over two thousand years. If the prophets could predict this war, they could predict other future events, too . . . and Michael intended to find out what would happen next.

He would never again waste time with doubt. He'd be ready.

Devorah reached out and pressed her hand to his shoulder in a compassionate caress. He did not look at her, for he knew what that touch, here in her father's house where such things were forbidden, had cost her.

The CNN camera was now focused on Adrian Romulus, who wore an expression of shocked sympathy as he toured the outskirts of the war-torn cities with William Blackstone. At one point in the photo op, Blackstone stopped and stared into the camera. "The blame for this devastation can be laid only at the feet of one man—Samuel Stedman. Stedman has been covertly aiding Israel throughout his term, and I promise to undertake a full investigation. As soon as I am inaugurated, we will discover the truth about what caused this tragedy and we will make reparation to the families who have suffered unspeakable loss. We will rebuild. We will overcome war and hate and destruction!"

The scene changed, and footage of a flaming Mississippi synagogue blazed across the television screen. "Bill Blackstone blames President Stedman, but most residents in this coastal town blame Israel for yesterday's horror," the news reporter said. "And though the Russian government has apologized for the deadly attacks, said to have been triggered by an outmoded automated defense system, Americans are in no mood for forgiveness."

Devorah lowered her head and pushed at a wayward dark curl. "My father always said anti-Semitism would run rampant in the last days."

Michael looked at her. "You sound like a believer."

"Perhaps I am." A smile trembled over her lips. "In the last two days I have seen things that cannot be explained by logic or reason or technology. They must have sprung from the hand of God." She trembled slightly, as though a chilly breeze had just blown over her. "Do you remember the Sukkot service? We recited the traditional psalms that night, and I haven't been able to get the words out of my mind."

She looked up at him, alert and present, but with the traces of memory in her eyes. "It is better to trust in the LORD than to put confidence in man," she whispered. "It is better to trust in the LORD than to put confidence in princes. All nations compassed me about: but in the name of the LORD will I destroy them. They compassed me about like bees; they are quenched as the fire of thorns: for in the name of the LORD I will destroy them."

She lifted her brows and smiled, waiting for him to respond, but Michael stared at her with deadly concentration. "I'm afraid I wasn't following much that night. Most of the prayers were in Hebrew."

Her smile deepened into laughter. "Sorry, I forgot. But don't you see? The psalmist wrote about the very thing that has happened in the State of Israel. We were surrounded by a swarm of nations, but God himself swatted them away. In the end, it wasn't our weapons or America or even luck that saved us—it was the hand of God. I see that now . . . so clearly."

Michael said nothing but reached out and ran his hand over her riotous hair as he pretended to turn his attention back to the television. Some part of him was thrilled that Devorah had found her way back to the faith of her father, but another part wanted to curl up and protect the place in his heart only she had managed to touch.

He pressed his hand to her head, his heart swelling with a feeling he had thought long dead. He loved her. He dredged the admission from a place beyond logic and reason and knew he could never confess the truth. Loving her would mean taking her away from her people and her home, and he could no more do that than he could remain in Israel. Soon he would be needed at home, in the service of his country, just as Devorah would be needed in Israel.

As the knowledge twisted and turned inside him, he sighed heavily and shoved his hands in his pockets. "Look, I'm really tired," he said, hunching forward. "Why don't you show me where I can bed down? I'll see you in the morning."

A new anguish seared his heart when she stood, her face bleak with hurt. "You can sleep in Asher's room," she said, her voice polite and distant. "Good night, Captain Reed."

-01001111100-

Adrian Romulus pressed the button on the limo, then closed his eyes in relief as the dark-tinted glass rose silently to block the sights, sounds, and smells of the devastation around him. For a few days he had actually hoped Gogol might pull it off, but then the dark voice whispered in Romulus's dream, and he knew Gogol would fail.

It was part of the Master's plan. One man would fall so another might rise. One nation would be humbled so others would be chastised and another would be thrust into the blinding white light of international attention.

Israel sat in the spotlight now, that valiant little nation whose capital, Jerusalem, would soon become Romulus's footstool. Jerusalem, the Holy City, would be his once he had wooed and won the Jewish people to his side. Like any intelligent suitor, Romulus knew just what would win the affections of a shy bride.

A temple. Rising white and gold on the mountain of God, dwarfing the sons of men.

"The driver wants to know where you want to go, Adrian." Elijah Reis's voice, dark and smooth, broke into Romulus's thoughts.

Romulus thought for a moment, then opened his eyes and gave his companion a confident smile. "The nearest functional airport," he said, letting his hand fall upon Elijah's. "We have important plans to make and a conference to organize. I want to go home."

He crossed his hands at his waist and closed his eyes again, settling back into the car's upholstery as Elijah lowered the slide and gave instructions to the driver.

Chapter Forty-three

0800 hours
Saturday, December 23

IN THE SPARE BEDROOM OF THE RABBI'S HOUSE, MICHAEL AWOKE ON A CLEAR
Sabbath morning to the sound of dancing and music. An odd impromptu
marching band moved down the cobbled length of Etyopya Street, the
clarinet and cymbals celebrating the defeat of General Gogol and his
multinational force.

Michael pulled on a pair of Asher's sweatpants and moved into the living room. Devorah stood at the window, one hand holding back the edge
of a curtain. The warm sunlight of early morning shone on her face, gild-
ing its loveliness, and Michael caught his breath.

He clenched his fists, restraining his natural impulses. Not now. Not
ever. He would ruin a beautiful friendship if he thought that way.

He tucked his hands securely under his arms and moved to stand
beside her, forcing his eyes to remain on the street outside. "Quite a celebration, hmm?"

She hit him with a sudden smile that made his heart turn over. "Quite.
The news has been playing on television since six. General Gogol is dead,
a victim of his own chemical weapon. It's too early to tell, but it would
appear that nearly 80 percent of the troops encamped around Israel are
dead."

"Eighty-three point thirty-three percent," Michael whispered, taking
pains to keep his eyes focused on the street musicians.

"You heard the report?"

"I read Ezekiel. The prophet predicted that only one in six of Gog's
army would survive the devastation. That's an 83.33 percent mortality
rate."

Devorah bit her lip and let the curtain fall. "I ought to wake Asher. He should be enjoying this, too."

"Wait." The word slipped from Michael's lips before he could stop it. "Before you go—"

Her steady gaze bore into him in silent expectation. "Yes, Michael?"

"Devorah." Against his will, his hands reached out, touched her shoulders, slipped down her arms. Even in her mother's old chenille robe and with her hair askew, she radiated a vitality that drew him like a magnet. "I'm sorry I hurt you last night. And before you wake Asher, there's something we need to discuss."

She looked away, but he knew she could tell what he meant.

Driven by a sense of urgency, he brought one hand to the warmth of her neck. "Devorah, my work here is finished. In less than a month, William Blackstone will be sworn in as the next U.S. president. He'll yank me back to Fort Meade as soon as he can."

A rush of pink stained her cheek. "Do you have to go?"

"Do I have a reason to stay?"

She looked at him then, and at the base of her throat a pulse beat and swelled as though her heart had risen from its usual place. Michael pulled her close, relishing the swirling heat that drew them together and the rush of blood through his veins. Her touch made him forget where he was even as his mind warned him he had no business pursuing a relationship that would destroy everything Devorah held dear.

She reached up, placed her hands along the sides of his face, and smiled at him through her tears. "You have given me so much," she whispered, admiration and affection radiating from the dark depths of her eyes. "Tell me what to do."

His arms tightened and drew her close as his common sense skittered into the shadows. He lowered his head, about to kiss her, then the abrupt slam of a car door brought him back to his senses.

As footsteps scraped over the cobblestones and the front door creaked open, Michael and Devorah reluctantly parted. Michael tensed as Rabbi Cohen walked into the room. With one glance the rabbi took in Devorah's sleep-tousled hair and robe, Michael's sweatpants, and the dark flushes on their faces. He nodded slowly, his expression a mask of stone.

"I am glad you are both here," he said, bringing his palms to rest on the cane in his hand. "Dress yourselves. We are going to take a drive."

A muscle quivered at Devorah's jaw as she stepped away from Michael and ran a hand through her hair. "Where are we going, Abba?"

"You will see."

As embarrassed as a preacher's kid caught with his hand in the collection plate, Michael gestured toward the bedroom where he had slept. "Asher's here, too. He and I shared a room last night."

The rabbi's implacable expression was unnerving. "Let Asher sleep. This trip is for the two of you only."

Devorah paused long enough to give Michael a single worried smile, then moved toward her room.

-0100111100-

The rabbi, who insisted upon riding in the backseat, gave Devorah directions to an obscure military base located in the emptiness of the Negev. "Abba, that base has been abandoned for years," she said, frowning at the printed directions.

"It is not abandoned." The rabbi stared out his window, a watchful fixity in his face. "It is where I have been living for the last three days. Drive, Daughter."

Devorah obeyed without another word, and soon they were on the open highway and driving south into the desert region. She switched on the radio as they drove, and Michael listened in amazement as Israeli Radio broadcast updates on the events of the previous three days. "Israeli emergency teams have been overtaxed as they attempt to clear the mountains of the more than one million dead," the broadcaster announced, his voice heavy. "Already there have been reports of vultures and buzzards gathering in the valleys, and authorities worry about plague-infected animals spreading disease in inhabited areas. The prime minister's cabinet is designating specially created government burial teams to rid the land of battle casualties. IDF officials have also expressed amazement at the sheer number of munitions left behind. It is estimated that a fortune in armaments has been abandoned in the valleys of Lebanon and on the plains of Jordan and Syria. Incredibly, a professor at Jerusalem University has pointed out that many of these weapons are made of a compressed wood product that could serve very well as fuel." The broadcaster broke into a wry chuckle. "Imagine that, ladies and gentlemen. We'll not have to import coal for *years*."

"Amazing," Devorah murmured.

"Predicted." Michael winked at her when she glanced at him. "Ezekiel. Israel will collect enough fuel from Gog's army to last seven years. For seven months those government cleanup teams will gather the dead and bury them in a place to be called the Valley of Hamon Gog. And all the nations will see the punishment of God, and Israel will know that God has delivered her from the hand of Gog and the nations who marched with him."

From the corner of his eye, Michael saw Rav Cohen's head turn in surprise. "You know the prophet Ezekiel?" the rabbi asked, one bushy brow lifting.

"I've been reading a lot of Ezekiel lately," Michael answered, shifting to look at the older man. "And I've found his prophecies very interesting."

A half smile crossed the rabbi's face, then he returned his gaze to the front of the car and remained silent until they reached the tall chain-link fence around what appeared to be an abandoned military installation. Despite the heavy rolls of concertina wire along the top of the tall fence, there were no cars in the parking lot, and only a single guard at the security checkpoint.

Devorah drove up to the gate, showed her ID, and waited while the guard walked around the car. When he saw Rabbi Cohen in the backseat, however, he halted his inspection and waved Devorah through.

"I never knew you had such pull with the military, Abba," Devorah said, glancing up in the rearview mirror.

"There are many things you have not known, my Devorah."

Devorah parked in the empty lot near a row of hangars, then she and Michael got out of the car and waited for Rabbi Cohen to lead the way. The rabbi set off at a quick pace, the wind blowing his earlocks and the edges of his fringes as he followed a sidewalk.

He called over his shoulder as he walked. "HaShem, blessed be his name, has saved our people."

"I know, Abba." Devorah gave Michael a quick smile, then lengthened her stride until she walked by her father's side. "Anyone with eyes to see has realized the truth."

Her father looked up as if surprised, then drew his lips in thoughtfully.

"So my wandering daughter has returned to the fold. Good. Now I will show you what will preserve Israel for all time."

Michael thrust his hands in his pockets and followed, more than a little curious about the rabbi's secretive manner. What had the Israelis hidden out here in this forsaken place, and why did Rabbi Cohen have access to it? Michael knew the man was revered as one of the descendants of Aaron, but he was no military expert, so why had they hidden him on this base during the invasion? And if they had some sort of weapon hidden out here, why hadn't they thought to use it during Gogol's attack?

The rabbi paused before a mammoth airplane hanger, then punched a keycode in the electronic lock on the door. The lock clicked open, and Michael stepped forward to open the door for the rabbi and his daughter. Devorah flashed him a smile of thanks, then lifted a brow as if to say she had no idea what her father was up to, either.

They followed the rabbi into a hangar the size of two football fields, their footsteps echoing weirdly in the vast empty space. The concrete floor was dark with oil stains and the footprints of those who had built this place, and the rabbi walked confidently through the gloom lit only by clerestory windows high in the curved roof. Halfway into the hanger, a deep access bay broke the concrete expanse. A staircase led into the empty well, and the rabbi turned to follow it without hesitation.

Devorah followed her father, but paused to give Michael a questioning look before taking the first step. He shrugged and followed. The rabbi moved slowly, one hand holding tight to the iron railing set into the wall on the railing, the other hand on his cane. Slowly he tapped his way down at least three dozen steps. At the base of the staircase, the rabbi opened a steel door that led to a narrow space of six inches, beyond which stood a pair of elevator doors. Michael looked and saw that there was no call button—only a small touchpad the size of a saltine cracker.

"This elevator," the rabbi explained as he pressed the flat area of his thumb to the panel, "can only be operated by one of the Kohein. We are allowed to bring visitors, of course—if we feel HaShem, blessed be his name, approves." He looked at Michael, and for the first time Michael saw the light of approval in the older man's eyes. "I am certain the Master of the universe understands what I am about to show you. It is important for you to see this."

Michael felt the vibration of machinery beneath his feet and heard the sound of a rising elevator. A moment later the steel doors parted. The rabbi stepped into the compartment, then held the door open while Devorah and Michael entered. Once inside, the rabbi touched another touchpad, and the elevator began to descend.

Rabbi Cohen smiled as he folded his arms. "The computer maintains a database of over 300,000 sons of Aaron," he explained. "There are even a few Kohein sprinkled throughout your country, Captain Reed. Any one of them could come and witness what I am about to show you—if they wanted to."

A sad note filled his voice, a surge of longing and regret. Michael said nothing, but waited until the elevator stopped and the doors opened into a brightly lit hallway. Ten feet away from the elevator, a pair of uniformed IDF soldiers stood at attention outside a pair of gleaming wooden doors.

The rabbi did not speak to the guards, but moved down the polished hallway with the confident air of a five-star general inspecting his troops. He paused outside the double doors, pressed his thumb to yet another sensor panel and spoke a few Hebrew words into an intercom mounted on the wall.

"Another protective device." He smiled at his daughter as the lock clicked. "In case someone decides to cut off my thumb and use it for a key. The biometrics of my thumb and voiceprint must match an established pattern in the computer before we can pass through this door."

"I'm surprised it doesn't read your retina," Michael remarked as they stepped into yet another room.

The rabbi's face brightened at the suggestion. "A very good idea, Captain. We will take it under advisement."

This chamber was completely unlike any room Michael had ever entered. The walls, floor, even the ceiling were made of white marble veined with threads of gold. The room seemed to shimmer with purity and power, and the rabbi stepped out of his shoes before moving carefully across the sparkling floor.

Michael looked at Devorah and lifted a brow. Shrugging, she slipped out of her leather shoes and left them on the mat by the door. Michael did the same, then followed the rabbi and his daughter.

The rabbi moved forward into the pure space, then disappeared behind a corner of white marble. As Michael followed, he found himself standing before a smooth and seamless wall of plate glass, as black as night.

The rabbi bent forward and bowed rapidly toward the space, murmuring in a stream of Hebrew. Devorah stopped as if hesitant to draw closer and Michael stood beside her, equally mystified. The air in this place seemed cool and fragrant, scented with sweet incense, though Michael could see no sign of candles or flames or lamps.

And then, before Michael's startled eyes, a glow rose from the darkness on the other side of the glass wall. It bloomed slowly at first, like a rare and radiant flower, then expanded and rose like a golden cloud hovering in the center of what appeared to be another chamber. In the fiery radiance Michael could see the shining forms of two angelic beings who faced each other with their wings outstretched, their wingtips separated only by a fraction of an inch.

The glowing sphere of light grew and rotated, throwing sparks of brilliant radiance throughout the chamber. As the light expanded, further illuminating the chamber, Michael saw that the angels sat upon a chest with two golden poles attached to its sides.

He blinked in astonished silence when he recognized the rabbi's secret.

Devorah recovered first and spoke in a voice soft with disbelief. "The Ark of the Covenant."

"The Shekinah," her father echoed. "The glory of God."

Ripples of shock were spreading from an epicenter in Michael's stomach, making the crown of his head tingle and his toes go numb. The ark of the Exodus? He couldn't believe it still existed. Most people didn't believe it had *ever* existed. Seeing it here, surrounded by the holy glory of God, was like discovering Noah's ark or the cross of Jesus Christ. It was *proof* that the Bible was truth, not myth, that God was real and not a by-product of mankind's yearning for significance.

Devorah sank to her knees, then bent low and pressed her hands to the floor, echoing her father's prayers. Michael knelt, too, his faith stirred and his hope restored. God did have a plan, and he was obviously at work in the lives of his people.

Chapter Forty-four

1205 hours
Tuesday, December 26

STANDING JUST OUTSIDE THE CUSTOMS AREA AT BEN GURION INTERNATIONAL Airport, Michael clutched his suitcase and struggled to wrap his thoughts around the necessity of saying his good-byes. In the wake of the war's nuclear devastation, President Samuel Stedman had requested that he return home immediately.

Devorah, Asher, and Rabbi Cohen stood before Michael now, their faces mirroring his own discomfort. Asher stepped forward first. "It's been a real pleasure to know you, Captain Reed. I will never forget that I owe you my life."

"Thank Devorah. She's the one who risked everything to save you."

Asher nodded, then stepped back and gave Michael a formal salute. Michael returned it, then lowered his suitcase as Rabbi Cohen came forward.

"Blessings be upon you, Michael Reed." The rabbi held Michael's hand for a long moment as his soulful eyes searched Michael's face. "I have spent many sleepless nights since your arrival."

Michael lowered his gaze, his feelings too raw to discuss even with Devorah's father. His heart was squeezed so tight he could barely draw breath to speak, but he forced the words out. "You have nothing to fear from me, sir. I love your daughter. I would suffer myself before I would allow anyone to hurt her."

A trace of unguarded affection shone in the rabbi's eyes as he looked at Michael. "You are a good man, Captain Reed, but you do not understand our ways. The Torah laws forbidding intermarriage are God's laws, and therefore they are just and good."

Michael looked away, unwilling to voice the words that rose to his tongue. This man had probably never experienced anything like the feelings that bound Michael and Devorah; he certainly had grown up in a different world.

"You think I am an old man, and you are right." The rabbi's words, murmured and uninflected, ran together in a soothing tune pitched to reach Michael's ear alone. "But I know love is more than the feeling of happiness that exists when you are with another person. It is an experience beyond emotion, a state of mind where you no longer distinguish between your own soul and that of the one you love."

Michael drew a deep breath and met the rabbi's brilliant gaze. The man was right, of course—and Michael was ready to love Devorah with every ounce of his energy, every reserve of his strength. But loving her would mean tearing her from the family she adored, from the heritage she had never been able to shed. Loving her would mean hurting her . . . and he could never willingly bring her pain.

"Thank you, sir." He shook the rabbi's hand in a warm grip. "I will never forget you."

"I hope you do not." A smile gathered up the wrinkles by the man's aged mouth. "The days are coming when Israel will be seen as the center of the world and Jerusalem as the center of Israel. HaShem, blessed be he, has shown me that the hour is fast approaching. May his will be done."

The rabbi moved away, nodding slightly at his daughter as Devorah moved toward Michael. For a moment they stood without speaking, the silence broken only by the monotonous inquiries of the nearby customs inspectors who asked "Is this your first or a returning trip to Israel?" about every thirty seconds.

"Well," she said, her voice artificially bright, "it will be quiet around here when you're gone. They'll have me back in the classroom, teaching reporters how to dodge bullets. But the PLO has been so cowed that we may not be faced with a challenging terrorist situation for years."

"You'll be wonderful, no matter where they assign you." Michael picked up his suitcase and shifted it from one hand to the other, deliberately giving himself something to do so he wouldn't be tempted to draw her into his arms.

She gave him a secret, understanding smile, then looked down at the floor.

"Devorah," Michael began. "I just want you to know—"

She cut him off with a warning glance. "Don't say anything, Michael. It's fine. I'll always be grateful I got to know you. And I'll be indebted to you for what you've done for my family and for Israel."

She looked down at the floor again, then absently scuffed the bottom of her shoe on the worn carpet. "So," her voice brightened again, "you'll be in touch with Daniel in the coming days, I'm sure."

"Of course." Michael smiled, glad that she had found a way out of the awkward conversation. "He's still tracking Romulus and still convinced that Romulus is the false messiah of the ancient literature."

Her eyes sparked with mischief. "Of course you believe he is the antichrist."

"I do."

"And you believe Jesus is coming back to earth, to snatch all the true believers away."

"That's the plan." He grinned and shifted his suitcase again. "So tell me, Devorah—what will you say to the Messiah when he arrives in Jerusalem?"

She paused and tilted her head, then a strange, faintly eager look flashed in her eyes. "I'll ask him," she said, her fascinating smile crinkling the corners of her eyes, "whether it's his first or a returning trip to Israel."

"You do that," Michael answered, grinning. "I'll be standing nearby, waiting to hear his answer."

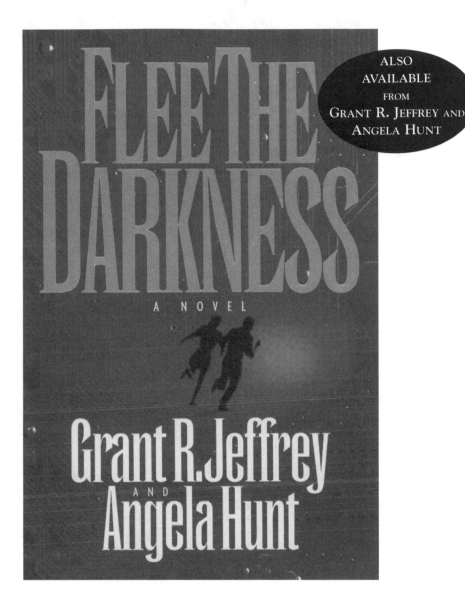

ALSO
AVAILABLE
FROM
GRANT R. JEFFREY AND
ANGELA HUNT

THE Y2K THEORY BECOMES REALITY
IN THIS THRILLING WORK OF FICTION

In a race against time, Daniel Prentice and his colleagues rush to meet a
gargantuan challenge: developing the software that will save the world from
chaos when the year 2000 arrives. But as the deadline looms even closer,
another source of chaos—and evil—arises from ancient roots, threatening
global enslavement and terror—and doom—if Daniel's plan succeeds.

 WORD PUBLISHING

Available at Bookstores Everywhere.